Edward B Hall

Memoir of Mary L. Ware, Wife of Henry Ware

Edward B Hall

Memoir of Mary L. Ware, Wife of Henry Ware

ISBN/EAN: 9783337012946

Printed in Europe, USA, Canada, Australia, Japan

Cover: Foto ©Raphael Reischuk / pixelio.de

More available books at **www.hansebooks.com**

MEMOIR

OF

MARY L. WARE,

WIFE OF

HENRY WARE, JR.

BY

EDWARD B. HALL.

Twelfth Thousand

BOSTON:
AMERICAN UNITARIAN ASSOCIATION.
1880.

CONTENTS.

VIII.

IX.

X.

XIII.

XIV.

MEMOIR.

I.

INTRODUCTION.

THE life of an unpretending Christian woman is never lost. Written or unwritten, it is and ever will be an active power among the elements that form and advance society. Yet the written life will speak to the larger number, will be wholly new to many, and to all may carry a healthy impulse. There are none who are not strengthened and blessed by the knowledge of a meek, firm, consistent character, formed by religious influences, and devoted to the highest ends. And where this character has belonged to a daughter, wife, and mother, who has been seen only in the retired domestic sphere, there may be the more reason that it be transferred to the printed page and an enduring form, because of the very modesty which adorned it, and which would never proclaim itself.

Such are our feelings in regard to the subject of

1

the following Memoir, and such our reasons for offering it to the public. It has not been without scruple,
and after an interval of years, that the family and
nearest friends of Mrs. Ware have consented to the
publication of facts and thoughts so private and
sacred as many which must appear in a faithful
transcript of her life. Perhaps this reluctance always
exists, particularly in regard to a woman and a
mother. In this instance it has been very strong,
and it is but just that it be made known. Never
was there a woman, we may believe, more retiring
or peculiarly domestic than she of whom we are to
speak. Never, we are sure, were the materials of a
life more entirely private, and in one sense confidential, than those which we are to use; for letters are
all the materials we have, and letters written in tne
unrestrained freedom of personal friendship, in the
midst of pressing cares, and with a rapidity and
unstudied naturalness, which will appear in all the
extracts, but are still more manifest in the entire
originals. Her correspondence was voluminous, to
an extent unsurpassed perhaps in a life so quiet,
with no pretence to literary character, and nothing
ever written except for the eye of the receiver. How
would the writer have felt, had she supposed these
letters were ever to be opened to the public eye? It
is a question which many ask, — some with pain,
some with decided disapproval. It is a question
which we have asked ourselves, and we prefer to
answer it before we enter upon the work.

To answer it unfavorably, to yield to this natural
reluctance to publish any thing designed to be pri-

vate, and in its nature personal, would deprive us of the best biographies that are written. It would restrict to single families, and to a brief period, the knowledge of facts and features, of all most reliable, most valuable. Indeed, it is this very fact of humility and reserve, of freedom and naturalness, indulged in confidential communion and the quiet of home, that reveals most the reality of virtue, force of character, disinterested nobleness, and the power of religion. Who is willing that the knowledge of such examples . should be withheld from the many who crave it, and whom it would stimulate and bless? Shall we make no sacrifice of our own feelings, supposing it to require one, shall we hoard exclusively for our own use the richest of God's gifts, when those by whom the gifts have come to us spent their lives in service and sacrifice for us? To these obvious considerations, we will add our firm faith in the knowledge which departed friends have of the motives from which we are acting, and of the influence which their own modest virtues and lowly efforts on earth may exert upon those remaining here; thus continuing, in a higher and surer way, the very work for which the loved and the pure always live, and are willing to die.

It is in point, not only for our immediate purpose, but for the exhibition in part of the character we would delineate, to say that these were the feelings of Mrs. Ware herself, in regard to a memoir of her husband. Public as a large portion of his life was, she shrunk from the exposure of that which was private, and which seemed to be sacredly committed to her own keeping. She remembered, too, his peculiar sensitiveness in this connection, and the injunctions he gave when under the influence of disease and depression. But another voice came to her from his present higher abode and larger vision; and thus she wrote to a friend, of the conflict and the decision, in language applicable now to her own case :—"I cannot tell you the agony it has given me at times, to realize that that sacred inner life, which I had felt was my own peculiar trust, was no longer mine, but was to be shared by the whole world. But this was sinful, selfish, earthly; and I have gradually left it all far behind, and can now only be glad that such a life is shown for the aid and encouragement of others."

It is our desire to give to this Memoir as much as possible of the character of an autobiography. We have few facts except those found in the letters, with the advantage of an intimate intercourse for more than twenty years. In the several hundred letters and notes that have been put into our hands, there is nothing that might not appear, so far as any one else is concerned. This fact is well worthy of note, as belonging to the character, and revealing a remarkable elevation and purity of thought, — that in such a mass of free epistolary writing, from different countries and to persons of every age, not a single severe stricture, not one unkind allusion or offensive personality, much less any approach to petty gossip, can be found. We feel the greater freedom in making copious extracts; and shall attempt little more than so to arrange and connect them as to give a fair view of the whole life, or rather of the mind and character that appear in every part of the life. That a life so private contained such a variety of incident, and a measure of unavoidable publicity, was the ordering of Providence ; and may serve to show that the sphere of woman, even the most domestic and silent, is broad enough for the most active intellect and the largest benevolence.

II.

CHILDHOOD.

MARY LOVELL PICKARD was an only child, her parents having but one other, who died an infant before the birth of Mary. She was born in Atkinson Street, Boston, on the 2d of October, 1798. Mark Pickard, her father, was an English merchant, who came to this country on business, and remained here. Her mother was Mary Lovell, daughter of James Lovell, and granddaughter of " Master Lovell," so long known as a classical teacher in Boston. James Lovell, the grandfather of the subject of this Memoir, was a man of mind and influence. He had been active in the Revolutionary war, and was once made prisoner at Halifax, sharing there, it is said, the prison of Ethan Allen. Subsequently he was a prominent member of the Continental Congress, and at the adoption of the Constitution received the appointment of Naval Officer in the Boston custom-house, a place which he retained until his death. A man of free and bold thought, associating much at one time with French officers, Mr. Lovell adopted some infidel principles, became familiar and fond of Paine's arguments, and, as we are led to infer, treated religion with little respect in his family ; the family in which Mary Pickard, as well as her mother,

passed her childhood and youth. James Lovell had
nine children, but only one daughter, Mary, who
grew up the idol of the family. At the age of
twenty-five she married Mark Pickard, who was
seventeen years her senior, but not her equal in intellect or energy, we infer, yet always kind and most
tenderly attached to her. She was a woman of rare
excellence, in whose character, as drawn by those
still living who knew her well, we can see, as usual,
much that accounts for the character of the daughter.

Mrs. Pickard had been educated in Boston, and
well educated, having a naturally vigorous mind and
strong common sense. She was a woman of self-
culture, loving books and choosing the best, conversing with marked propriety as well as ease, and ex-
hibiting decided energy and generosity of character.
In person, she is described as remarkable; of so
commanding figure, benignant countenance, and
dignified demeanor, as to draw general observation
in public, and suggest the thought once expressed
by a gentleman of intelligence, — "She seems to
me as if she were born for an empress." Yet her
empire was only the home, and her life peculiarly
domestic; with enough of discipline and change to
prove her fortitude, but never to damp her cheerfulness. She was a Christian. In early life, perhaps
from causes already referred to, her mind had been
disturbed, and apparently doubts raised, though
never fixed, by sceptical writers and so-called philosophical reasoners, — more common in good society
then than now, and more bold and insidious, notwithstanding our complaints of present degeneracy

A gentleman to whom Mrs. Pickard had once com
municated her difficulties, and who was less a be
liever than she, spoke of her the day after her death
in reference to that conflict, as " one of strong mind,
who took nothing upon trust" even at that early
age when she approached him with " obstinate
questionings." Whatever the effect upon his faith,
her own was strengthened by all inquiry and experience. She was a member of the Episcopal
Church, though apparently less a devotee to its
ritual than Mr. Pickard. Not sect, but piety, was
the source of her power and peace. " In religion,"
says one most intimate, " she was unostentatious
and charitable, but decided and sincere ; and her
whole life was an exhibition of the ascendancy of
principle over mere taste and feeling."

Such was the mother, who was the constant companion and instructor of an only daughter, through
the whole of childhood ; for Mary never attended
school, that we can find, until she was nearly thirteen
years old. But in that best of schools for the very
young, an intelligent and quiet home, she was well
instructed in the common branches, in habits of
order, refinement, and frugality, in principles of undeviating truth and integrity, and in that most essential of all accomplishments for a girl, whether in
ordinary or exalted station, the use of the needle.
Her mother also taught her to sing, being herself
passionately fond of music, with one of the sweetest
voices, and, though not a great performer, enough so
to impart a love of it to her child which always continued, associated with holy recollections. " Often,"

says one, " at early evening, just before going to rest have I seen the little girl upon her mother's lap, and have heard her singing her evening hymn : —

' Teach me to live, that I may dread
The grave as little as my bed '; &c."

In January, 1802, Mr. Pickard was called to England on business, and took with him his wife and the little Mary, then but three years old. They remained there a year and a half, visiting both his and her relatives, in different parts of the kingdom; Mrs. Pickard being connected, on her mother's side, with Alexander Middleton, a Scotch farmer, in whose family Ferguson, the astronomer, lived as a shepherd boy, and of whom, with his wife and three children, there are still existing likenesses drawn in pencil by that lad, so celebrated as a man. Among such friends, and in such new scenes, we can believe a deep impression would be taken by an observing, thoughtful child, though at an age when it is considered of little consequence what a child sees or hears. Mary never forgot the enjoyment or the instruction of that visit. When she was again in England, twenty years later, she wrote her friends here that she was surprised to find herself recognizing her old home in Guildford Street, London, and other objects with which she was then familiar. And years afterwards, when her own children came round her with the never-satisfied request, " Mother, do tell us about when you were a little girl," the standing favorites were incidents which occurred either in England or on the voyage home, and particularly the following. During the voyage, her fifth birthday came round, and the captain promised her baked potatoes for her dinner, but, as the cook burnt them, threatened to give him the "cat-o'-nine-tails"; when poor little Mary, not taking the joke, burst into tears, and begged him "not to hurt the kind, good sailor, who did n't mean to burn the potatoes."

A lady who came as passenger in the same vessel, has told us of the peculiar sweetness of little Mary, and the universal interest and love inspired by her in the ship's company. And this from no outward attractions, or efforts to commend herself, but by the simple power of goodness, and her ever-prompt obedience. If inclined to go anywhere, or do any thing, not approved by her mother, it was always enough to say, — "It will make me unhappy, my child, if you do that."

A few extracts which we are permitted to make from letters that passed, during this absence abroad, between Mrs. Pickard and her parents, will help to show the respect and affection which the daughter inspired, as well as the interest felt in the little granddaughter.

Under date of January 10, 1802, James Lovell writes from Boston to his daughter in England : —

"I constantly recur to the joyful consideration, that you though absent, are still left to me, an amiable object, within he reach of hope, and a source of expected comfort for ny last days. I think of you, at this moment, as safely arrived with your most worthy husband, and my *None-such*, in health, and happy among your friends. My engage-ments in office, especially since General Lincoln has been confined by sickness at Hingham, have occupied me very much. Though it is evening, little Dickey is bristling up and attempting to sing, that I may not forget to tell my dear little *Molly Pitty* how constantly he looks for her in the morning, at the rattling of the tongs and fender. Kiss the dear child for me.   JAMES LOVELL, — need I add, your affectionate father ? "

In February, 1803, Mrs. Pickard writes home to her mother : —

" Your pickles and berries came in good order, and were very acceptable, particularly to my darling Mary. She often thanks you for them, and is now writing to you, and interrupts me every minute to hear her read her letter. My father must not laugh, and say I call my goose a swan ; every one allows she is a charming child. You will not be able to deny her a large portion of your love, though you have so many lovely ones with you. She has been an inexhaustible source of comfort to me since I left you ; and, as if she knew it would please us all, most of her conversation is of home and the friends she left there. She has a sad cold, but she says she is always happy. Farewell, dear mother. God bless you all."

March, 1803. From the same : —

" We are still in Guildford Street, but think of going into the country, where Mary may have more field for exercise. She is pretty well, but wants a little country air. I wish you knew all her little chat about you, so pleasing to hear, but so foolish to write. She is very tall and lively. . . . . . Mr. P. is even more anxious than I to go home. Mary is the only contented one. She is happy all the time. She nas a very sweet disposition, and I hope will one day be as great a comfort to you as she is to me. She is telling me a thousand little affectionate things to say to you."

In the fall of this year the family returned to
Boston, and lived with Mrs. Lovell in Pearl Street;
and there, with parents and grandparents, Mary
found a home, whose blessing filled her heart, and
never left her to the day of her death. The home
of her childhood, — how reverently and tenderly did
she revert to it, through all the scenes of a changing
and eventful life! Often has she said, that she was
continually carried back, not only in her waking, but
her sleeping hours, "to the old Pearl Street house
and garden; assembling the various friends of all
the different periods of her life, in dream-like incon-
gruity, in the little parlor, with its black-oak wain-
scoting." There also were formed some of those
first friendships, which do not cease with childhood,
but affect the happiness of a lifetime. The other
half of the block in which they lived was occupied
by Colonel T. H. Perkins, and with his children, of
whom some were near her own age, she grew up in
terms of daily intimacy. In the partition between
the two houses there were doors which were entirely
closed, except their keyholes; and through these,
Mary and her favorite companion used to sing to
each other "all the songs we could muster," and
exchange notes and experiences, the pleasure enhanced, no doubt, by the excitement of the little
mystery occasioned by so peculiar a mode of communication.

So far as our scanty materials of this period enable us to judge, we infer that in the training of this
favorite child there was a singularly wise union of
control and indulgence. Mrs. Pickard seems not to

have been one of the parents who think control and indulgence incompatible; nor does it appear that Mary was inclined to refuse the one, or abuse the other. The true training, we suppose, — if there be any rule for all, — is that which allows to children all the freedom and enjoyment consistent with deference to authority, refined manners, and fixed principles of truth, gentleness, and unselfishness. That these principles may be inculcated without sternness or perpetual restraint, indeed with a large allowance for the necessary activity and often irrepressible exuberance of childhood's spirit, few can doubt, though so many deny or forget it in practice. From the views which Mrs. Ware herself always expressed on this subject, and the reverence and gratitude with which she adverted to her own childhood, we are confirmed in the impression, that such was her uniform experience at home, and with the happiest effect. "It has been said," writes a friend of her mother, "that she was much indulged; and I believe it may be said so with truth. But she was not indulged in idleness, selfishness, and rudeness; she was indulged in healthful sports, in abundance of playthings, in pleasant excursions, and in companionship with other children, as much as might be convenient. I never knew her to be teasing and importunate, obstinate or contradictory." Nor is this to be ascribed, as many will be ready to ascribe it, to natural temperament and a peculiar exemption from ordinary temptations and trials. Of few persons, perhaps, would this be more generally inferred or confidently asserted, from a knowledge merely of

2

her subsequent character.   It is on this account that
we refer to it particularly, and for this not least that
we value the example.   For we know it was *not* a
case of peculiar exemption and easy control, but
rather a remarkable instance of early conflict, the
power of principle, and perpetual self-discipline.
This we gather from occasional hints in conversation, and from letters to her own children, some of
which will appear in their proper place.   At present,
we only adduce, for the right understanding both of
this and later periods of her life, one or two short
passages, like the following, from a letter to a
daughter.   " The tendency to self-indulgence was
also one of my trials, in early life, when I grew rapidly and had poor health."   " My trials of temper
were different from yours, but they were very great."
" What a comfort it is, that, although those who see
only the outside can never compute *what is resisted,*
all our struggles are known and appreciated by Him
who looketh on the heart as it is; and that He who
alone can give us strength is thus enabled to know
when and how it is needed."

To this brief sketch of her childhood we venture
to add an extract from a letter just written us, by a
gentleman than whom no one living, probably, was
more intimate with Mary and her home, at that
early period.   After a warm tribute to the character
of the mother, confirming all we have said of her, he
speaks thus of the daughter: —

" When I first remember her, it is as a gentle, loving,
active child, always doing some little useful thing, and the
darling of her parents' hearts.   When her character first

shone on me in its higher attributes, I do not know. But I seem to myself to remember, that there never was a time when I could have supposed it possible that she would do any thing that was not exactly right ; when I had not perfect confidence in her tact and judgment to discern duty, and the prompt and unhesitating determination to do it, as *the only thing to be done.*"

III.

MENTAL AND MORAL CULTURE.

REMAINING in Boston, with little change, until she was thirteen years of age, Mary Pickard was then taken by her parents to Hingham, Massachusetts, to be under the care of the Misses Cushing, whose school for girls enjoyed at that time, and as long as it continued, a very high reputation. Her instructors there, who still live, seem to have regarded her as a friend and companion, rather than a child and pupil; and the fresh recollections and tender love with which they always speak of her, and delight to dwell upon her early and mature character, give us an impression of more than common excellence. This will best be shown by an extract from a letter written since her death to one of her children.

"Your dear mother came to us first in June, 1811; a sweet, interesting girl, thirteen years old, tall for that age, and with the same sweet expression of countenance she ever retained; remarkable even then for her disinterestedness and forgetfulness of self, and her power of gaining the love of all around her. She went home in November of the same year, and returned to us again in 1814. . . . . . She was with us but little more than one year in the whole, and in that short period endeared herself to us in a remarkable manner. For with the love which we could not but feel for her was mingled a respect and admiration for her high principles, and the piety which shone through all her conduct, in a degree very uncommon for a girl of her age. As a scholar she was exceedingly bright, and quick to comprehend, and would, I always thought, have made an excellent mathematical scholar, had she pursued the study of that branch. Her capacity for accomplishing a great deal in a short time was always remarkable, and I believe she never undertook any thing that she thought worth her attention, that she did not go through to the satisfaction of others, if not of herself. Her chief object, even when a young girl, seemed to be to do good, in some way or other, to her fellow-beings, and she considered nothing too difficult for her to undertake, if it could benefit another person either in a temporal or moral view. You have had sufficient evidence of this, since you have been old enough to judge for yourself, and I can only tell you that it seemed to be, at an early period of her life, a living principle with her. Yet, with all this devotedness to the highest objects and purposes of our existence, she was one of the most lively and playful girls among her companions, and a very great favorite with them all."

Mary had been but five or six months in the school at Hingham, when she was called back to Boston by the threatening illness of her mother, who continued feeble through the winter, and died in the month of May following. That winter must have been one of peculiar experience to Mary. It was her first great trial. She loved her mother, not only as every true child must, but with a reverence and affection heightened by the unusual circumstance of having been always the pupil of that mother alone, regarded as a companion also, and

called now to the tender offices of a nurse, at an age
when most children can ill bear confinement and
devotion to the sick.   Mary was never happier than
when thus occupied, as her whole life has shown.
To her it was no task, but a grateful privilege, to
spend all her time at the side of a revered and departing mother.   For six months was she allowed
to give herself to this blessed ministry; and when it
closed, she was left, a girl of thirteen, the sole comfort and chief companion of her father, now past the
prime of life, broken in spirits and in fortune, clinging to this only child with doating and dependent
affection.   She now became an important member
of the family in Pearl Street, with her desolate
father, and her venerable grandparents, who were
still living, depending themselves more upon her for
their comfort than upon the only son that remained
with them, a young man whose fine talents and affectionate disposition were perverted and ruined by
sad habits.   These were circumstances to call out
all her energy, and make full proof of her judgment
and gentleness.   Mr. Pickard had for some time
been embarrassed in business, and, from a state of
easy competence, was then and afterwards reduced
to the necessity of the strictest economy.   Of his
daughter's essential service to him in this respect,
we have frequent intimations in his own letters; and
not only by her prudent management, but also by
her generous and active aid, as will be seen still
more a few years later.   For her father survived her
mother eleven years, and during the whole of that
period, though not always together, Mary was his

efficient helper, and his devoted nurse in sickness, of which he had a large share.

For two years after her mother's death, she remained wholly in Boston, enjoying part of the time a new privilege, which she greatly prized, — admission to the best school for young ladies then in New England, or the country, — Dr. Park's. That she would improve such an opportunity to the best of her ability, we need not say. Of her proficiency as a scholar, there are no particular proofs. She was never a prodigy, but she never slighted opportunity or duty. She appeared always well, distinguished at least for faithful preparation and uniform accuracy. And especially was she distinguished for moral excellence. She was the friend and favorite of all. If petty difficulties occurred, Mary Pickard was the peacemaker. Her impartiality, amiableness, kindness to all, and perfect truthfulness, endeared her to the teacher and all the pupils; from several of whom we have had the testimony, that no one ever exerted a better influence upon any school.

The earliest letters we have from Mary were written in 1813, the year after her mother's death, and about the time of her first going to school in Boston. They are the letters of a school-girl, but not of a child. While there is in them no indication of remarkable powers, to which she did not pretend, nor her friends for her, they show a habit of reflection and power of discrimination, with a choice of topics not usual at that age. A few passages may be given, very simple and juvenile, but indicative of character.

"Boston, February 27, 1813.

" My dear N——:

" I am determined another day shall not pass before I answer your letter. I think it is the best way, when we receive a letter, to sit down immediately and answer it ; at least I find it so, though I do not always practise it. . . . . . We talk so much when we meet, that there is little left to write, and I am now at a loss what to say. The folly of the fashionable world is an old story, and if not, is too *vast* a subject for our limited views of it. Of our school plan we have said much, but we can say more. I had no idea that such insignificant beings as we are, in comparison, could ever afford matter for so much conversation as there has been on this subject. Although opinions could not alter the case, yet it is certainly very satisfactory to know that our doings are approved by those whose good opinion we value. I look forward with much pleasure to the day on which we shall commence our studies. We shall feel very awkward at first, but it will soon be over, and then we must endeavor to keep ourselves exempt from the condemnation that falls on the whole school for the faults of two or three. . . . . .

" I am reading ' Temper,' and like it much better than I expected to, having heard nothing in its favor, and, besides that, being *prejudiced* against it. I have condemned prejudice in others, but never felt the effects of it before ; I dislike it now more than ever, — it is certainly a most unreasonable thing. I like some of the characters very much, and it is not as yet very tedious, but contains many good lessons. I find many that I can apply to myself, and (as usual) some to other people. It cannot, however, be compared to ' The Absentee ' or ' Vivian.' Novels are generally said to be improper books for young people, as they take up the time which ought to be employed in more useful pursuits; which is certainly very true; but as a recreation to the mind, such books as these cannot possibly do any hurt, as they are good moral lessons. Indeed, I think there is scarcely any book from which some good may not be derived; though it cannot be expected that any young person has judgment enough to leave all the bad and take only the good, when there is a great proportion of the former. I know we are too young to hold up an opinion of our own, independent of the superior judgment of those older, and this I would not do. I have collected mine from observation, and, if it is not right, would thank any one to correct it; nor would I offer it at all to any one but you, or those of my own age."

That last sentiment will seem *very* juvenile to many young people of the present day, but it is none the worse for that. Nor by this writer was the expression of such sentiments restricted to that age; for modesty and deference, combined with self-respect and decision, were marked features and peculiar graces of the character we are presenting. They are features and graces of a strong mind. Superciliousness, in youth or maturity, is a sign of weakness. And it says little for the improvement or the promise of the present, if it be true that respect for experience, reverence for age, and meekness of expression, are rare qualities in the young. Mary was still young, when she wrote to her father, — " I am no advocate for destroying that delicacy which forms, or ought to form, so great a part of the female character. But such a degree of it as is not compatible with sufficient firmness to command one's self in danger, appears to me to be false modesty, or ' sickly sensibility of soul,' — beneath the dignity of beings endowed with power for higher feelings." Here is that union of humility and courage which marked her whole course.

In all her early letters there is an entire absence of that trivial talk about dress, parties, and the gossip of the day, so common at her age. Instead of it, we find remarks either upon moral and religious themes, or upon her reading and studies. In the very earliest letter we have, written in a child's hand, she speaks of her interest in the " Life of Washington, in five large octavo volumes," and expresses the opinion, that " the history of one's country ought to be the first historical lesson of a child." About the same time, we find her deeply engaged in an argument upon the moral influence of the study of astronomy; and her mind rises to the highest and the largest views.

" The hand of Almighty God certainly should raise in our souls such unbounded adoration and love, that our only object would be, to be worthy to appear before the presence of such excellent goodness, and partake of the joys of heaven. It seems unaccountable, that any one could for a moment raise his eyes to the sky and not be convinced of the being of some superior power, who rules and directs the paths of the planets and the ways of the children of men. If we for a moment transport ourselves to another part of the universe, and behold our little insignificant Earth in comparison with the rest, or with any other planet, and consider how highly favored it has been with the presence of the Son of its Creator, are we to think that we alone are thus honored, and that superior worlds are not endowed

.n the same manner with a knowledge of heavenly things? But I find myself getting into an argument, on which, though the subject may be interesting, the style of the writer must be tedious."

These extracts are from letters written to a friend near her own age, with whom there began at this time the longest and most confiding intimacy of her life, out of the circle of immediate connections, if indeed any exception need be made. To this friend are addressed some of the first and last letters that Mary ever wrote, and by far the larger number of all which we use for this sketch. It is an evidence of the faithfulness of her friendships, that from the date of the earliest letter we have, through nearly forty years, she wrote to that same friend, beside other occasional letters, " a New Year's epistle," every year, to the last in her life. And to her were confided her first and deepest trials, disclosed to no one else, and beginning while at school. There is something both ingenuous and magnanimous in such sentiments as the following, from a girl of fifteen, whom the death of a mother had placed in circumstances of peculiar responsibility, and often painful perplexity.

" I expose to you my weaknesses, my faults, my passions. There is but one thing of which I have the slightest apprehension. You may sometimes hear me blamed for deeds which you know are right. You will hear my lot in life envied, as apparently all that the reasonable wishes of any being could desire. And sometimes, too, busy Scanda', which honors even the most insignificant with her notice, will glance at me. Your generous, affectionate heart will

prompt, I well know, on those occasions, some defence of
your friend. But never give way to it; never whisper to
the winds that she has any trials. It will necessarily in-
volve the question, What are they? You are the only person to whom I ever communicated them, and my conscience
almost reproaches me for it. I try to think my peculiar
loneliness sanctions it, but my very uneasiness proves it
was not strictly right, and I would not for worlds sin farther. You will bear with me. All this is foolish, but I
must say it. I defy any one to tell from my appearance
that I have not every thing to make me happy. I have
much, and I am happy. My little trials are essential to my
happiness. They teach me to value the only true sources
of enjoyment this life can afford, — the affection of the
good, the cultivation of the better feelings of the soul in the
service of their Creator, and the joyful hope of a better,
purer state of existence. Blessings and peace go with you,
and pure, unalloyed felicity be your portion for ever.

" Mary."

In the latter part of the year 1814, Mary left Boston for Hingham, to be again in the family and
under the tuition of the Misses Cushing. Of her
character then, and the renewed impression made
upon her instructors, a letter which we have recently received from one of them will give the best
idea; though, from regard to the writer's wishes, we
quote but a small part.

" I can hardly give you an idea of my feelings towards
her, during the whole of her residence with us, without
seeming to speak extravagantly. Every day's experience
confirmed our first impressions of her, and showed in some
form the sweetness of her disposition, her self-sacrificing
spirit, and untiring devotion to the claims of those about

her. She possessed such purity of heart, and elevation of principle, as were certainly uncommon at such an early period of life, and which, it seemed to me then, could only arise from a constant sense of the Divine presence, and an habitual communion with the Source of all good. Love was always, with her, the predominant feeling in her thought of God, and I have heard her say she never remembered the time when she did not feel that she loved God. This was said, you may be sure, not boastingly, but from surprise at hearing some one speak of the difficulty of giving the heart to God."

And now came a crisis in that inner life, which was always greater to Mary Pickard than the outward. Always thoughtful as well as cheerful, her interest in religion, and her wish to be wholly a follower of Christ, led her to an act, too rare with the young, and requiring, in school and college particularly, courage as well as principle. She desired to connect herself publicly with the Church. And the convictions by which she was brought to this purpose, with the views she entertained of the nature and importance of the act, we make no apology for giving, as fully as we find them expressed in her own letters; for there are older minds that might be instructed, and doubters who might be admonished and aided, even by so youthful a believer. Mary had received baptism in Trinity Church, Boston, but it is evident that in her moral training more heed had been given to the cultivation of piety than to adherence to forms and special doctrines. The preaching that she usually heard, in the church of her parents, did not edify or satisfy her; a fact

3

which we give, without comment, as part of a faithful record, and as we find it in her own account to a
son, in one of the last years of her life. The lan
guage in which she there describes her early religious
wants is unusually strong for her, and might seem
extravagant. We give only the result of her dissatisfaction with what she heard from the pulpit.
" The final effect upon me was, by throwing me
more upon myself, to open a new source of religious
instruction to my mind; and I can now remember
with great pleasure, and a longing desire for the
same vivid enjoyment, the hours I passed in 'my
little room,' in striving, by reading, meditation, and
prayer, to find that knowledge and stimulus to virtue
which I failed to find in the ministrations of the
Sabbath." And then most earnestly does she ex-
hort her son not to let these things, or any thing,
tempt him " to treat sacred things with levity and
disrespect."

Few minds have kept themselves, through life,
more free both from levity and bigotry. At the time
of which we speak, she seems to have thought only
of her own unworthiness, her need of religion, and
the greatness of the privilege offered her. A long
note which she wrote to one of the teachers with
whom she was living, and to whom she confided all
her feelings, will explain the whole. It bears no
date, but must have been written in the autumn of
1814, when she was about sixteen.

" Saturday Morning.

" Will you, my dear Miss C., pardon my addressing you
in this way, when under the same roof; but as I could not

speak on the subject I have now most at heart, in the presence of any one, I did not think it right to engross exclusively so much of your valuable time as would be necessary
to say all I wish to. I could not feel satisfied with my own
conclusions, until I had appealed to you, and I hope this
will excuse the liberty I take. Though still young, I have
tasted the bitter cup of affliction and disappointment, and
have found thus early that all worldly enjoyments are incapable of promoting happiness, or even of securing present
gratifications ; and in every deprivation have felt the healing balm of religion to be the only source of consolation to .
the wounded spirit and afflicted mind. But I may, indeed,
say with sincerity, ' It is good for me that I have been
afflicted,' for it led me to reflect on the end for which I
was created, to examine my own heart, and, by comparing
it with the Christian standard, to prove its weakness and
awake to a sense of my danger. A very little reflection
convinced me I had been leading a very different life from
that which was requisite to form the character of a true
Christian, and that I must exercise my utmost powers to
redeem the time which I had lost, and which could never
be recalled. Though I cannot think the observance of any
religious ceremonies sufficient to secure future happiness,
unless the motive for their performance is founded on faith
in the word of God, as revealed to us by his Son, yet they
seem to me necessary, not only in a moral, but religious
point of view, to the attainment of that degree of perfection
which we are taught it is in the power of every one to attain.

" Ever since I have thought at all on the subject, it has
been my earnest wish to be admitted a member of the
Church of Christ. It is a duty which I cannot but think is
of the highest importance, both as it is fulfilling the last
request of one to whom we owe all we enjoy here or hope
for hereafter, and as it continually reminds us of our obli-

gations to obey his precepts, tends to make us better, and
more worthy our high calling. If we assume the name
of Christians, and obey not those positive commands of our
Saviour which are in the power of every one who is sincere
how can we expect to receive a continuance of his favors?
Fearing I was too young fully to comprehend the use and
importance of so solemn a rite, I have delayed saying or
doing any thing about it. I have thought much on it, and
summed up all the reasons which appeared to me to prove
it absolutely necessary to our happiness and well-being, and
all the objections that arose in my mind against the propriety of young persons joining in it. I then read every
book on the subject I could meet with, and found in none
of them half as many objections as I had raised, and very
few arguments in its favor which I had not thought of. Do
not think it has made me think better of myself than I deserve, — far from it; it made me feel more sensibly my
own unworthiness, when compared with what I continually
saw I ought to be. Still, as I could not give up all thoughts
of it, I determined to appeal to you. Tell me, my dear
Miss C., if you should consider it a violation of the sacredness of the institution, to think I might with impunity be a
member? I am well aware of the condemnation denounced
on those who partake unworthily, and I tremble to think
how liable I shall be to fall into error and sin, and how
much greater will be my responsibility. These reflections
have hitherto prevented my proposing it to my father or
any one, and now almost make me fear I am doing wrong
in writing to you. I am afraid I am presumptuous, and,
did I not view it rather as a means of religion than the end,
I should hardly suppose there were many who could say
they were worthy of it. I cannot think there is any *mystery*
connected with it, as some are so eager to prove, and its
very simplicity renders it the more interesting and useful,
and increases the obligation to perform it.

"Forgive me, my dear Miss C., if I have said any thing wrong, and correct me if you see any seeds of vice in me. Recollect I have been the guardian of myself too long not to have erred very much in my ideas of every thing; pity, and make me better, if the task is not too discouraging; and be assured, the purest love and gratitude of which I am capable will be the sincere offering of your affectionate young friend,

"MARY."

The self-scrutiny and humility evinced in this note prevented any hasty action. Mary seems still to have deliberated, and sought all the light and direction she could obtain. A long letter, of which we give a portion, to her true friend, N. C. S., in Boston, shows her state of inquiry and progress.

"*Hingham, January* 13*th*, 1815.

"You could not possibly have received more pleasure from hearing Mr. Thacher's sermon, than I did from reading your abstract of it. Nothing could be more satisfactory to me, who still doubted whether it would not be a violation of the sacredness of the institution, for any one so thoughtless and liable to fall into sin and folly to join in such a holy offering, with the good and faithful of the earth. But that was enough to convince any one who believed the obligation in any degree to be great, that it extended to young as well as old, and would be an effectual means of turning them from error to a knowledge of truth, would make them happy here, and be almost a security of it hereafter. And though the punishment of those who outwardly profess themselves disciples of Christ, and yet devote their time and thoughts to the world, is inevitable, I cannot but think it will be in a much greater degree inflicted on those who wholly neglect it, particularly when once convinced of its

3 *

importance. We have both felt the power which only the sight of others performing this duty has had on our minds; what then will it be, when we join in it ourselves, and feel the direct influence of those heavenly rays, which enlighten the Christian at the altar of his God, and guide him in his dreary progress through the world to heaven! Surely then we should not hesitate; now, while it is in our power, it would be absolute wickedness to neglect the performance of such a reasonable and delightful act of duty.

" MARY."

But one doubt now remained in her mind; that caused by the many differences among believers, and the numerous branches of the Christian Church. But this she soon answered for herself, with her usual simplicity and largeness of view. " I have considered the Church of Christ to be one body diffused through the whole world, and that sects, form, and opinion made in truth no essential difference; — that all the various denominations of Christians on the earth were united in one spirit and one mind, in all the important doctrines of religion." Not long after, she received from her confiding friend an account of similar feelings in herself, together with an excellent note from the Rev. John E. Abbot, encouraging their serious purpose. Mary's reply follows.

" Hingham, April 1st, 1815.

"I do, indeed, my dear friend, rejoice with you in the unexpected and happy event your last letter informed me of. I had felt all your doubts and fears as though they were my own, and, I do assure you, participated in your joy with the same sincerity. How much reason have we to be grateful for this instance of the overruling Providence! Does it not sufficiently prove, that, if with sincerity and pureness of heart we undertake to perform any duty, we may rely on the assistance of the Holy Spirit to guide our steps, and to cause all things to concur to render it easy and delightful?

" I cannot tell you how much it increased my own happiness to know that you, too, felt happy; for there is in the sympathy of friends something that increases all our pleasures and alleviates all our pains. It is to this I owe half that I enjoy in this life, and without it wretched must be existence, even in prosperity, and all other earthly blessings.

" I believe I have mentioned often to you the desire I had of becoming one of the church here, if I could be sure of remaining here this summer. When I found there was no doubt of that, I had only to overcome the fears which a consciousness of weakness and liability to relapse into former coldness still kept alive in my mind. Now all have subsided, and I am convinced that it is dangerous to delay so important a service. From the moment I had decided what to do, not a feeling arose which I could wish to suppress; conscious of pure motives, all within was calm, and I wondered how I could for a moment hesitate. They were feelings I never before experienced, and for once I *realized* that it is only when we are at peace with ourselves that we can enjoy true happiness.

" . . . . . I think, all things considered, I was never more happy in my life. It was a bright, clear night, and the moon which rose just as I went to bed, shining full on me, seemed to reflect the tranquillity of my soul, and appeared to me an emblem of the mild light that was just dawning on my soul. I could not sleep, and actually laid awake all night out of pure happiness.

" I will not trouble you with any more of my feelings at present. On Sunday we were proposed, and the next

Sabbath will see the completion of all my hopes **and** wishes relating to myself for two years past.

"I cannot at present write more, but will finish this next week.

"MARY."

The church with which Mary connected herself was the Third Church in Hingham, under the pastoral care of the Rev. Henry Coleman, with whom she speaks of delightful interviews, receiving from him the best instruction and counsel at that important period. She shows at the same time her habit of thinking for herself, as well as her liberal and humble spirit, in the casual remark, "Though I could not agree exactly with him in every thing he said, as they were not essential points I thought nothing of it, and received his advice with as much pleasure and satisfaction as could possibly be." The same month she records the completion of her wishes and her happiness.

"Last Sunday witnessed the accomplishment of my highest desires; for I joined for the first time with those who compose the church here, in commemorating the death of our blessed Saviour. The feelings it excited are not easily described, and as you will so soon experience them, you will thus be able more fully to conceive of them than by any thing I could say. I know you will derive much, very much satisfaction and happiness from it; and I sincerely pray that it may be to us both a means of becoming more like its heavenly Founder, and finding acceptance with God through his intercession. I wish you could have heard our dear Mr. C——. He was particularly interesting and affecting; his prayers, too, are better than any I ever heard (always excepting Mr. Channing); they breathe more of the true spirit of Christian humility than is commonly to be found in these days of pride.

"MARY."

About this time we find mention of an incident which appeared then of little importance, but to which subsequent events, though quite remote, have given so peculiar an interest, that it seems not right to omit it. Mary Pickard, still a school-girl, saw for the first time the individual with whom, twelve years after, her fortunes were to be connected for life, but with whom, during that interval, she had no intercourse. HENRY WARE, then a theological student at Cambridge, was on a visit to Hingham, his native town, and passed an evening at Miss Cushing's. Mary does not appear to have had any conversation with him, but simply saw and heard him, and wrote to her friend in Boston a frank account of the opinion she formed of him.

"*Hingham, April 9th*, 1815.

"Again, my dear N——, I resume the delightful task of writing to you, which, I assure you, gives me a degree of pleasure next to that of talking with you, however you may judge from my writing so seldom. Since Saturday I have experienced a pleasure I never expected, the desire of which I have often expressed to you. I have seen, heard, and consequently admired, your Exeter friend, *H. Ware;* [*] and though his errand took something from the delight his presence would otherwise have completed, it was sufficiently great for the safety of so large an assembly of young

---

[*] He spent two years at Exeter, as teacher in the Academy.

ladies. He was as agreeable as he could possibly be, und fully satisfied all the expectations you had raised in my mind. He spent Sunday evening here, and as ho is very fond of music, and it is usual for us to spend a part of this evening in singing, we sung psalms from dusk until eight, when he was obliged to leave us. He joined in all, and added very much to the harmony and melody of our little choir. On Monday evening, too, he was here, and much increased the good opinion that had been formed of him. I thought his face indicated the greatest purity and goodness; I never saw a more benign, delightful expression on any face before, and much less any thing like it in a gentleman. I will not, however, judge any one by their face, particularly as I have not proved myself a good physiognomist. Yet I cannot help being in some measure influenced by it. How can I look at such a countenance as his, and not be confident that there is a mind within correspondent to it? There is, though, a want of energy in it, which I hope is not in his character; but it is sometimes the case, that a love of poetry, and habit of writing it, effeminate the mind of man, while they only render more attractive and interesting that of woman.

" He came for his sister Harriet, who has left us, very much to my sorrow as well as that of all the family. She has an uncommon mind, and possesses much original genius: it is very seldom you see such proofs of it in one so young, as to put it beyond doubt, that, under any circumstances, love of literature would have been predominant. She is a great loss to us, and to myself particularly so, as I can never hope to have it in my power to cultivate her acquaintance as I should wish. But I must be content, and if I can only have the power of appreciating as they deserve those friends I now have, I think it will be my own fault if I am not happy.

" With love to all friends, I must conclude by assuring vou of the firm affection of your friend,

" M. Pickard."

This was written the same month, and within a few days of the date of that remarkable religious paper, which Henry Ware wrote for his own sacred use, — " To be opened and read for improvement, once a month," * — seen by no other eye, probably, until Mary herself opened it, as his widow! From this time they did not meet, as personal acquaintance, until the year of their marriage.

---

* Memoir of Henry Ware, p. 83.

IV.

DISCIPLINE AND CHARACTER

WITH all her deep happiness and cheerful aspect, Mary had many anxieties and trials at this time. These were caused by her father's loss of property and depression of spirits. Mr. Pickard seems never to have had a large property, but was connected with one of the best firms in Boston, and enjoyed a good reputation as a merchant and a man. In what way reverses came upon him, we are not informed ; but the period of which we speak, just at the close of the war with Great Britain, may be a sufficient explanation. Either from his own letters, or through others, his daughter heard of his losses, and had written him a letter which we do not find, but of which the following reply indicates the character.

" Boston, April 17, 1815.

" I have just opened your letter. You are every thing that is amiable and good ; it is not possible to have a better child. But you cannot enter into my feelings, because you know not my situation. I will not trouble you with any more complaints, if I can help it ; I will only tell you that I have done nothing that should make you ashamed of your father. If I have not enough to pay every one their just dues, it is owing to misfortune and events that I could not control. No one, however, except the estate, is likely to suffer by me, and you of course will be a joint loser; the whole, I hope, will not be much. My anxiety is, how I shall get a living, — what I shall subsist on. Without any capital, I can do no business. I long for the time to come when I shall see you here. . . . . . I am about making inquiry amongst my acquaintance for employment. If I succeed, my mind will be easier; if not, what shall I do? I know not. I had a long talk alone with cousin N—— last evening. She tried to encourage me with the hope of being able to support myself, as we calculated you would, after some time, have enough to support yourself without mental or bodily exertion. Yet I know, my dear child, that you would exert both for me ; but how much more satisfactory would it be to me to support myself while I am able. It is not the change of circumstances, but the dread of want, tha depresses me. I did hope, too, that you would have been in a better situation; but you have a mind and spirits, I hope, to keep your heart at ease ; for you will be esteemed for your virtues. You see I cannot help writing what is uppermost in my thoughts.

"Your very affectionate father,

"M. P."

We have not many of Mr. Pickard's letters, but all we have, even those in which he writes in rather an unreasonable mood, as if expecting too much of this endeared and devoted daughter, yet contain incidental expressions which show his exalted opinion and almost respectful regard for her, as well as a tender and grateful affection. He speaks of having shown one of her letters to a friend, who was " highly gratified with the seriousness and piety of your disposition; but she did not need that proof of it; and in the troubles and vexations of this world, it is

4

a great consolation to me to have so good a child, whom I look forward to as the comfort of my declining years; you know how much your letters please me, and console me for your absence." This we can understand when we read the letter which follows, probably in reply to that which we have given above.

" Hingham, April 22, 1815.

" I did not receive your letter, my dear father, until Thursday afternoon, and cannot delay for a moment answering it. I should be sorry to think you considered me so weak as to bend under a change of fortune to which all are liable, and which does not affect the interest of my friends or myself, while a self-approving conscience is their support. I trust nothing which can befall them with respect to the world will wholly overcome their fortitude and confidence in the protection and care of a Supreme Being. I can, I think, enter in some measure into your feelings, and believe I can feel as you do with regard to being dependent on others. I am prepared for almost any trial; if my ability is equal to my desire of being of service to you in misfortune, I do not fear but that I shall be able to support myself, and at least not be a burden to you. I am sorry you think so much of my situation. I shall never regret the loss of indulgences which I have never been taught to consider as essential to my happiness, and which do not in any great degree conduce to it. I shall be content in any circumstances, while I know you have not brought on yourself calamity. I am not so proud that I should feel the least repugnance to gaining a living in any useful employment whatever; I feel that kind of pride which assures me that local situation will not disturb my peace within, and with that I could combat almost any thing. I can only regret the loss of property, when it makes me an encumbrance to my friends, and limits my power of communicating good. As to the former, I think, while I can possibly do it, I had better remain here, rather than burden any of my friends with my company, and I will retrench other expenses for the sake of being independent; for I do not think that any service I could do would compensate for the trouble I should give; and with regard to the latter, the *will* will be present with me, and though the money means were denied me, I do not despair of doing good in some way or other I shall do very well; my only anxiety is for you, lest you give up hope of better times, and thus put a stop to the mainspring of human action. I cannot but regret that what belongs to the estate should be lost, for the obligations we are under already to the family are more than can ever be repaid, and obligations are to some people oppressive I shall see you soon, and will then make some arrangements. Till then, I know not what to propose. I hope to hear from you soon. And do write in better spirits; it will do no good to be discouraged. With love to all, I remain your affectionate daughter,

" MARY."

Those only who have experienced reverses, or have seen parents suffer from them undeservedly, know how hard it is to sustain, beneath their pressure, a cheerful and buoyant spirit. We can moralize upon the comparative worthlessness of this world's goods, and call poverty and pain light evils. It is a false view. Poverty and pain are positive and great evils. Sin only is greater, and sin, it may be, is as often engendered by these as by the opposite state of health and affluence. In setting forth the dangers of prosperity, we are not to forget the temptations and conflicts of adversity. Honor to the man or woman, who maintains integrity and serenity in the hour of misfortune!

We mean not to intimate that the pecuniary perplexities of Mr. Pickard and his daughter were extreme. But we believe them to have been enough to test the power of character, and to throw a delicate and difficult duty upon a daughter, so young, and so connected with friends who were able and willing to help, but on whom she was not willing to lean. She preferred to lean upon herself, though not in unaided strength. Seldom do we find such evidence of early and entire reliance on a higher Power. She had made her election. With the deliberation and firmness of mature conviction, she had given herself to God, and was at peace. How complete, though quiet, was that surrender, and how full and permanent the peace, every subsequent year of her life bore witness. And there were those who saw this in the beginning, and predicted its future power. We are struck with the confidence expressed by judicious friends in Mary's "piety," — a word of deeper and larger import than belongs to many beginners in the school of religion and life. It is an incomparable blessing, when a faithful and experienced teacher can write to a pupil thus: —

"Could I in any way serve you, how gladly would I do it! But when I take my pen to write you, and my heart would dictate something, which, to most of your age (particularly when so early deprived of a mother's care), might be useful, I am deterred by the thought of your maturity of mind, your well-regulated affections, and correct and dignified deportment. This is not flattery; you know me too well, I hope, to believe me capable of that, where my heart is interested. It is an opinion founded on a long, and for some time close observation. May you feel in your own bosom the reward you so richly deserve, and be sensible of those joys with which 'a stranger intermeddleth not.' So early disciplined in the school of affliction, your heart has felt the need of consolation which the world has not to bestow; and at a period of life when the follies and vanities of the world most commonly engross us, you have been led to an attention to those things which are unseen and eternal. God grant that you may be induced to persevere in the path of *piety*, to reach forward continually to higher attainments, nor ever rest satisfied till you have attained the glorious prize which is reserved for the followers of the blessed Jesus. . . . . . I should not, to many of your age, write so much on so serious a subject; but I believe you have a feeling persuasion of its reality and importance, and therefore will not deem me intrusive."

In the summer of 1815, Mary left Hingham, and returned to her home in Pearl Street, Boston, where another change had just occurred in the death of her grandfather, James Lovell. This left her grandmother very lonely, and for the remaining two years of her life Mary devoted herself to her care, and ministered to her wants, with the same assiduity and affection that marked her devotion in her mother's sickness. Not that she was wholly confined to the sick-room, or the house. Mrs. Lovell's health varied, and allowed occasional visits to friends in and near Boston, for several weeks together. One of these visits took Mary as far as Northampton;

4 *

and in a pleasant letter to her father she gives a full account of her journey thither, a very different matter then from what it now is. Going from the presence of sickness and sorrow into that beautiful region, her heart expanded with joy and gratitude, — gratitude to God, and to those generous friends whose guest she was, and whose hospitality she describes in a way that would leave no doubt to what family she refers, even if there were not a direct mention of one whom so many love to recall. " Mr. Lyman is, without exception, the most agreeable man 1 ever met with; and if I could only overcome feelings of restraint which his infinite superiority makes me have before him, I might be able to enjoy his conversation more. I may overcome it, but as yet I cannot, and therefore fear I appear stupid." This diffidence she never did wholly overcome, and we can conceive of its having been very great, at that age. Yet it seems never to have prevented her from going forward to the performance of any duty, or appearing with propriety and dignity in any position. She had a keen relish for all the beauties of nature,·and no less for the refinements and pleasures of society. But her highest enjoyment, even at that age, was evidently sought and found in the company of the devout, and the joys of religion. Her father gently reproves her, in one of his letters, for indulging too much in " sombre " thoughts, and talking of " trials presenting themselves everywhere." But it is evident that it was to his own trials that she referred, and his depression may have extended sometimes, though very seldom, to her. He himself says of this state of feeling, "I was not without fear that I had imparted it to you, which would grieve me much."

During the long period of her grandmother's sickness, Mary formed a new attachment, opening to her a fountain of the purest enjoyment. She was a constant attendant on the preaching of Dr. Channing. When a child, she loved to go to his church with that relative and devoted friend of the family, who, though of the same age as her mother, still lives to mourn the loss of all of them. Led by that hand, which was to her as the hand of a mother to the very end of life, (may we not so far depart from our rule, in regard to the living, as to give the venerable name of Ann Bent?) Mary listened very early and intently to the man who has moved multitudes of every age. As she grew up, her evident and strong preference for his preaching over all other is said to have been the subject of "a little affectionate bantering on her mother's part," while to her more rigid father it was so little agreeable as to cause at times some trial of feeling and a conflict of duty. But where duty pertained to God and the whole existence, she never doubted long. Her decision was taken deliberately, with respect and gentleness, but with a force and faith that never wavered, and never failed to supply strength and consolation in her varied trials. Indeed, it was amid trials, as we have seen, that she first consecrated herself to Christ, soon after her mother's death. And now that she was daily watching the decline of another life very dear to her, at the bedside of her aged grand mother, her letters are chiefly filled with accounts of her vivid interest in the *preaching* she hears, and the effect it has upon her character. Two of these letters we give together, as relating to the same subject, though written several months apart.

" *Boston, Sunday Evening, Sept.* 15, 1816.

"How frequently have I heard it said, that we never feel the true happiness of having a friend more than when, overwhelmed with feelings it cannot control, the heart seeks relief in the sympathizing bosom of that Being who alone can comprehend them ; and never, my dear N——, did I feel this truth more than at the present moment, never did I feel more eager to open to your view my whole heart, to *show* you the emotions excited in it, for I feel sensible that I cannot describe them. It will not surprise you that Mr. Channing's sermons are the cause ; but no account that I can give could convey any idea of them. You have heard some of the same class ; they so entirely absorb the feelings as to render the mind incapable of action, and consequently leave on the memory at times no distinct impression. That in the morning from this text, ' He that forsaketh not all that he hath, cannot be my disciple,' was calculated more than any thing I had *then* heard, to exalt the Christian character ; but that this afternoon was as if an angel spoke,—' Come unto me, all ye that labor and are heavy laden, and I will give you rest. Learn of me, for I am meek and lowly of heart, and ye shall find rest to your souls.' Happiness, or, as it is here expressed, ' rest to the soul,' does not, it is evident, depend on our situation, as may be proved by a slight view of the condition of mankind in general. We see them constantly aspiring to something beyond what they possess, but which, when attained, adds not to their peace, but rather increases their discontent. . . . . .

"I doubt whether I have succeeded in giving you any idea of what Mr. Channing's sermon really contained, as I cannot remember any thing of it but the impression it made on my feelings, and I have, I find, given you rather a transcript of them than any of his original ideas, as you will readily perceive. The object of it, however, was to prove that the only real happiness to be enjoyed in the world was to be found in that peace of mind which a true and lively faith in the wisdom and mercy of God necessarily inspires in the Christian, and without which all the pleasures this world can give will fail to convey to the heart even one transient gleam of real enjoyment. Could you only have been here, you would, I know, have been much benefited by it; but you could not feel it as I did, for you do not so much require it. My reason and conscience have always told me that it was not right to let any of the trials I have met, and still meet with, destroy for a moment my peace; and though they have sometimes conquered my weaker feelings, yet there are times when I find my own strength so insufficient that I am almost tempted to doubt whether it be in my power to attain. This morning, I felt more than ever my weakness, from having had a long and unsuccessful struggle the whole of yesterday with myself. That the precious privileges this day has afforded me are not lost upon me, I hope to prove in the day of future trial. Forgive my egotism, but I know to whom I write.

" MARY."

" You said to me, as we were returning from meeting to-day, in answer to my observation that ' I had been depending on this day during the whole week, and had unexpectedly realized all the feelings I anticipated,' that you, too, had expected much, thinking that Mr. Channing would give us the sermon he did. I have often thought that the very great pleasure we take in hearing him preach has given us other feelings and motives in our attendance on church than ought to be allowed by the devout Christian. The good which is to be obtained from one of *his* sermons particularly is indeed a great object, and sufficient to induce us to attend the hearing of them whenever there is an opportunity ; but in our eagerness to hear the sermon, to admire it, and endeavor to improve by it, the original intention of public worship, I fear, is in a manner lost on us. Do we, when we go to the house of God, feel that we are as it were entering his more immediate presence ? He is, it is true, present with us in all places, and at all times ; but in the world it is not required, neither is it practicable, that our whole thoughts should be devoted to any one subject ; but when we go to the house of worship, is it not that we may, by shutting out of our minds the world and all that it contains, give to the Lord of the Sabbath every thought ? Was it not for this end he gave us the day, and renews our strength every week ? We are called together to worship, not merely with our lips, but to unite every thought and feeling in adoration. It is a privilege thus to be enabled to call our minds entirely from the cares and troubles of life ; it gives to those who are oppressed by them some idea of heaven, when all the trials which now torture them will be for ever forgotten ; and to all it should be esteemed a high and holy privilege, setting aside the delightful instruction we receive, thus to hold communion with Heaven, for I can compare it to nothing else. It seems often to me, while in the hour of prayer I give myself up to the thought of heaven, as though I had in reality left the world, and was enjoying that which is promised to the Christian. I fear, however, these feelings are too often delusive ; we substitute the love of holiness for the actual possession, and often deceive ourselves. But if we can keep our reason unclouded, we have nothing to fear from feeling too much. I would not be understood to mean, that the delightful, improving preaching we are in the habit of hearing is not a good motive for carrying us to meeting; but it is not enough, if it be the only one; if the happiness of an unreserved devotion of thought to God is not sufficiently great to induce us to seek every opportunity of enjoying it, I fear the true, vital piety, which is the only support of religion, is imperfectly gained by us.

"I have not time to write more. I doubt if I have explained myself intelligibly, but more of this at some future period. I presume there is an appearance of vanity in one paragraph, which I will some time explain.

" MARY."

This fervid religious interest and enjoyment seems to have filled her heart, and absorbed her thoughts, more and more, until, in the following summer, it led to a personal interview with Dr. Channing, of the most interesting kind, to be described only in her own words.

" *Boston, July* 10, 1817.

" There is a certain state of feeling, or I may now say passion, in which the heart must either find relief in utterance, or burst; when all the powers of mind and body are suspended, and thought, feeling, sensation, are all centred in one sole object. It is at such moments as these that we feel the true value of a friend who will submit patiently to our detail, and sympathize in all. I have just had a long — (I do not know what to call it) — with our dear minister. You know how long I have wished, yet dreaded it. That I should ever have *dreaded* it appears now a most astonishing fact, except that I knew it would humble me to the dust. And why should I not be so humbled ?

"It chanced that grandma was too unwell to see him; and I, though not in the most composed state of mind that can be imagined, was to sit down alone with him, fully determined to improve the opportunity and say all that I had so long wished. I put on as collected an appearance as could possibly be required, and, trembling at the very centre of my heart, met him with a smile of joy. Indifferent subjects soon entirely subdued all kind of internal embarrassment, (external, I did not permit,) when, to my great annoyance, C—— walked in! O that I could have rendered him invisible, — deaf, dumb, — any thing, for the time being! But patience triumphed; I contrived at last to let him understand that I wished him far away. He took the hint, but when he rose to go, Mr. Channing did so also! I could not but detain him. How I did it, or what followed on my part, I know not; I heard all he said, I laid every word carefully aside in my mind to be enjoyed at some future period, but how foolish, how weak, how every thing irrational *I* was, I cannot, dare not, think. I told him as well as I could, with what views and feelings I presumed to deviate from the path in which I had been led by my parents, what he had done for me, and what I hoped to do for myself. I could not have been intelligible, but I will not regret that I attempted, though I could not succeed. I am relieved by what he said of many unpleasant, oppressive feelings. I felt that I was detaining him, or I might have been rather more collected. What a state has he left me in! O, could I for ever preserve the remembrance of what now fills my heart, could I ever feel as I now do, that I am one of the least of all beings, capable of being better but shamefully neglecting my best interests, awfully responsible for the inestimable privileges I enjoy, but wholly unmindful of them.

"Dearest N——, I am wrong to impose on your patience

but I am too selfish to resist. Forgive this sentence. I do not doubt your interest, but I may talk too long. This is not the fervor of sudden enthusiasm; no, I have long felt my sinfulness, but the excitement of talking to Mr. Channing has made me now utter it. Give me your prayers, give me your advice, assist me in elevating my heart to higher objects, purer joys, than this world can give. I love it too well; I want the severing hand of trial to rend asunder the thousand evil passions which connect me with it.

"I have scribbled this at your desk; this quiet retreat has calmed me. It is, perhaps, fortunate that you were not at home, except that you would have been saved this fine specimen of what an egotist can write. O dear, how weak I am! excitement is so new to me, that it almost deprives me of the use of my understanding, or I should not thus betray myself. I know not what I am coming to; I was very foolish yesterday; I have been worse to-day. Do come and see me to-morrow and lend me a little sense, or if you cannot spare it, exercise it yourself over the mind of your senseless friend,

"MARY."

During this season of peculiar experience, Mary sought the confidence, and enjoyed the sympathy, not only of the one friend to whom the last letters were written, but also of her late instructors in Hingham. The correspondence between them is of the most confiding character, and shows a mutual respect and sense of obligation in pupil and teacher. "Talk not of gratitude, my dear Mary," the latter writes; "has not every kindness we have ever had it in our power to show you been more than cancelled by your unremitting assiduities to serve and please us? The uniform disposition you have ever

5

shown to promote the ease and happiness of all around you, will long remain a sweet remembrance of one whose image is connected in my mind with every softer virtue, accompanied by that strength of mind which would enable you, if called upon, to sustain uncommon trials. No, I shall not, I cannot, be disappointed in you, my dear young friend; you will be all that your opening character now promises, because you have built on a sure foundation. If my life is spared, I anticipate much pleasure from the continuation of a friendship thus commenced. May it be increased and strengthened while we sojourn together on earth, and may we have the happiness of exciting each other to a higher standard of excellence than is generally adopted by the world, and thus be prepared for the society of those pure and holy beings we hope hereafter to join." These expressions of confidence and encouragement were probably induced by the trying circumstances in which Mary was then placed, partly from her father's misfortunes and feeble health, and partly from the weight of her responsibilities in a household where there was not only sickness, but other and sorer trials. She went very little into society, and was thrown entirely upon her own resources, in the midst of arduous and delicate duties. Some of her struggles, and the sources of her peace, are intimated in the following letters to Miss Cushing.

"*Boston, June* 19, 1817.

" As I can neither see you nor hear from you, my dear Miss Cushing, I must write you, if it be only to say how much I think of and desire to see you. I know too well that I do not deserve any indulgence from you, but there is something so solitary, and at times almost overpowering, in the idea that those whom we have best loved, with whom we have passed happy hours of intercourse and sympathy, are, though still dear, divided from us, not perhaps by distance, but by circumstances which we cannot control, that I am almost tempted to repine that such must be our situation. You will, I know, be ready to ask why I have so neglected the only means in my power of continuing that intercourse? I would not complain of it, but I have little time, and so many occupations which the call of duty bids me not neglect, that I seldom write to any one, and always in so much haste that I should be ashamed to send such epistles to you. Beside all this, I have so little intercourse with the world, or those in it in whom I think you would be interested, that I must, from a dearth of ideas in this poor brain, write almost wholly of self, the most odious and wearisome of all topics. But this very isolation makes me depend so much on every little iota of external excitement, that I should be satisfied, or rather content, with any thing in the form of a letter you would find time to give me. . . . . .

" I have felt, and I believe have expressed to you, or Miss P——, a kind of discontent sometimes operating on my mind at the want of opportunity to become what I have vainly thought I might be. But this is all over, and I am satisfied that I must be content with a very low degree in the scale of knowledge. But I trust I may be good, though never great, and am confident that the peculiar situation in which I am placed is one more calculated for me than any I could choose for myself. Trial is necessary to me, and I am happy in it, except when I am conscious it is not improved as it should be. It is not for us, who have so many blessings, to murmur if our faith is sometimes put to the test; did we view things aright, what now seems judgment is in truth mercy. What should we be, were we not sometimes reminded of our sins and the weakness of our minds? Surely, then, whatever may be the trials which bring us to a true sense of our accountability to our Father in heaven, they are the kindest expressions of his goodness. I never could have any gloomy views of religion, and the more experience I have of its cheering influences in the hearts of its votaries, the more I am convinced that it is the only sure guide to happiness even in this world; how much more in another!

"You will forgive me for writing you just what happened to occupy my mind. It is an indulgence that I cannot resist, to be able to communicate a few of my feelings and thoughts. I fear you will think I impose too much on your goodness.

"MARY."

"*Boston, August* 20, 1817.

"MY DEAR MISS CUSHING: —

"There are, I believe, moments in the lives of all human beings, when, from some cause or other, the heart is saddened by a feeling of peculiar loneliness, which, though perhaps rather a disease of the imagination than the effect of real circumstances, is nevertheless irresistible. I have felt this in the gayest period of my life, and it is not strange that I should now often experience it. Leading a perfectly monotonous existence, my resources of animal spirits are not entirely sufficient to supply the call of duty and the hour of solitude too. And when evening closes, and my beloved charge is laid peacefully to rest, excitement ceases, and I am thrown on myself for pleasure. Then it is that I long to be with friends, whom I can only visit in imagination; then I long to annihilate distance, and talk with you. It is, I know, imposing on your goodness to attempt to write you under the influence of such feelings, but it is an indulgence I can hardly resist, convinced as I am that, when you are assured it is a relief to a poor solitary, your benevolent heart will pardon me. I would not convey that I am unhappy in this situation. O, no!—there is such a thing as being 'pleased, and yet sad'; and though sometimes

> 'The heart will feel, the tear will steal,
> For auld lang syne sae dear,'

yet I rejoice with joy unspeakable that the present is still filled with many privileges and pleasures, and that I can with perfect trust refer the future to Him who appointeth all things in mercy. I wish most sincerely I could communicate something interesting to you, to redeem my miserable letters from the charge of perfect egotism, but I live so wholly out of the sphere of the interesting part of the world, that I am as ignorant of all that passes within it as those who know not that it exists. It is this reason which has often withheld me from writing you when indeed I wished for my own sake to indulge in it, and I think you will be fully convinced of the wisdom of my forbearance after the perusal of this.

" M. L. P."

And now another trial impended, to be followed by other and important changes in her condition of life. In the autumn of this year her grandmother died. For the event itself, so long expected and not to be lamented, she was prepared. But some of its circumstances were unusually trying, and she well knew that its consequences might be still more sad. Yet how little these considerations affected her, in comparison with the moral aspects and spiritual lessons of the change, may be seen in her own account of the last sickness, to N. C. S.

" You have so long indulged my selfish propensity of communicating to you every feeling that chances to be excited in my heart, that I find it difficult, when under the influence of any peculiar emotion, to resist the ever-present desire to impart all to you.   But this would be the height of folly and weakness, and I therefore contend against it with all my powers.   There are, however, certain kinds of feeling of such a doubtful nature, that the agency of some external power is absolutely necessary for the proper man- agement of them. · Of this nature, I am persuaded, are those by which I am now overpowered; and lest I should be too much led away by them, I must beg your assist- ance in ascertaining their origin and tendency.   This may seem too systematic for any one who feels *much*, but the violence of the tempest has passed, and that deadly calm which always succeeds the raging of the elements natu- rally inclines the mind to thought and reflection.

" I have lived for the last few months in the hourly con- templation of a most striking picture of the end of human life, the termination of all its joys and sorrows, the anni- hilation of its hopes and wishes.   This could not fail to im- press with sadness a mind in full possession of its powers of enjoyment, and for a time to give it almost a disgust of all those pleasures and pursuits which must so soon fail before the dim eye and feeble energies of approaching age.   It had, in a great degree, this effect on me ; for the moments have been when I would willingly have surren- dered life rather than live in the expectation of such an end, — to outlive the ability to engage in its duties.   I now tremble at the thought of ever having suffered such feelings for a moment to possess my mind.   Continued and deep reflection on the object of all this, the comparative nothing- ness of every thing in this world, the hopes and prospects ot another and better, meditation on the spiritual life, and occasional experience of the real happiness of that elevation of soul above earthly things which religion alone can impart, have overcome this melancholy, and sometimes produced almost a feeling of triumph. I have this evening been almost overwhelmed with a variety of emotions, of which this was the most prominent. Grandma has thought herself dying, and has been conversing with me on her approaching change with that most heavenly calmness which those only who rely on the mercy of God, through the merits of his Son, can experience at this trying hour. This, together with joining in prayer with her that we might all welcome this hour as she did, and her final parting with all in the house, has elevated my mind so much above this transitory scene, that I can scarcely believe I shall ever be so weak as again to be engrossed by it. I cannot describe the state of my mind. I never *felt* so before, though I have often imagined that others have. It is almost a kind of transport at the thought that this mortal shall put on immortality, that there is within us an ethereal spark which can never be extinguished or grow dim, capable of rising superior to the pains and weakness which bend these frail bodies to the ground. O, it is a joy unspeakable! Viewed through this medium, death loses its sting, and the idea of a glorious immortality alone presents itself with the view of its approach.

"But alas! I can place no dependence on the continuance of my feelings beyond the moment that excites them. My life is a mere vision; the world in which I act has no connection with that in which I think. My pleasure, my happiness, is so far independent of the objects around me, that I can hardly associate them together. Having little else to do than meditate, I exist almost in imagination, and communicate so little with others on the subject cf my thoughts,

4

that it seems like living two beings; the greater part of my time is passed in this ideal world, and I am consequently unfitted to mix in the real one in which I am placed. This is a misfortune and a fault. Which has the greatest share of blame? It is most unfavorable to true Christian humility; for, as Mr. Channing says of the effects of a diseased imagination, ' We feel superiority to the world in ascending the airy height, and pride ourselves in this refinement of the mind. After arraying ourselves in the robes of glory, we cannot take the lowly seat which Christianity assigns us.' Thus, then, although this elevation above the objects of this vain world may be a right spirit when it rises from the pure flow of real piety, if it be only the enthusiasm of the moment, which rises for a time and then vanishes away, an abstract theory which would not be practised upon in the hour of temptation, it had better never have been. When we have once been imposed on, we know not what to trust. All my purposes of goodness and high resolves are as yet but theories, which I fear I should never put in practice should temptation assail me. O, I dare not be thus happy!

" MARY."

V.

CHANGES AT HOME.

THE first change consequent upon the death of old Mrs. Lovell, was the leaving of the house in Pearl Street. This, to Mary, was not a small matter. It was not the mere moving of furniture, nor the living in one street rather than another, of the same town. It was the loss of the earliest and only HOME that she had ever known; and none are to be envied who cannot enter into the feelings which such an event must awaken in a heart like hers. With little of the romantic in her nature, and as great independence of the merely local and external as is often seen, her love of family and early friends, her memory of childhood and all its associations, the very changes and sufferings which had made so large a part of her life, were all identified with "that house" as the place of their birth, and bound her to it by the strongest chords. Within a month of the day of her grandmother's death, she wrote her last letter there, which, with the first that was written out of the house, will show what she felt, and why.

"*Boston, November,* 1817.

"It is with many new and peculiar feelings that I attempt to write you for the last time from this blessed spot, rendered doubly sacred to me from having been the scene of that intimacy which ever has been, and I trust ever will be, one of the purest sources of happiness which it has pleased my Heavenly Father to bestow on me......It has been *one* of the happy effects of the trials which, during the last few years, have fallen to my lot, to produce a more unreserved acquaintance between us than under any other circumstances could have been effected. I bless them in all their influences, but particularly in this, that they have brought me the knowledge and affection of such a friend. I should blush at the recollection of the numberless follies, weaknesses, and sins which this frail heart has discovered to you, but I wish you to know me entirely ; the candid confession of faults is the greatest proof of confidence I could give. But that delightful intercourse which has so much conduced to this must for a time be broken off, perhaps never again to be renewed in this changing world. Change of situation will necessarily preclude the possibility of that continued intercourse of thought and feeling, which has been the joy of the past. I cannot admit the idea that this will weaken the bonds that unite us, much less can I think it will break them. But I have been the creature of situation ; my character (if any thing I possess can be entitled to the name) has been moulded by circumstances peculiar in their nature, and which will soon cease to exist. What I shall be in the wide world into which I am going to enter, I know not. I hope, yet fear to change. Without a guide to lead me in the right path, I fear my inexperienced steps will stray into some of the many fascinating, delusive snares which are found in every direction. My course has hitherto been over an old and beaten track, secure by its remoteness from all temptation. What, then, shall I do, when the whole host of the world's allurements are presented at once to my weakness ?

I wish I could describe to you the feelings which the very prospect of leaving this house excites in this poor, weak heart, — so weak that it cannot subdue or control its emotions. It would seem romantic and visionary to any one who had been accustomed to change; but this house supplied in a great measure the relation of instructor, parent, and friend. And it is true, that in every part are recorded by association the admonitions of those friends I have known in it or lessons which the experience of repeated trials has impressed in indelible characters on these scenes. Here, when temptation assailed, and this frail heart was on the point of surrendering to it, would the remembrance of former good resolutions, presented by the very walls around me, recall my wandering virtue, and strengthen me to new exertions. And to that sacred retreat, that sanctuary of all my joys and sorrows, I owe, if not the creation, at least the preservation of the best feelings I possess. There I find the history of the most important moments of my life, for in that spot did the first sincere and heartfelt aspirations of my soul to its Creator find utterance; and there, too, have I always found support under trial, in prayer. It were an endless work to recount all the associations which attach me to this only home I have ever known; it would be to give you a minute account of every transaction which has taken place since I lived here.

" Mary."

" *Boston, December*, 1817.

" For the first time since I left that loved spot in Pearl Street have I seated myself at my *desk ;* and, although my object in now doing so was a very different one, I cannot resist the impulse which the sight of it gives, to renew the employment, so wont to be pursued at it, of pouring forth a few of my feelings to my friend. It is so long since I have had an opportunity to do so, and so various have been the occurrences, and still more various the feelings which it has been my lot to experience in the course of the last two months, that, though my mind is full of what I wish to communicate, I am as much at a loss what to write as if all was vacancy. This poor little, unconscious desk has carried me back, against my will, to scenes which it were wise seldom to think of. The last time I wrote at it was the last evening I spent in the 'oaken parlor,' when all was sad and solitary. But I cannot dwell on it. I find in the record of that evening prophecies which are hour.y fulfilling. I felt deeply impressed with a sense of insufficiency to meet with, and bear aright, the temptations which a life of indulgence would present. I felt that I was not fit for society, and I feel so still, but more sensibly, more truly, for it is now the lesson of experience, sad indeed. But a truce with such feelings ;—it is not of them I wish to write. This wicked desk has conjured up the old complaining spirit which so used to haunt me whenever I attempted scribbling to you. I am happy, contented with any change that has or may take place. I only ask a less selfish, more disinterested frame of mind, — to be more independent of the opinion of others, when a consciousness of sincere endeavor to do right acquits me of actual transgression. Selfish are all my regrets, all my trials, and wherefore, then, trouble another with a detail of what self alone can sympathize in, or ameliorate, or cure ? I will not ;— for once, I will follow reason rather than inclination.

"The more I know of the world, the more I see of the beings who constitute what is so called, the more the hopes and wishes which excite and keep alive their energies sink into insignificance, and the more my own restlessness and anxiety about the cares and pursuits of life excite my astonishment and contempt. We surely were not placed in this world solely to be occupied by its allurements, or, without reference to the design of our Creator in placing us here, to pursue that which seems to us the most easy and pleasant path. And with our reasons convinced, how can we so unweariedly pursue that phantom happiness which has here no fixed abode? We acknowledge that nothing here can satisfy us, and yet vainly delude ourselves with the hope of soon attaining some ideal joy which, like the philosopher's stone, will convert all into solid happiness. One would think I had been disappointed in some fond hope, or found too late *my* fancied joy a dream. But no, I am not disappointed, for I have never anticipated; and if aught I have said savors of this temper of mind, I would recall it.

" Mr. Colman advised me never to write in the evening, lest I should deceive myself and my friend with an exaggerated account of what in the light of day would prove false. I am half asleep, and therefore will take his advice, and I already find myself on the verge of the gulf, — self-deception.

" M. L. P."

To some it will seem strange, that one of such faith and principle, with no proneness or taste for the follies of the world, should express fear of " fascinating, delusive snares," or think for a moment of the " whole host of the world's allurements." But this will be understood by those who remember that strength does not lie in a sense of security, nor wisdom in assurance. It seems to have been ever a part of Mary Pickard's wisdom, to own her weakness. And more than this, the evil that she feared was not that coarse, palpable thing usually called " vice," but the invisible, subtle evil, so serious to the sensitive and pure mind, though by the many lightly

6

regarded. " I fear not actual vice," she said at this very time, " but to become thoughtless, forgetful of duty, unmindful of my highest interests, is to my mind a more deadly sin than many which are accounted by the world *crimes*. It is this I most dread. My conscience, or, should that fail, my friends, would save me from the first, but who can control the thoughts of my heart?" Thus fearing, thus armed, she went out into the world, beginning at this point her life of self-guidance. Of her means of support we know little. She was not dependent From her grandparents, to whom she had been so true a child, she received enough to enable her to assist her father in his depression, though it is evident that he took no more than was absolutely necessary, and that she retained enough for her wants, more than she used to the time of her marriage. This could have been accomplished, however, only by a uniform and strict economy, whose necessity she never regretted, except as it curtailed her charities.

And now began a life of business and of motion. Since her return from England, at the age of five, Mary had been from home very little, and only for her schooling. Hereafter she is to become a traveller, to a greater degree than was then common for a lady, and greater than she desired. Her journeyings, we infer, were always more for others than herself; either for the gratification of friends, or in aid of her father. For she seems to have become, in various ways, his active as well as domestic helper, and was intrusted by him, we should judge from their letters, with important business. For some purpose of this kind, in the year following our last date, she went, for the first time, to New York. And the account she gives of the preparations and the journey, while it shows what changes there have been since, shows also how much there was on her mind and her hands. She speaks of getting but four hours for sleep from having " so great a variety of occupation, — so much for my poor, weak head to think of." And then, half playfully, half in earnest, she writes of being " at last equipped for a journey probably of two months." But we must give a part of the letter itself; showing, as it does, how near to her, even in her busiest moments and most fatiguing labors, were the higher cares of the mind and the soul.

" I am glad of having a great deal to do ; any thing that will call my little powers into exercise gives me a transient feeling of consequence, which, as it is highly flattering to vanity, produces rather pleasant sensations. I will not enter on the subject of leaving home, and setting out on an expedition fraught with untried temptations, and presenting even in the most favorable view a scene of life little calcu-lated to satisfy my taste or warm my heart. But I believe there may be instruction found in every situation, and I hope that seeing eyes and an understanding heart will be given me, to discern and improve it. I cannot tell you how much more I feel than I ever did before, at leaving home ; —I cannot; it is in vain to attempt so vast a subject at such a time. I have been highly favored the last two Sun-days in hearing two of Mr. Channing's most delightful ser-mons, which I hope will not be soon forgotten. Last

Sunday was the anniversary of many eventful days to me. The first Sabbath in September has for many years been a memorable day to me, and this last, I think, exceeds them all. It is three months since I have been at home on Communion-day, and the coldness which I had felt creeping through my very soul gave me a feeling of hope that I should find something to excite and elevate my affections. I never felt more entirely humbled to the dust, or more sensible of the immense privilege we enjoy, in having such a man to guide us on our way. But I am so excessively weary that I cannot write more, — scarcely to assure you of the warm affection of your

" M. L. P."

The journey to New York, by way of Providence and Norwich, was " a week's work," though it seems to have been all used in travelling, but with many " adventures " and delays incident to the beginning of steamboats, — against which, notwithstanding the discomforts and perils, Mary expresses herself " not so prejudiced that I should be unwilling to step on board one again." The letters she writes from the great city, so new and strange, are almost exclusively business letters to her father, and his replies show that he had given her important commissions, to be discharged in person, and in her own discretion. Directions are given for the sale or purchase, not only of muslins and moreens, but also of skins, saltpetre, and the like. And at the end of several weeks, in which she seems not to have indulged herself in much recreation, she speaks of returning as soon as she " has seen the city."

But instead of returning, she was induced by a

tempting opportunity to go still farther from home, and with no time to get her father's permission, — a liberty evidently new on her part, and receiving at first severe reproof from him. The incident is not important, except as showing their relation to each other, and the manner in which she incurred and endured (being now a woman) the only harsh language that we find addressed to her by her father, — though it is clear that he always inclined to be exacting. The trouble in this case was, that he first heard from another of her being seen on her way to Baltimore, when he thought her safe with friends in New York, if not on her way home. The fact was easily explained. A gentleman with whom she was intimate invited her to accompany him to Baltimore, where she had long wished to visit a cousin newly married and settled there; and, with the approval of those with whom she was staying, she accepted the invitation as suddenly as she received it, "and in two hours was in the stage for Baltimore," to ride night and day till she arrived there. As soon as possible after her arrival, she wrote to her father all the circumstances, giving her reasons in a way that should and did avert his displeasure entirely. But unfortunately he had already heard of the runaway by accident, and one is forced to smile at the manner in which it affected him. Not waiting to hear from Mary, he instantly wrote to the lady in New York with whom she had staid, — " I am exceedingly vexed and mortified that she should do any thing so foolish, and cannot conceive how she will be able to justify herself; had I had any idea she would

6*

have been so indiscreet, I would not have consented to her leaving Boston. I have been expecting daily to hear what was likely to be done with some muslins she had the charge of; but instead of attending to that, she is flying like a wild goose about the country. These girls in their teens [Mary was just twenty] should not be let out of their leading-strings; nor would her's have been let loose, but from confidence in her discretion." Yet in company with this letter he sent a note for his daughter, which begins with saying he can hardly call her " dear," but ends in a very different tone; and the first letter he receives sets all right. His only anxiety now is to have her with him, coupled, however, with a fear as to her companion home, and again making us smile by a prediction which has been singularly reversed in the fulfilment. " If you are well, pray come by the first *good* opportunity. I am afraid you will wait till the end of the month for the parson; your being so fond of parsons is rather ominous, and you had better almost be any man's wife than a parson's." The parson referred to was Mr. Colman of Hingham, now returning from a visit to Baltimore. It is a pleasant conclusion of this little episode, and offers a hint to children as well as parents, that, when Mary found how much her father had felt, without blaming herself for doing what seemed right and a duty, she expressed such sorrow for the pain she had given him, in terms so respectful and filial, as to turn all his severity against himself, and increase his admiration and love for her. The next time he refers to her fondness for the " clergy," it is in a vein of pleasantry which seldom relieves his merchant-like letters. " Could you not, my dear, enliven your letters by writing of persons and things which you have seen ? I think your letters are too much tinctured with what may be called moral philosophy, for so young a person. You are so fond of the clergy, you will get into a habit of writing like one of them, and if you were to turn Quaker, I have no doubt but you would preach yourself. Tell us something of Baltimore, how it is situated, &c.; and, as Mrs. Slipslop says, something of the 'contagious country.' Pray take care of your own health, and get the family well soon."

The last words refer to the actual cause of Mary's protracted absence. On returning to New York, intending to go home by the first opportunity, she found her good friend, Mrs. Harman, whom she was visiting before, dangerously ill, the husband absent, and the family in great confusion and trouble. At once she became the director and nurse, — offices which she seemed destined to fill wherever she went, as her subsequent life will show. All thought now of herself and her plans yielded to the present duty. And not an easy duty could it have been, as she describes the severity of the mother's sickness, the care of difficult children, and her responsibility in another's house and a strange city. As soon as they were in a condition to be left, she returned to Boston, though Mr. Pickard even urged her to stay longer, for rest and her own gratification.

For a year or more Mary and her father remained together in Boston, with no change or incident to be noticed. They were living at board, so far as we find, though they may have taken a house, as he seemed very anxious before her return to be alone with her, having an aversion to company, and preferring her society and care to all other.

In her correspondence at this time, the prevailing theme and object, as usual, were religion and its influences, for herself and others. We cannot but observe the preponderance of this theme, and yet its perfectly natural and healthy tone. With nothing dark or melancholy in her religious views, with an habitual horror of ostentation and cant, she lost no opportunity to cherish and diffuse an all-comprehending faith. The letters which follow, addressed to her constant friend, declare their own occasion and design.

                              " Boston, August 12, 1819.

" There was something in the strain of your last letter to me which has given me some feelings of anxiety. You refer to the course of medical discipline which has been pursued with Mr. —— with expressions of regret, which, though natural, must add greatly to every other painful feeling that his present situation, and perhaps loss, must inevitably excite. I cannot reprehend you for what I know but too well is the natural impulse under such circumstances ; but I would, if it were possible, point to a healing balm for that worst of all wounds, — fruitless regret.

" I am no fatalist, but the continual influence of an unerring Providence is a truth which was early impressed on my heart, and which daily observation has confirmed and strengthened. The simple order of nature speaks it with a powerful voice ; the sacred pages of God's own book proclaim it in terms which cannot be misconstrued ; and would we impartially review our own lives, should we not see in them incontrovertible proofs of an unseen power, that guided and directed many things for our happiness which our blindness would have wished otherwise? And are we to assent to this truth only when our minds can clearly see its reality? Are we to withhold our confidence in Him whom we have always found mighty to save, because we cannot in a single instance see its practicability? O, no! far be it from us, who profess to acknowledge the being and attributes of a merciful God, to shrink when he puts our faith to the test. Are his so often repeated expressions of love towards his creatures mere empty sounds to deceive the credulous, or assist the imagination in forming a perfect model of moral sublimity, but to wither into airy nothing when we dwell on them for support? This we would not, most certainly, admit in our actions, and why should we even in our thoughts? Surely, believing, as we do, that his promises are sure and steadfast, we may in the darkest hours of adversity find consolation in the thought, that, however mysterious may be his decrees, there *must* be some good result, some benevolent design, concealed beneath the most doubtful appearances.

"Cowper has beautifully versified this idea in his hymn, beginning

> 'God moves in a mysterious way,
> His wonders to perform';

you will find it in Belknap. Read it for the sake of one whom in all trials it has animated and consoled. Forgive me for dwelling so long on this subject. Do not infer that I think it new to you, but it is one in which I have felt most deeply, on which, too, I have had the most severe contentions with the spirit that warreth within, and one which, of all others, it is necessary for our happiness and goodness to establish in our hearts, that it may effectually influence our lives.

"MARY."

" It is now a month since the date of your last letter, during which time I think I have at least once written you ; but our intercourse is now so different from what I would desire at this peculiarly eventful period, that it seems as if I did nothing, if I do not tell you every day how much depends on its events. I have been with you in a happy vision, and awake to the sad disappointment that it is but a dream, and to the consciousness that for a long time my unfruitful pen will be my only means of communication. It would be weak to repine at what is inevitable ; I will not give way to it. How often have you told me that you were almost tempted to pray for trial, that you might know the true state of your religious life, that you might have your faith put to the test, and the veil of self-deception taken from your eyes! Often have I prayed that, whenever it should please the Disposer of all things to send to you sorrow and affliction, you might find strength and support where least expected, not from your own resources, but in that arm which is mighty to save to the uttermost all who seek. It is not, however, simply in the belief that whatever He appoints is right, that you are to receive his dispensations ; difficult as is the task, we must not rest satisfied with ourselves until we have learned to receive with cheerful acquiescence what the world calls trials ; until we have learned to view all events as tending to the same great end, and be thankful for what is denied, as well as what is received ; knowing that there is but one great object in each. This may at first seem too high an aim, even above human powers to attain. But it calls not on us to give up natural feeling, only to guide it aright, and the higher our standard of excellence is fixed, the greater will be our efforts to attain it, and our success unquestionably proportioned to it.

" But why talk to you of what you have already more

knowledge? Forgive me; I lost, in the interest I felt in your present happiness, the remembrance that you were not in want of counsel on a subject on which you have already experienced enough to feel its importance. But do not, my dear friend, look only on the dark side of the picture; do not suffer your mind to lose its activity, because confined at present to one subject. It is not to contract our feelings, but to expand and teach them to enter . into the feelings of others, that we are made thus to experience what it is to suffer. Should it not quicken our efforts to alleviate, to our utmost endeavor, those who are tried also, and by a cheerful example lighten the hearts of fellow-sufferers? I have felt, and *know* therefore too well, the tendency of severe trial to enervate the mind, and lead us insensibly to give up our ambition to act on any other subject; but our general duties are not the less imposing, because a particular one requires more attention, nor are we to give way for a moment to the impulse of self-indulgence, because we feel any peculiar right to it. . . . . .
All this is unnecessary, but you can conceive how deeply I feel interested in the result of this great trial of your Christian faith. I know its difficulties, therefore can appreciate its triumphs.

" MARY."

" *Boston*, 1819.

"I leave the dismal beginning of a letter, intended to excite your compassion for my suffering under the confinement of a cold, and it would be rather *mal apropos*, after what has passed, to proceed in due form to give an account of myself during the long period since I last saw you. But in order to preserve the unity of time and place, I must first revert to the accident which brought us together so opportunely. I will not pretend to defend the prudence of the action, but acknowledge it was rather the impulse of strong desire to give some one a little pleasure, than the sober dictate of reason, and I felt that, in M——'s solitary state, she would be glad to see any one. I know it was wrong in one point of view, but right in another. I was rewarded for a severe sickness, as far as regarded my own sufferings, should one have ensued. I had a very pleasant ride, and became more acquainted with J—— than I could in any other way. I was agreeably surprised to find in his conversation so much depth of thought and knowledge of mankind. I am glad of any opportunity to extend my acquaintance with character, in its infinite variety. There is no human knowledge, I am persuaded, which has so great an influence on our happiness. We learn to estimate ourselves more justly, and in the formation of our own characters we are enabled to discriminate between right and wrong more accurately; for in nothing are we more liable to confound them, than as respects our own feelings and motives. Is it not wilful blindness that leads us so often to ridicule in others what we unconsciously practise ourselves? Why are we not as cautious to ascertain the motives of the conduct of others as of our own? We console ourselves, when we have done any thing which to the eyes of the world appears weak and foolish, with the thought that our motives are good, and with a consciousness of having done what was right. All else is of little importance; but did we believe that our friends were as much influenced by appearances, in their judgment of us, as we are in ours of them, I doubt if the approving smile of conscience would always compensate for the loss of the good opinion of those we love. Let us not, then, judge solely by the conduct of any what are their real characters; peculiar circumstances may prevent even our most intimate friends from disclosing to us their particular reasons for every action; but in that case, if it be a tried friend, it were surely a proof of friendship to believe that it is at least felt by him to be right. And with regard to people in general, let charity have its perfect work, and let us think all are free from deliberate faults, till we have good reason to suppose otherwise. This is, perhaps, if understood literally, rather too liberal a plan for this world of sin and wickedness; but as far as is consistent with reason, and our previous knowledge of men and manners, is it not just to judge of all as we would be judged? I have *felt* the want of this spirit of impartial justice, and speak from experience in some respects; in one, I hope never to be tried. I have been what you call mysterious; could you understand me, you would, I am sure, approve. Believe me, I am not governed by caprice in my treatment of friends; if any thing may have appeared so, there has always been a motive, and I feel that I may confidently rely on your friendship for all charitable construction. . . . . .

" I am in a sad state. I long to see you, in hopes of procuring some remedy in your better regulated mind. I am so much under the dominion of certain sickly feelings of late, that I begin to think my mind will never recover its healthy tone again; active employment for the good of others is the only preventive for such disorders. I have not at present any prospect of such a means towards my own recovery, but trust the vital energy of my being is not quite extinct, and that ere long it will rise and subdue the weaker powers. . . . . . I have just thought that it is the spring-like feeling of the day that has such a weakening effect on my mind. Why do we indulge so much in idealism, instead of the real pleasure of our existence? I have no opinion of this giving way to imagination in our estimate of life.

" MARY."

7

In the month of October a death occurred which awakened all her sympathy, and the sympathy and sorrow of a large community. The Rev. John E. Abbot, whose life and character Henry Ware has made familiar to us all, died in October, at his father's in Exeter, where Mary's friend was staying as a relative. To both of them he had been a Christian helper when they most needed Christian counsel and encouragement. His short life was, indeed, a blessing to all who knew him, and his death full of "joy and peace in believing." Again was the pen taken, and solace offered.

"Boston, October 15, 1819.

" I attempted, my dear friend, to write you on Tuesday, for I felt then that, all being over, I could calmly write of what had passed, and direct your feelings and my own to the future. But I knew from experience that a few days' delay would find you more in want of a letter ; as the necessary exertion which attends a scene like that you have passed through occupies the whole mind while it is necessary to support it, but leaves, when it is passed, a vacuity which needs some external power to fill it. Perhaps I too easily found in this an excuse for leaving my letter unfinished, and now that I review it, I blush at my own weakness. I sought to relieve my own heart, instead of strengthening yours. I have been with you every moment since I last wrote you, and too fully realized all that you have suffered. At the moment I was writing you, that pure spirit was taking its flight. I felt it as by intuition, and needed not further confirmation. But it was a relief to know that his blessed spirit was for ever beyond the reach of pain and anguish; that it was exalted to its native home, there to realize all that his brightest hopes could anticipate of a glorious immortality.

" I feel an almost total inability to write you on this sub-ject. Could I talk to you, there would be time to enlarge on all the thoughts which it suggests. But they are so vari-ous, so interesting, so overpowering, that I know not on which to dwell. His virtues are too deeply imprinted on our hearts to receive any additional weight by enumeration. We can only go forward with them to that world where they shall meet a reward proportionate to their value. The remembrance of his character, while it awakens every emotion of affection which he excited while on earth, sheds on the heart a light which unfolds to the eye of faith its glorious perfection in heaven. Nothing in him can have escaped the mind of one so closely connected with him; friends need not to be reminded of what is imprinted in indel-ible characters on their hearts. But the thought that what we so loved and cherished is gone for ever from us, that the form by which we have held communion with the spirit is hid for ever from our view, the chilling realities of death and decay, as they appeal to our purest earthly feelings, are the most difficult to contend with. Our brightest visions of the future have a most powerful drawback in the horror with which nature shrinks from the sad appendages of death.

" It is this, I think, which more than any thing else makes us look forward to our own dissolution with instinctive dread, and leads us to avoid, if possible, every thing that reminds us of it. But when we view it as it really is, but a step in the ceaseless progression which is to carry us on to eternity, as a mere change of the external habitation of our spirits, a removal of the greatest impediments in our pro-gress towards perfection, then, indeed, it loses all its terror, and we think of our friends who have passed through it as absent only in body, but present in spirit. Our own souls, though still connected with an earthly load, form by their derivation from heaven a part of the spiritual world, and in proportion as they become purified from the corruption of the world, they approach the state of those beatified beings who have finished their course. And therefore, though separated from them in this world, we are allied to them more closely than earthly ties could bind us, and must patiently wait for the fulfilment of our Father's plans for our joyful removal to them. This is, indeed, a new incentive to exertion, to prepare ourselves for this change. I have feared it might supersede a still higher motive; but how far it may be permitted to influence us, I dare not determine. That our earthly affections *may* be a means of leading us to the Creator of them and of all our powers of thinking and feeling, I believe must be true, or they would not have been given us as sources of such pure enjoyment here. But their tendency to make us forget all other considerations, to absorb those thoughts which should be directed to higher objects, is the trial which always attends every means of worldly enjoyment we possess, and as such should be combated with our utmost powers. . . . . . .

" Yours, most truly,

" M. L. P."

In the summer of 1821 Mary went with her father to live in Dorchester. And the change from town to country, and from a life of business and care to the free and still enjoyment of nature, seems to have had both a favorable and unfavorable effect upon her mind. Unfavorable in part, if we may trust her own account of herself. In this account, however, there is a nearer approach to morbidness than we have before seen, and a kind of self-disparagement, which must have been sincere at the time,

but was not, we think, a part of her essential character. Humble she was always; truly, deeply humble;
yet no one knew better than she, or acted more upon
the truth, that genuine humility says very little about
itself. And the expressions of it which appear in the
letters that follow were made, we are to remember,
to a confiding friend, to whom she declared all that
she felt, though it were but the feeling of the moment, and the next moment recalled. She says herself, in this connection, — " I believe I have given an
extravagant detail of my danger; and I may be under the influence of one of those fits of distempered
mind, to which I have always been prone." If this
were so, it shows the more what efforts she made,
and how completely she brought every such disposition under the sway of principle, so that few who
knew her ever suspected, we imagine, that any effort
was necessary.

But we are ourselves overstating, it may be, the
disposition to which we refer. Wherever it appears,
as here, it is connected with such just and exalted
sentiments, that it seems incidental and unimpor-
tant.

" Dorchester, June 18, 1821.

" The first line which I date from this place is to you,
my friend, to whom my first feelings, on all occasions of
self-interest, turn for sympathy. Your friendly curiosity is
awake to know what effect a new kind of life is to have on
a character which I know you feel of some importance to
yourself. I would not imply that this selfish reason is the
only motive of your interest, but I seek rather to find in it
some pretence for indulging myself in the egotism which is

creeping over me ; and which led me to this desk for relief. How much will one short week of quiet reflection teach of our own hearts ! How deceived are we, if we imagine we know ourselves thoroughly, when we have been but partially exposed to that change of circumstances and situation which alone can develop character even to one's self ! I have found, indeed, just what I anticipated, that the change from constant activity to perfect stillness and inaction would of course produce a vacuity which time and habit would alone overcome ; but I knew not the whole weakness of my mind. In the bustle of a busy life (idly busy, perhaps, but not the less exciting) I had almost lost sight of my natural propensities. Accustomed to find objects to occupy my powers wherever I turned, I mistook the simple love of being employed for real energy of mind, and therefore did not even apprehend the want of power to direct these energies to whatever I pleased. But it is not as I thought. My natural turn of mind (if I may so call what is perhaps more a weakness of heart) is for that calm, saddened view of things, which seeks enjoyment from the contemplative in character, and lives rather on the food of imagination than reality. I never found in words a more accurate description of the prevailing mood of my natural feelings than in that exquisite little poem, ' I 'm pleased, and yet I 'm sad,' — yet not of an uneasy, discontented temperament, but simply inclined to the purest refinement of melancholy. Trials which called for vigor of mind and cheerfulness of manner, a situation whose duties required the full employment of time which might otherwise have been wasted in cultivating this propensity, and perhaps a little pride lest those who could not understand it should discover it, and I hope a principle which taught me to wage war with what must interfere with higher duties, — all these combined to stifle the propensity, and I sometimes thought had almost extinguished it. But now, removed from those occupations which demanded thought as well as action, thrown entirely upon myself, with every thing around to inspire the enthusiastic indulgence of fancy, my imagination has suddenly taken the reins, and I find it will not be without a struggle that reason and principle will recover them.

"I suppose I must set about some new study or dry book, if I cannot find some animate subject to interest and fix my mind. There is a little deaf and dumb girl just opposite us, and if I knew the process I would teach her to read. I must have something to do which will rouse my mind to exertion. I have employment enough, but it is not of my *mind*, and that is unfortunately one which will retrograde if it does not progress. I am delighted with our situation, and cannot describe to you the sensations of first realizing that I am living in the pure, unconfined atmosphere of nature. It has a power, which I hope familiarity will never efface, of elevating the heart to Him whose ' hand I see, wrought in each flower, inscribed on every tree.' It is a privilege which I hope I shall fully estimate, to be thus reminded at every glance of the love and power of our Father in heaven. I am grateful for that goodness which has appointed me so much of the purest enjoyment of life, and I would testify it by devoting all my powers to his best service. I was not made for solitude of heart, and I would find all that my heart requires in the love of divine perfection. I think Foster will do me good, — ' On the Epithet Romantic.'

" I have just been taking a delightful walk, as the sun was setting gloriously, and I think if you were only with me I should enjoy it tenfold. I wish you could arrange matters to come out with father one night before you go, and we will go to Milton.

"MARY."

" *Dorchester, July* 25, 1821.

" I wrote you last rather a monotonous round of sedentary employments, occasionally interrupted by a visit to the city, or a ride about the country. On the whole I enjoy life highly, although my present mode is so novel a one, that I am sometimes at a loss to decide whether it is actual enjoyment or negative indulgence of ease. But country life is a privilege I estimate most highly ; that I can at all times, when I raise my eyes, find my thoughts so forcibly directed, by all I behold, to that ' still communion which transcends the imperfect offices of prayer and praise ' ! I am persuaded that it is far easier to cultivate a devotional spirit here than in the confusion of life, and to have a deeper sense of the presence of God in the heart. Feeling is little, to be sure, unless it fortifies for action ; but in the hour of trial, we find great assistance in recalling past exercises, and in spiritual as well as temporal concerns habit is a powerful coadjutor. That high-wrought state of feeling which some of the splendid appearances of nature often produce on a heart which has once felt the power of piety, is ridiculed as enthusiasm of the most dangerous kind ; and I do not myself think it is any test of religious character ; but as far as the enjoyment of the present moment is of any importance, what can exceed it ? We are, indeed, too apt to feel that we have been on the mount, when it was but a vision which we saw ; but where it does not so deceive us, nothing but a good effect can result from its indulgence. I recollect part of a description of this state of mind in Wordsworth's Excursion, which from its accuracy has remained in my mind, though I forget the scene which suggested it : —

' Sound needed none,
Nor any form of words ; his spirit drank
The spectacle ; sensation, soul, and form
All melted in him ; they swallowed up

His animal being; in them did he live,
And by them did he live; they were his life.
In such access of mind, in such high hour
Of visitation from the living God,
Thought was not; in enjoyment it expired.
No thanks he breathed, he proffered no request.
Rapt into still communion that transcends
The imperfect offices of prayer and praise,
His mind was a thanksgiving to the Power
That made him; it was blessedness and love.'

" I have got Samor to read, because you recommend it,
and am shocked to find how unfit my mind has become for
every kind of application in the way of reading. I know
you think I am greatly deficient in that kind of literary taste
which fits one for an agreeable companion, — and I feel
most sensibly that it is true. But I am fully persuaded that
if the *sentimental* requisites of an interesting character are
only to be derived from books, I must go through life the
plain matter-of-fact lady I now am; it is too late for me to
work a reform.

" MARY."

Not long afterward, an event occurred of no little
interest and importance to Mary, — the marriage of
her true friend, now Mrs. Paine, who went to reside
in Worcester. In a letter dated May, 1822, we
find a full expression of the thoughts and wishes
caused by this event, but of too personal and private
a character to be used. The letter closes with ·an
allusion to herself, showing that she had trials and
experiences of her own, not to be disclosed to the
public eye. She speaks of the previous winter, as
" a remarkable era, never to be forgotten. Its perplexities have passed away, but its blessings have increased and become consummated. We have all

found it an important period, and to some of us the
most so of life. How far it has improved us, He
who searcheth the heart alone knows ; but for myself,
I feel that it has been a scene of more mental suffering than I ever before knew. You have seen it, and
will not misunderstand me when I say that, had I
been more indifferent, I should have escaped much
torture. But it has been a good lesson for me."

There are few greater demands upon the exercise
of a sound discretion and practical wisdom, than the
giving counsel and exerting a right influence on *sceptical* minds. Nor is it often that such minds are
willing to open themselves, and confide their doubts
or indifference to a Christian friend. Unfortunately,
Christians are apt to be either too careless in their
conduct, or too morose in their manners and severe
of judgment, to make a favorable impression on the
sceptical, and win their confidence in the assurance
of a generous sympathy. We dare not conjecture
how much of the infidelity of the world, and the un-
happiness of the unbelieving, is owing to this cause.
We are sometimes driven to the fear, that Christians
themselves may have as much to answer for as those
whom they exclude for their unbelief, and whom
they fail to impress with the power of their own faith,
or the beauty of their holiness. We have many intimations that this was felt peculiarly by her of whom
we write. And it is one indication of character, and
of the aspect and influence of her faith, that many
came to her freely with their doubts and difficulties.
Some of the particular cases cannot be published.

But where no names are used in her account of them, nor a hint given of the persons intended, there can be no impropriety in offering the facts as related. The reflections with which she accompanies them may be profitable to both classes of minds, the believing and the doubting.

Under date of August, 1822, Mary writes to her former instructors in Hingham, giving with other incidents the following case of hard indifference, if not infidelity.

" This leads me to a subject upon which I want assistance. I have lately met with a person of my own age, who, though living in a Christian land, under the public dispensations of the Word, from the more powerful influence of those with whom she has lived and the want of education, is as it were wholly ignorant of what religion is, in any form, except as it is in some way connected with going to church, but without the least *feeling* of what that connection is. She is not deficient in strength of mind, or capacity to receive instruction on the subject, but without any idea of the necessity of any other principle of action than she already possesses ; that is, a firmness of purpose proceeding from natural decision, and a patience under trial, because experience has taught the weakness and uselessness of irritation. Now this seems to me an opportunity of doing some real good. I have almost unlimited influence over her from the strong affection she feels, and, as my opportunities are few, I cannot neglect this one without reproach. But that dreadful consciousness of incapacity will place its iron hand on my wishes. I am aware that much might and ought to be done, but that much, if not every thing, depends on the first impression. She must be made to feel the *necessity*, in order to be excited to the pursuit of piety ; and how this is to be done I know not. Never did I feel so forcibly the imperfection of the characters of Christians, as on this occasion. To be able to point to one example of the power of religion in producing that uniform loveliness of character and happiness of life of which it is capable, would do more than volumes of argument to such a mind and heart. It has made me shrink at my own unworthiness of the name I bear. Could you find a moment to assist me in this undertaking, you would confer an unspeakable kindness.

" M. L. P."

Another more decided and serious case came to her knowledge about the same time, — a case of avowed atheism, confided to her for relief, and most kindly and wisely met by her; so that, while she supposed no effect had been produced, the work was going on, and an intelligent, troubled spirit came out of darkness into marvellous light. This success, which seems to have surprised her, was apparently owing to the beauty of her own religion, and the harmony and happiness of her life, which the doubter could not fail to see, which indeed first induced the confession, and was more effectual than any formal arguments; another evidence of the power and responsibility of the Christian course and character. " What a responsibility did this trust impose on me!" Mary writes; " for I knew that no human being but myself was aware of it. It was too much to bear alone; I was unequal to it, I dared not attempt it for a time, I knew that so much depended on the very first step in such cases."

The counsellor to whom she would gladly have gone for aid, her beloved pastor, was then absent, travelling in Europe for his health. He returned the following summer; and the account she gives of that happy event, familiar as the facts may be to the readers of the Memoir of Channing, will be interesting to many, as the impression of one who saw and heard for herself.

"*Dorchester, August* 25, 1823.

"MY DEAR N——:

"I have just returned from passing the day with E——, and although it is late, and I am very tired, I cannot resist the strong desire I have to send you a few lines by her to-morrow, that I may give you some faint idea, at least, of what you would have felt, had you heard Mr. Channing yesterday. But to begin at the right end of the tale, I passed Thursday in town, and learned that Mr. Channing would possibly come in a vessel which was expected daily. On Friday I was at Nahant, and saw a ship enter the harbor which might be that. Saturday I went to Newton, and on my return was told that he had actually arrived, and was to preach the next morning. I could scarcely credit it, and it was not until my arrival at home, when I received a note from George requesting me to come in to hear him, and pass the day in Pearl Street, that I could be convinced it was actually true. I went in on Sunday morning, and with what sensations I saw the church filling, and every one looking round in anxious expectation, you may perhaps imagine; it was a feeling more of dread than pleasure, lest the first glance at his face should destroy all our hopes. He wisely waited until all had entered, and when his quick step was heard (for you might have heard a leaf fall), the whole body of people rose, as it were with one impulse, to welcome him. He was much affected by this, and it was some seconds before he could raise his head; but when he did, it made the eyes that gazed on him rejoice to see him, seated in his accustomed corner, looking round on his people with the most animated expression of joy glowing on his face, and with the evidences of improved health stamped on every feature. His skin was much burned, to be sure, which may have given him an appearance of health that did not belong to him, but the increase of his flesh and the animation of his countenance promised much.

"Mr. Dewey commenced the services as he used to do, but when, after the prayer, Mr. Channing rose and read his favorite psalm, —

'My soul, repeat His praise,
  Whose mercies are so great,'

I could hardly realize that he had been absent, his voice and manner and action were so exactly like himself in his very best days. He stood through the whole psalm, and seemed to join in and enjoy every note of the music. He could not control a smile of joy. But of what followed I can tell you little. You have heard him when he felt obliged, as then, to dismiss the restraints of form, and speak freely the thoughts that filled his mind, and have perhaps often thought with others that he went too far, was too particular, too personal ; but yesterday, I believe the most uninterested person present could not find fault. I thought it was the most deeply affecting address I ever heard ; it was also deeply and decidedly practical. There are few occasions which will authorize a minister to excite the feelings of his audience in a very great degree, and none which can make it allowable for him to rest in mere excitement. But when their minds, from any peculiar circumstance, are particularly susceptible, I know no reason why it should not be permitted that they be addressed familiarly and affectionately on the subject of it. But you need not that I should defend Mr. Channing from the charge of egotism. You understand his motives too well to require it.

"His text was from the hundred and sixteenth Psalm: 'What shall I render unto God for all his mercies? I will offer the sacrifice of thanksgiving, I will call on the name of the Lord, I will pay my vows unto the Lord now in the presence of his people.' Returning, as he said, under such peculiar circumstances of mercy to his home and his people, he trusted no apology was necessary for waiving the common forms of the pulpit, that he might speak to his people as to his friends, that he might in the fulness of his heart utter its emotions to those who, he trusted, could understand and sympathize with them. As he slightly reviewed the views with which he left us, the mercies that had followed him, and the blessings which were showered on his return, he seemed almost overpowered with the fulness of his feelings, and I feared he would not be able to go on. But his voice rose as he said, 'And now what shall I render for all these benefits? I will first pay my vows unto Him, whose mighty arm hath been stretched out to save, whose never failing love hath everywhere attended me.' The ascription of praise which followed was more truly sublime than any thing I ever heard or read. His solemn dedication of his renewed life to the service of Him. who had borne him in safety over the great deep, who had sustained him in sickness, comforted him in affliction, and crowned all his gifts by giving him strength to return to his duties, was almost too much to bear. It was a testimony to the power of religion, which spoke more loudly than all the books that ever were written to prove it. But he meant not to speak of his past experiences merely to relieve his own heart ; he had but one great object in view, the good of his people, and he would not lose sight of that even when the fulness of his own feelings might almost be allowed to engage his whole mind. He could not be expected to enumerate all that he had learned during his absence, but one thing he could assure us ; that at every step, under all circumstances, in every country, and with every variety of character, he had become more and more convinced of the value and necessity of the Christian revelation."

The last of that succession of bereavements which Mary was so early called to meet, and by which she was left as alone in the world, was now at hand Since the death of her mother, in 1812, when there devolved mainly upon her, at the age of fourteen, the care of a dispirited and feeble father, and two aged grandparents, with other members of the family in a most trying condition, she had lived either in the sick-room, or in a press of domestic cares and business avocations.   That these often made a severer demand upon her strength and patience, as well as affection, than any one knew at the time, or indeed ever knew, appears from various intimations in her letters and life.   And all this was now to be brought to a crisis by the death of her *father*, leaving her without one near relative, or proper home. They had been boarding for some time in Dorchester, in the family of Mr. Barnard ; where she received, as she says, "the greatest kindness and affection," — and she felt the need of it.   But let her give the circumstances in her own words.

Boston, November 1, 1823.

" MY DEAR FRIEND : —

" I have been wishing this whole week to find time to write you, but it has been wholly impracticable. I have been in a perpetual agitation from sundry unexpected occurrences and continual interruptions from visitors. In fact, at no moment of my whole existence have I more wanted your counsel and sympathy. You know it is my lot to be assailed in more than one direction if in any, and it has been more remarkably the case now than ever. . . . . . I thank you most sincerely for your two good letters; it was more than I dared expect, and it was a cordial to me to receive the kind expression of your sympathy, though I should not have doubted its existence without it. You say you ' have heard but little of me,' and it was scarcely possible that you should hear of the immediate circumstances that attended my trial. It was so sudden that I was, as it were, alone, and I have feared that, in indulging myself in writing to you of it, I should give way too far, and distress and weary you. I have realized more than I ever did in any of the various changes I have met with, that ' the wind is tempered to the shorn lamb,' and even in the very extremity of trial we can be strengthened to support all with calmness.

" For the first three days of my father's sickness he seemed to have only a severe cold and slightly disordered stomach, and though I had called Dr. Thaxter, it was more to satisfy him that the medicine I gave was necessary for him, than from any doubt that I could do all that was needed; for he had often appeared more sick, and I had administered to him without any advice. On the morning of the fourth he appeared to be a little wandering, but remained quiet until night, when he was very violent for two or three hours; and the following day I was told by the physician that nothing but a miracle could preserve his life until the next morning. I heard it calmly, I believe because I could not realize it. He did not seem to be conscious that he was sick; he did all that I asked him to, but did not seem to know me. I soon found that the doctor's prediction was but too true, for symptoms of decay increased very rapidly, and at three the next morning he breathed his last, as a child would go to sleep. Not a struggle indicated the approach of the destroyer. I held his hand, and gazed at him until I was taken from him senseless. No one was with me but Mr. B——, and Mr. E——, his son-in-law. I recovered myself in a few moments and found Mr. E—— fainting ; this obliged me instantly to rouse myself to action, which was all mercifully disposed, and I sat down quietly with them for the remainder of the night, giving directions when any thing passed my mind, or remaining silent, knowing all would be done just as I wished.

" It would have seemed dreadful to me had I anticipated passing through such a scene with only two gentlemen, who a few months before were perfect strangers to me ; but it never passed my mind that I was not with my nearest friends. I could not in volumes tell you of all their kindness. It was one of the striking testimonies of God's merciful care of me, that He placed me with them. Indeed, His goodness towards me has been most wonderful, and above all, that He has enabled me to feel it continually ; even in the awful stillness of that night I never lost sight of it. I could feel as it were His arm beneath me ; and I can truly say I never experienced that fulness of heavenly peace which results from undeviating confidence in Him, which I then did. It was an hour of peculiar elevation which I can never forget, and which I trust will ever be a source of unfailing support, as it must be of gratitude. What beside could have sustained me amidst its horrors ? All that I could call my own was departing from me, and I was standing as it were alone in the universe ; but I felt that I was the object of His care who was all-sufficient, and I found in that consciousness a calmness which nothing could move. I stood firm and erect, though the storms of life seemed to have concentrated their power to overthrow me, and I felt that the Power which enabled me to do this would never forsake me, for it was not my own. We may talk of the resolution and fortitude which some possess, but what would it all be at such an hour? Nothing, — less than nothing. I gave up all reliance upon myself, or I should have utterly failed. Every thing was directed with the utmost mercy. Even his unconsciousness, which I thought at first I could not bear, was a mercy to him, for how much was he spared by it; he could not have left me alone without a severe struggle.

"I am now fixed for the winter, and shall soon feel, I doubt not, as much at home as it is possible for me to feel; and if the greatest kindness and affection that ever were shown to any human being can make me happy, I shall be so, for I have it.

"With love, I am yours,
"M. L. P"

VI.

VISIT ABROAD.

MARY PICKARD was now alone. Every member
of her own family had gone, and she had witnessed
and smoothed the passage of every one. She had
only entered mature life, but her twenty-five years
of experience and change had been equal to double
that period of common life. Already had she learned
the great truth, which to many comes late, if at all, —

> " We live in deeds, not years; in thoughts, not breaths;
>   In feelings, not in figures on a dial."

Heretofore she had always had an object to live
for, — some one dependent upon her affection and
exertions, to whom it was happiness enough to minister. Now there was no one; and we wonder not
that she said, " I seem to hang so loosely on the
world, that it is of little importance where I am."
It was indeed a singular providence which at this
moment opened to her an entirely new field, yet one
vholly congenial with her tastes and wishes.

Her only relatives on the father's side were in
England, connections whom she had seen only as a
child twenty years before, but had always hoped to
see again. And not for her own gratification only,
but that she might be of service, if possible, to those

who were in depressed and obscure condition, as some of them were. This consideration, which would have offered least inducement to most young minds, perhaps have kept them away, was an incentive to Mary, and gave her a right to find in the opportunity a duty as well as a pleasure; especially as the occasion given her was itself an opportunity to serve an invalid friend. The circumstances will appear in the following letters to Miss Cushing and Mrs. Paine.

"*Boston, March* 8, 1824.

" My dear Miss Cushing : —

" If sorrow for sin is any ground for forgiveness, I trust you will grant it to me, for my shameful neglect of you. Do not think that forgetfulness or want of interest has led to this; you know me, I trust, better than to believe that, and you know my faults too well not to be able to account for it, from my too deeply rooted habit of procrastinating. Often during the past winter have I thought, if I could only see you, I should be sure to find the guidance and sympathy which I have longed for ; but when I thought of writing to you, I felt the selfishness of troubling you with my own perplexities, knowing that, as my mind was so much occupied by them, I could not compensate you for it by any other communications I could make. The last six months have indeed brought to me a constant struggle of feeling. Left as I was to choose my own path on the wide ocean of life, with health, strength, and some means of influence, the responsibility which it imposed to use to the best possible advantage the powers that God had given me, to promote the end for which I knew they were given, was almost overpowering, — and at times I would have given myself up willingly to the control of any one who would relieve me from the burden. I have experienced in so many striking ways the great goodness of God in giving me light to guide, and strength to sustain me in hours of trial, that it is, I know, but practical infidelity to doubt for one moment that his protecting influence will still be extended towards me, if I try my utmost to attain a knowledge of duty, and persevere to my best ability in the path which conscience dictates. But the difficulty is, that, though in great events where we see at once that no human power can aid us we cannot but acknowledge that He is sufficient for all things, we are too apt to lose sight of this truth in cases in which human agency must be exerted, forgetting that God is as surely the operating cause in one case as the other. When it appears that our fate may be determined by a single word which we feel the power of uttering, we can scarcely help thinking that upon our own heads must be all the consequences which may follow; and thinking thus, we must realize our weakness and insufficiency.

" All this has been preying upon my mind, and its effects have been deplorably contracting to my thoughts. I have, indeed, been outwardly much occupied by various pursuits, trying to do something for others, but my thinking has been nearly all for myself. This is my only excuse for not writing you more, and I think with this specimen you will be satisfied that I have not before attempted it. I believe that all the events that befall us are exactly such as are best adapted to improve us; and I find, in a perfect confidence in the wisdom and love which I know directs them, a source of peace which no other thing can give; and in the difficulty I find in acting upon this belief I see a weakness of nature, which those very trials are designed to assist us in overcoming, and which trial alone can conquer. Whatever is in store for me, I trust that I shall not forget that the first and only important object of existence is to promote, as far as my powers may extend, the cause of holiness. That every one, however humble their station and limited their capacity, has some power to do this, I doubt not, as I find in every line of God's word a command to do so; and I pray that my feeble efforts may be fully devoted to this end.

" *March* 15. What changes a few days may produce in one's prospects ! Little could I think, a week ago, that the conclusion of this letter was to tell you, that in less than another week I should be floating on the vast ocean, on my way to England. But so it is, and I hope that the suddenness of the determination to go has not shut from my eyes any very important consideration against it. It seems to me like a dream, for it is only in my dreams that I have ever thought of it as a possibility. I have wished to see my relations there, having always kept up a constant correspondence with them, and felt very much interested in them ; but since my father's death, I have viewed the accomplishment of this wish as an impossibility. But now that so good an opportunity has offered, I cannot hesitate to accept it. I seem to hang so loosely on the world, that it is of little importance where I am, as it regards duties, and it is an advantage to enlarge one's ideas, which I feel ought to be improved. To tell you all that I feel at leaving home would be impossible ; it is a most solemn undertaking, and when I glance at the possibilities connected with such a step, it almost overwhelms me.

' I wish I could see every one of you once more. My heart is indeed too full to tell you half that I wish.

" Yours most affectionately,

" M. L. P "

"*Boston, March* 13, 1824

" My dear N——:

" I have been sitting many minutes with my pen in my hand and paper before me, trying to bring to myself sufficient resolution to tell you the new and surprising turn which has taken place in my wayward destiny. I have been so long the creature of circumstances that you must be prepared for changes of all kinds in my lot; but I know not how it will strike you when you learn for truth, that in one week from to-morrow I sail for England. I thought that I was entirely willing to go, but as I find myself telling you of it, and think that it is utterly impossible for me to see you again, my heart sinks within me, and I almost shrink from it. In fact, this is the first moment I have realized it. I knew nothing of it until the day before yesterday, when Edward Robbins sent to me, to say that his physicians and friends advised his taking a voyage, and that, if I could go with him, it would decide him to take their advice. I had thought of the subject so much, that I was prepared at once to answer. It is a very desirable thing for me to visit the few relations which I have there, and I could never give up the expectation and endeavor to accomplish it. My dependent state was the only barrier, as I could never go unless under the protection of one of the few male friends from whom I should be willing to receive such an obligation, and it was so unlikely that either of those few would ever think of going, that I had but little hope I should ever realize my wishes. But this proposition at once removed all difficulties. Our families have been so long connected, and Edward himself has been so particularly kind to me through life, and more than ever since I have been without a parent's protection, and is in every respect so exactly calculated to make one feel willing and happy to be under obligation, that I could not but feel that now was the time

(if ever) for me to accomplish this great object. Doubts
about the sufficiency of my means, and some scruples about
my right to employ them in this way, made me hesitate a
few hours; but in less than four I decided, with the advice
of all whom it was necessary to consult, that it was right to
improve the present, as all future opportunities were uncertain. That it cost me a deep inward struggle to make my
feelings acquiesce, you will not doubt. The first day I felt
like a child. I could not glance even at the reasons which
favored my going without sad and overpowering retrospection, and the thought of the uncertainty of the result, the
thousand possibilities involved in such a change, almost
turned my brain; and yet every one was wondering how I
could look so composed and keep so still. It is singular
how much little things sometimes concur to aid us. It was
Thursday, and I was just going to lecture, as Mr. Robbins
came in with his proposal. I went still, and Mr. Walker
gave us one of the most delightful, strengthening sermons
upon the influence of the Spirit, and the all-sufficiency of
trust in its guidance, that I ever heard in my life. I believe
no other subject could have fixed my attention, and it did
fix it most effectually.

"I know it is utterly impossible that I should see you,
therefore I will not dwell for a moment on the thought. I
have, of course, a great deal to think about, although little personal preparation; but I must leave every thing in
which I have the least concern just as I should wish if I was
certain I should never return. God only knows what the
future will bring to me, but I hope to find myself wholly
willing to yield myself to the disposal of his providence.
We think of these changes for others, and feel little doubt
about their safety, but when the case becomes our own, it
is another thing. To embark on the wide ocean in a little,
frail vessel with perfect calmness, requires a firmness of

faith of which no one can boast until they have stood the test. I have no fear of it now, and I trust I shall find that the ground of confidence in the all-powerful God, which the experience of my life has given me, will be sufficient to support me in all events. I am willing to be put to the test, for if all that I think I feel is but delusion, I had better discover the delusion before it is too late.

"We have taken passage in the Emerald. If I feel alone here, I don't know what I shall do in a land of strangers. We go to Liverpool, and probably immediately to London from there. I go with very moderate hopes about seeing the wonders and beauties. I must be satisfied with seeing people, not things. I shall have no right to travel much, and shall have no advantages not common to the most insignificant; nevertheless, if I can attain my prin cipal object, all the rest will be unexpected gain. It is most probable we shall be gone a year, but it is possible we may return in the fall.

"What a variety for one poor soul in the last four months! It absolutely makes me giddy to think of it all. But what a source of comfort is it, that in all things I have sought guidance where I believe it is ever freely given; · and I do believe, whatever is the event of all this, it must be the direction of Him who knows and governs all things I must not write more.

"Yours most affectionately,

"M. L. P."

A particular friend in Milton, one of the truest and noblest friends that Mary or any one ever had, describes her as at this time "worn to the bone' with care and trial; and then breaks forth in praise of her, in unmeasured terms; adding, "Yet, with all this superiority, where is the other being on whom

any poor fool can repose with such trust and confidence, as on her?. My meanest thought is not
checked in the utterance, because her mind is so
flexible it stoops to the lowest. I am only afraid of
adoring her, so I may as well hold my peace." This
was said in earnest, and is one of many expressions of admiration and affection called out by her
departure.

Of her progress' and occupations abroad, our
knowledge is drawn exclusively from her own letters.
These, therefore, we shall use freely, leaving them
to show their connection as far as they can, and
make their own impression; begging the reader to
remember, however, that they were all written in the
haste of travelling or the fatigues of watching, and
that their literary merit or public appearance was the
last thought to occur to the mind of the writer. She
wrote a great deal, and we confine our selection
chiefly to passages relating to personal experience,
rather than descriptions of places or works of art.
For these last she allowed herself little time, though
keenly alive to the enjoyment of all grandeur and
beauty, and giving passing indications of her power
of appreciating and delineating.

Arriving in Liverpool in April, she was made to
feel at home immediately, by the kindness and sympathy of a kindred mind, in one to whom Dr. Channing had given her a letter, and whose name and
sad fate are familiar to many, — Mrs. Freme, daughter of the Rev. Dr. Wells, who settled in Brattleboro',
Vermont, where she afterward perished by fire. Mary's account of her interview with that excellent

woman is characteristic, as her first interest in a new country.

"London, April 19, 1824.

"In Liverpool, I went with Mrs. Frome to visit the Female Penitentiary, and took a long walk with her. She had relinquished an engagement out of town to go with me, and I know not that I ever felt more grateful to a stranger in my life. She is an uncommonly sensible, kind woman, extremely interested in the encouragement of all good works, a warm Unitarian, and a truly liberal, benevolent Christian. I never enjoyed any thing in my life more than the conversation I had with her. I had begun to feel the want of that free intercourse upon those subjects upon which we can speak only to those who we are sure are equally interested in them; and in a strange land, to meet with one who not only entered fully into every thing I wished to say, but carried me on to higher, more improving and elevated thoughts, was indeed a privilege."

"London, May 6, 1824.

"My dear Ann : —

"It was a great deprivation to me to be unable to write at sea. I hoped to have had a large packet for the many kind friends who aided and blessed my departure, expressing something of the gratitude which overpowered me. I have sometimes feared that you thought me insensible to it all, for I dared not try to utter even a word of what I felt lest I should lose my self-possession entirely, and trouble them more than my thanks would please them. God alone knows how fully I appreciated it all, and when I look back upon the period which elapsed after my father's death until I left you, I know not how to speak my astonishment that such a one as myself should have been so signally favored. For your Aunt Nancy I can only say her reward must be beyond this world; nothing that I or any one here can do,

is adequate to it. Never was a human being so blessed
with kind friends, and could I feel that I had been as grateful as I ought to have been, I should be happy. But the
entire absorption of every thought in self, during the past
winter, is now a subject of much reproach.

"I had time to think of all this during the long days and
wakeful nights on the voyage, and I do assure you I took
a new view of every thing connected with it. Whether it
was the absence of every thing else to interest my mind, or
the natural increase of our attachment to all objects when
we are going from them, I know not, but there were moments of acute agony, when I thought of the return I had
made for the kindness manifested towards me. How often
I longed to be for a little time on the little stool in the drawing-room, giving utterance to my spirit! There was so
little in the monotony of sea-life to interrupt the train of
one's thoughts, that I could not sometimes get rid of an idea
which possessed me, and I often woke up, wearied with the
continuation of one and the same dream, night after night.
But I did enjoy a great deal at sea, there was so much to
elevate the mind in the very situation; and the want of confidence which I felt from the first evening in the head of
the concern tended most powerfully to raise my thoughts
above all second causes, to the One Great Cause and Sup-
porter of all things. Never did I so deeply feel our entire
dependence upon the power of God, never did I so fully
realize the impotence of human skill, as when I saw it
contending with the winds; and yet there was something
ennobling in the idea, that human skill had contrived and
taught to guide such a vehicle as a ship upon the trackless
waste of waters; and while we trace all this power to the
original source of it, we cannot but feel that He has given
to us a noble nature. Often when the sea was rising in
immense waves on every side, and the ship tossed about as

though it were but a little shell which the waters would soon overwhelm, have I felt as I never before did the immense value of that religion which was able to calm all fears, and raise the mind to a state even of enjoyment, under such terrific circumstances. What but a firm confidence that, whether we live or die, or whatever event befall us, it is in Infinite Wisdom that it is so, can give this composure? Shall we not then hold fast and cherish such a faith? shall we not seek to understand its nature, and endeavor with our whole hearts to ingraft its principles upon our characters?

"Tell me as much about Mr. Channing and his sermons as you can. I went to chapel on Sunday with Mrs. Kinder, but heard very poor preaching, to very poor houses. But Mr. Channing told me just what to expect, therefore I was prepared for it. Poor as it was, however, the delight of finding myself once more in a place of public worship overbalanced all, and when I heard the same tunes sung to the same words which I had heard in Federal Street, it was a little more than I could bear firmly. I am charmed with the whole Kinder family; they are too literary to make me feel able to communicate the least pleasure, on account of my ignorance upon all literary subjects, but they are every thing that is kind, and very agreeable, and I find a good lesson for my humility when I am there.

" MARY."

" *London, May* 26, 1824.

" MY DEAR FRIENDS: —

" For the first four weeks I resisted all the entreaties of my cousins to go to them, because Dr. R—— was so depressed and ill, and it was so bad for Mrs. R—— to be left alone. But the third week Dr. R—— improved very much in health, and somewhat in spirits. And though he offered me many great inducements to accompany them to Leamington, ould not think it quite right to do so, as my society would not be as necessary to them as it had been, and they were going to a fashionable watering-place. I had seen nothing of my own friends, and as Mrs. Bates and Mrs. Morton had asked me to stay with them when I first arrived, I took the liberty of accepting their invitation for a few days.

"I believe I told you I had a kind letter from Uncle Ben, and have since had a visit from his son, who heard of our arrival, and came up the next day, in true Lovell style, to take me home with him to Waltham Abbey, near Enfield.

"Through the kindness of Mr. Kinder's family I have had many privileges. By their intercession I have been admitted to Newgate, and though Mrs. Fry was not there, I was very much gratified. I met with a young Quakeress, who was rather handsome, was very intelligent and kind, and has been very attentive to me. Mrs. Fry is too much out of health to go often, but I am to be informed by my little friend when she next goes.

"Walking to Newington with the Kinders, to return a call, they asked me if I would go with them to see Mrs. Barbauld. To be sure, it made my heart beat, but I could not say no. It was indeed a privilege, and I wish I could tell you all about it. She spoke with great feeling of those of our ministers whom she had seen, — Buckminster, Thacher, and Channing. Having never seen Mr. Thacher's sermons, I had the honor of sending them to her, and of writing her a note. A note to Mrs. Barbauld! What presumption! Yet I was asked afterward to dine with her. She is remarkably bright for her age, speaks of death with the firmest hope, and I really felt as if I were communing with a spiritual body. Though now eighty-two, she possesses all her faculties in full perfection. Her manner is peculiarly gentle, her voice low, and very sweet.

" I went with the Kinders to see some rich Quakers, who are very active in the school concern, and also to a meeting of the British and Foreign School Society, where I saw the Duke of Sussex, and heard some fine speaking. They go upon the Lancaster and Bell system, and truly wonderful is their success and usefulness. I have heard Madame Catalani, and some of the finest singers, at a concert at the Opera House, and was as much amazed as it was possible to be, notwithstanding all I had heard. But some of those with less power pleased me more. No one can equal *her*, or be compared with her. Braham sung with her, with a full band, and her voice was heard above all; it is tremendous, for the house is immense, and she entirely filled it. At a meeting of the Sons of the Clergy at St. Paul's, I heard some very fine sacred music. About thirty little boys sang the high parts, and chanted the responses. The church was very full. The Duke of Clarence, Lord Mayor, and a goodly company of the dignitaries of the Church, filled the seats of honor. Nothing could be more solemn than the whole scene, and when at parts of the service the whole congregation joined in the chant, the dome rung with the sound, and one almost looked to see if the statues around were not roused.

" Do you fear that my head is growing giddy, with all this variety? At present there is no danger. My thoughts turn too often homeward, to be very much engrossed by any thing here, and my heart will feel sad when I think of the time which must elapse ere I see it again."

" *Broadwater, Worthing, June* 11, 1824.

" My dear Cousin : —

" On Saturday, the 29th, I received a letter from Dr. R—— saying that Leamington did not agree with him, that Mrs. R—— was quite unwell, and they begged, if possible, that I would come to them the next day, with some plan of proceeding for them, for he felt wholly unable to decide what to do. After some debate with Mrs. S——— I concluded that it was a duty to give up all my own views, and do what I could for him, as there was no one else who could assist them in this land of strangers. Accordingly I wrote him that I would join them on Tuesday, as it was not in my power to make such an entire change in my arrangements before. I had just prepared on Monday to start, when another letter arrived, saying they should be in London at night.

" We propose going from here to the Isle of Wight, and round to the western part of England, Bristol, Bath, and Wales. I hope on the way to have a peep at Mrs. McAdam, who is now at Plymouth, for it is rather tantalizing for us to be kept so long separated. I would not have believed that any thing would have kept me so long from my friends after I had found myself in England. But it is well to be obliged to control our selfishness in England, as elsewhere. The little I have seen of my relations has only increased my desire to know them and be loved by them. My reception at Uncle Ben's was more like that which I hope to have at home, than any thing I could have expected in this strange land. He is a warm-hearted old man, with all the best of the Lovell feelings in full vigor. He was very much attached to my mother, and retains a stronger interest in his Transatlantic relations than I could have thought possible after an absence of fifty years. He was very much overcome at seeing me, and wept over me like a child. They demand three months, at least, from me, but I am afraid I shall not have half that time for them. You don't know how delightful it was to be among people who seemed so like my own home friends."

"*Broadwater, June* 11, 1824

" My dear Ann : —

" You have been sorely afflicted indeed, doubtless for
some good purpose. I am rejoiced to find by your letter
that you are disposed to view it so, and improve by the
chastisement. I hope it will lead the way to a more free
communication with our good minister. It is a great privilege, and one which ought to be improved. I have learned
since I have been here to estimate our advantages in this
and all other religious affairs, as I could never have done at
home. In London, it seems to me that there is no more
connection between minister and people, in the Established
Church, than if they had no influence whatever to exercise ;
and among the Dissenters I have met with, the case is not
much better. They are so scattered, and wander about so
much, that it is difficult to have much intercourse, or keep
up much interest among them. . . . . .

" I have heard but one sermon since I have been in this
country which made the least impression upon my mind,
and that was from one from whom I expected nothing that
would satisfy me. This was Mr. Irving, whom Mr. Channing mentioned as the popular favorite in London. He is
a most singular-looking Scotchman, a pupil of Dr. Chal-
mers, and now so much the fashion, that tickets of admission are sold, to enable those who wish to hear him to go
in before the hour when the doors are thrown open. Even
in this way it is like the theatre of a Kean night, and for
two hours before the service commences the crowd is immense. His manner is very like Kean's, most impassioned,
and when he commenced I turned from him in disgust.
But there was that in the subject and substance of the sermon which made me forget the manner in which it was
delivered. It was, I understood, one of the least flowery of
his productions. I shall never forget it, I think ; but I

would not be obliged to go to such a place for the best sermons that ever were written. It was just like the theatre or
some great exhibition.

" You cannot think how I long, when the Sabbath comes
round, to have an ear in Federal Street. I find, as Mr.
Channing warned me, that travelling is a sad enemy to the
cultivation of religious knowledge and improvement ; it
does so derange the regularity of one's habits of thinking
and acting. The day is too confused, and the nights too
wearied. But there is much in the experience of every
day to excite a strong sense of gratitude to that Providence
whose care is extended over us in all places ; in the consciousness which we must have, even when the idea of
separation from those we love presses most heavily upon
us, that there is One, ever present, whose love for us is
infinite. Yet it is not of feelings that I ought to speak ; I
could fill volumes with the variety of thoughts which every
day suggests, but I am learning to do without the communication of them."

From Broadwater the party of four went to the
Isle of Wight, and made the usual circuit, in their
little open carriage, through that charming region,
" with nothing wanting but health, and with that
deficiency all was a blank." Dr. R—— was too
unwell to enjoy any thing, and Mary herself, for a
wonder, speaks of suffering from a cough which she
had had a month. But it did not prevent her from
making what she calls " a break-neck excursion "
up a precipice of about four hundred feet, at the
southern part of the island. Of the country she
gives a glowing description, for which we have not
room On leaving the island, Dr. R—— found it

necessary to return to Broadwater for medical advice, and Mary, who had arranged to meet some
of her relations at Plymouth at this time, readily,
though not without regret, gave up her own plans,
and went back with the family to Broadwater. The
place had little interest for her, and she writes of
" useless idleness " as a new thing to her, and uncomfortable. But others did not think her presence
useless, nor did she fail to find employment. From
the wife of the clergyman, who had lately established
schools in the parish on a new plan, she learned a
good deal of the national system of education. After a short time, Dr. R—— determined to go to Paris,
and she accompanied him. But of Paris itself she
saw very little, being chiefly devoted to the care of
her friend. And except for him, she had no wish to
be there. " It may seem strange," she writes, " that
I should not wish to see Paris, but the pleasure of
every thing depends upon the circumstances which
immediately surround us. Yet I am very glad I
came, for, though I cannot be of much use, any one
is better than none."

Their stay in Paris was short. In view of all
considerations, Dr. R—— found it best to return at
once to America, and sailed that same month from
Havre, Mary remaining to make her visit to her
friends in England. Her next letters are from Chatham.

"Chatham, September 7, 1824.

" MY DEAR ANN : —

" You may easily suppose that my sensations at leaving
Havre were not the most cheering. I knew that I could

have been of but little comfort to our friends on the voyage, but I could not help wishing that it had been so ordered that I might have returned with them. There was something, too, so very lonely in the idea of being left in a strange land, with no chance of escape for a certain length of time, even if my friends should take it into their heads to dislike me; and worse than all, under my own sole direction, to govern myself and my actions only by my own judgment. Indeed, I did feel as though I should almost shrink from the effort it required; but this did not trouble me long. I thought of the mercies of my past life, the great goodness and preserving care which had hitherto upheld me in many times of danger and difficulty. The night was a most beautiful one, and the very motion of the little vessel recalled so much which had once given me support under similar circumstances, that my mind seemed to acquire a degree of calmness and firmness which was almost sublime. For this I have great cause of gratitude; it was the gift of a Power mightier than I, and prepared me for the coming danger. We were two nights and a day crossing to Southampton, about twice the usual length of the passage, the greater part of the time in a violent storm and most dangerous situation. I suffered more from sickness than in crossing the Atlantic, but met with very great attention from the ladies who were in the same state-room, and much entertainment beside; but I never was more rejoiced than when I found myself in a clean bed on *terra firma*, upon the second morning.

" My first attempt at journeying alone was a very encouraging one. A good old clergyman was my companion, and after three weeks in France, I assure you, I enjoyed any thing like serious conversation; though he happened to be a Methodist, he was a rational and learned one, and I believe I learned much that was useful from him. I had

10

apprised my good cousin of my intended descent upon **her**
family, and was received with open arms and much kind
greeting by all her flock.   Here I am, then, at last, and I
know you are impatient to know all about them, and the
place in which they live.   Mrs. S—— is in appearance but
the shadow of what she was when her picture was taken.
Trouble and age have made her thin and pale.   But the
perfect symmetry of her pretty little figure, and the brightness of her still beautiful eyes, enable one to see in her the
remains of one of nature's fairest works.   Her naturally
good spirits are almost wholly subdued by the trials and
perplexities which have followed her in constant succession
for many years, and ill health and an anxious mind have
created a disposition to despondency which even her piety
cannot at all times overcome.   This has unfitted her for
great exertion, and, not possessing much natural force of
character, it is impossible for her to make much effort even
for herself.   She is all gentleness, and full of affectionate
feeling, and I often think, in looking at her in her happiest
moments, that she would be a good personification of Shak-
speare's Patience smiling at Grief.   Her situation here is
that of matron to the hospital, but it is almost a nominal
office, a perfect sinecure, for she has scarcely any duty,
and a comfortable income.   She is now peculiarly tried,
and seems to consider it an especial mercy that she has
one to whom she can turn in her loneliness with something
like a claim for sympathy.

"..... There is a small Unitarian chapel here, and
cousin N—— will say, ' Why do you not go to that?
Merely because I found out but yesterday that there was
such an one ; hearing a lady say, ' We ought to tolerate all
denominations but those dangerous enemies to religion, the
Unitarians,— I cannot pass their chapel without shuddering,'
— next Sunday I shall endeavor to ascertain the grounds of

this pious hatred. But in truth, if I had not learned liberality before, I have had experience enough to teach it to me since I have been in this country, I have met with so many good Christians, of such a variety of sects; and found that the bond of union created by a mutual desire to aid in the cause of benevolence was sufficient to excite interest, without any regard to different creeds or doctrinal points.

" I am constantly hearing now from all my little circle of relations, who seem determined to prevent my feeling alone, if their attentions can prevent it. Do not suspect me of vanity in mentioning all these attentions; this is not the case, for the effect is rather humbling, and I fear when they know me better they will find a poor return for it all; but I do feel such gratitude for so many unlooked for, undeserved blessings, that I want you all to know it, that you too may unite with me in thanksgiving to God for his watchful care of me, a solitary orphan in a foreign land.

" *September* 14. The day after I wrote the above, I received a letter from Mr. and Mrs. C——, then at Ramsgate, a town upon the eastern shore of Kent, saying that they were making a short tour, and had intended coming to Chatham to see me on their way home, but thinking I might like to see Dover and its castle, proposed that I should join them there, and pass a few days with them. So, without hesitation, I got into one of the many coaches which daily pass through Chatham, and in six hours was with them. The ride was delightful, through a richly wooded and highly cultivated country, the fine old city of Canterbury, and a number of pretty towns. My companions in the coach were very genteel, intelligent people, and I was quite pleased with finding that it was a very customary thing for a lady to travel inside a coach without escort; I wished it were equally so to travel outside, I do so much prefer to see all I can. This was on Thursday last, the 9th, and I remained with them until to-day, receiving every attention and kindness from them, and much satisfaction from seeing the place. . . . . .

" I returned here to-day. My cousin was to have met me at Canterbury, but was prevented by the weather. I rode the greater part of the way alone, inside, though the outside was full; and you may tell Mary that my thoughts were often turned to her; for a guideboard with the name of ' Milton ' upon it reminded me of my shameful neglect of our sweet *tune* of that name. I had not once sung it since I left her, and found full employment for some miles in trying to bring it to mind; and it was not until after recalling her looks and voice, and beating three strokes in a bar, over and over again, to try the power of association, that I could bring it to my recollection. But I sung it enough, when I did get it, to make up for all past deficiencies. It carried me back to last winter, and all your happy family, so fully, that my empty coach was soon peopled, and I had as pleasant a ride as need be.

" I had the gratification of seeing the famous actress, Mrs. Siddons, at Dover, — a rare sight indeed; she is a wonderfully handsome woman for her age, living in elegant retirement, in handsome style.

" MARY."

"*Chatham, October* 4, 1824.

" MY DEAR COUSIN : —

" I am delighted that Mr. Gannett pleases you all, and to hear such good accounts of Mr. Channing. The very idea of a letter from him was almost too much for my poor brain; the reality would overpower me, I believe. I greatly fear, unless the spring should bring me some kind American friend with whom I can travel, that I shall see little more of England. But I will be satisfied, at any rate, if I can but find the means of seeing my poor aunt S——.

" The return of this season brings so forcibly to my mind the recollection of the trying events of which it is the anniversary, that I find it difficult to prevent myself from dwelling too much upon it. I would not lose the remembrance of it, for every hour of that time was filled with valuable experience of the goodness and loving-kindness of my Heavenly Father. I love to dwell upon it, and recall every act of the many friends who then surrounded me with renewed feelings of gratitude towards them. May I yet be enabled to prove in my actions what I cannot express in words.

" MARY."

Mary Pickard is now among her kindred, those relatives of her father whom she had so long desired to know, and whom she hoped in some way to benefit. For her idea of conferring benefits was never defined by the thought of wealth, or excluded by the want of it. That she gave most liberally, according to her means, at this very time, we learn from others; her letters would never suggest it. In other and better ways, by most unexpected opportunities, did she render service to many before she left England, where her stay was greatly prolonged beyond the first intention, for this very purpose. For ten weeks she remained in Chatham; and though she does not say it, we infer from other intimations that much of that time was occupied with the care of the sick, or in relieving some kind of trouble. It is in reference to Chatham that she says, " I am fated to find trouble wherever I go,"— which is true of all who are willing to *take* trouble, that they may relieve others.

From Chatham Mary went to Waltham Abbey, and passed three weeks with the son of the only surviving brother of James Lovell. And in December, unwilling to be detained longer from the cousin to whom she designed to make one of her chief visits in England, and finding that sickness in the family prevented any one from coming for her, she took the coach alone, leaving London before daylight and riding to Salisbury, where some of her friends met her, and conducted her to their home at " Burcombe House," in that vicinity. And there she spent the next three or four months, in a way that her letters will best tell. These letters we give as we find them, without excluding the personal allusions and occasional descriptions of character ; since it is in just such descriptions, natural and easy, that we best read the mind of the writer and of those whom she portrays, as well as the features and ways of a common English household. And should these letters chance to fall under the eye of any to whom they allude, if any still survive, we trust they will pardon a liberty which exposes nothing that is not to their honor.

" Burcombe House, December 8, 1824.

" Congratulate me, my good friends, that I am at last under this roof, and have seen cousin Jane and all her dear family. I left London at five o'clock on Saturday, the 4th, and I found myself at Salisbury at three o'clock, not at all fatigued. Cousin Jane and her son came to meet me ; but as their carriage was from home, they were in an open gig, and we thought it expedient to take a postchaise, as Burcombe is five miles from the town. But before I proceed to the events of my ride, I must tell you something of my cousin, as I know you are wishing to hear how she received me. Our meeting was just what you could easily imagine it would be, knowing her to be a person of ardent feelings, strongly attached to her dear uncle, and conse- quently determined to love his daughter, let her be what she might; and after the frequent disappointments we have had, with regard to meeting, we both had an almost super- stitious fear that something might yet happen to separate us But we were at last together, and, if it took us both some time to realize it, we were not the less rejoiced to find it true. She has suffered much, and it has subdued her mind and spirits, and softened her manners. She is certainly one of the most entertaining women I ever saw, and one of the most interesting. She has strong powers of mind, and of course strong passions, warm-hearted, enthusiastic, prone to extremes, almost without restraint in youth, and the sport of adverse circumstances through life, ignorant of the only sure Guide to direct and guard the soul under the temptations to which such trials subject it. Imagine, then, what such a mind must be when brought by suffering to a deep sense of religious obligation, turning all its energies to the accomplishment of good to others and the subjection of self, not content with feeling until every feeling leads to active exertion,—and you have my dear cousin before you. You will not be surprised that I should already dearly love her, and feel that it was worth coming so far to know and give her pleasure. Her mind is just in that state which requires free discussion upon subjects of faith and practice, and shut out as she is here from society, and almost wholly without ministerial instruction, she suffers from the want of a companion who feels a like interest in the matter. How often do I wish for her the same privileges which I have had in Mr. Channing, or that you, my dear cousin, could step in and pour forth a little from your fund of knowledge.

"But I have digressed vastly from my tale. To return to the inn at Salisbury. We soon seated ourselves in a chaise, trunks, boxes, and all, and were driving on at a furious rate towards Burcombe House, when, lo! in a quiet lane, a mile at least from any houses, the axle of the front wheels gave way; off went one wheel, and down went we, just at dark, and the rain falling in torrents. We soon found it was only a subject for laughter; we had but one resource, which was to send the postboy back to Salisbury for another coach, and to sit quietly in the broken one until he returned. We had not, however, sat long, before Lord Pembroke's carriage came to our relief; it had passed us full at the commencement of our disaster, and was sent back to take us home, or to Wilton House. As we did not like to take all the baggage with us, we left it in the care of a servant, and, glad to get out of the cold, we proceeded to my Lord's house. I could not but be amused, that my first introduction to this region should be to Wilton House, in an Earl's carriage. I was not sorry to have an opportunity of seeing a place of which I have heard so much, and should have been quite pleased to have seen the great folks themselves; but they chanced to be dressing for dinner, and as our chaise soon came up for us, I had but little time to survey the place. The house is filled with pictures, statues, and ancient armor. I hope to have an opportunity of seeing it more leisurely.

"This whole family gave me a most hearty welcome, and I found that it would be my own fault if I was not loved by them, and happy with them. Jane has, indeed, a remarkably fine family, of steady principles and habits, and sufficiently accomplished to be agreeable and well fitted for society. This is a very retired spot, and except a call from

Lord and Lady Pembroke when they are in the neighborhood, or a visit from some travelling acquaintance, scarcely
any one enters the house except the family.

" . . . . . The state of the poor in this country is so
very different from any thing we see at home, that I can
scarcely give you any idea of the striking difference everywhere observable in their manners and habits. The immense sum which is collected for their support, under the
form of poor rates, must lessen their exertion for themselves, and the very dependence which is thus created
makes them servile. Some great man owns the village
and lands about it, his steward lets them to farmers, and
of course it depends upon sundry contingencies whether
they retain possession even during life ; and how can they
feel as much interest as if it were their own freehold, and
they knew their children would reap the benefit of their
improvements upon it ? "

" *Burcombe House, December* 31, 1824,
Half past Eleven.

" MY DEAR FRIEND : —

" This hour has for so many years found me at my desk
pouring forth to you, that, although in a new hemisphere
and under new influences, I instinctively turn to the pen
and ink, with a feeling that something remains to be done
before the old year can be allowed to take its departure. I
am not, as I was wont to be, seated quietly alone by my
' ain fireside,' cogitating upon the past, and, for the only
time in the twelve months, daring to look forward and hope
for the future. It is the custom here for all the family to
sit out the old year, and I am in the parlor, surrounded by
the whole tribe. On one side is my cousin's eldest daughter, playing ' God save the King ' as if all possibility of ever
doing it again was going with the year ; on the other, an
animated Miss C——, acting the old-maid aunt, giving her

nephews and nieces sage advice upon the occasion, who are all laughing most heartily. In fact, the whole house is in a bustle; so you need not expect a very connected epistle, as I am obliged to turn to one or the other, every other word, to join in the merriment.

" The changes which the past year has made in my life are so amazing, when I view them in a body, that I cannot but be astonished that we should ever attempt to look forward with any thing like calculation or plan. You can easily conceive that the contrast between this night and its past anniversary is enough to excite the few nerves I have; and you will not at all wonder, that, whatever attractions there may be around me, thought will wander back to home and its interests, and it requires some effort to restrain my impatience to be again restored to them, that I may make up, if possible, for my abuse of some of them. Yet do not imagine me discontented or homesick; I am not in the least, for every hour's experience makes me rejoice that I am here; and, if kindness and attention could make up for old acquaintance, I could be as contented to pass my life here as anywhere. I would not return without seeing and doing all that may be in my power; but that I do look forward with a feeling of desire, such as I never knew before, to the period when, all this being accomplished, I shall find myself again at home, it would be folly to deny. But this is just what I expected to feel, and of course was prepared for with some degree of firmness; and when thus prepared, it is astonishing how indifferently we go through with what, under any other circumstances, would destroy one's self-possession entirely. The greatest evil I find in this state of constant preparation for enduring is, that I am getting into a quiescent state of inaction; not being quite enough at ease to exert my own powers freely, I am losing that activity of mind which I rather hoped to increase. But I have long since learned that youthful habits are not easily displaced, and I am sure now that I never shall learn to be loquacious. You know how much I felt the inconvenience of my silent habits at home, and will readily believe that I must suffer still more among strangers, with whom agreeability is a necessary passport.

" It is so long since I have written you, that I scarcely know where to take up the thread of my discourse. I was then, I believe, at Dover, and you probably have learned from my letters to Boston how much I found to please me in my cousin's family at Chatham. It was my good fortune to have it in my power to be of some service to them, and I assure you I was most thankful for any opportunity of redeeming my time from entire uselessness. I am fated to find trouble wherever I go, and ought to be truly grateful when it is such as I can relieve. I staid ten weeks at Chatham, and went then to Waltham Abbey, about sixteen miles from London, and spent three weeks with George Lovell and his most lovely wife. He is the son of the only re maining brother of my grandfather, with all the warmth and generosity which characterized the family in America. He unites good judgment and firm principles, an uncommon versatility of talent, and consequent power of pleasing.

" I came here upon the 4th of December; and if I have ever told you enough of cousin Jane and her concerns to give you any idea of the strong interest I have always felt in her, you will fully understand how intense was the excitement of my mind when I found myself at last approaching her mansion. She had been the greatest attraction to me on this side of the water, indeed the principal object of my visit; the constant impediments which had prevented our meeting during the past summer of course increased our interest and impatience about it, and I can scarcely tell whether pain or pleasure predominated when I felt that the

crisis was near which would decide how far it was well
that I had come. . . . . . She has had a life of trial, and
being without that only comforter under suffering which
can teach us to submit patiently to it, the effect has been
unhappy. And now that she is just awaking from her
dream of darkness, you can easily conceive that the effect
of the bright sunshine which is breaking upon her mind
should be most powerful, and apt to carry such a mind to
the extreme of enthusiasm. She has but few connections,
and almost idolized my father as the guardian of her youth,
and therefore inclined to extend to his child all the strong
affection she felt for him, so that her delight at seeing me
was little short of mine to be with her. Here, then, I am
enjoying much with her and her family.

" The house itself is one of those ancient stone edifices
which abound in all parts of the kingdom, in connection
with the houses of the great ; probably built for some
younger and less affluent branches of the family. The
grounds are laid out with taste, and the lawn behind it has
not probably been disturbed since the house was built, and
is covered with a turf which might rival velvet in beauty.
The fir-trees, elms, and walnuts which surround it, and the
yew hedge which divides the garden from it, all speak its
antiquity and add to its loveliness. We have no neighbors ;
but the occasional visits of the different branches of the
family give us some variety."

" *Burcombe House, January* 1, 1825.

" MY DEAR MARY : —

" A happy new year to you, and all the good people at
Marlborough House, South Street, Newton, and Canton !
Although I cannot have the pleasure, as I had at this time
last year, of waking you out of a sound sleep upon the occasion, I have taken the liberty of thinking of you almost

all the night, and wishing you in my heart all possible blessings during the year upon which we have entered. I do not dare to look forward, but I cannot help hoping that it may witness my return to you, to find you in the enjoyment of all that is worth possessing in life. It is the custom here to sit out the old year, and as we were expecting Mr. McAdam and William home last night, we determined to s.. up for them. They did not arrive until nearly five this morning, so that I had time enough to reflect upon the past and hope for the future; and every thought and action of the last anniversary were lived over again in full reality. I only wanted liberty to pour forth to some one, to be a most eloquent egotist; but as it was, I just thought on quietly to ' my ain sel,' and enjoyed what was going on around me as well as I could.

" Our only neighbor is the farmer's wife, a most excellent woman of sixty, one of the old primitive people of the country, of good sense and sound judgment, just such a body as cousin N—— would delight in. Her husband is the church-warden, overseer of the poor, and indeed the principal man in all parish concerns ; and their goodness to the cottagers makes them beloved by all. You may imagine Mrs. L—— as about dear aunty's size, of pale complexion like her, white hair, just parted under a neat white cap, always surmounted with a neat black-satin bonnet, stuff gown, made as grandma used to wear hers, with a plain double muslin neckerchief within and a black or calico shawl outside, and a full linen apron, as white as the snow itself. Her face is all benevolence, and her voice, even with the broad provincial pronunciation of the country, sweet and musical. They have a large family of sons and daughters ; one of the former, a very interesting young man, is now going in a consumption. It is the best specimen of an English farmer's family that I have yet seen.

11

" I went on Christmas day to the Cathedral at Salisbury. It is a very fine building, and the part appropriated to tho services of the church is fitted up in a much better style than any thing I have seen, being of black oak, and in unison with the style of the building. The organ is a remarkably fine one, and I think I never felt music more powerful than the first symphony, played as the bishop and clergymen entered. It was at first so soft, that in that immense building it seemed rather as if it were the sound of the air itself than any earthly creation ; and as the tones swelled, the very building trembled, and one involuntarily held tho breath with awe."

Burcombe House, February 24, 1825.

" MY DEAR COUSIN : —

" The winter months have passed very quickly, and, as spring approaches, I begin to look forward with much anxiety to the period when, having completed all for which I came, I may prepare to return to my beloved home, and join again the many dear friends I may find there. I thank God that he has been pleased to spare so many of them for such a length of time, for it is remarkable that among so large a circle there should have been so few changes in ten long months. You cannot conceive of the gratitude which I feel whenever I hear from you, for you know not the anxiety which the consciousness of being at such a distance inevitably excites. I know not why it is, for were I ever so near, I could do nothing to save even one of the least of them all ; but so it is, and it is a greater exercise of reliance and trust than I could have ever known, had I not left you. I try to look forward without fear, and I never doubt that, whatever trials may be in store for me, it will be in mercy that they will come, and I will be patient and submissive.

" With regard to the probable time of my return, it is impossible for me to speak with any certainty. The first four months that I was in England were lost, so far as the accomplishment of the immediate object for which I came was concerned ; and it retarded my progress more than that time, as it is impossible to do as much in winter as might be done in half the time in summer. I do not speak of this as regretting it, for I have no doubt that it was for some good object that I was so employed ; and I saw much which I should not have otherwise seen at all. But it makes it necessary that I should prolong my stay here, in order to do even what I calculated upon when I named a year for the probable limit of my absence. In addition to this, many objects of interest have been presented to me of which I knew nothing, and peculiar circumstances have occurred since I have been here to make me desirous of remaining longer than I had anticipated. For I consider myself a sort of isolated, unconnected being, who, having no immediate duties in life, is bound to improve all opportunities of usefulness which may offer themselves."

In April Mary received the welcome intelligence that her very dear friend, E. P. F., from America, had arrived in Liverpool. Being at this time at Ash, Surrey, the residence of her father's uncle, she immediately arranged to meet E—— in London, making, as she says, " a desperate effort " to break away from her friends at Burcombe House, to whom she had become so strongly attached as to make it no easy matter, as we may believe there was some attachment on the other side also. Again and again was she constrained to alter her plans and defer her purpose of returning, by the entreaties of those whom she wished to gratify, and who urged upon her, when other arguments failed, one that was unanswerable; namely, that she had no *duty* to call her home. With sadness did she admit it, and nobly too. "I feel that I have many ties which have to *me* the force of duties, in drawing me back; but I cannot forget that I am indeed without bond of any kind in life which can be called peculiar duty."

The two friends met in London, and, after a few days of delightful interview, Mary was called to Sydenham, where are dated two letters, from which we take portions, referring to widely different subjects and scenes.

"*Sydenham, June,* 1825.

"Dear Emma : —

"It is so evident, from many circumstances of which you must be fully sensible, that this is an appointment by that Providence who guides even the sparrows in their course, that you have only to seek to fulfil its duties to the best of your powers, and humbly leave the event in His hands without whose blessing the best endeavors of the mightiest must be ineffectual. Do not be thinking how much more this or that one might have done ; we should do what we can for the sake of obeying God, not for our pleasure ; and acting from this motive, we may learn to be ' willing even to be useless,' if it be His will. This may seem more than the Gospel requires, but I believe, if we knew ourselves thoroughly, we should ever be suspicious of all feelings which led to personal comparisons. We should, as you say, be thankful for the one talent, not dissatisfied that we have not the many, knowing that we may please God, and accomplish the end of our being in the one case as well as in the other. And as it regards the good we may do, do we not often see Him using feeble means to effect great ends? At all events, it is our duty to be satisfied with what He has thought sufficient for us. But you need no urging to induce you to do your utmost; the only difficulty is, to know in what manner it is to be done."

"*Sydenham, June* 9, 1825.

" MY DEAR MARY :—

" I made a call with some friends one day upon the clergyman's lady, when our names were carried along by a row of livery servants, each one sounding it louder and louder, until it was announced by my lady's own servant at the door of the drawing-room, in a voice that made me start at the fellow's impudence in speaking so loud to his mistress; but I found that the poor lady was very deaf, yet a good, easy, old-fashioned body, as sociable and kind as need be. My risibles unfortunately took alarm at the similarity of this train of servants to a line at a fire handing buckets, and I had much ado to look indifferent and dignified, as if I were used to it; but I had my laugh out when I got into the room, for the good-natured body soon gave me a pretence for it by her whimsical stories.

" I went to St. Paul's last week to see the annual gathering of the parochial schools, and I could not have conceived any thing so striking as the sight was. That part of the church which is fitted up for service is not used, but temporary seats are erected for the children under the great dome, and the spectators sit in the body of the church, quite down to the western door. The children, about eight thousand, all clothed in the uniform of their several schools, are arranged one row above another to the number of sixteen, and to the height of at least fifty feet, within the pillars of the dome and on each side of the aisles. The appearance of

11 *

the children was most deeply affecting; all between seven
and fourteen, not half of what belonged to the schools, for
want of room; all clothed and educated by charity; taken,
for the most part, from the poorest classes, and perhaps
saved from destruction; it was a delightful sight for a
Christian, a striking testimony to the power of religion.
They were directed by the motions of one mar and it
seemed as if one impulse moved the whole, so perfectly
did they keep time together.   And when at last all were
assembled, and the solemn silence was suddenly broken by
one swell of their united voices in a hymn of thanksgiving,
I think the most insensible there must have been melted;
the sound filled the whole of that vast building, and rever-
berated again and again along its aisles.   The morning
service was performed by the clergyman, choristers, and
children; the minister's voice was almost powerless in
that vast place, and the organ, and voices of the singers,
sixteen in number, could scarcely be heard at the end of
the aisle; the children only could fill the space, and as they
occasionally burst out in different parts, the effect was wonderfully fine."

At this point, Mary received a cordial invitation
from a party of American friends, to go with them
to Scotland.   It was an opportunity which she
hardly expected, but most earnestly desired; not
only for its own sake, but as facilitating a cherished
purpose of visiting her father's only sister in the
North of England, — a visit of which she thought
more than any other, and which was to prove more
important than any other, though in a way which
she could little anticipate.   The journey thither,
which was almost her only pure recreation, and was

shared with a friend of all others desirable, was a high enjoyment; and her unstudied account of it, written from Chester and Gretna Green, we give at length, as we have allowed but little room to this kind of description. We claim for it no distinction, except that of naturalness and ease.

" Chester, July 22, 1825.

" MY DEAR COUSIN : —

"From sundry letters from Emma and myself, which will, I trust, have reached you long before this does, you will be able to guess how I have found my way to this place ; but I am very glad that I have time and opportunity to tell you, not only how, but why, I am here. I wrote to Ann the last of June, mentioning Mr. Perkins's kind proposition, that I should join his party and go with them to Scotland. I received your delightful letter the day after, and, I assure you, the encouragement you gave me to see and do all I could, with the promise of the approbation of those kind friends whose wishes it is my greatest desire to fulfil, did not a little in deciding me to use the means placed within my power of acquiring the information, which I probably should never again have an opportunity of getting. I try to be satisfied in having done what appeared best, by the thought that it is my duty to improve all the means of doing good which may fall in my way. But I do not like to think that any thing is to keep me from you much longer. I had made up my mind when I came, to go on bravely to the end, let it take what time it might, but my hope was that a year would be sufficient, and I still hope that it will ; yet I know you would not think me right to leave my work half finished, for any childish weakness, or homesick feeling. Be assured that I am as industrious as I can be, for my stimulant to exertion is a most powerful one, that of being again united to the beloved friends which that blessed spot, home, contains.   We have had a most delightful tour so far, and I daily feel that I am a highly favored mortal, to have such an opportunity of witnessing the wonders of this goodly world ; and I cannot but be grieved that I can make so little use of such a privilege.

" We left Bath upon the 9th, and have since passed through South and North Wales, and to-day took leave of the interesting scenery and people we found there, with much regret.   At Chepstow we passed a day, seeing the ruins of its old castle, upon some sublime rocks on the banks of the river Wye, and walking through the grounds of Piercefield, a gentleman's seat in the neighborhood, finely situated upon the rocky, yet thickly wooded heights, which border the river for a long distance from its mouth. On our ride from Chepstow to Hereford, we stopped to see the ruins of Tintern Abbey and Ragland Castle, both very famous, and I should think as fine as it was possible any thing of the kind could be.   Of the former, the walls and pillars of the church are nearly all that remain, but they are so perfect as to give one an exact idea of the beauty which it once possessed, built in the purest Gothic style, in the bottom of a quiet, beautiful valley, watered by the Wye, and protected on all sides by rocks and hills, which seem to defy any power that should dare to approach.   But the hand of Time has worked silently and effectually, and what was once a most noble temple is now but a tumbling ruin, sublime, indeed, even in its decay, covered almost with ivy, and shaded from within by trees which have grown upon the very spots consecrated to the prayers and confessions of its former possessors.   Its situation, and the peculiar lightness and beauty of its architecture, have made it very much talked of by travellers ; but all my ex pectations were fully answered, although they were very great.

" After riding all day over hill and dale, with only the sheep for our companions, we came at once upon one of the most romantic scenes imaginable; the singular pass called the Devil's Bridge, a stone structure thrown over a chasm in the rocks of one hundred and fifty feet depth, through the bottom of which runs a very rapid stream, dashing over rocks which at some seasons must make quite a grand cataract; but at this time the water is low. The banks are thickly wooded, even to the edge of the water, and altogether it is very attractive. At A—— we passed a night, and came through much glorious scenery to Dal-gelly, where we performed the mighty feat of mounting Cader Idris, the highest mountain in Wales, except Snow-don, and two thousand eight hundred feet from the point we left in the plain below. Imagine me mounted on horse back, for the first time in my life, for such a perilous un-dertaking, fortunately without any fear, and much amused by the novelty of the situation. The day happened to be very hot, but the atmosphere was clear; and we should have been amply repaid for tenfold the fatigue we endured by the grand scene we beheld from the summit. Never having before been on a great elevation, I knew not what to expect; and if the sensations were not just what I had supposed, they were sufficiently solemn to make me sensi-ble that it was ' good to be there.' A birdseye view of a circuit of five hundred miles could not fail to fill one with an idea of the power and majesty of Him who formed these wondrous glories, such as no common scenes could ever have inspired. I think I shall never look back upon that hour without recalling emotions which should make one better for ever.

" MARY."

" MY DEAR MARY : —

" My last, I think, was from Lancaster, just as we were about commencing our journey among the beautiful lakes of Cumberland and Westmoreland. We crossed what are called the Ulverstone and Lancaster Sands to Ulverstone. The shore is very hard at this place, and when the tide is down the ride is perfectly safe and free from water, except in the centre, where a river passes through. At this place is always found a guide, who conducts the carriage through the ford. I confess I did not much like the sensation, for though there is no danger in a heavy carriage, the current of the river is so strong that it seems as if the carriage were swimming. It was an odd feeling, too, after having been so recently three thousand feet in the air, to find one's self walking on the very bed of the ocean. We had about twelve miles of this kind of travelling. The coast is very bold, and we were quite delighted with the variety.

" The next day's ride, from Ambleside to Keswick, was a very interesting one ; the scenery of the grandest, and at times most beautiful, character. At Rydal we stopped to see what would have been a beautiful cascade if there had been any water, but we have had such a long period of dry weather that the stream had almost disappeared. The scenery about it was fine, and the thing itself could not but interest us under any circumstances, for it borders upon Wordsworth's grounds, and has no doubt been a favorite resort of his, and the suggestion of much of his fine poetry. His house is just below, and we could not help stopping at the gate, to look at the abode of one whose writings we so much admired. He was not at home, but his sister came out and invited us to see the place, and take a view from the Mount which gives the name to his place. This we could not do, but it was some consolation for our disap-

pointment to have spoken to her, although it was very tantalizing not to be able to avail ourselves of her polite invitation. The lakes of Rydal, Grasmere, Windermere, came
in succession on our way, all beautiful, but Grassmere with
its little island in the centre the most so, by far; the banks
being much wooded and ornamented by gentlemen's seats.
And Emma and I fancied that, after searching the greater
part of England, we had at length found a spot in which
we should be willing to take up our abode for life. The
mighty Helvellyn tempted us mountain-climbers to ascend
its rough sides, but with Skiddaw before us we were satisfied to pass it, in the hope of accomplishing the ascent of
that. At Keswick we staid one night, riding to Bassen-
thwaite in the afternoon, and sailing upon the lake in the
evening. Nothing could exceed the beauty and sublimity
of the latter excursion. When we first went upon it, the
sun was just setting behind the immense mountains which
bound this lake on the west, throwing their shadows upon
its smooth surface, and lighting those beyond with that purple, misty hue, which is not to be described but by the brush
of an artist, this again giving way to the sober hue of evening, until all view of them would have been lost, had not
the moon risen in full-orbed glory, to enlighten the scene
with her paler, but not less beautiful light. We sailed about
four hours upon the lake, landing upon one of the islands
upon which is a gentleman's seat, and going to the other
extremity to see the falls of dark Lodore, and to hear the
singular effect produced by firing a cannon on the shore; it
seemed like the rumbling of thunder, and was distinctly
echoed five times. I don't think I have enjoyed any one
thing so much as this sail, since we commenced our
journey.

" We came on through Carlisle, and passed the boundary
line between Scotland and England, and reached this place

before dark, — the first town over the border. It is a very small village, consisting of scarcely more than a dozen white cottages, but it has, perhaps, been the scene of as many critical events as many a larger one. We are at a very comfortable inn, got up for the accommodation of the fugitives who fly hither to seal their fate with the blacksmith's unholy blessing. Do not be alarmed for me, although I am quietly seated in the very room which has witnessed the consummation 'so devoutly wished' by most young dames. It is, indeed, mortifying to find one's self so near the goal, with so many requisites, obliged to miss the glorious opportunity for the want of one trifling article, — a husband; but so it is, and notwithstanding I am treading fairy land, I in vain look for some kind godmother to conjure up the needful, and must even submit to single blessedness a little longer. But I must stop; and have not time to look this over.

" MARY."

VII

SCENES OF SUFFERING.

VERY different from its beginning was the termination of the pleasant tour through Scotland. Mary felt it a duty to suppress all longings to go on with her good friend, who was soon to leave the country. Gladly would she have returned with her to America at once. But the great purpose, certainly one of the chief objects, for which she had gone abroad, was not yet accomplished. Her father's only sister, who had been left a widow in a very destitute condition, was still living in a distant and obscure village of Yorkshire. Mr. Pickard had made an annual provision for her support while he lived, and his daughter determined to carry out his intentions, so far as she could. Yet she felt that no aid in her power to send would be as much to her poor aunt as a visit, and she had been anxiously looking for an escort to the place, which was so remote as to make it hardly prudent for a lady and a stranger to venture alone. She was therefore the more ready to accompany her friends to Scotland, as on their return they would go within eighty miles of Osmotherly, her aunt's residence. Accord-

12

ingly she parted from them at Penrith, and went the rest of the way alone.

The visit that followed forms the most remarkable, and in some respects the most interesting and important, chapter in the story of her life. Instead of three weeks, which she had set apart for this purpose, she remained three months at Osmotherly. And it is not the least noticeable fact in that experience, that she wrote on the spot a very full account of the whole, in the midst of cares and the sight and sound of sufferings which are ordinarily allowed to excuse, if they do not wholly prevent, any use of the pen or effort of mind. But we will not anticipate. Nor will we interrupt the narrative, which we have drawn from various letters, by any comments of our own.

"*Osmotherly, September* 2, 1825

" My dear Emma : —

" I wish I could relieve your mind about my undertaking and prospects as quickly as my own was set at rest. I will not recapitulate all or any thing that I felt at parting from you yesterday, but you know me well enough to believe that it was with no common degree of regret and anxiety, which the uncertainty of the path before me tended not a little to increase. But I did recollect that I had never yet been forsaken in any difficulty ; supposing the worst, there could be no fear of real evil, and anxiety and distrust only made all that real which might after all be merely imaginary. In order to obtain the quiet feeling which this view of things should create, I turned my attention to my fellow-passenger, who proved a very respectable, well-informed woman, and my only companion to North Allerton. Her experiences helped to make me more comfortable, for she had come from London alone, travelled all night, and had a very long distance farther to go. She said she found no difficulty in travelling alone, and gave me some useful hints upon the subject. Our route lay over a different road from that by which we approached York, and as the day was so fine, we had a more tolerable ride than I expected. At North Allerton I found a quiet room at the inn, and a civil landlady, — went directly to the post-office, where a long and delightful letter from Jane McAdam awaited me. Not a word there of my aunt's letter, and I then went to a gentleman, through whom I had formerly transmitted letters to her, and found that he had sent the day before a letter from her to me, and that she was then well. This set me quite at ease, and I took a chaise and rode hither with a comparatively light heart. And then I wished it had so chanced that you could have taken this ride with me, for a more beautiful one I have seldom seen. This town lies upon one of those hills which we saw at a distance towards the east the day we rode from Richmond; and the ride from North Allerton is a gradual ascent, giving at every step a more extended view of the rich country which we passed through, with the additional beauty of numberless little streams which we could not see, and highly cultivated hills rising on one side to a great height.

"I found my aunt much better than I expected, and, as you may suppose, almost overpowered with joy to see me. I did wish you could have seen her, — a small, thin old lady, with a pale complexion, like Aunt Whipple, and the very brightest black eyes, which sparkle when she speaks with a degree of animation almost amusing in such an old lady. She lives in a comfortable little two-story cottage of four rooms, which far exceeds any thing I ever saw for neatness. I find that I could not have come at a better time to do good, or a worse for gaining spirits. My aunt's two daughters are married and live in this village; one of them, with three children, has a husband at the point of death with a fever; his brother died yesterday of the small-pox, and two of her children have the whooping-cough; added to this, their whole dependence is upon their own exertions, which are of course entirely stopped now. One of the children, a year and a half old, is with the grandmother, but so ill with the cough that she is almost sick with taking care of it. It has fortunately taken a fancy to me at once, and I can relieve her a little. But worse than all, one of her sons had come home in a very gloomy state of mind, and all her efforts had failed to rouse him to exertion. I hope to be more successful, for he seems will ing to listen to me. You may suppose, under such a state of things, I shall find enough to do. My aunt's mind is in a much better state than I expected, and if she does not get worn out with care to do more for me than ever was done for any body before, I shall be most thankful that I came. She tells me of many neighboring places which it would interest me to visit, as resorts of my dear father, and I think, next week, if possible to get a vehicle, I shall take her off upon a jaunt round the country for a few days, in home style, driving myself.

" I have not seen half the multitude of cousins that I find are to be seen, but so far they are kind and affectionate, and disposed to make me comfortable and happy. I feel just like a child who has left home for the first time ; the change is so sudden and so great, that the last eight weeks seem to me very like a dream of some distant age, and a most interesting one too. I never was more thankful for the varieties of life through which I have passed, for with-out actual experience I never could have adapted myself to the new order of beings I now have to deal with. I shall

find full employment for my fingers, in making my poor
aunt as comfortable as I wish to leave her.

" Yours,

"M. L. P."

" *Osmotherly, September* 8, 1825.

" MY DEAR EMMA : ——

" Watching all night by a death-bed is but a poor preparation for writing; and yet I am not willing to lose the
first leisure moment that I have had since I wrote you, lest
you should be alarmed at my long silence. But I think,
from the account I gave you of the state of affairs here,
you will naturally conclude that I should have had constant occupation, and will not be uneasy about me. I have
indeed found quite as much employment for mind and
body as either were able to perform, and have not had one
moment to devote to you, although my heart has been with
you, and my thoughts have often followed you. The poor
sick man, of whom I told you, has been growing worse
daily, and it was with feelings of almost joy that I last
night closed his eyes, knowing that his sufferings were at
an end ; and yet he is so great a loss to his family, that I
seldom knew a case in which it was so difficult to feel that
' it is right.' His wife, who is but a slender woman, is
left with three little boys, without a penny to support them,
and almost without the power of gaining it, for the youngest, which is but three weeks old, is dreadfully ill with the
whooping-cough. She is a calm and patient sufferer, however, and it does one good to see how trouble can be borne
by the most unlettered and uninformed, when the spirit is
right. I have not been able to do much for him, but the
little baby has been my constant care, and I have got to
loving it dearly. Every thing around me is sad and sor-
rowful, and nothing but the effort, which it is absolutely
necessary for me to make, to cheer and assist others, gives

12 *

me the least pleasure. My poor aunt, weakened in mind and body by continued and most severe afflictions, is almost a child; her son is nearly insane, and keeps her in constant fear lest he may destroy himself; and the trials of this poor daughter are enough to break her heart. Another of my cousins is well married, and wishes me to be with her at her quiet and happy home; but I cannot think of deserting this post, however painful, for any prospect of ease to myself. In fact, it seems to me that posts of difficulty are my appointed lot and my element, for I do feel lighter and happier when I have difficulties to overcome. Could you look in upon me, you would think it was impossible that I could be even tolerably comfortable, and yet I am cheerful, and get on as easily as possible, and am in truth happy.

"This village is the most primitive place I ever was in, and a very obscure, out-of-the way place; the inhabitants almost entirely of one class, and that of the poorer kind of laboring people, ignorant as possible, but simple and social. You may conceive of their simple manners, when I tell you they 'never saw such a lady as Miss Pickard' among them before; and of course Miss Pickard is an object of as much curiosity and speculation as if she were Empress of all the Russias; but they are kind-hearted and civil. The peculiar situation of things has taken me more among them than I should have been in twice the time, under common circumstances, and it has been a good exercise for my faculty of adaptation. I have succeeded, I believe, in pleasing them, for it seems as if they only vied with each other in trying to do the most for me, and I really think, if they had a parson to write the 'Annals of their Parish,' the arrival of the 'American lady' would stand as the most remarkable event in the year 1825. This amuses me, and gives me an opportunity of doing much good with little trouble, for it gives me influence; and, moreover, it shows me human nature under a new form. But I am entirely destitute of every thing like companionship, and having had so much in this way lately with you, of the most satisfactory and delightful kind, you will readily believe that I must feel a great deficiency. There is not even a clergyman's family for me to associate with, for the curate of the place is of the very worst class of that set whose existence is a standing disgrace to the Church; an ignorant, drinking man, as careless and negligent of the duties of his station as if he considered it of no consequence whatever. I hope to have a little leisure soon, and then reading and writing will make up to me in some measure for the loss of society; but as yet I have literally had to work hard, and have not found time even to look at 'the journal.' I have a nice, little, quiet room, however, and feel quite at home in it.

" I have thought much, very, very much, of your voyage back without me. I will not say I regret the circumstances which have led to my disappointment, for it seemed to be my appointed path, and when one follows the dictates of conscience it must be right; and when it is right, why should we wish it otherwise ? But I am weak, and there are times when the thought of another six, perhaps nine, months' absence from home, with all the uncertainties which attend the future, makes my heart sink, and the tear start, in spite of myself. Yet it could not be otherwise; it would have been wrong to have neglected coming here. I am more convinced of this now than ever, for though it was said that I could do as much good by sending money as by coming myself, I do not think so; and though I may be thought foolishly scrupulous for subjecting myself to the evils I must meet with here, when I might have avoided them, I am sure I never could have felt satisfied that all was don· for my poor aunt as well as it could be, unless I had seen and managed it. But I am allowing myself in talking of self in a most unwarrantable manner; you will pardon me, in consideration of the difficulty of giving up at once the habit of self-indulgence which your kindness has created and fixed."

Osmotherly, September 10 1825.

" MY DEAR EMMA : —

" I do not mean to act modest and beg a compliment for it, but in sober truth you do overrate me. Just because you happen to have seen more deeply into my ' inner man ' than you are wont to do with others, and have your feelings strongly interested, you let them carry you off, upon their liberal and expanded wings, to a region of romance peopled by ideal spirits with which you identify your poor friend Mary, who has in truth no business there. But I do indeed rejoice, if the experience which God in his goodness has given me has been in any measure useful. I do consider it a privilege to have learned so much of His character and will as in the wisdom of His providence He has enabled me to do, though it has been by fiery trial. I feel responsible for the right use of such a privilege, not only for my own, but others' good ; and if in the fulness of my heart I have been tempted to show you more of myself than a cooler judgment would have approved, I trust that it may not have been without its advantages to both ; to me, in teaching a lesson of humility ; to you, as a warning, perhaps. But I must not yield to this propensity to egotism ; I have too much beside to talk about.

" Our poor man was buried yesterday, and, as clergymen rarely come here, my cousin thought she would have her infant christened on the same day. It was a most affecting sight. I stood as its godmother at her request, because I could not refuse her at such a time ; but it is too great a responsibility to be lightly taken. The child, however, cannot live, for it has begun already to have fits with its cough.

" *September* 12. In three days you are to be gone from the country, and I shall not have this means of communicating. Dear Emma, you cannot tell how much I shall miss you. You seem to be a connecting link with home, which I have a fearful dread of losing. I don't know how it is, but these coming six months seem to me a worse separation than all the past eighteen. Yet do not think, because I feel so sad about not going home, that I dread staying. You know enough of the interests I have here, to feel satisfied that I shall have much to occupy me pleasantly. It is only the protracted separation from home that I feel sorry for, and that is unavoidable, and will perhaps prove best on many accounts. Farewell "

" *Osmotherly, September* 13, 1825.

    " DEAR EMMA : —
    " I had determined to write last night, as I found it quite out of the question to attempt it in the daytime. I had been up with the little boy a great part of the night before ; yet I knew I could keep awake writing, I wanted to do it so much. But in the true spirit of Polly Pickard, attempting more than any one would think reasonable, I was quite persuaded that, as I was to sit up, it was as well to do all I could ; and as poor cousin Bessy had not had a quiet night since her child was born, and was going to sleep alone in her house for the first time since her husband's death, I thought it would do her good, and me no harm, to sit up in her parlor, and take care of the baby in the cradle, that she might have a little sleep, and not feel alone. The dear little baby had been better than for some time, during the day, and I doubted not it would lie in the cradle or on

my knee very quietly, except during its coughing fits.
Bessy went to bed, but the poor little creature grew worse,
and coughed itself into a fit, in which it lay so long that I
thought it dead, and awoke its mother; but its little heart
began to beat again, and it seemed to be reviving, though
slowly, and I sent her off again. It appeared for some time
to be recovering, but all at once it sunk away and died in
my arms, so peacefully and sweetly that I could scarcely
be persuaded that it had not fallen into a still slumber, or
had another fit. But it was indeed gone, and when I could
bring myself to give it up, I arranged its little body for its
last home. I don't know when I have had my feelings
more excited. It was a lovely little creature, and I have
nursed it so much since I have been here, that I found it
had become an object of great interest to me; not a day
has passed that I have not given three or four hours to it,
and it was always so quiet with me that it seemed almost
to know when I took it. The circumstances of the family,
too, made it singularly affecting that it should be taken
away, and the suddenness of its death seemed almost to
bewilder me. Its poor mother is ill, and between comforting her and coming home to my aunt, who is very feeble, I
scarcely know how to find time enough for either. I have
been up three nights since Wednesday last, and, with two
children to manage, I am almost mazed.

" I have tried to write this morning, for the baby was not
out of my arms a moment last night, but I cannot collect
my thoughts, — I don't know what I mean to say. You
must state the case for me. Could you look in upon me
you might wonder I was not crazy, but I shall do very well
when I get a little sleep. Do not feel uneasy about me; I
am not in danger of being sick, unless the prophecies of
the old women here will kill me, for they think, I believe,
that I am too kind to live, and they shake their heads most

knowingly, — one proof among a thousand how much more frequently our characters are estimated by the circumstances in which we happen to be placed, than by any other criterion. Do write, to the last minute. I cannot bear to part with you in this unsatisfactory manner, but indeed I am incapable of any thing more ; my eyes are dazzled as I write, and I must lie down. I shall write by the packet of the 24th from Liverpool, so that you will hear of me almost as soon as you get home ; and I pray God that in safety and health and increased happiness you may all reach ' that haven where you would be, with a grateful sense of His mercies.' May God for ever bless you, my dear, kind friend, and strengthen you by His grace to pursue with success that path of virtue and holiness which it is your wish to follow, and enable you to perform all the duties which lie before you, consistently with His divine will, and worthy of His acceptance. This can only be done by humble reliance upon Him who is the way, the truth, and the life, for guidance, support, and reward. He alone can enable us to do that which we ought to do, and, feeling our own weakness, let us rely with faith upon His promises, neither doubting nor fearing the certainty of their accomplishment. But I cannot write or think ; I seem to feel that ' bonnie little bairnie ' in my arms still, and my nerves are something shaken. The worst of the whole is that poor, unhappy young man, whose low moans are continually sounding in my ears ; but I send him away to-morrow for his own sake, as well as ours, and all will go well. Again, dearest Emma, Heaven bless you ! Ever your

" M. L. P."

" Osmotherly, September 14, 1825.

" Dear Emma : —

" I have had a grand night's sleep, and am better to-day, — should be well, but for this lazy feeling, and a dull headache. Don't fear for me. I do not think I am going to be sick, and it will be for some good purpose if I am. I could not regret what I have done; I could almost say, as Mr. Thacher once said, 'I had better live a shorter life, and a useful one.' But I am not inclined to throw away life either; I enjoy it much, and think it right for all to endeavor to preserve it, for we may all do some good if we try, and that is reason enough for keeping it, were there no enjoyment to be had; as there is, even for the most distressed. But I must leave you, for I am not able to write more.

" . . . . . We buried the dear little baby to-day, which has been a wet, uncomfortable one, and I do not feel the better for the exposure, but on the whole am very well; nothing but a trifling cold, scarcely worth minding. I feel with you that it is as well, if not *better*, that I should stay. But you must not judge of its importance by cousin Jane's representation; her warm heart runs away with her judgment where she feels so much.

" A truce with your ' feelings of inferiority.' Who scolds me for the same feelings? It is Pride, my dear, depend upon it. I know it of old. Do not let it triumph.

" Ever sincerely yours,

" M. L. P."

" *Osmotherly, October* 3, 1825.

" My dear Emma : —

" I have just received your farewell blessing, and could you look in upon me, and know the peculiar circumstances and situation in which I am placed, you would not be surprised that it has made a very child of me, and that for the time I feel as if all my connection with my home and its interests was severed by your departure. I would not write under these impressions, for I know it is a diseased state of mind. did I not fear that, unless I improve this one leisure evening, I shall not have another opportunity of writing for a long time ; and I know you will be anxious to hear from me, from the uncomfortable feeling which you express at not receiving late letters. I did at first regret that I had not written upon the chances of your being detained, but on the whole it was best that I did not, for I could not at any moment since my last date have relieved your anxiety, had I told you the truth, and I think your imagination could not picture any evil so bad as the reality has been.

" But to proceed in order. I wrote you last, I think, the day after the dear little infant was buried, and I believe I mentioned to you that I had taken up my night quarters with my poor cousin Bessy. She had never been left alone since her husband died, and now that she had no longer her baby to occupy her attention, she felt her desolateness more forcibly. I therefore gave the day to my aunt, having Bessy and her two little boys as much with us as possible, and passed the night with her. She was the most patient sufferer I ever saw ; not a word of repining ever escaped her, and she went about her occupations and duties with a steadiness which spoke a determination to sacrifice every selfish consideration to the good of her children. Scarcely a tear could be seen on her cheek, and a common observer would have accused her of want of feeling, if he had not understood that the settled calm which sat upon her face might hide more real agony than is ever shown by any ' sounds of woe.' Her resolution astonished her friends, for they knew her to have a very timid and self-distrusting character, and the situation in which she was thus suddenly placed would have appalled even a stout heart. But I saw the true state of the case. When the duties of the day were past, and the necessity for exerting herself over, and all at rest but ourselves, she felt at liberty to indulge herself in talking of that of which she would not speak to any one beside ; and I found that what seemed

13

insensibility was in reality a degree of fortitude and reso
lution which I never saw equalled. I thought it best, too,
to encourage her thus to open her heart, for I believe that
concealed grief is always the most destructive to the mind,
and her situation really required the advice and assistance
of any one who could aid her, as she was inexperienced
and felt her own deficiencies to a most overpowering degree. She had had but little instruction upon religious
subjects, and would listen to my reading of the Scriptures,
and detail of my own experience of the power of religious
consolations, as if a new light were opened to her soul. I
did not then know how much she was affected, but the
readiness with which she adopted advice upon the subject
gave me much hope that it would in time become as valuable to her as it had been to me.

" I told you that her infant was only a fortnight old when
her husband was taken ill, and only a month when it died.
Its mother had never recovered her strength, and distress
having destroyed her appetite, and watching deprived her
of sleep, she was as thin and weak as possible, and but ill
able to bear the consequences of the sudden death of the
child. This, added to a cold which she took, made her
very feverish, and the absence of the physician from town
obliged her to confine herself to such simple remedies as
we could prescribe, to avert further evil and restore her
strength. But the benefit which she derived from them
was but temporary. A week from the day upon which her
baby died, while passing the afternoon with us, she was
taken very ill, and it was with great difficulty that her
brother and myself carried her to her own house, only a
few rods distant. I lost no time in administering the pre-
scriptions of the physician, and for a few days she seemed
to mend ; but I soon felt convinced that her disease was
the worst form of typhus fever, and was sure that she had

not strength to get through it. The doctor confirmed my suspicions, but told me that such was the dread of it among the country people, that, if it were known, I should be left to myself, for no one would come near the house. I had not then required any assistance, for I was very well, and, knowing her situation to be a critical one, did not like to trust her to any one beside. By some means, however, the story was sounded abroad and spread like wildfire, and the suspicion of (what was in fact the truth) the two broth ers having died of the same disorder added to the evil.

"The day after Bessy was taken, Jemmy, her youngest child, a boy of three, fell ill too, and though it was doubt-ful whether whooping-cough or typhus had the greater share in his malady, to the fearful minds of the villagers it was all one and the same, and the family were thought to be doomed to destruction. One by one fell off from com-ing near the house, till I at last scarcely saw a person ex-cept the doctor during the day. This I did not mind, for I preferred being constantly with my cousin, and the actual labor of attending her was not great; she took but little, and all the help which I wished for I had. She died, how-ever, on the 30th of September, eleven days after she was taken, and during that time I had never left her, night or day, except to change my clothes occasionally at my aunt's. I had watched with her seven nights, and been up part of every other; for so accustomed was she to my care, that she did not like to be touched by any other person. I had sent the two little boys to their grandmother's, and the youngest was very ill during the whole of his mother' sickness, and still continues so. My cousin's little cottag was so small, that I felt unwilling that any one should sleep in it, lest they should suffer from infection; and often did i sit up with her alone in the house. I had been so exposed to the disease that I felt no fears for myself, and I believe this helped to preserve me, and the good doctor watched me very narrowly. I could not in a month tell you half the interesting circumstances attending this trying scene. Her senses never forsook her for a moment, nor her deep sense of gratitude to God for the mercies which he had bestowed on her amid all her sufferings. It seemed to her His immediate providence which had sent me to them just at this time, and her expressions of affection and thankfulness were indeed most delightful to me. It does appear most singular that I should have come just now, for the fact is, poor Bessy would have suffered for want of a nurse, beside many other necessaries, had I not been here. Her mother was fully occupied with the little boy, and her sister too distant, and of too much importance at home, to be with her, and the people of the place are too ignorant and frightened to have been all to her that she required.

"It was necessary to bury her immediately; and thus is this family entirely broken up, in the short space of three weeks, by the death of both its heads. She left her children to my sole direction and care, and the settlement of all their affairs, so that I have still much to do, beside the care of the sick child. His grandmother is almost worn out with it, and left his mother's death-bed only to nurse him. I have now stolen away from him for an hour to visit this deserted place, and am sitting by the fire in the lonely parlor, without any other being in the house but the eldest boy of seven, who is amusing himself by my side, interrupting me now and then by saying, 'Cousin Mary, you will let me live with you, wont you?' Every thing is still without, and so strongly is my poor cousin's voice associated with every thing I see around me, that it would not require any very strong effort of imagination to fancy I still heard her blessing me from what is now, I trust, her abode of peace and joy. But I must not indulge myself in

writing about feelings, for I have much else to say; but I
really think, since the last solemn evening that I spent alone
in the old oak parlor in Pearl Street, I have never felt so
forcibly the mutability of all earthly things; and had I any
one to listen, I could talk all night upon the subject.

"This is by far the most primitive, uncivilized place I
was ever in; I cannot liken it to any thing I know at home,
for even Worthington has lawyers and a clergyman's family
to redeem it; and, moreover, the general inhabitants of our
little towns have more information and education than is
to be found in these out-of-the-way villages, to which the
modern improvement of national and free schools has not
yet been extended. I am glad to see all the varieties of
life, but under present circumstances this is a very solitary
one. Were it not for the physician's visits, which he kindly
makes every day, I should live totally without conversation
in its true sense. The people are good and honest-hearted,
and treat me as if I belonged to a higher order of animals,—
and this is a novel situation! I am very free from complaints, and take care not to do more than I feel able to,
and if I am superstitious in feeling that Providence directed
me hither at this time, it is a useful superstition, inasmuch
as it gives me a feeling of security that I shall be guided
and strengthened to accomplish the work appointed for me.
Do not fear, but hope and pray for me.

"I cannot tell you how much your visit to Burcombe
gratified me; you could not have obliged me more, for I
should have been so suspicious that my own description of
it and its inhabitants might be a partial one, that I doubt if
I should really have done them justice at home. Jane was
as much pleased with the effort you made to see them, as
any one could possibly be, and more pleased with the visit
itself than I choose to tell you. I have most kind letters
from the family at Penrith, offering to come for me when-

13 *

ever I give the word of command ; it is a delightful **rest to**
look forward to, but it will, I fear, be long before I can avail
myself of it. The thoughts of home are to me now something like the dreams one has of heaven, in the twilight
hours between sleeping and waking ; I dare not form any
definite picture, and yet the idea will not be wholly dis-
carded. But with so much around me to make me realize
the uncertainty of life, and exposed to actual danger every
moment, how can I presume even to hope ? May I be able
to say from the heart, ' Thy will be done.'

" MARY."

" Osmotherly, October 23, 1825.

    " MY DEAR COUSIN : —

"I wrote Emma a hurried letter a few weeks since,
giving an account of my poor cousin's illness and death,
and then hoped that I should soon be able to tell a happier
tale, to relieve the anxiety which that might have produced.
But it is not yet in my power, and I should not venture to
write at all, did I not hope that all your uneasiness on my
account will find an antidote in the confidence which daily
experience increases in my heart, that He whose arm is
mighty to save, and who has hitherto protected me from all
danger, will still extend to me his fatherly care, and guide
and guard me under all the events of his providence. You
will readily believe that I have need of this confidence to
strengthen me, when I tell you that I am writing this by
the bedside of the eldest of those two dear little orphans
whom my cousin left in my care. His little brother had
scarcely recovered from his fever, when I was obliged to
leave him to attend this poor child with the same fever, and
have now been for more than a week his sole nurse, night
and day.

" But to give you an adequate idea of the peculiarly trying situation in which I have been placed for the last seven

weeks, I must recapitulate the story, which you may perhaps have gathered in unconnected details from my letters
to Emma. It is indeed a melancholy one, but proves to
me most painfully that our steps are oftentimes guided by
a wisdom from above, far beyond our own limited conceptions. You know that one of my objects in coming to
England was to try to do something more than I had hitherto been enabled to, for the comfort of my poor old aunt,
and you will not therefore be surprised that it was my fixed
resolution not to return until I had an opportunity of ascertaining how to do this most effectually. When at last I did
get here, it was with the expectation of staying only just
long enough to see that she was made comfortable. I knew
nothing of her family even by name, and of herself only
that she was old and feeble, and subject to fits of extreme
melancholy. I had not any anticipations of pleasure, except from the feeling that I was doing what my dear father
would have done, and fulfilling one of the duties of my life.
My father had been her idol through life, and, as I have
now found, almost her sole dependence; her children could
do little for her, and the relations she had in England knew
nothing of her. She was of course most delighted to see
me, and prepared to devote herself with all her faculties to
my comfort. But, poor body, she stood in need of all that
I could do to comfort to her.

. . . . .

" I have written this in the intervals of attendance upon
the little boy, and, as you may perceive, at different periods,
for I seldom sit five minutes at once. It is now the 25th, and
I am happy to say he is a little better; but I scarcely dare
hope, he is of so feeble a constitution. I left him yesterday
under the influence of opium, so that I was sure he would
not miss me, to go to North Allerton, seven miles distant,
to meet old Mr. McAdam and my cousin S——, who had

come from Penrith in their carriage for me. They did not come hither, fearing that strangers would be but intruders in such distress, but stopped at North Allerton, and sent an express to me on Sunday night, begging me to return with them if possible, for they had known of all the sickness which surrounded me, and feared I should suffer from contagion. It was most kind in them, and I should have been most happy for the release could I have gone with an easy conscience. But it would have been worse than inhuman to have left this poor little sufferer, beside that much of the business which I have undertaken is unfinished, and I should not think I had done my duty until I had settled these orphans permanently. But I thought I ought to go to them to explain this, as I should have been afraid to have had them come here, and I took a chaise and passed the day with them. My patient did not wake up enough to know I was away, and it was quite a refreshment to me. Am I not most fortunate to have such kind friends in this strange land? It is a comfort to feel that I have such a resting-place when my labors here are over, and cheers me even in this most solitary of all the situations in which I have ever been placed. Were it not for the good little doctor who attends my patients, I know not what I should do My cousin cannot leave home for an instant, and my poor aunt is overwhelmed with all these distressing events, added to the continual trial which the melancholy young man is to all of us. I get on without much fatigue, however, and have not yet been obliged to sit up all night; and with the sleep which I get whenever the little fellow is quiet, I do very well. He has been very much out of his head the greater part of the time, but very patient when he is sensible. It is now ten days since he became ill, and you may suppose he is somewhat attached to his cousin by this time, and I to him. O, if you could look in upon me, what would you say!

" *October* 30. You would pity me now if you could look
upon me, for I have this night closed the eyes of the dear
child whom I was watching when I wrote the above. He
seemed better daily after my last date, and on Friday, the
28th, sat up and appeared in every respect on the recovery ;
his appetite was good, his fever reduced, and his strength
improving. He awoke on Saturday early, and begged for
his breakfast, ate a light one, and fell asleep. His nose had
bled a little the evening before, but not much ; but about
eleven, he suddenly threw off from his stomach such a
quantity of blood, as proved to us that there was some internal rupture in the head. This continued through the
day and night, increasing in violence. No earthly power
could save him ; all was done that could be, but certain
spots which appeared upon him soon after the bleeding
commenced decided the physician that he could not live.
He lingered until this evening, and died from absolute exhaustion at ten o'clock, of what is called spotted fever
here ; — and I laid with him after the spots had come out, .
without knowing what they meant. It is a great shock, for
I felt almost secure that he was getting better, and his poor
grandmother is nearly distracted. This seems to affect
her more than all ; being under her own roof, it is brought
more home to her senses, and it is indeed shocking to lose
five of one family in so short a time. I am sitting up,
while a woman, who has been with me through this dreadful day, gets a little rest by the side of my aunt ; but as I
was up last night, I am in such an agitated state that I am
not fit to write. To have seen four human beings die in
the short space of eight weeks is enough of itself to solem-
nize one's mind ; but with all the additional circumstances
which have attended these, no wonder that my heart is full
to overflowing. This was a fine boy, and you know that
the endearing ways of a sick child are most engaging under

any circumstances, and when that child is an orphan, and dependent upon one's self entirely, the interest is indeed intense. I never met with so violent a case of fever, and the poor sufferer was sensible to the last of all its horrors. One cannot indeed lament for him, for he would have probably had but a hard life. Little James is now indeed alone in the world, happily too young to be conscious of his loss; but it is very affecting to think of his being deprived of father, mother, and two brothers in eight weeks, and left so perfectly alone.

"*November* 2. I add a line to say that I am quite well, therefore do not feel anxious about me. There are very many cases of the fever in the village, and as I am almost the only person in it who is not afraid of infection, I still have full employment in assisting the poor sufferers. My cousin's little niece is still very ill. I have indeed been wonderfully preserved and strengthened. Heaven save me from presumption, but I cannot help feeling that I could not have lived through all that I have, unless God had protected me.

"Yours affectionately,

"M. L. P."

We need not attempt to add any thing to this simple and affecting narrative of events that seem to belong to a more remote place and period than England and our own day. With all their naturalness and the stamp of reality, it would not be difficult — as indeed has been done — to clothe them with the drapery of fiction, and weave them into a romantic, improbable tale.

But the tale is not all told. The scene shifts at this point, only to be succeeded by another not unlike, nor far apart. Near the end of November, Mary was released from present duty at Osmotherly, took a reluctant leave — yes, with her generous and clinging affections, a *reluctant* leave — of the family in which she had closed the eyes of five members, and was carried by eager, anxious friends to Penrith. There, in the bosom of a charming household already known and dear to her, every thing within and without presented as strong a contrast to the situation she had just left, as words could express. Her own words give us some idea of it, in the first letter she wrote after leaving a place associated " with images of danger and death," and leaving it, as she supposed, for ever. But the very next letter after that surprises us with the old date of " Osmotherly "; and we find that hardly a month had passed before she was recalled to the same spot, the same painful responsibilities, and far greater danger than before, as the result proved. But again we leave her to tell her own story.

" *Penrith, Cumberland, November* 29, 1825

" My dear Cousin : —

" After all my melancholy letters from Osmotherly, you will be glad to receive one of another date, and under happier circumstances. My last letter was just after the death of the dear little boy, and I then thought I should be able to leave there very shortly ; but it was not until the 26th, (after I had been there twelve weeks instead of the three which I intended when I went,) that I could arrange matters so that I could give up my charge conscientiously ; and, after all my efforts, I could not succeed in settling the business for my poor, unfortunate cousin. I left it, however, in a fair way for completion, clothed the dear little orpnan fcr the winter, and placed him with his aunt, making all the arrangements which my limited means allowed for his future support ; and notwithstanding the incessant trial which I had there, I assure you it was not without many painful feelings that I took leave of the place, for ever. I had been for the last five weeks constantly with my aunt, and could not bear to leave her in the solitary situation to which she was reduced by the death of so many of her family. My dear little Jamie had become an object of affection to me, heightened to an extreme degree, since he was, like myself, left without parents or brother or sister. I longed to take him as my own, for he is a child of very uncommon capacity, and I fear will not have the education which he deserves. But I could only commit him in faith to Him who is the Father of the fatherless, who will not suffer even the least of his creatures to want his care. I think I never shall forget his screams of agony when he saw me drive away ; I thought his little heart would burst. But childish sorrow is soon over, and he will forget me long before I shall cease to love him.

" According to an arrangement previously made, my cousin S—— met me at Greta Bridge, in her grandfather's carriage. I came to that place on Thursday in a postchaise, passed the night, and came on hither the next day, so that I had only about thirty miles to ride alone, and as I got a postboy from the neighborhood to drive me all the way, I felt perfectly safe, and found no inconvenience whatever. Nothing can exceed the kindness of this family to me ; indeed, I am made to feel that I am at home with them as it I had always belonged to them. After all I have had to suffer, it is almost like the rest of the Sabbath to the weary laborer, and if kindness and petting will cure one, I shall soon recover all I may have lost during my dreadful siege at Osmotherly. To be sure, I am almost bewildered at the change from constant anxiety and labor to a state of perfect idleness and indulgence, but I will try and make a good use of it; and I feel so entirely convinced that this most amazing preservation of my life must be for some useful end, that I think I never can fall into an insensible or cold state again. I was almost glad to stay from here, until I was quite sure I had not suffered from infection, for although I cannot feel much faith in the doctrine of contagion, I would not run any risk of communicating the disease to others. It is the opinion of many physicians here, (and my little doctor among the number,) that change of air may bring out the fever which would lie dormant in the system for a long time without it, and he warned me not to feel too secure until I had tried it. But I do not yet feel any symptoms; weak and weary I am, but not feverish, and having no fear am the more safe.

"But do not think I am so much occupied by the distresses I have experienced here, as to be unmindful of those which have visited my friends at home. Your letter of the 20th of October, and Ann's of the 18th, reached me on the 16th of November. The account of poor Maria's death shocked me very much, and made me long to fly home, that I might, if possible, do something for her dear little children. I wish I could assist them, and feel that there is no one of the family to whom the duty of doing it is so great. I beg you will use my name in any case in which you think I could act with usefulness, and if God spare me to return to you, I promise you I will fulfil all you may engage for me to the best of my powers. . . . . . It tires me so much, that I can scarcely write intelligibly. God bless you!

" MARY."

14

" MY DEAREST FRIEND: —

" I have often welcomed this anniversary with delight, but under all the various circumstances in which it has found me, I think I never felt the value of the privilege which it gives me of writing to you more deeply than I do at this moment.

" But I will first account to you for my being again at this place, the very name of which is no doubt by this time associated in your mind, as it is in mine, with images of danger and death. Of the events which took place during my former visit here, you have no doubt been informed by my letters to Boston, and of my departure from it, as I thought for ever, for the hospitable abode of my kind friends at Penrith, where I was enjoying much when I last wrote home. I intended staying with them until the middle of January, when Mr. McAdam's appointed journey south would secure me an escort to Birmingham, and I was, among other things, anticipating writing this under the influence of the same most delightful society which was operating upon my mind on this night last year. But I was doomed in this, as in many more important concerns, to feel the uncertainty of all calculations for the future ; for on the 23d of December I received a letter from the physician of this place, written at the request of my aunt, who was apparently dying of typhus fever, begging me if possible to let her see me once more. I knew there were many reasons which made it important that I should come, if that were indeed her situation ; and at the advanced age of sixty-eight, with a most feeble frame, I could not dare to expect a favorable termination. The risk of returning to such an infected region was, of course, much greater than my former residence there, but thus summoned I could not hesitate, and my good friends, even more fearful and anxious than I was, could not attempt to dissuade me. It was indeed an appalling undertaking, knowing so fully the evils to which I was coming which could not be avoided, and all that might ensue could not be kept out of sight.

" It was, I assure you, with many solemn thoughts, though hid by cheerful looks, that I took my leave, probably for ever, of that good family, and got into the mail alone on the morning of the 26th. My route lay across the dreary hill Stanmoor, and, as I had not even a single companion the whole eighty miles hither, you may be sure my cogitations were many and various. Among other things, I was struck by the singular coincidence which has always given to Christmas week a peculiar interest ; neither could I fail to consider, on recollecting the various circumstances that had occurred in it, how deep was my debt of gratitude to that Being who had guided me through them all in safety. Dear N——, this is an overwhelming thought, and one which every day's experience forces upon my mind with increasing power, a power of which, it seems to me, it would have been impossible to conceive under any other than the very peculiar circumstances in which I have been, and, it would seem, am still doomed to live, while in this country. Imagine me, at this distance from all to whom I have been accustomed to look for dependence, a being alone in creation almost, literally alone in this strange land, making an excursion of eighty miles across the country, partly in coaches, partly in postchaises, without a being to protect me or appeal to, and upon such an errand, — and yet as safe as if a host were escorting me, calm, quiet, and perfectly easy as if I were taking a ride to Hingham ; and then tell me, if the confiding spirit which our sacred religion creates in our souls is not worth all that we could possess besides.

" I arrived here in eight hours after I left Penrith, and found the poor old lady rather better, and not a little de-

lighted that I had cared enough for her to come. She has
had many and severe trials through life, to which those of
the last summer were but a sequel. I was the only one of
her own relations with whom she had come in contact for
many years, and the poor soul's heart warmed towards me
with the whole force of her long shut up affections. I at
once installed myself as sole nurse in the very room in
which I had watched the progress of disease and death
upon that poor child, whose case I mentioned in my letter
to Emma ; and here am I now writing you by the light of
a rush candle, with my little work-box for a desk, almost
afraid to breathe lest I should disturb my aunt's slumbers.
We two are the only beings in this little cottage, for I have
sent her sons out to sleep, as a precaution against the fever,
and put a bed into the corner of the room for myself.
Could you see me acting in the fourfold capacity which I
adopt in this humble cottage, you would hardly believe me
to be the same being, who, a week ago, was installed in
all the honors of a privileged visitor, amid the luxuries of
Cockel House, acting ' lady ' solely, to the utmost of my
ability. It amuses me to find how easily it all sits upon me,
and how readily we may adapt ourselves to varieties of
situation and find something to enjoy in all. Aunty is much
better, and I think there is a good chance for her recovery,
at least to as good a state of health as she was in before this
illness. I feel little evil in the contrast, great as it is to
myself, except a slight cold, which the very sudden change
in the weather, from warm and damp to excessive cold,
has brought me. The fields to-day are covered with snow,
the first time I have seen them so in this country, and it
looked so homeish, and so much like your happy home
the last time I saw it, that I have been enjoying the sight
highly to-day, while every one beside was looking blank at
it. I am in one respect more comfortable than when I was

here before, for I have one companion. The 'little doctor' has his only sister to keep his house, and she has
already made herself most important and agreeable to me;
she has only been here a week, and being as much a
stranger as myself, we have some feelings in common.
She is a very lovely little creature, twenty-one only in
years, but older in experience. Her manner is suited to
the style of her face,— gentle, winning, and at the same time
indicating cultivation and elegance of mind. Without the
slightest shade of affectation or consciousness of beauty,
she not only gives me a new study of character, but is a
most convenient and pleasant associate; living in the next
house but one, I can call upon her at any moment. Something always comes to me in all situations to prove to me
the care which is taken even of the most insignificant; and
surely the whole of my experience in this place has been
but a continued lesson of it. Indeed, I certainly have great
cause of thankfulness, for that only dark passage in my
progress since I left home, trying as it was, was full of admonition. It showed me a part of the great plan of creation of which I knew little or nothing before, a class of
beings whose characters, duties, motives, and views I had
never before understood; and above all, it showed me how
perfectly the various links in the great chain of existences
are adapted to aid, and strengthen, and apply to each other,
adding another to the many proofs of the Supreme Wisdom
which formed and governs all.

"The only remnant of my poor cousin Bessy's family
is a boy of just William's age; he was ill at the time his
mother died, and became my immediate charge until his
brother was taken sick, and grew so fond of me that it was
long before even his aunt, whom he had been used to seeing, could make him content to be separated from me. He
is a very engaging child, bright, and of a noble disposition

14*

and temper. The similarity of our situations was enough
to make me feel more than common tenderness for him,
his dependence upon me increased it, and his strong attachment to me completed it. I think I never felt so much
for a little creature before, and were it not for the great
distance I should have to take him, I never would leave
him behind. I thought he would have broken his little
heart when I drove away, and when I came back his
ecstasy was really affecting ; he ran round me, jumped up
in my lap, stroked and kissed my face, as if he could not
trust to the evidence of one sense, and at last burst out a
crying, 'Uncle Mady wont go away again ; Uncle Mady
live with Jamie every day, wont you, Uncle Mady ? ' He
had always a trick of calling me ' Uncle.' Do not think
I am made melancholy by all this. I have no recollection
of ever having the same degree of good spirits as I have
been blessed with for the last six months, — I may say nine ;
and save my longing for home, I have had no cause to wish
any one thing relating to me different from what it has
been. God grant that I may not be tempted to great presumption ! I hope my wishes are humble, though my confidence may be great.

" May God be with you, my dear friend, and guide and
guard, and bless you, through the year on which we have
now entered, and for ever, — is the earnest prayer of your
sincere

"MARY."

But with all her cheerfulness, and self-forgetting,
heroic courage, Mary was not proof against danger
and disease. It is well for us to learn that the laws
of nature are not suspended nor diverted from their
course, even by the strongest faith, or for the sake of
the most noble and useful laborer. Such a laborer

there was here; but it was hardly to be expected that she would pass unharmed, the second time, through such exposure, fatigue, and painful anxiety. If the transition was great, at first, from that barren and comfortless place to the luxuries of Penrith, the change back again must have been peculiarly trying. She speaks of the difference between the two places as equal to that between the most sumptuous dwelling in Boston and the farm-house at Brush Hill. Nay, the contrast there was yet greater; for the common cottages in Yorkshire had no floors for the first story, except of clay and sand. Such was the house in which all that previous sickness and death had occurred, and in which the nurse and servant of all now found herself again. Sending away to another house the melancholy and moaning young man, and fixing up a bed for herself in a corner of her aunt's small room, she endeavored to keep herself from the night air, particularly as the weather, after a long course of warm rains, became intensely cold. But in vain did she shun exposure. There was work to be done out of doors as well as in, and no one but herself to do it. A sudden and severe cramp seized her, and she at last fell upon the floor, when alone in the night, and there lay a long time, utterly helpless, striving to make her groans heard by some one in or out of the house. This left her in a state of extreme debility, from which nothing could for a long time raise her. She would make it appear a light matter when it was over, but it is evident, from her own expressions and other facts, that she was in great danger.

"Penrith, February 10, 1826.

" My dear Emma : —

" Your last letter was a cordial to me, and came at a time when I greatly needed it ; for I was actually suffering under all the evil which you were fearing for me when you wrote it, — confined to the chamber of that little cottage which I have described to you, weak and languid, the mere shadow of what I was when I parted from you. But for the cause and effect of my last visit to Osmotherly I must refer you to my letters to N. C. P. and Mrs. B——— ; you know I cannot bear to tell the same tale twice, more especially if it be a melancholy tale.

" But do not imagine me to have been in a very forlorn and disconsolate predicament, for I had many blessings to rejoice in all the while. The sun shone brightly all the day full upon the windows of our comfortable, neat apartment, furnished with what, in her former prosperous days, had been the furniture of the 'spare chamber' (the museum of precious articles, you know) of Aunty's ' bien house '; Aunty sitting by the fire in her easy chair, her bright eyes glistening with the exhilaration of returning health ; and my ladyship lying on the bed, thin and pale enough I grant, but in as high glee as strength would permit, and not for one minute depressed ; if any change came, it was for the better, and my nurses remarked that my worst days were my gayest ones. Then I had two visits each day from the ' little doctor,' the very essence of good-humor and cheerfulness, and as I had in reality but little pain, I could manage to enjoy a good deal. Besides, I had the comfort of a female companion, with whom I could associate with something like equality of feeling. This was the sister of the ' little doctor,' who had just come to Osmotherly to keep house for him. My dear little Jemmy, too, was a source of great amusement and delight to me ;

he had improved even in the short time I had been from him, and showed some new and interesting trait every time I saw him. I left all behind me, however, on the 30th of January, not without many regrets as you may believe, for I felt it was now certainly for ever; and no one can part from those who have been kind to the utmost of their power, however small that power may be, without sad feelings. This is certainly a great drawback upon the pleasure one takes in travelling, and I sometimes think, when the time comes that I must do the same to all I have known here I shall wish I had never come. But I do not like to think of it.

"I am indeed much better than I could have dared to hope, but I always gain fast if at all, and this week of eating has made a great change in me. I cannot tell you how I rejoice at this, for I began to be heartily tired of my fictitious character; I did not realize my identity when toddling about, catching hold of chairs and tables like a child just going alone, as I did last week; I longed to shake myself of the encumbrance, or that the scene would drop, and let me scamper away, Mary Pickard again.

"I am glad you have seen this house, for it will aid your imagination a little; but you can scarcely conceive of the appearance of comfort which pervades this room as it is now arranged. The gentlemen have all deserted us, and just now Aunty George, Selina, and I are seated in true spinster style round a large fire in the drawing-room up stairs, (which by the way was any thing but comfortable when you saw it,) Aunty at full length upon the sofa reading on one side, Selina on the other writing, and I in the front doing the same, at the same table with her. Around us are arranged, in the most convenient places, piano, flowers, tables covered with books, writing-desks, &c., ottomans ditto, all sorts of comfortable chairs, — easy, rocking, &c.;

in the corners, shelves with collections of shells, minerals, and other odd things, to say nothing of the living ornaments. It is the very picture of comfort, and I could tell you of certain sensual luxuries which make their appearance upon the centre-table, some three, four, five, or perhaps six times a day, now that I am prohibited from descending to the dining-room; but that would destroy the intellectual charm which must hang round the image of Aunty George. Mrs. McAdam writes me that she received your letter, and really begins to imagine herself a ' monstrously agreeable woman.' You must have given her a good dose, I think. She has been in a fine taking about this illness of mine, but is cooling a little, now she finds I am not satisfied with less than four meals per day. How shamefully I have treated Emma's kind letter; but there is no end to my wickedness of this sort. I must not begin with confessions, but end them by confessing myself very tired, and ever your sincere friend,

"M. L. P."

" Erdington, near Birmingham, March 3, 1826.

" My dear Cousin : —

"I have continued to gain strength daily since I last wrote. Miss McAdam passed a week in Liverpool, during which time Selina and I kept house at Cockel; and after passing my last few days there in the most delightful manner, with all the good inmates, I left them on the 26th. Mr. McAdam kindly insisted on coming by the way of Erdington, that I might not be obliged to travel all the way alone. We found a great change on this side the hills of Westmoreland; the grass is green, and every thing putting forth, the lambs bleating and the birds singing as if it were May.

" . . . . . I had given Mr. B—— notice of my intenuon to come to him at this time, and found him looking out for me even at the gate, with characteristic impatience, on Tuesday about noon, and not a little delighted to see me at last. You know how strongly attached he was to my father and mother, and indeed to the whole family; his enthusiastic feelings have fully retained the remembrance of what he enjoyed with them, and any one who belonged to them would have been most welcome to him. Besides this, he used to pet me, and took a great deal of pains to teach me, and I thought the little body would have lost his wits when he saw me; he is a kind-hearted man, and with all his peculiarities one cannot but respect and love him. You may remember what a little oddity he was in appearance when he was in Boston, and I assure you increasing years have not at all lessened his peculiarity His face is not, I think, altered in the least; his hair is still a bright brown, cut as short as scissors can do it, upon which he usually mounts a small sailor's wove hat, from beneath the narrow rim of which his little bright, gray eyes twinkle in a most animated manner. His common dress is a pepper-and-salt frock-coat, which has been apparently in the service many long years, the waist of which just divides his height, coming down to the chair when he sits; a straight, long waistcoat of the same materials, and a colored neckerchief tied as tightly as possible round his little neck; breeches of purple-corded velvet, fastened at the knee with a little steel buckle, white worsted stockings, and a pair of what have been long leather gaiters, pushed down over the ankles *à la negligée*. Fancy this little odd figure moving about as briskly as if he were a boy just loose from school, the vivacity of his manner and looks corresponding exactly with the quickness of his motions, and you have my little friend Mr. B——. You would think all this must be ludicrous, but it is not. There is so much good sense and kind feeling about him, and so much real benevolence in his manner towards every one, that all his peculiarity is forgotten in a very short time.   He is one of the most intelligent, entertaining men I ever met with, and certainly one of the most warm-hearted.   He has passed a very un settled life since he left America, and is now living in a poor cottage, quite out of the way of all society, with no amusement but his little garden, which he cultivates entirely himself, and a fine library of most valuable books.   This is quite enough for him, and he seems as happy and contented as possible, because he is independent.   His *sanctum* is more like grandpa's than any I ever saw ; he reminds me of him in many things, and we have talked over old times until I have fancied myself young again.

" You may form some idea of my strength, when I tell you I was yesterday tempted by the pleasure of my own company to a walk of eight miles, and did not suspect I had done half of it.   I have indeed recovered my strength rapidly, and do not care about the flesh.   I believe I am as well as I ever was, and should forget that I had been ill, were it not for certain feelings of inefficiency and reluctance to move, — the consequence of the indulgences .I have had, I presume.   I have indeed had enough to make a spoiled child of me, had I not been one before.   It is no light burden upon my mind, that I can do nothing to show my gratitude for all the kindness I have received here.   I do begin to dread parting for ever from all these good friends ; but do not think that *any thing* can efface the remembrance of what I owe my dearest friends at home.

" Mary."

" *London, May* 26, 1826.

" My dear Mrs. Barnard : —

" Mr. Bond had a letter yesterday from Mrs. B. of April

21st, in which she says you had heard of my illness at Osmotherly. I am glad to remember that you would at the same time hear of my entire recovery, and I hope before this you have received other letters to tell you how complete was that recovery. It is indeed overpowering to me, when I look back upon the events which have taken place since I came to England. How many and great have been the blessings which have attended me!

'I staid here with Mrs. Bates from the 4th to the 30th of April, seeing and doing very diligently, and, with Mr. Paine's assistance, examining many of the wonders and curiosities of this great place, which I had not before seen. I then went to Chatham to make my farewell visit to my cousin, Mrs. Stokes, intending to stay only a fortnight; for I did not then know at what time precisely Mr. Palfrey intended to embark for home, and was making my arrangements to be ready the latter part of June at the farthest. I was not, however, able to return at the time I intended, for I was attacked very violently with spasms from being very bilious, and the heavy doses administered by the physician kept me housed for more than a week. I returned to town on Monday last, the 22d, and came again to Mrs. Bates, as she begged me to make her house my home in London, as long as I staid. I was very much wearied with the journey, and Mr. Palfrey and Mr. Bond, who came in soon after, thought I must be ill, and may say so, but I assure you I am not. I gain strength very fast, and, as a proof of it, I was nearly seven hours on my feet yesterday, without food, and not fatigued by it. I shall stay here only just long enough to see the friends I have about London, and pack up my duds for the voyage, and then go to Ash and Uncle Ben for a few days, and thence to Burcombe to stay as long as I can.

"I feel now that my work here is finished. (that is, all

the most important part, — I could find enough to do were I to stay ever so long,) and I assure you I should feel most impatient of delay beyond the time appointed. Mr. Bond brought me Mr. Channing's Review *from himself;* you may believe I was not a little pleased that he should think of me. I beg you will thank him for me. How I shall enjoy hearing him, if such a blessing is in store for me! Love to you and the household.

" M. L. P."

During the progress of events recorded in these different letters, covering the space of a whole winter, we can imagine that some anxiety was felt by friends on both sides of the water. Communication with remote towns and obscure hamlets, even in England, was not frequent or easy ; and across the ocean we all know how different was the correspondence then and now. Accordingly, we find the deepest solicitude. expressed, and painful suspense, in both lands. The manner in which the English friends write shows the extent of Mary's danger, as well as the amount of her services and their exalted and tender estimate of her worth. We are not in possession of as many letters from England, relating to any period, as we have wished to obtain ; and the few we have we hesitate to use freely, because of their allusions to domestic incidents and persons who may be still living. But abundant is the testimony, if we need it, to their appreciation of Mary's character, warm and enthusiastic their love and admiration. A few sentences we take from the letters of Mrs. McAdam, the ' Aunt Jane' so often named, to a friend here.

October, 1825. "I have a letter this morning from our blessed Mary, dated the 3d of October. She has laid her poor cousin in the grave, after a fortnight's illness, during which time she appears to have been her sole nurse. I dread she is doing far more than she can bear. The younger of the two boys left is taken ill, and she talks of taking him home to nurse him; but I shall by this post write Miss McAdam to send for her and insist on her removal. Her life is of so much more consequence than any which are now left, that I can no longer hesitate. You, who love her as well as I do, can imagine my uneasiness. Rest assured, however, that I will keep you informed of every thing. When she wrote, she said she had so much to do she could not write home, and begged me to write. Now, my dear friend, all we have to do is to rely on that God who orders all things for the best, and to whom I constantly and ardently pray that He would spare and reward our and His own Mary, to guide more of us to Him; and I feel comforted when I rely with confidence on His love and wisdom. She is such a blessing, that I would fain hope the rest of my days may be influenced by her."

From the same: —

November, 1825. "Since I last wrote you, my dear Emma, I have had various accounts from our incomparable Mary. I feel much anxiety on her account, for which I have been frequently reproved by her, whose higher feelings and better regulated judgment give her such wonderful advantage over me, and so constantly produce in her the tranquil security of inward peace. She is so excellent, and so truly set in the midst of difficulties, that it sometimes appears to me as if she had been graciously lent to us for our guide to that heaven which we *all* pretend to seek. When she wrote, she was perfectly well; but though our friends went for her, she would not leave for several days, lest she should take the disease with her to Penrith. I dare not say I wish she were removed, for all is assuredly for the best, however it may appear to our imperfect minds. I feel confident she is the peculiar care of the God she loves and serves; but when she gets to Penrith, I know I shall be almost too happy. Her mind has taken such complete possession of my affections, that I appear to myself a new creature; I have totally changed since I became actually acquainted with her. . . . . . Our correspondence will not drop here, I hope; and I may at some future period give you a faint idea of the interest she has excited for every thing that lives and breathes her atmosphere."

From the letters written in America at this time, to Mary or her friends in England, many touching passages might be borrowed. How much is conveyed in a single fact communicated to her, at the moment of the greatest anxiety! "With all their desire for your return, nobody murmurs; every body says it is much better for you to stay. And Mrs. Barnard says, when she expressed her sorrow about it to Dr. Channing, he gave her for the only time in his life almost an angry look!" The writer of this passage, when at last assured of Mary's perfect safety after all her labors and perils, sent her such a full, hearty outpouring of joy and love, that we must be pardoned for citing a part of it, as showing the depth of the interest she awakened and the affection she secured.

"MY DEAREST *LIVE* MARY: —

"The pleasure and gratitude I feel in the confidence I now have that I am writing to an inhabitant of this world,

you can scarcely imagine. The dread I felt about your
fate weighed upon me so heavily, in spite of all the reasoning and hope about which I sedulously employed myself,
that it was a great effort to write; and I fear our letters of
late have not served to animate you. I shall not enter
upon the long history of my anxiety, which was inwardly
greater than any body's, I believe, because I knew more
about it. I will only tell you, that a question about you was
sure to damp the best spirits I could be in; and if people I
visited undertook to talk about you, it was a signal for my
call to terminate. At one time, I determined not to go to
town till I heard from you, but was induced to alter my
plans, and did go and pass a month, doing all I could to be
at ease, and acting just as if I knew you were *safe;* — how
you want to scold me for using that word! as if you could
be any thing but safe in the hands of your God, and when
you were serving him to the utmost of your power......
On Monday night, the 13th of this month, M——, E——
B——, and I found our way to Milton Hill in the 'evening coach.' The next day, that most valued of couriers,
the milkman, brought us a bundle from Pearl Street; two
letters fell out on opening it, — one from Exeter, the other
from the Sandwich Isles, — a long one from B——, which
I employed all the daylight in reading. Would you believe
me so insatiable, when one such blessing as hearing from
that distant spot of earth had been allowed? I was not
yet satisfied, although we had left town but the day before; presentiment drove me to the pile of clean clothes
on the floor, when my hand made its way through the chaos
to a letter! Mother says it was the sense of feeling that
discovered it to be yours, for the room was quite dark. I
needed but half a glimmer of fire-light to show me the characters I had so longed and prayed to see once more. I
screeched, ' Mary Pickard!' and flew to the kitchen fire to

15 *

assure myself still farther ; and never, dearest Mary, did ı
feel a warmer flood of joy and gratitude than when ' Penrith, 8th December,' convinced me you were alive and
well, and in just the hands you ought to be ! And when l
came to know, too, that my fears had not been unfounded,
that you had so narrowly escaped, had passed through such
trying scenes, and done more, much more, than almost any
body ever did before, I was too happy ! Though you don't
tell me so, I know under such circumstances what efforts
you made. But you have earned the privilege of being an
instrument, in the hands of the All-powerful, of good to
every human being you come in contact with. And when
l knew this, why did I feel so forlornly whenever I thought
of you in that remote place, alone, and exposed to fatigue
and illness ? If it had been you, how much higher views
would you have taken !

"Emma."

So ended the visit to England. How unlike most
visits there ! It is not often that two years are spent
abroad chiefly in confinement with the sick and
devotion to the dying. We wonder not that Mary
Pickard thought that such employment was her
" destiny." More appropriate does the word seem
than the common term, " mission "; for that expresses too much of design and consciousness to be
associated with her. She projected no large plans,
or distant enterprises. She simply held herself ready
for the work to which she might be summoned,
abroad as well as at home, and with an ambition
as easily satisfied at home as abroad. All her ministrations might seem to have been accidental, if
any thing were accidental; — the occasions sought
her, more than they were sought by her. Yet in

some way or other the occasions were sure to appear, and equally sure to be used. Nor were her charities merely those of the hand, or of time and toil alone. There was benevolence, as well as diligence. No one knew, no one will ever know, the amount of her direct gifts at Osmotherly. But we know, from various sources, that they were free and large. And by no means were they restricted to her kindred. There is reason to believe that the whole village shared her bounty; in moderate measure, of necessity, but in decided liberality. From the nature and power of the disorder, a general panic prevailed, aggravated by ignorance and superstition, and followed by improvidence and want. We have seen the statement, that a large proportion of the inhabitants either perished or became helpless and a burden. And when the sufferings of her own connections ceased, by death or recovery, Mary went out to do what she could among the diseased and destitute generally. She toiled till the alarm abated, and aimed particularly to remove from the minds and dwellings of the people those fruitful feeders, if not sources, of the calamity, — superstition and uncleanness. Is it too much to believe, that Osmotherly will always feel the blessing of that Providence which sent there the " good lady " ?

It was a beautiful termination of her whole experience among that people, — whose very dialect differed so much from hers, that they could scarcely understand her words, but easily read her actions, — that, when she recovered her own strength sufficiently to take a final leave of them, the whole village came out in a body, young and old, and escorted her on her way.

VIII.

NEW RELATIONS.

MARY PICKARD returned from England in the summer of 1826, and was warmly welcomed by her many friends in Boston. Her last home before going abroad had been at Miss Bent's in Washington Street, where she now went, and stayed through the fall and winter with the exception of short visits to friends in the vicinity. Thronged with visitors, and occupied with business of her own which she never left to others if she could do it herself, she had no time for large correspondence, and we find few letters for some months. But there are brief notes which show the fulness of her enjoyment and gratitude, enhanced by the recollection of the trying scenes through which she had passed, but which she rarely named and never magnified, as we are assured by some who were constantly with her. The mercies of the past, more than the trials, filled her thoughts. " My whole absence has been but a succession of mercies, for which I could not in a long life show the gratitude I feel ; and this the greatest of all, the safe restoration to my beloved home and blessed friends, — it is indeed overwhelming. I have been borne through afflictive trials by that Power which alone can enable us to bear them, may I also find the same strength sufficient to keep me firm and uninjured, amid the greater trial of prosperity and joy." This was said to one of her former instructors in Hingham, with whom she spent a week in November, reviving the memory of the " first awaking of the mind to high and holy thoughts and resolves."

To the trial of prosperity of which she speaks, she may have been exposed at this time, if at any. She had returned after a long absence, in which she had accomplished all that she proposed, and more than to most minds would have seemed possible. She was again in the midst of endeared and delighted friends, more free from care and solicitude for others than she had ever been before; her society sought by a larger circle of devoted and admiring acquaintance, paying her marked attention. There was every thing to gratify, and much to flatter. And she was happy, very happy, — " more lively and joyous, I think, than at any time of her life," writes an intimate friend. But she did not remain long unemployed, or live for herself. She sought other objects of interest, places and ways of laboring for those in need. She took classes of poor children in more than one Sunday school, and visited the houses of the poor during the week; of several families in Sea Street she is said to have taken particular care through that first season, though a season crowded with engagements of friendship and society, and occupied before its close with an unexpected and absorbing interest.

The last night of the year, Mary made one of that

great congregation who listened to that discourse
of HENRY WARE on the "Duty of Improvement,"
which few who heard have forgotten, and of which
one hearer has said, "No words from mortal lips
ever affected me like those." We may conceive
the emotions with which they were heard by her, in
whose mind religious concerns were always para-
mount, and who already, as we have reason to believe, was compelled to feel a personal interest in
the preacher. For we now approach that event
which is considered the crisis of a woman's life, and
which was certainly to change the whole aspect of
a life that was felt to be peculiarly insulated. But
we may be anticipating. No engagement yet existed, and in the letter written after the services of the
"last night" to one who was never forgotten on that
occasion, there is no allusion to new events, unless
in the close.

"*Boston, December* 31, 1826.

"Were I by your side, dearest N——, I might be able
to satisfy myself by talking; but when I think of committing to paper what I wish to say to you, I am almost discouraged, and have a great mind to give up the attempt.
I do verily believe I should for once play truant, and shut
up my desk, did I not fear, should I do so, that the ghost of
the departing year would start up in visible form before
me and pronounce a fearful malediction upon me for my
apostasy. Indeed, so wedded am I to old customs, and
really superstitious about the fulfilment of certain vows,
that I should not dare to hope for peace or prosperity for
the year to come, if I allowed myself to yield to the
tempter.

' When I look back only upon the past month, I feel as
if it were the work of an age to give you any idea of its
interest; and when the year, nay, years, of which I wish
to speak come in array before my mind's eye, it is not
strange that I know not how to begin, or how to confine
myself to the limits of a sheet of paper. You know, however, enough of the circumstances of the past year to
understand something of the feelings which this period has
brought with it. Perhaps I am inclined to exaggerate the
peculiarity of the events of my life, which, after all, may
have been no more exciting than every body meets with;
but be that as it may, there can be no harm in magnifying
the blessings. And as there is more hope of attaining a
high degree of excellence, if our standard of comparison
be high (even if it be beyond our reach), so I will hope
that the more enlarged is our estimate of our subjects for
gratitude, the more deep and heartfelt will our gratitude be.
It does seem to me, that no being can have *more* for which
to give thanks, than I have in past and present blessings;
and that no one can fall as far short as I do of the effect
that should follow such a belief.

"I have been reading the letter I was writing you at this
time last year, and it does make me tremble to the very
soul, when I contrast my situation now with what it then
was, to think how much is required of one, who has been
saved from such peril, and brought back to so much good.
But it is in vain to attempt to tell you what I think or feel
at this hour. One idea above all the rest will rise, and this
you will join me in, — that the proofs which the experience
of the past year gives of the never-ceasing, all-sufficient
care of God should make us look forward with perfect
trust to whatever the future may bring, without a doubt
that all will be well that He directs, — that our weakness
will be strengthened, our fear removed, and our spirits sus-

tained and soothed under all trials, if we will but rest in faith upon his almighty arm. I have felt this so much, that I had begun to be presumptuous, and almost thought that no possible temptation could make me doubt its sufficiency. But I dare not hope so much. I find there are temptations of which I have hitherto known nothing, and under the influence of which I may have to learn a new lesson. It is said of Bishop Sewell, who once most strangely departed from his faith, that his fall was necessary to teach him humility, and improve his character. Perhaps it may be so with me. If I do fall, I hope it may have the same good effect.

"I have wished to-day, as I often do, that you could have an ear where mine was. Mr. Channing gave us a most useful sermon this morning upon the office of Christ, from the words, 'I am the way, the truth, and the life.' Mr. Gannett this afternoon upon the retrospect of the past, — good and solemn. And this eve, notwithstanding the violence of the snow-storm, Mr. Ware's house has been filled to overflowing, to hear his usual address. It was one of the most eloquent and impressive I ever heard from him ; a powerful exhortation on the necessity of Progress, delivered with an energy which gave it great effect. I have heard but one of those discourses before this, but I should think it a most profitable service. The occasion is certainly one by which all who are capable of feeling seriously must be solemnly impressed ; and the great interest which is generally felt in Mr. Ware gives him the power of making a good use of such a predisposition. And now that it is *possible* that he may accept the call to New York, his influence is greater than ever.

"I have passed a quiet, delightful week at Hingham, made my long talked of visit to Mrs. P——, and returned on Christmas day to be quiet at home (if possible) until I go to you; and yet I ought to be stationary for a time for business' sake. I need not tell you how much you have been in my thoughts during the past week, so strongly are all the singular events which have taken place in it associated with you. It has not been suffered to pass without its own special interest; to me it has indeed been *full*.

"Most heartily yours, with best wishes for the coming year.

"M. L. P."

The year 1827 opened upon Mary differently from any previous year of her life. Its first month was to witness the consummation of a purpose, which could not be lightly regarded by a mind like hers. Strange that it can be by any! Yet we have such reason to fear it, that we deem it a sufficient apology, if any be needed, for disclosing her own thoughts at this time more fully than might otherwise seem right. Sure we are of *her* permission, whose conversations on the forming of a connection so often made the subject of trivial jesting were as free as they were serious. By nothing earthly is the social or moral community more deeply affected than by the prevalent views of Marriage, and the feelings with which its momentous obligations are assumed. And when there are revealed to us by death, under that seal of sacredness which deepens our conviction of their sincerity, such sentiments as those which Mary Pickard brought to this relation, our view of duty, and even of delicacy, moves us to impart rather than withhold them. Not that we suppose them peculiar to her, or that she has given them any remarkable expression. They may be common to every

16

right and earnest mind. But various considerations prevent their being publicly presented with that personal reality which adds so much to their power. Thankful would all be, and none more than those perfected spirits of which we now speak, if the young and the mature would take exalted and sober views of the holiest and happiest relation in life.

Mary's views were expressed to her two most intimate female friends, the same night; to one in a short note, to the other more at length.

"*January* 30, 1827. Dearest Emma, I am not willing that any other than my own pen should communicate to you the events of this day. I would not that you should think it possible for me, under any circumstances, so far to lose my identity as to be unmindful of the feelings of one whom I so love; and though it requires some effort, I will do the thing with my own hand. Know, then, dear E., that a change has passed over the spirit of my earthly dreams, and, instead of the self-dependent, self-governed being you have known me, I have learned to look to another for guidance and happiness; and, more than that, nave bound myself, by an irrevocable vow, to live for the future in the exercise of the great and responsible duties which such a connection inevitably brings with it. . . . . . You need no explanation, nor have I time to give any; it would require one of our long nights to trace the rise and progress of the influences that have thus terminated. At present, the idea of the change I am making is so solemn, so appalling, that my faculties are almost paralyzed.

"*Boston, January* 30, 1827.

"My dear N——:

"I have been sitting with this sheet before me for the

last half-hour, trying to find out in what way to begin the long and eventful story which I wish to convey to your mind as clearly as I see it in my own. I am in truth hardly able to write at all, from absolute exhaustion of body and mind, and therefore am driven to the necessity of beginning at the end of the chapter, lest I should not have time to tell the whole. Will it be an entire surprise to you to hear that this day has been to me the most important of my whole life, the turning-point of existence, the witness of my solemn and irrevocable promise to unite for the future my fate with that being, who, when we last met, I thought was doomed to be a stranger to me for ever? It seems, indeed, like a dream, and yet it is true, dreadfully true, that I have taken upon myself great and unknown duties for which I feel incompetent, — true that I have gained the best blessing life can give.

"You need no explanation to teach you the progress of this in my own mind, for you know me well enough to read it without book, and you may easily imagine how I feel at such a crisis. O, it is solemn, it is awful, thus to bind one's self for life! and yet I am conscious my whole heart is with the act, and my happiness intimately dependent upon it. This feeling of distrust and fearfulness will soon pass away. I have not been used to its interference in any case where I have known it was my *duty* to act; it is only when we seem to have the direction of events in our own hands, that the feeling of doubt as to what *is* duty weakens our confidence in our success. You will say, feeling must be the guide; and so it must so far as this, that we may be sure that that path is not the right one to which it does *not* impel; but there is danger of its tempting to the wrong one notwithstanding, and it cannot be safe unhesitatingly to follow its impulses.

"Mr. Ware goes to New York on Thursday, for four

weeks, to preach; he will, I suppose, return by the way of Northampton, and I hope you will not object to a visit from him on the way. But I must put an end to this. I am in truth unable to write more.

" Yours most truly,

" M. L. P."

The relation thus viewed by a Christian woman has often one aspect, as in the present instance, which is thought more delicate and unapproachable than any other. Mary was to take the place, not only of a wife, but of a "step-mother," — a name that should be redeemed from the inconsiderate and unjust odium to which it is commonly subjected. Why should that odium attach to this, more than to all *unfaithful* use of the conjugal relation? Does not this, the more difficult office, exhibit proportionably as many noble wives and true mothers as the other? According to the difficulty and the delicacy, is the greatness of the trust and the merit of fidelity. Let honor be rendered where honor is due; and let no vulgar prejudice or unkind prediction hide a beauty and excellence of woman that are less rare than may be supposed.

In aid of these thoughts, as well as in illustration of the character we are delineating, we are glad to be allowed to quote from two letters of Henry Ware himself; the first bearing the same date as Mary's just given, the other written after a more intimate acquaintance. They are both addressed to his sister at Northampton, to whom he had confided the care of his children while they were without a mother. The mother whom they had lost three years before had left a void not easily filled. A woman of more than common qualities and powers, doomed for several years to more than ordinary suffering from an insidious and fatal disease, she had still given much time to the parish, and discharged to the last the duties of a wife and mother, with a fidelity and affection whose loss was very grievous, and was felt more and more by Mr. Ware from the necessity of separation from his children, and their own growing years and needs. We can understand, therefore, the feelings with which he formed another connection, and made it known to one who was now to resign her charge to other hands.

" Boston, January 30, 1827

" DEAR SISTER : —

" There is no one who will have more sincere and hearty pleasure in the tidings I am going to communicate than you, or from whom I shall receive more sincere and affectionate congratulations. I therefore lose not a moment in telling you that I am to build up again my family hearth, and bring my children to their father's side, and have a home once more. With whom, I need not tell you. Providence has thrown in my way one woman, whose character is all that man can ask, of a singular and exalted excellence. You know how admirable she is, and how well suited to fill the vacant place by my side. She consents to do it; and that I feel grateful and happy, a privileged man, you will not doubt. . . . . . Write me at New York. Love to you all. Affectionately,

" HENRY WARE, JR."

" Saturday Evening, March 3, 1827.

" MY DEAR HARRIET : —

" You will not be troubled, I hope, if I pour out from my

16 *

mind a little of the satisfaction which I feel, and in which I am rejoicing more and more every day. Since my return the congratulations of my friends have been absolutely overpowering; and from seeing more and more of Miss Pickard, I am made to feel more and more grateful for the kind providence which has led me to this result. You know all my feelings and views, and the process of my mind, and I shall therefore be understood by you as by nobody else. It is not a common feeling which fills me; it is something peculiar, sacred, as if I had been under a supernatural guidance, and been made to act from pure and elevated and disinterested motives, for the purpose of accomplishing some great good. Every thing is connected with the memory of the past and with my former happiness, in such a way as not to sadden the present, but to give to it a singular spirituality, if I may so say; and I feel that, if the departed know what is transacting here, my own Elizabeth would congratulate me as sincerely as any of my friends. I have sought for the best mother to her children, and the best I have found. I have desired a pattern and blessing for my parish, and I have found one. I have wished some one to bear my load with me, and to help, confirm, and strengthen my principle by her own high and experienced piety, and such I have found. All these things, meeting in one person, — I might have looked for each alone, but where else are they to be all found in such excellent proportions united? I surveyed them with cool judgment, and I shall by and by love them ardently.

Dear Harriet, I must have somebody to pour out myself to; so bear the infliction charitably. Good by. Yours ever lovingly.

"HENRY."

The character of Mary Pickard would not be drawn, but one of her noblest traits be left out of

view, if we failed to speak frankly of the former
affection to which Mr. Ware refers, and the memory
of which she herself cherished, at first and always.
She had no sympathy, and little respect, for that
narrow view which insists that one affection must
crowd out another; that the departed and the living
cannot share the same pure love of the same true
heart. The happiness of husband and wife and
household has sometimes been impaired by a mistaken apprehension on this subject, and a suspicion
of feelings in each other which had no real existence,
or existed only from the want of mutual and free
expression. We have even known cruel attempts
made by others to prejudice the minds of those most
concerned, and especially the children of a former
mother. For such attempts, and all thoughts of the
kind, we cannot repress our indignant reproof. No
false delicacy should prevent the utterance of truth,
where the best affections and dearest interests are
involved. Instead of avoiding the subject, we are
grateful for the opportunity which such characters as
Henry and Mary Ware give us, of presenting the
just, generous, and Christian view. One of her own
children has said of her: " Perhaps no one thing in
her character and conduct has oftener struck common
minds with surprise, and superior ones with admiration, than this entire freedom and frankness in regard
to the first wife? ' She was the nearest and dearest
to *him*,' she would say, ' how, then, can I do otherwise than love her and cherish her memory?' And
her children she received as a precious legacy; they
were to her from the first moment like her own;
neither she nor they knew any distinction."

We are permitted to add one other letter of Henry Ware, beautifully illustrating the character of Mary, and showing his own large and holy view of this particular relation. It was addressed to Mrs. William Ware, sister of that first wife the memory of whose excellence and love he so blended with the new affection.

" May 15, 1827.

" MY DEAR MARY : —

" I believe that I have said to you, two or three times, how much I had calculated on your long visit, as a means of making you and Miss Pickard well acquainted. . . . . . And I am not sure that I should have said even as much as this, were it not for one circumstance, which has given me a satisfaction that I never had hoped to enjoy, and which will be increased by imparting it to you. I have known so much of the selfishness of human love, and heard so much of the sensitiveness with which women are apt to regard a former affection, that I had not dared to hope that I ever should be able to speak as I feel of former days, and the memory of my earliest love. Yet, as I longed to cherish it, and as all my present plans and feelings are interwoven with the thoughts and images of the past, it would have been an exceeding pain to me to feel that there was any reserve, or any of that — I don't know what to call it — which would compel me to hide such feelings, and seem not to have them. I cannot tell you, then, how happy I have been in finding Miss Pickard entirely above all mean and selfish feelings, which I have supposed to be so common. She enters into my views, and we have talked freely of other days ; and she helps to keep me right by speaking of the pleasant impressions she used to receive from Elizabeth's character, and what she has heard of her. I wish I could go into particulars. So unexpected a communication between us has been a source of gratification to me unspeakably great; and I do not know when I have felt more truly exalted and spiritualized, than when, after such a conversation which has freed us from every selfish and earthly feeling, we have knelt down together and prayed for blessing from that world, where, I·feel sure, if the departed regard those whom they left behind, there is no sorrow or displeasure at the course I am pursuing. I take pleasure in telling you this, because nothing can or shall divide me from you, or lessen that feeling in which I have so long regarded you as one of the nearest, the very nearest, to me; and I long that all who are near to me should be so to you. Best love to you, and all happiness with you and yours. Till I see you, adieu.

" Yours,

" HENRY."

Immediately after her engagement, Mary visited her friend in Worcester; and from that place we find a very long letter, relating more to others than to herself, written in a cheerful mood, but showing how deep and sober had been her meditations on the change that was before her, of which she writes more fully in the first letter after her return to Boston.

" Worcester, February 18, 1827.

" DEAR EMMA : —

" I have been hunting round the room to find a small sheet of paper upon which to do the pretty thing, and pay a troublesome debt. But my search has been in vain, so I have e'en changed the object of my pen, and determined to let it follow the dictates of my inclination, in covering a sheet of Grandpa McAdam's ' Bristol-best ' with such lines

and scratches as it may be impelled to make; nothing
doubting but its impulses will give you some satisfaction, if
they go no further than the expression of the sincere sympathy felt with you by your friends here, in your present
state of joyful excitement. I do indeed rej e with you in
your happiness at the return of your brother; and you
may be assured I am joined in this by the whole household.
Although I have never known from experience what are
the precise feelings you may have, I think I can enter into
them at all times. And now, whether it is that my mind is
more than usually attuned to joy, or whether it is more interested for you than it ever has been in similar cases with
respect to others, I know not; but sure I am, that I never
felt so much before, or seemed to myself so wholly awake
to the feelings and interests of my friends, as at this moment. You must enjoy a great deal in the next few months,
and I know you will not let so much cause for gratitude
pass without its full effect. It has always seemed to me a
most humiliating fact, that so much *suffering* should be necessary to teach us our dependence. Why should we not
be equally taught by the blessings which are bestowed upon
us, that we are and have nothing but as He wills it to be;
and does it not seem a natural effect of such testimonies
of love, to draw our hearts towards a Being who is so good
to us? Let us at least, dear Emma, prove that it may have
this influence.

" Nancy is very well, and bright and happy; and could
I drive away from her a foolish feeling of a parting visit
which hangs upon her mind, and fills her eyes whenever
she speaks to me, we should be in a very merry key. As
it is, however, we enjoy much, for I have much to tell her
of the adventures of the last three years, which takes her
away from the present; and she is at heart so truly satisfied and happy, that we cannot get up any thing like real
melancholy.

" I wish indeed, with you, that I could attain something of your animation, and for a longer period .han that you prescribe ; for I do not hold it in such contempt as you do. It might not, perhaps, add to my individual happiness, for it seems to me I am as happy as mortal can be ; but I do feel sure it would give me the means of communicating more pleasure to others, and this could not fail to increase my own. I have always considered that buoyancy of spirit of which you speak as a great and valuable gift ; perhaps I have exaggerated its power, as we are apt to do every thing in which we are deficient. But its effects in chasing away the vapors which will sometimes gather, almost without cause, around the feelings of even the best and happiest, are not to be questioned, and are in my view of great worth. My happiest moments have always been my quietest, and this does little for others' comfort. I have in a great measure overcome the solemnity which oppressed me when I saw you ; and were you only here, I think I could join with you in one of your merry laughs, as gayly as you could desire. I do indeed wish you were here.

" You were right in thinking that one of my letters was from cousin Jane ; the other was from Aunty, quite a happy one, not one complaint, and directed by the ' little Doctor,' — so I conclude he is in the land of the living. Jane writes in good spirits ; all things there in a better state than usual.

" Yours truly,

" M. L. P."

" Boston, March 20, 1827.

" My dear N——:

" Were I near you, it would be an unspeakable relief to pour forth to you, for every moment is so filled with constantly increasing interest, that at times I am oppressed and overpowered as I do not like to be ; and there are moments when doubt and distrust of myself so entirely possess me, that I feel almost tempted to doubt my *right* to undertake what I have. My mind is slow in all its processes, you know, and in this matter it seems to me more slow than is common, it may be from the magnitude of the change ; but certain it is, I have suffered more, and labored more to bring myself into the right state, than I ever did in my life in the same time. My cause for happiness is increasing every day, and this tempts me to dwell too exclusively upon concerns connected with self. I am seeing daily more and more of the immense responsibility under which I am placing myself, and feeling more and more my own incapacity, and this tempts me to be anxious and doubtful. I am understanding more of what *might* be done in the station I am to fill, and this makes me ambitious to satisfy all who will look to me with hope. O, if I could feel as I should, that if I do my utmost with my whole heart, from the right motive, I shall gain that approbation which should be the first object of my desire, be my efforts successful or not ! But I am getting to depend too much upon the approbation of those I love.

" In one respect, this new and strong and satisfying interest is not having the influence I feared ; instead of engrossing, absorbing, and making me selfish, excluding all other interests, it seems to enlarge the capacity of affection. I feel warmed more than ever towards every living being whom I ever loved. And it has done much towards exalting and enlightening my mind upon the point which has been a greater trial to me than any thing I ever met with. I mean, it has made me more willing to leave the world, and enjoy the happiness of heaven, than I ever thought I should be. Strange that the thing from which, of all others, I should have expected the very opposite effect, should have done this !

" I have been through all the forms and ceremonies of

'introduction,' very quietly. I have been to Cambridge, and the family have been here; and, better than that, I have laid siege to the venerable Doctor in his study, and had a most delightful conversation of nearly two hours in length; which made me feel that I was not a little privileged, to have any claim, however small, upon his interest. . . . . . I wish you could have heard Mr. Channing this morning on the 'Glory of Jesus Christ'; it was one of his highest flights. We have great preaching now-a-days from many quarters.

" Yours ever the same,
" MARY."

The marriage of the Rev. HENRY WARE, Jr. and MARY L. PICKARD took place at the house of Miss Bent in Boston, on the 11th of June, 1827, Dr. Gannett uniting and blessing them. They were absent a fortnight, journeying to New York and Northampton; and then returned to Boston with the two children, and entered upon their new home in Sheafe Street, at the North End. And there began a new life, — to Mary wholly new, and intensely busy. She gave herself up to all its duties, at once and unreservedly. Of her standard of duty we know something already; and they who also know the demands of a large parish upon a minister's wife, who resolves not only to make her house free and pleasant to all who will enter it, but also to share all of her husband's labors for which she is competent, can form an idea of what Mary found to do. " Mrs. Ware, at home and abroad, was the *busiest* woman of my acquaintance," is the reason given by one of her female friends for not seeking her society

as much as she desired.   It will be remembered that
she began with a family, as well as parish, and that
the duty of a "mother" was one which she held very
sacred, and would never slight for any other.   But we
will let her tell the story of her first labors, as she does
in a letter to Mrs. Hall, at Northampton, who had had
the care of the children, and another to Mrs. Paine.
We ought to say of these, and all the letters to be
offered, that they are not given as recording great
events or rare qualities, but simply for what they
are, — expressions of the daily thought and domestic
life of a conscientious woman, in common relations
and quiet duty.

                                    "*Boston, July* 20, 1827.

   " DEAR HARRIET : —

   " You will be glad, I know, to hear from my own pen
how we all prosper, and I sincerely wish I had time enough
to tell you all I wish you to know of my various arrangements and avocations, hopes and fears, wishes and success-
es.   Of the latter I cannot boast much ; I am, however,
much delighted to find that many things which I expected
would perplex me, and take more time and thought than I
should be willing to give them, do not trouble me in the least
degree, — such as household affairs, eating, drinking, and
keeping matters moving methodically.   I did not, to be sure,
indulge anxiety about it, as from my utter ignorance I had
some reason to do ; but I did not suppose it possible that such
a *young novice* could be inducted into the important station
of housekeeper without suffering for a time a degree of
martyrdom.   But thus far I get on easily, and hope to
learn by experience sufficient to meet future wants.   My
parish matters have gone on so far just as I wished.   I
gave up all last week to receiving visitors, and they came

in just the manner I wished, morning, noon, or evening, as might be most convenient to themselves. It was the best way for me, for it gave me a better opportunity of getting acquainted with their looks, and they seemed to like it very much themselves. I am at liberty now, but prefer staying at home, and still have enough to do to say ' Welcome ' to my friends.

" But this is all play-work in comparison with the other duties that belong to my lot. They are just what I knew they would be, — most delicate, most difficult, for one so utterly ignorant ; but I see the difficulties, and do not find them greater than I have always known they would be ; am neither discouraged nor faint-hearted, but hope and trust that power will yet be granted for all exigencies. I do not find myself as much discomposed by the task as I expected, considering I have had so little to do with children. But I do feel the importance of the relation in which I stand to them more deeply, more oppressively, than I could have conceived, and I am more than ever certain that I have a great deal to learn, and a long work before me. Do let me hear from you sometimes; we may not have much communication at present, but, as the Quaker said, ' we can meditate on each other.' I beg you to understand that I consider myself one whose lot has more than a common share of blessing, and daily and hourly do I thank God for guiding me to this pleasant path. I find I shall realize all you promised me of comfort, and much more too.

" Yours in sincerity.

" M. L. W."

" Boston, July 22, 1827.

" DEAR NANCY : —

" Your letter was given me this morning in meeting, and has just been read in one of the few quiet moments which fall to my lot, and one of the most peaceful and refreshing and I am rejoiced to add to its pleasure, by turning to my little table and writing to you. I have indeed longed to give you a peep into my almost too delightful *home ;* but it has been entirely beyond possibility to find an opportunity to write. How much I wish you could look in upon us, and see the whole detail of affairs from Monday morning to Saturday night, and that still more delightful season, the holy Sabbath, I need not tell you. But I fear you will never fully understand it, unless you can make yourself invisible and come among us. . . . . .

" We came on in the same stage, next day, and found all in readiness, perfect readiness, for us ; and made so, too, by the efforts of our friends, which added not a little to the comfort. The ladies of the parish would not let Miss B—— hire workwomen, but came and did things with their own hands. All looked more comfortable and neat and appropriate than I expected, as I had picked matters up with no small degree of carelessness. Miss B—— and Mrs. B—— were on the spot to receive us ; and oh ! Nancy, to enter *one's own home,* in which was to be known all of experience which might be hid in the future, — to come to it, too, as I did, after so long floating on a changeful sea, — and to come to it under all the interesting circumstances of grateful joy and fearful responsibilities, — it was a moment not to be described or forgotten.

" H—— told you of our Sunday. The transfer to a new place of worship was trying and affecting ; but I forgot the people, and did not suffer because every eye in the house might be directed towards me. I need not add, that the excitement in church is much more than it ever was to me, though not what it will be when I am more at home there. Sunday gave me truly the rest of the soul. I arranged that it should be a quiet day. We prepared dinner on Saturday,

and locked up the house ; Mr. Ware in his study after breakfast, and the children with me, reading and studying. They
were easily interested, and, the excitement of common days
being removed, they were more as I wished, and gave me
much pleasure. So it was at noon; and at night they go to
their father, and I have my own hour of peaceful thought.
And then in the evening we are all together, talking or
reading or singing. It is realizing so exactly what I have
always wished to have the day, and what I never before
knew, that I enjoy it doubly. A friend, perhaps, drops in
and joins our singing.

" . . . . . All classes have come to see me, even the poorest, and seem quite disposed to be pleased. I have said
distinctly that I wish ours to be entirely a social intercourse,
and they take me at my word. I have not told you of my
own private joys, nor can I in this little space. That they are
great, immensely great, you can believe ; and even with
the ——. *August* 16. Here I was interrupted more than
a fortnight ago, and·do not now remember what was to
have been the close of the sentence. I might add, that I
feel it happy for me, that, with all these blessings and pleasant circumstances, I have so much of responsibility and
anxiety as will effectually prevent my head being turned by
it. But I have not room for further detail. Yours ever.

"MARY."

The sense of "responsibility" just referred to
might be called one of Mary's characteristics. And
it had this peculiarity, if no other, that she felt it to
be a blessing rather than a burden. Indeed, in cases
where others would speak, as almost all do speak, of
"the *burden* of responsibility," she used the other
and brighter word. As, at this time, she said, in a
note to a friend, — " My fate is a singular one in this

17 *

respect,—that, whatever may be the variety of the scene, it is always filled with the extremes of blessing and responsibility; and I know not that I ever felt more fully the *blessing* of responsibility than now. Had I not great and almost overpowering duties and cares, my head would almost of necessity be dizzy with the bright prospect before me. As it is, I rejoice with a serious, but most grateful spirit, —a *sober* bliss certainly, but not the less valuable." There was one utterance of her "sober bliss" of which we have not spoken as we might, for it was habitual with her through life. We refer to her love of singing, and her use of sacred hymns in the family, which began, as we have seen, with the first Sabbath in her new home, and, as we are to see, ended only with life. One who lived with her just before her marriage tells us how much she indulged and enjoyed in this devotional, but cheerful melody, for "it seemed in her to be truly singing hymns of *praise*." She would sing after withdrawing for the night, at the close of the busiest and most distracting days; and sometimes, "after having actually retired, she would think of a charming tune, always selecting the most beautiful words, and joined by Miss K——, they would enjoy an hour in this way." Distinct are the echoes which linger in many hearts still, from her soft and expressive voice,—the voice of the soul!

The biographer of Henry Ware says that the year of which we are speaking, that which followed this second marriage, "was one of the most active, and also, to all human appearance, one of the most successful, of his ministry." It was marked by the efficiency of his labors, increased attention to his preaching, a growing congregation, and many proofs of favor with the community in general. He repeated, that winter, and enlarged, his Lectures on the Geography of Palestine; and, beside his Bible class and vestry service, his house was open to his parish every Tuesday evening for social intercourse and religious conversation. In this last, as in other parochial ways, Mrs. Ware was an efficient helper. Nothing could be more to her taste, or in unison with her best powers, nothing certainly could contribute more to her deepest joys, than this whole manner of life. If we may not believe that she was reserved for this very position, we may confidently say that she could have filled no other with more ease, more energy, or happier results. We attempt no enumeration of the relations and offices in which she endeavored to serve her husband's society, or the larger community. Boston is not more remarkable for its noble charities, than for the noble women who find sphere and activity enough in devising or directing so many of those charities. Mrs. Ware sought no publicity or distinction in these movements, and was less prominent, perhaps less efficient, than many others. Comparisons she seldom attempted, and never made them a rule of conduct. Her rule seems to have been, to refuse no service asked of her for which she was competent, if it interfered not with any duty to her family or parish. From the opportunities she had enjoyed and improved, when abroad, of visiting various charitable institutions, she was frequently consulted in regard to them, and she sent to England for plans and hints. She was a directress of a Charity Sewing School; and always regretted that sewing was not taught in the public schools, and made-essential to a complete education with every class. In all her views and efforts there was that practical good sense, which is better than the best theories or brightest abstractions. Yet she did not despise theory and abstraction, nor suppose that either she or her own generation had learned all there was to be learned. Indeed, we use no great boldness in saying, that, without the slightest tendency to reckless innovation or foolish experiment, there never was man or woman more interested in reform, or anxious for progress, or fearless for truth, than Henry and Mary Ware.

Of Mary's ideas of the *reward* which the benevolent and the good should desire, an amusing illustration has been given us by one who heard the remark at the time. A motion being made in a charitable Society for a " vote of thanks for the minister's prayer," Mrs. Ware said to a lady near her, " While I was secretary of the Society for the Employment of Female Poor, I never recorded votes of thanks. I thought members should do *all they could*, and when that was done, they might make their courtesy to each other ! "

In March, 1828, Mrs. Ware, after the labors and anxieties of the first winter, made a visit to Mrs Hall in Northampton, where she wrote her first letter to her husband, containing expressions whose full import we cannot know, but whose intimations of self-distrust and increasing sense of responsibility many will understand.

"*Northampton, March* 19, 1828.

" DEAR HENRY : —

" No letter from you yesterday ; but I did not expect
one, knowing that Saturday and Sunday are busy days. I
feel sure of one to-day, however, and while waiting its
arrival with all the patience I can summon, I cannot please
myself better than by talking a little to you ; and if I am
willing to believe that in this, as in many other matters, our
tastes may correspond, pity my delusion, but do not destroy
it, — it is the brightest dream of life to me.

" I find it is a very different thing to be lone Polly Pickard, beating about the world, conscious that it could not
interfere with any one's comfort or convenience if she
were out of it, and to call myself Mary Ware, with all the
appendages which belong to her, — the cares and comforts,
the duties and privileges, from which she cannot disconnect
herself. It is almost incredible to me that a short year
should have made one who was before utterly reckless
of danger so careful and cautious, — I had almost said,
anxious. And, oh! what a lesson it has taught me! I
thought I was deeply sensible of my danger; I thought I
realized fully the strength of the temptation which assailed
me to rest satisfied with my earthly blessings, and to depend upon them entirely for my happiness. But this little
separation has shown me the state of my mind in a truer
light than I ever saw it before, and compelled me to confess,
with deep sorrow, that my trial was greater than I could
bear. I had borne sorrow and deprivation, loneliness and
calumny, unmoved, erect, fearless, — but had sunk before
the greater trial of satisfied affection. May this knowledge
do me real good ! And if it should please our kind Father
to restore us to each other, let us strive with greater zeal to
conquer this enemy. While we rejoice, as we must, in the
blessings of His providence in calling us together, may we

use our comforts without so abusing them as shall make them instruments of evil instead of good to our souls.

"Do not think I am nervous or inclined to croak. I am perfectly well, and while I look at these things seriously, I feel a cheerful courage to contend manfully, nothing doubting that strength will be given in aid of all right effort, and that all these trials, if rightly used, will be so many additional aids in attaining that heavenly-mindedness which alone can satisfy.

"All blessings attend you, dearest Henry. All send love. Your own

"MARY."

Expressions of self-distrust and extreme discouragement seem strangely unintelligible to many minds, when they come from those who are thought better than others, and are always striving and advancing. Yet these are the very persons to feel discouraged, because of the high mark they set for themselves. And the fact that they are thought better than others, with their keen insight of their own failings, is more apt to mortify and depress than to exalt the humble and earnest spirit. Never, perhaps, was Henry Ware doing more for others or himself than in the winter and spring of the year we are reviewing. Yet in a letter to his wife, written a few weeks after that which we just gave from her, we find the expression of a dissatisfaction with himself, even greater than hers. It was written on his birthday, and shows also his sense of the great blessing which the last year had brought him. "I never yet was satisfied with my mode of life for one year, — perhaps I may except one. But since that I have been growing worse and worse. I did think soberly, that, when I was settled down with you, I should turn over a new leaf; and I began; but, by foolish degrees, I have got back to all my accustomed carelessness and waste of powers, and am doing nothing in proportion to what I ought to do. Yet other people tell me I do a great deal, and I am stupid enough to take their judgment instead of my own. . . . . . These, dear Mary, are the morning reflections with which I open my thirty-fifth year. Will the year be any better for them? I hope so, but I fear not; for I do not *feel* the weight and solemnity of these considerations as they ought to be felt."

Different, indeed, from the anticipations of either did the opening year prove. The season which had been the first of Mary's coöperation with Mr. Ware, was the last of his active service as a pastor. He had overtasked his energies, and that change was impending which affected the whole of their remaining work in life. On his return from Northampton, where he had been preaching, in the month of May, 1828, he was arrested at Ware by a violent fever, which was followed by extreme prostration, and confined him there several weeks. His wife was in Boston, and in a state of health that made travelling neither easy nor wholly safe. But she wrote so persuasively to the physician for leave to join her husband, that it could not be refused, and she was soon at his side. Under date of June 16th, she writes from Ware: "How grateful and happy I am, to be here! All the few feelings of doubt about the expediency of the jaunt, which others' fears forced upon my notice, have vanished, and my own strong convictions that it was best have become perfect certainty.   With the unspeakable satisfaction of being with my husband, so unexpected to him, and scarcely hoped for by me, what can there be to dread which can be a balance for such blessings ? "

As soon as Mr. Ware was well enough, they went on to Worcester, where they remained six weeks. And there, on the 13th of July, Mrs. Ware's first child was born; a son, who lived but few years, yet long enough to leave a deep impression of beauty and promise.   Toward the last of August, Mr. Ware set out alone on a horseback journey for his health, riding through New Hampshire and Vermont to Montreal and Quebec, and returning in October. During the first part of this interval, his wife and infant child were at lodgings in Newton, where her next letter is dated, referring in the opening to a poetical epistle which she had received from her husband.   That epistle, as published at length in the Memoir of Mr. Ware,* many will remember ; but its tenderness, and its allusions to their common experience at this period, will furnish an excuse, if we insert a part of it, as a preface to the letter which follows.

> " Dear Mary, 't is the fourteenth day
>   Since I was parted from your side;
> And still upon my lengthening way
>   In solitude I ride;
> But not a word has come to tell
> If those I left at home are well.

---

* Memoir of Henry Ware, p. 220.

"I am not of an anxious mind,
   Nor prone to cherish useless fear;
Yet oft methinks the very wind
   Is whispering in my ear,
That many an evil may take place
Within a fortnight's narrow space.

"But no,—a happier thought is mine;
   The absent, like the present scene,
Is guided by a Friend Divine,
   Who bids us wait, serene,
The issues of that gracious will,
Which mingles good with every ill.

"And who should feel this tranquil trust
   In that Benignant One above—
Who ne'er forgets that we are dust,
   And rules with pitying love—
Like us, who both have just been led
Back from the confines of the dead?

"Then, dearest, present or apart,
   An equal calmness let us wear;
Let steadfast Faith control the heart,
   And still its throbs of care.
We may not lean on things of dust,—
But Heaven is worthy all our trust."

                    "*Newton, September* 13, 1828.

   "Thank you, dearest, for the pleasure your good long
letters have given me; and if I am the more pleased that
you called your Muse to aid you in my behalf, I hope it is
one of the pardonable weaknesses of womankind, and trust
your vanity will not take the alarm lest I should undervalue
your own unassisted powers of pleasing.   It is indeed a
great and unceasing source of delight to me, that, although
separated externally in our way, our thoughts, our spirits,
are pursuing the same course, and we may meet in medi-

tation and prayer, sure that the same feelings of gratitude
and trust are ever present to us both. I thought much of
this, last Sunday, when I made my first attempt to attend
public worship.   I had felt a great desire to go to meeting
upon that day, being the eighth week from the birth of my
child ; and, moreover, because the first Sunday in September
ber has been a memorable day to me every year since
1813.   I did not attempt it in the morning, but in the afternoon rode over to hear Mr. Wallcut at the Upper Falls.   I
had felt well and strong at home, but it was quite too much
for me ; my mind was too weak to bear it quietly.   The
reflection upon all that had passed since I last entered the
house of God, which was forced upon me at one view, was
indeed overwhelming.   I could scarcely control myself
sufficiently to join in the services.   I longed to put every
one out of the house, that I might prostrate myself bodily,
and I did mentally, before that Being whose goodness had
brought me to that hour.   I did indeed think much of *you ;*
and there was a high and holy satisfaction in the idea that
you were at the same time employed in the same way ;
and although all was uncertainty with regard to you, I
doubted not, that, whether on earth or in heaven, I might
safely rely upon this.   How did I rejoice in that faith
which could remove from me all anxiety and fear concerning you, which could enable me so calmly to suffer you to
go from me for such a length of time, notwithstanding the
very many uncertainties which must belong to your situation.   I sometimes wonder at the peace which pervades
my mind, but I know I have a right to feel it ; it has its
basis upon an immovable foundation.   Mr. Wallcut gave
us a very useful, solemn discourse, and I was strengthened
by the service, and not injured by the excitement.

 " Heaven bless you !   Your own

                                                    " MARY."

In September, Mrs. Ware returned to their own house in Boston, — that house in which she had been so happy, and to which she hoped soon to welcome her husband back again, in restored health. She writes at once.

" Sheafe Street, September 26, 1828.

" Here we are, dear Henry, as comfortable as you could wish, in our own dear house, more grateful and happy than I could easily describe, every thing looking just as if we had not been away. Never did the place look more comfortable, — I had almost said, beautiful ; — I will say so, for there were so many delightful associations with it that it possessed a moral beauty, if I may say so, exceeding any other it *could* have had. I feel finely, and am sure I am as able to do all that is necessary as I ever was. It is not necessary just now that I should make any violent efforts ; there is no call for it. Elizabeth is with me, as happy as a child can be ; and the ' young rogue ' likes his home so well that he has turned over a new leaf at once, and I believe means to behave well. All we want now is your presence, and that I trust we shall have in the right time. O, how willing does all this experience make one to leave all things in His hands, who has brought us through such troubled waters so safely, so joyfully ! I have gained since Sunday ; at least, I have none of the confused feeling I then had, which made me fear my head was too light for Boston. It is getting *home*, I believe ; home and its peacefulness are the best restoratives. I trust you will find it so. I shall walk a little every day, and call first on those in affliction and the sick ; there are but few, astonishingly few for the time ; none that you have not heard of, I believe Peace be with you, dearest ! Your

" MARY."

Mr. Ware did return to Sheafe Street in October, but not to remain. His health was not restored; he could not resume his pastoral duties, and he was not willing to remain in Boston and among his people unemployed. A friend's house in Brookline was kindly offered them, and early in November they took leave — as it proved, a final leave — of their parish, and of that house where they had passed but a single year, yet one of the happiest of their lives. In the mind and memory of both of them, that abode seems to have been invested with peculiar interest. They have been heard to speak of the " Eden of Sheafe Street." Their children always revert to it with a tender fondness; and, beside theirs, there are many eyes that fill with tears even now, as they look back upon the happy hours and blessed influences enjoyed there, in their pastor's home. And she who helped to make that home what it was to pastor and people, loved to the last to live over again that precious season, though to her crowded with peculiar cares and trembling responsibilities.

They remained in Brookline that winter. In the spring of 1829, Mr. Ware virtually resigned his pastoral charge, and a colleague pastor was chosen, while a new professorship was planned for him in the Divinity School at Cambridge. At the same time, he was urged by generous friends, who offered the means, to go first with his wife to Europe, for entire rest and the recovery of his health. This unexpected opportunity he felt it right to use. And his wife, who was herself not well, thus speaks of it to Mrs. Paine, in a letter of several dates : —

" Brookline, December 31, 1828.

" My dear, kind Friend : —

" I have been for a long time prohibited from using my eyes, or should ere this have despatched to you the epistle which for many a weary week has been prepared in my brain for you; and now being still under the same interdict, I can only venture to remind you that there is still in existence the same old friend, who has been wont upon this eve to pour forth to you a copious stream of egotism, who never longed for the time to come when she might do so, more than at this present; but who, for the trial of her patience, must lay aside her pen, and, wishing you every blessing, wait until she is at liberty to use her eyes to say more.

" *January* 23. Although still unable to use my eyes without suffering, I am strongly tempted, by an empty house and an unoccupied hour, to renew, in some small measure, the intercourse which has so long ceased between us, and cannot help seating myself, pen in hand, to give you a few moments. I have ——

" *March* 30. I was interrupted by company at the above pauses; and since then, dear N——, what a revolution in the state of things around me ! It seems like a dream that I am again on the eve of departure for Europe. It is indeed a dream from which I should like to awake; and yet I am so sure that it is right to do just what we are doing, that the spirit faints not, nor even falters. I do not, indeed, dare to think, but have busied myself in visiting my parish, and do not fear but that power will be given. Yet, dear N——, what a lot is mine ! Surely I ought to be better for all this various blessing.

" Ever yours.

" M. L. W."

In closing the first and only year of Mary Ware's
" parish life," we remember that it was also the first
year of her married life, and an immediate entrance
upon the office of a mother.   To her views of this
office we have already referred, but have feared to
say all we know to be true of her discharge of its
duties.   There is a veil which we may not raise, a
sanctuary which none can enter.   Yet it is due to
her and to her children, — it is due to the greatness of
a trust whose difficulties all see, but few estimate
kindly, — to speak of the glowing filial love, the reverent and grateful obligation, expressed by those who
were permitted to call her " mother," and whose
sense of indebtedness grows with their days.   By
the exercise of a sound discretion in exigencies unavoidable and seldom allowed for, — by freedom of
intercourse through the day, and prayer and blessing
at night, — by a tenderness that made counsel always
kind and discipline never disheartening, — in a word,
by a yearning affection which has caused a start
and regret at any allusion to her not being " their
own mother," she took possession of their hearts for
life; and her death called forth, in the simple words
of one, the unutterable sentiment of both, — " Surely
God never gave a boy such a mother, or a man
such a friend."

IX.

EUROPEAN TOUR.

On the 1st of April, 1829, Mrs. Ware sailed from Boston, with her husband, in the ship Dover, for Liverpool. One of the older children was left at board and in school, the other in Mr. William Ware's family, in New York; while the infant was confided to Mr. Ware's sister, Mrs. Lincoln, — an arrangement that relieved the mother of anxiety, as far as was possible with any separation. But no parent will need to be told what she must have suffered, at best, in leaving behind her her first babe, not a year old, to cross the ocean and go into distant lands for an indefinite time, with a sick husband on whose restoration or return no calculation could be made. Yet we see in her not a moment's hesitation, we hear from her no expression of doubt or the least despondence. Physicians and judicious friends advised the step, her husband's health and power of usefulness, if not his life, might depend upon it; and this was enough, even if her own judgment had differed, as we have no reason to think it did. It was a feature of her mind very prominent, as it must be of every well-balanced mind, that she never suffered herself to be tortured with doubts or fears for the future when the present duty was clear,

and never lamented that she had done that which
seemed right and best, whatever the issue. As she
writes, on one occasion, of her own habits of mind
and long experience : — " There is no one thing that
has been more important to my comfort, under any
result of my plans, than the consciousness that they
were decided upon after a full and careful deliberation of all other possible plans, and a calm judgment
concerning them all. Then I felt I had done all that
poor human nature could do; the rest was in God's
hands, — it was all in God's hands. I was satisfied
that this decision was in the order of his providence,
and, come what might, I could never regret it, or
spend one vain, impious *wish* that I had taken another course. But, in order to make this decision
satisfactory, I have always desired to know the whole
truth, and be convinced that I had a perfect view of
the whole case in hand; and have sought suggestions
from others, not for my guidance, but that I might
be sure I had deliberated upon all the varieties of
plan which could be thought of."

This principle was now to be put to a severe test,
the severest, perhaps, of her whole life. We have
seen what she did, and what she suffered, in her former visit abroad. Totally different were the circumstances now, but none of them such as to make the
trial less. Then she had been alone as a traveller,
and also alone as to all exposure and peril. Now
she was to feel and fear for the one most dear to her
in life, one who was ill able to bear the fatigues and
discomforts to which he must be subjected, and
whom neither his own faith nor her serenity could

keep from depression and discouragement. Through the whole period of their absence, which proved to be a year and a half, Mr. Ware could not be said to be well for a single day. Much of the time, he yielded to dejection and apprehension, as she had never known him before. He enjoyed much, but suffered more. Not bodily suffering wholly, or chiefly; but that which is much harder to bear, — the hardest of all, — a sense of helplessness and the increasing fear of uselessness; the conviction, in the very prime of life, that life's work must be left undone, a calling which he dearly loved be relinquished, and he either remain abroad a wanderer in search of health, or return home with only the capacity of projecting numerous plans and labors, not one of which would be ever accomplished. All this his wife shared, at least in its effect; against all this she had constantly to contend, bearing most of the responsibility of measures and results, her own health not strong, and soon subjected to peculiar and most anxious trials.

We have no desire to magnify these trials. We only wish to set them in their true light, as making an unusual — not an unprecedented, but an unusual — demand upon the trust, endurance, and energy of a wife and mother. She herself has been heard to say, that this was the most trying period of her life; that no other experience equalled it. Yet this would hardly be inferred from her letters at the time. They were necessarily few, but written with her usual cheerfulness and unfailing hopefulness. Not all of them, however. One or two we have seen, such as cannot be used, that intimate, rather than express, peculiar suffering and solicitude. But this was in confidence, and for counsel; it being one of the peculiarities of the case that it presented many points where it was very difficult to decide whether wisdom and duty should carry them farther on, or turn them instantly back, — and the decision was with her.

We will not attempt to follow them closely in their foreign tour. Those who wish to trace its progress, and note the dates and incidents, will find them in the Memoir of Henry Ware by his brother. They visited England, Scotland, Ireland, Holland, Switzerland, Italy, and France, spending the winter in Italy. The first summer they passed over much of the ground and sought the spots, in England, so familiar and memorable to Mary from her former experience. They visited Wordsworth, Southey, Mrs. Hemans, Miss Edgeworth; and passed much time with Unitarian ministers, whom Mr. Ware wished particularly to see, that he might learn all he could of their position, cultivate a fraternal feeling, and open the way for a more frequent and friendly correspondence between those of the same household of faith in England and America. About the last of August they went to the Continent, taking Holland first, and thence through Switzerland into Italy reaching Rome in December, and remaining there until April.

The few letters that Mrs. Ware wrote home will be given in the order of their dates, with little explanation or comment. Some are in the form of a journal; and here and there we see the hand of Mr.

Ware, taking up the thread which his wife had dropped, and then leaving her to resume.

" *Greta Bridge, July* 8, 1829.

"MY DEAR EMMA:—

"I slept last night in the very same room, at Barnard Castle, which you and I occupied four years ago. And having been in many places lately where we had been together, such as Studley, Ripon, and the George Inn at York, where we parted, and moreover, as you have visited me in my dreams, night after night, for a long time past, I feel that I must yield to the desire of writing to you, although it may be but a few lines of uninteresting matter. This place will, however, insure to the letter some value, for I remember well how you wished that the rain would abate, that you might see something of its beauties. I wished it also then, but I wish it much more now, that I have had an opportunity of ——

" Here the arrival of the coach which was to take us from this paradise cut short Mary's opportunity, and I dare say she will not remember what she was going to write ; so that I, her substitute and lieutenant, go on to tell you how much we have mentioned your name while on these romantic grounds, and how glad we should have been to trace with you the paths of Rokeby and Greta in memory ——

" My lieutenant seems to have been cut off in his march rather abruptly also ; so I must beg you to imagine what beautiful associations of persons or things he was about to recall, and proceed with my own plain story, — just to tell you that we were more than satisfied with our walk ; it quite meets Scott's description. We trod the same path by which Bertram and Wycliffe wound their way from Barnard Castle to Mortham, and a wilder or more witching scene could scarcely be imagined. We had walked from

Stockton to the Castle by the side of the Tees, sixteen
miles, stopping for refreshment and rest at the little, humble
inns which alone are to be found on this unfrequented
route; and truly, after the parade and luxury of large ho-
tels, it was a delightful change to see something of simple
country life. You would have enjoyed it, too, notwithstanding the novelty of carrying the equipments of one's toilet in
our pockets.

" At Penrith we found our letters by the May packet, and
yours, dear Emma, was most welcome, not only for the
news you gave me of my darling children, but for the kind
feelings which dictated it, and the great entertainment it
gave us. It was just such a letter as we wanted just at that
time; it was the latest account, too, that we had had, for
though one from Mrs. Barnard, and another from Dr. John
and William, reached us at the same time, they were of
earlier date. You brought my little Robert more vividly
before my eyes than any thing I have heard of him. I
could see his little hand resting on Clarissa's shoulder, looking half coaxingly at you; and if the picture made me long
to try if he would notice me any better, I was amply compensated for my inability to do so by the knowledge that he
was doing so well, and under such kind care. At Penrith
I had an attack similar to that which I had when you were
at Brookline with me, which detained us a day; but, as it
rained, it was not of much consequence. We had projected a drive round the lakes in a gig, and this plan we
entered upon the next day (Saturday, 11th), — just such a
day as we should have asked for. We went to Ambleside,
via Ullswater and Patterdale, where we spent Sunday;
heard Wordsworth's son preach, and looked at Windermere. Monday we breakfasted with Wordsworth at that
lovely place, which I doubt not is still visible to your mind's
eye, as we saw it that beautiful morning. It looked just as

beautiful without, and as perfectly in keeping within, as we had imagined it. I confessed our theft, to the no small amusement of Mrs. Wordsworth, who did not, however, seem surprised at our feelings. Wordsworth, his wife, son, and daughter, composed the party. I wished I could have seen him again.

" *July* 16. Dear me, what a careless child ! I have just discovered that I began my letter on a sheet which Mr. Ware had one quarter filled to another person; and, having no time to rewrite, I must send it piecemeal. I was going to say, that I wished I could have seen Wordsworth again, because he did not meet my expectation; and therefore I felt disappointed, in spite of all my reasoning with myself that my imagination should not be the standard in such a case Besides, such a man could not be seen at one view; that which is most delightful in him would not be delightful if it were external.

" The ride to Keswick you will remember well. It lost nothing by being seen a second time. We were at the same inn at which we formerly stopped; and I could hear, perhaps, the same horses tramping along the same pavement over which our nags paced their way for us that memorable morning.

" We drank tea at Southey's, whose residence is much more like a poet's than it appeared at a distance, having a fine view of the lake between the trees with which it is almost enveloped. I heard him talk but little, as there was a party at the house; but was more pleased with that little than I expected to be. His study is just the most enviable one that I ever have seen. The next day we went upon an expedition to Crummock and Buttermere, which, though fatiguing, we enjoyed highly, having a fine row upon the lake. We returned to Keswick by a road which gigs

19

seldom pass over, the Crag through Borrowdale. It was
just such an expedition as you would have enjoyed on
horseback, perhaps on foot, as we took it for three of the
worst miles I ever passed over for roughness and wildness.
The last part amply repaid us for our toil. We rode by
the side of the Keswick lake for the whole length, just as
the sun was setting, yesterday.

"*July* 17. O, what would you not give for the sight
which is before me now! — 'fair Melrose,' not by the
' pale moonlight,' but by the light of as beautiful a sunset
as you could ask for upon such a scene. I have not been
out of the house yet, having contented myself with looking
at it from my window, and am now, with all diligence,
scribbling for the next Boston packet, while Mr. Ware has
gone to see Mrs. Hemans, who wrote us that we should
find her in this neighborhood. This is no small addition to
the attractions of Melrose. I feel very much as if I were
going to see an old friend, so near does sympathy with a
person's writings bring one to the writer himself, in soul at
least, if not in the outward expression. On our way hither
from Selkirk, we passed Abbotsford. A motley group of
towers and chimneys did it appear; and it verily made me
hold up my head, and feel stronger, at the thought of
breathing the same atmosphere with its mighty inhabitant.
We passed Branksome also to-day, and came through Tev-
iotdale, — classic ground every inch of it. But it will not
answer for me to run on at this rate; I shall scarcely complete one letter beside, when I wish to write fifty.

" Just at this point Henry returned from his call, with the
original ' Dominie Sampson,' and the intelligence that Mrs.
Hemans would join us in our intended visit to the Abbey.
The moon is just now in full-orbed splendor. Thither,
therefore, we repaired; and I met Mrs. Hemans for the

nrst time on the top of one of the towers, in such a scene
as beggars all powers of description. Never were mortals
more favored by the heavens and the earth for such an
expedition. The air was very mild; not a sound disturbed
the midnight stillness but the chirping of the —— (I cannot remember its Scotch name; its sound is somewhat like
a cricket's). There were just clouds enough to give us all
the varieties of light and shade. We did enjoy it highly.
And yet we almost wished we had been alone. One did
not want to have the interest divided; and the Dominie's
dry sayings and droll manner had such an effect upon our
risibles, that we had, in spite of ourselves, a little too much
of the ridiculous with the sublime. This Dominie, whose
real name is Thomson, junior minister of the kirk of Melrose, is unique, not *exactly* such as Sir Walter has described, but quite as original.

But I have come to the end of my letter, that is, my time.
Love to all, at Canton, Milton, Brookline, Nahant, Rox-
bury, Boston, — a goodly company truly. We have just
had a ride to Dryburgh Abbey, on the Tweed, a fine ruin
beautifully situated. The river here answers Scott's description better than at Berwick. There are very many
lovely situations upon its banks. But I *must* close. With
Mr. Ware's united love, and sincere wishes that you were
with us, yours most affectionately,

" MARY L. WARE."

"TO MRS. LUCY ALLEN AND MRS. HARRIET HALL.

" *Geneva, October* 11, 1829.

" MY DEAR GOOD SISTERS: —

" Wishing to say very much the same things to you both,
and finding that the expense and trouble of transporting
letters from this place across the Atlantic are *pretty considerable,* I am induced to address you both at once; hoping

that the question of title to the possession of this valuable
document will not give rise to a more severe litigation than
the lawyers of Massachusetts will be able to settle.   Your
letters reached us in the course of time ; yours, Lucy,
while we were in London, and Harriet's just three months
after its last date ; both most welcome.   It is a pleasure
which none but a pilgrim can understand, to see the veri-
table handwriting of a friend when separated by such a
space.   You say much of the pleasure we shall receive
in these foreign parts from the novelty, &c. of what we
may encounter.   So it is ; and I trust that I shall enjoy all
that we should do from the privilege allowed us.   But I
can tell you, under the rose, that there is no pleasure in all
this wide creation like that of sitting down in a quiet corner,
no matter what may be around us, holding communion
with *home ;* and I fully believe that all travellers would tell
you the same, if their pride would let them.

" We have, as you may have learned, fulfilled in part
your first wish, Harriet, — we have seen Miss Edgeworth,
but not Sir Walter.   She is a short, rather fat, extremely
homely, perhaps I might say ugly woman, without a spark
of intellectual expression in her still face, and not over-
much in her most animated moments ; but as full of animation, kind feeling, good sense, and intelligence, in her conversation, as one could desire ; a great talker, and a very
good listener ; not an item of pedantry or self-sufficiency,
or indeed any thing of what one would fear to find in her
father's daughter, or in any woman who had been so celebrated ; easy, playful, natural.   We forgot it was the re-
nowned Miss Edgeworth, and felt only that it was somebody who must be loved and admired.   We found her in
the old family mansion at Edgeworthstown, whither we
went fifty miles only out of our way to see her ; but all the
awkwardness of such a lion-seeking visit was entirely taken

off by the reception we met with from the whole family, and we should have felt quite at our ease to have passed a week there. We could stay only a part of three days; that is, part of two, and the whole of the intermediate one. The only impediment to our comfort was, that, being constantly in the family circle, which is a large one, we could not talk with the lady herself upon many points which would have been most interesting. Perhaps we saw her to peculiar advantage, but we certainly do feel that she has been greatly scandalized in having the reputation of acting the pedantic authoress, and partaking of her father's scepticism. So much for Miss Edgeworth.

" I wish I could tell you half as much of Sir Walter from personal observation, but he was out when Henry called with his friend, Mr. Hamilton; and he is so overpowered with visitors, that we were not willing to add ourselves to the list of the curious who persecute him. We were delighted with all that we heard of him; indeed, the nearer we viewed his character, through the medium of those who knew him, the more our admiration and desire to see him increased. It would really seem that his vast intellect is his least remarkable feature. We saw many of his familiar letters to Miss Edgeworth, and that was next best to hearing him talk, for they are just like conversation. Mrs. Hemans, too, we have seen, and Bowring a great deal, and some others of the noted of the present day; and we shall treasure the remembrance of the few, for they have been but few.

" It has been truly tantalizing to pass through Switzerland in clouds and darkness, now and then catching a glimpse of its beauties to show us what we were losing, but the far greater part of the time passing through the very finest portions of the Alpine scenery without any visible indications that we were not in a level country. But we have

19 *

proceeded thus far free from sickness, danger, or even difficulty, and have therefore too much reason to be grateful to
find it possible to complain.

" We find a great deal to amuse us in the various habits
and customs of the countries through which we pass, particularly since we left England; and the eating and drinking part of the business is not the least entertaining. We,
however, manage to please ourselves, and our entertainers,
too, pretty well. Henry eats his bread and milk as com-
fortably as he would at home, and I do what justice I can
to the various dishes which are set before me, though,
when they amount, as they have done, to twenty in number,
in spite of all the 'J'ai fini's' I could utter, I have excited
a smile of contempt from the waiter, who wondered at the
barbarism of dining from one dish. We have not seen a
carpet since we left Holland, except upon the sitting-room
of an English lady here, and we have been in some hand-
somely furnished houses. . . . . . O this pen, ink, and
paper! I will have no more to do with them, but leave them
to Henry. Your sister   MARY.

" Dear girls, women, or wives: My loquacious helpmate
has merely left me a place to send my love, and to say I
wish I had room to write to you and your husbands. By
way of supplement, I will just say of myself, that I am now
able to talk while riding, without pain, which I never could
do before we left England; and can also read loud a little
while. This is something worth telling of. My visit to
Geneva, owing to circumstances, is the least satisfactory that
I have made. You will perhaps hear again from the land
of the Cæsars, whence I will dictate a letter full of 'ettas,'
and 'inas,' and 'issimas,' and 'ulinas,' and other satin eu-
phonisms. Meanwhile, peace be with you! Your brother
         " HENRY."

We have added Mr. Ware's pleasant little post-script to the last letter, chiefly to show, by his own confession, how very feeble he must have been, and how great her anxiety and care. Indeed, she says of him at this time, " His system requires rest; it will be long before it is fit for use again." She herself was far from well, and had the depressing prospect of a more serious sickness, in a foreign land, with added cares. And yet neither of them was idle, during any period of that trial. They accomplished a great deal in various ways, and prepared one distinct work for publication. We say, *they* did it; for Mrs. Ware seems to have joined in that labor which afterward gave us one of the most useful of Henry Ware's works. We refer to his treatise on the "Formation of the Christian Character." It is probably known that this book was written almost entirely in travelling; first in this country, during the horseback jaunt which Mr. Ware took alone through New England to Canada, in 1828, and then abroad, at various stages of this European tour. And here it was in Mrs. Ware's power to be of essential service to her husband, in a way which she explains in a letter written late in life, half jestingly taking to herself a part of the credit for the work to which we refer. To Dr. John Ware she writes, in 1844, in reference to her husband's labors in this and other ways, at the time of which we are speaking: —

"You will gather from the letters of European friends in what estimate he was held by them. That is of little import; but it shows how faithfully he preserved his identity as a minister of the Gospel. In looking back upon the jaunt, as a whole, nothing is so prominent to my mind as the perpetual indications of his ruling passion, if I may call it so, — his love of his profession, — the eagerness with which he sought out his ministerial brethren wherever he heard of them, stopping by the way-side to introduce himself and extend to them the hand of fellowship, often going out of the way many miles for that purpose, and making all other objects subservient to that of increasing his knowledge of men and things pertaining to the ministerial life.   I *know* his visit was a useful one to his brethren in many respects. . . . . . .

" You know, I believe, that the greater part of his work upon the ' Christian Character' was written on that tour.   Its pages are to my memory a sort of diary of our progress, associated as they are with the pleasant evenings, when, after our autumnal day's journey, having despatched our supper, we settled ourselves at a little table before a cheerful wood-fire in our inn, and he with his writing materials, and I with my work, or writing or reading, could almost imagine ourselves at home.   Thus were my even‧ ings spent in alternate writing, reading, and criticism, until I almost felt as if I had written the book myself ! "

The end of the year 1829 found Mr. and Mrs Ware travelling from Rome to Naples; and on the " last night," faithful to her friendships everywhere, she began the regular " annual " to Mrs. Paine, which she did not finish till after their return to Rome, thus giving some account of their condition in both places.

" St. Agatha,* December* 31, 1829

" MY DEAR NANCY : —

" This is not the first annual which you have received
with a foreign date ; neither can you be surprised at any
aberration in my orbit. And yet methinks you will have
to consider twice before you can quite realize that it is
' Pearl Street Mary Pickard,' who is writing you from this
region of ancient glory and far-famed beauty. But so it is ;
and could you look in upon me, you would wonder, as I do,
that the very peculiar changes of the eighteen years you
have known me should leave me so precisely the same.
I begin to think that I am made of most invulnerable materials ; for here I sit — surrounded by as singular and trying circumstances as any which I have ever known — as
easy and happy, I had almost said as indifferent, as if the
world were jogging on with me in the tamest way imaginable. At no period of my life have I had more for which
to be thankful in reviewing the year which has passed, —
that we should have travelled so far without the slightest
accident, leaving our dearest interests so well provided for,
finding so much kindness wherever we have been, and so
many facilities for our enjoyment ; and above all, that my
husband, though not much better, should not have been
made much worse by all the disadvantages under which he
has labored of climate and weather. If I were at your
elbow, how I should love to give you a detail of some of
our experiences during the year. You know enough of the
outlines to guess at the minutiæ in many instances, and
enough of us both to imagine the internal effects produced
by them.

" *Rome, March 2d.* Back in Rome again, after a five

---

* " A little village, or rather almost solitary inn, between Rome and
Naples."

weeks' sojourn in Naples, from which place 1 should have despatched this, but that I did not think it quite worth while to send such a piece of egotism so far by mail. We had almost incessant rain while at Naples, which prevented our doing and seeing as much as we wished; but the few fine days we had, we enjoyed and employed to the utmost. Although in January, they were like our June days. A shawl was too warm a garment to be borne in the sun, and upon our out-of-town expeditions we took our lunch in the open air. These were rare days, to be sure, but they gave us some idea of what the climate would have been had the season been a common one, for so much rain at that time, they told us, was almost unprecedented. We went of course to Pompeii, where I had many and pleasant recollections of your husband, tell him; for the explanations which he gave me, when we saw the panorama of that place together in London, had made it all so familiar to my mind that I could not easily overcome the impression that I had been there before. Vesuvius we were content to admire at a distance, fearing the ascent would be injurious to my husband. But the classical regions of Avernus and the Elysian fields, the abode of the Cumæan Sibyl, and the beautiful temples of Baiæ, we explored at our leisure.

"I can scarcely fancy any locality more beautiful for a city than that of Naples, and, viewed at a distance, it has a very imposing appearance; but in itself it is noisy, dirty, and disagreeable, with the exception of the modern part of the street which borders upon the bay. We had rooms in that street, within forty feet of the water, and in rain or sunshine enjoyed the beauty of the bay with equal delight. We returned hither in company with Mr. and Mrs. Grinnell, and Mr. and Mrs. Rollins, with whom we have been the greater part of the time since we arrived in Florence in November. We are at lodgings with them here, and, as you may suppose, very much enjoy our quiet family party. We have also Dr. and Mrs. Kirkland, and Mr. and Mrs. Gould, from our part of the country, and many from New York.

" There is so much to be done here, and my husband is obliged to do things so leisurely, that I know not that we shall ever see half that is to be seen. There is a great difference between travelling for health and mere pleasure. Almost all our friends will be on the wing before us, but I trust we shall find our way home in good time, and be the better for having come. Mr. Ware's is just such an uncertain case, that it is impossible to have any very decided opinion about it, — he sometimes seeming almost as well as ever, then again prostrated by some very trifle. On the whole, there is still much to hope from time and care, but nothing to flatter one into the hope of speedy restoration. May we have patience to wait with cheerfulness the full development of the designs of Heaven with regard to us, hoping for good, and willing to submit to trial !

" This is the season of Lent, which makes no apparent change in the state of things, and before we leave Rome we shall have the famous solemnities of Holy Week, when, if the Pope does not die (which it is reported he is about doing), I hope to witness the illumination of St. Peter's, and to listen to the *Miserere*. So far, I have not heard any music in Italy which satisfied me, except once the vespers of the nuns in one of the churches here ; it is all too loud, rapid, and theatrical. But it is time to despatch my letter, so good by.

" Yours, most affectionately,

" M. L. WARE."

The last date of the above letter is the 2d of March ; and before the close of that month Mrs.

Ware's second child was born, — a daughter, who still lives. Mr. Ware's letter, announcing the event to his brother in Boston, expresses his gratitude for the many mercies that surrounded them, among excellent friends, making " as pretty a little, quiet domestic circle as ever Rome has seen since the days of the twin founders." At the same time, he confesses his entire discouragement in regard to his own health, and their great embarrassment at what course to pursue. "I am weary of this miserably idle life, and yet I am fit for no other. I am afraid to go home, because I know I shall only be able to do half the requisite work, and to do that not more than half; yet to stay away is altogether out of the question." As usual, Mary was ready to do any thing that seemed best, even to go home alone with her new charge, if her husband would be benefited by remaining longer and acting freely. Some prompt and decided course she advised, at whatever sacrifice. " We have talked over this matter together, and the only relief which Mary is able to suggest is, that I should state my case exactly, resign the professorship, so as not to be a burden or hindrance to those for whom I care more than for myself, send her home from Havre, and spend a year in travelling Europe on foot and on horseback. This might be done at a very small expense, an expense which we could meet without taxing College or friends."

We can easily conceive of the anxiety of a high-minded woman, a devoted wife and mother, at such a crisis. We have said that Mrs. Ware has been known to refer to this experience as the great trial of her life, and we suppose the period of which we are speaking was the most trying of all; especially if we comprise in it the few months that preceded the birth of her child, — a season of which she has written more freely than of any other of her trials. Nor can we show the full power of her endurance at that time, and her wonderful energy, — such as is common only to woman, — unless by giving part of a letter written to her physician, describing this experience.

" Not for a single day free from positive pain, I felt determined to keep out of sight all physical as well as mental distress. In this I believe I succeeded, excepting when occasionally nature was overpowered, and I lost for a time my consciousness. But the effort to keep a cheerful outside, when the body was undergoing so great suffering, and the mind fully awake to all the uncertainties and possibilities which lay before us, can only be appreciated or known by one similarly situated. My faith never failed me, nor my confidence that the course I had adopted was the right one. But the degree of tension to which every faculty was stretched, all the time, was just as much as my reason could bear unshaken; and more than it could have borne, I believe, had not my nerves found relief in hours of tearful prostration, when Henry was asleep, or so far out of the way as not to detect it."

We have no further particulars to give of the sojourn in Rome. The travellers gladly turned their faces toward home the moment the season and their strength would permit. Early in May we hear of them in Geneva, and at the end of that month in

Paris. From both those places Mr. Ware writes home, in a disheartened, yet decided tone, as to his return, showing what a burden of anxiety they were still bearing. " I have only spoken out more plainly what has for some time been my conviction, that I am gaining nothing; and I simply wish to have you prepared for a proper reception of my *miserability* when I shall return." " I am sure I need not stay away; I am sure I am not fit to do any hard work; I do not think I could edit the Examiner. But I will come home by the packet of July 20th, and you shall judge. It will be the hardest of all I have yet done, to abstain from Cambridge, especially as Mr. Norton vacates his place, and there is the more need of other laborers."

In June, Mr. and Mrs. Ware were separated for a time, she taking lodgings with her infant at Waltham Abbey, and he making an excursion alone for his health. Soon after he left her, Mary wrote to him thus: — " I am quite sure it was best for you to go, though there was some risk in it. If you only keep a sharp watch upon your ' excitables,' not mistaking the effect of them for strength, and so do not overdo, you will, I doubt not, be better for the jaunt; you will be gaining much mental satisfaction, and I am sure that will help the body...... Yours to ' Miss Pickard ' is just received. The dear little Miss is as good as possible; she knows how much I wish I were with you, and coos and smiles all the time to make me contented. I am thankful you are so well, and though I should have richly enjoyed being with you, I am sure it is better for you to be alone. I want to go to Chatham next week, if I feel better, but it is such a luxury to be at rest! O, dearest, how we shall enjoy it! I have had time to think a little, and collect my scattered wits, and I could pour out volumes of the result of my cogitations — but *voila!* the end of my paper! Do all you can, see all you can without injury, gain all that is possible to gain, and above all, *feel* that you have time enough; that is, don't feel ' hurried'; it is destructive to comfort and profit."

In this letter we find also a hint, which tells something of Mary's continued thoughtfulness and generous provision for that poor old aunt whom she left at Osmotherly five years before. On first arriving in England, she had again visited, with her husband, that scene of singular interest and mingled recollections. And now that Mr. Ware is journeying alone in that direction, she writes to him: " Should you go to Osmotherly (which is not quite worth while, as it would take you two days), give Aunty her yearly allowance, if you can, — ten pounds. But no, I remember you did not take enough with you. Write her a word, — it will please her; and pay the postage." This was said at the very time that Mrs. Ware had denied herself the pleasure of going with her husband, on account of the added expense of travelling with an infant. She continued that annuity to her aunt as long as she lived, and a friend thinks it was doubled part of the time. We bring the fact to notice, because, from a delicacy which ought not, perhaps, to sup-

press facts so illustrative of character, we have forborne to give half the proof we found, in letters and
in conversation with friends, of her noble generosity
in connection with the strictest domestic economy,
and withal a personal self-denial and simplicity that
caused remark, if not censure. Could all the facts
be given of her early surrender of property to a
considerable amount, when she might have held it,
and the rigid restriction of her personal expenditure,
through life, within the limits of bare comfort and
respectability, while there were times when she could
have done much more for herself, and no time when
her hospitalities were not without stint, — were it
right, or were it desirable, to refer to facts and instances confirming this general statement, — we are
sure it would be seen to be at the least worthy of
honor and imitation. But the very thought of her
disinterestedness, and *secret* charities, checks and re-
bukes us.

Before leaving England, she wrote the following
letter to the two children in America.

Waltham Abbey, June 19, 1830.

"MY DEAR CHILDREN : —

"It is a long time since I wrote to either of you, for I
was ill for some weeks, and since I got well, I have been
travelling almost every day, and have not had time to sit
down quietly. But all this while I have thought much of
you, particularly when I was lying on the bed sick. When
I remembered how great was the distance which separated
us from you, and how uncertain it was if we ever saw you
again, I wished that I could be sure that you would always
be good, doing that which would please God, that I might

hope to be united to you again in heaven. You do not know how often your father and I have talked about you since we left you, or how anxious we have felt that you should improve; we hope to find that you have made a good use of the time of our absence, if we are ever permitted to see our home again; and how happy we shall be to have you with us, not to be separated again, I trust, for a long time!

"You will be glad to know that your dear father is better than when he left home. He has gone now to Manchester for a few days, and I have come with little Baby from London to stay with a cousin while he is absent. Baby will have been a great traveller by the time she gets home, but she will not be any the wiser for it; when she knows how many wonderful things she has passed by, she will wish she had been old enough to observe them. I have seen a great many grown-up people in our travels, who, I think, will not know much more than she does of what they have passed by, because they have not the habit of observing and thinking about what they see; they remind me of the story in ' Evenings at Home,' entitled ' Eyes and no Eyes.' I dare say you recollect it. Others are not wiser for their travels, because they have not prepared themselves to understand what they see, by reading; they care nothing about the antiquities of a country, because they know nothing about its history; or the works of art which they meet with, because they do not know how they are made, or their uses. You will be surprised to find, as you grow older and know more, how much every thing which you have learned will add to your pleasure. I dare say you have many lessons given you, of which you do not see the use at present, but you will by and by, and if you fix them well in your memory you will be very glad then.

"It is now the 26th of June, and we have just heard that
20*

the king of England died this morning, and his brother, the
Duke of Clarence, was proclaimed king, at twelve o'clock,
at Westminster. On Monday he will be proclaimed at
three places in London, by heralds dressed in very gay cos-
tume, such as has always been worn on like occasions for
many centuries, of course very different from modern
dresses. They will use trumpets in order to be heard by
as many people as possible, who will no doubt collect in
great crowds to hear them. The new king is called William
the Fourth. There will be a great parade at the king's
funeral, and the new king's coronation, but we shall not
see either. I hope we shall be on the water before they
take place, for the preparations are to be so great, that it
is said three weeks at least will be necessary for the funeral, and perhaps months for the coronation. The next
heir to the crown is a little girl, only a year older than you,
Elizabeth.

" Good by, my dear children.

" Your loving Mother."

On the passage home, in August, Mrs. Ware had
another severe trial of her physical and mental energies, — a trial that is supposed to have essentially
impaired the vigor of a remarkably strong and enduring frame. Mr. Ware, who had gained little if
any strength during their whole absence, became
severely ill from a painful and alarming attack of
acute disease. His wife was his only nurse, and, if
we recollect right, the only physician. And there,
amid all the deprivations and discomforts of the *sea*,
confined to the narrow range of a small state-room,
carrying in her arms a restless infant, of which those
most willing could but seldom relieve her, and with

the whole weight of the responsibility upon her saddened heart, that wife and mother performed offices
and made exertions, which, by some acquainted
with all the circumstances, have been called "almost
superhuman." One fearful night especially, the night
which was to determine the result, she watched
over the flickering and apparently expiring light
of the life most dear to her, in anxious and most
arduous services, until the crisis had passed. Her
husband recovered from this attack almost entirely,
before the end of the voyage; but the effect upon
herself, of all she had done and endured in the last
seventeen months, was a prostrating and protracted
sickness soon after her return. Up to this time, we
suppose Mrs. Ware to have possessed a power of
action and endurance seldom equalled in her own
sex or in the same walk of life. Yet she used to
say that her natural temperament was sluggish
rather than active, and that her activity was an exertion. Recurring, some years later, to this same
season, she writes: " You do not know me as well
as you might, or you would not talk of my *activity*.
Naturally I am essentially indolent; and to this
day no one knows the effort it often costs me to
rouse myself from my lethargy. Still I have had a
pride in my physical ability, which has sometimes
impelled me when better motives ought to have op-
erated. But that pride had a fall, when I went to
Europe with Mr. Ware, from which, it seems to me,
it can never rise again. Yet it may influence me
when I do not suspect it, and I shall look out sharp
for it."

It was in this connection also that Mrs. Ware
repelled the idea of "sacrifice" in such relations.
"The phrase 'sacrifice for those we love,' I do not
quite understand. I should think the thing intended
was more nearly allied to the germ of selfish gratification, and therefore as little entitled to the appel-
lation of a virtue as any other selfish propensity."
Just before leaving America for this European tour,
when not strong herself, she had written to her husband, "I am very much afraid of becoming too
thoughtful of this poor body of mine." And now,
on her return, she was compelled to think of it more
than ever before.

X.

LIFE IN CAMBRIDGE.

Mr. Ware's connection with his parish in Boston had been continued, at the earnest request of the people, in the hope, that, if he removed to Cambridge, he might still retain the pastoral office, and perform such of the duties as should be perfectly easy. A connection which had existed thirteen years, in perfect harmony and mutual attachment, could not be sundered without mutual pain. To no man living did permanence in the pastoral office seem more desirable or more important than to Henry Ware; and the time had not then quite come when pastor and people could separate in a day, with or without cause. Nor could Mrs. Ware be indifferent to such a change. It was the extinguishment of many hopes which she had fondly cherished, in becoming the wife of one whose earliest choice and highest ambition had been for the ministry and a parish life, — a life which had attractions hardly less strong for herself. But now they had no choice. Whatever the sacrifice required, neither of them was willing to remain in an office, whose duties they could not perform with vigor and entire devotion. A dissolution of the connection was therefore asked, immediately after their return from Europe. And the society, in yielding to the obvious duty of granting the request, expressed earnestly their sense of obligation and gratitude, not only to their pastor, but also to her who had been his co-laborer in their service. In their final letter, they say: "We should do injustice to our feelings if we failed, on this occasion, to make mention of her also, who has laid us under such obligations by her devotedness to you when we looked upon you as belonging to ourselves, and who, though not long with us, had already taught us how highly to value and how deeply to regret her."

In October, 1830, Mr. and Mrs. Ware took up their abode in Cambridge; where he entered at once, in improved, but still feeble health, upon the duties of the new Professorship of " Pulpit Eloquence and Pastoral Care." And except the place which they had been compelled to resign, for which they both retained, we think, as long as they lived, a strong preference and lingering desire, no situation could have been found more acceptable than this at Cambridge. A post of great responsibility, calling for all the strength and labor that any could bestow, it was yet a position of peculiar privilege and opportunity, in the midst of family connections, near to all their friends, and having close relations to the ministry which they so loved. In many ways, too, would these relations afford to Mrs. Ware herself facilities for action, and the exercise of her peculiar powers and affections.

Yet there were two great anxieties which Mrs. Ware brought to this new situation; one, relating to the health of her husband; the other, to their straitened pecuniary means. The first of these was known, and could be understood by all. The last will never be understood, except by those similarly situated, and as high-minded, generous, and desirous of usefulness. We speak of this as a general truth. There is more mental suffering, more physical feebleness, and greater loss to the community in regard to the energy and activity of those who would serve it, resulting from this one cause, than perhaps from any other. We say it in no temper of complaint, much less of censure; for we know not where the fault lies, if there be any. But we do know the fact, and there can be few who have not seen it in some of every calling, — that the necessity of incessant thoughtfulness and extreme carefulness for the things of this world, with the dread of debt or dependence of any kind, in the midst, too, of sickness and the utmost uncertainty, is a weight upon the heart, and an obstacle to the energies, such as no faith, or fortitude, or philosophy can wholly overcome; no, nor even the experience, as in this instance, of ceaseless kindness, and a liberality ready to do all that delicacy would permit. The fact remains, — better known than explained, and inseparable, it may be, from the constitution of society, possibly from the nature of man, — aggravated, as the trial often is, by the infirmity and helplessness which God himself appoints.

The beginning of their life in Cambridge was made memorable by one of the longest and most serious sicknesses that Mrs. Ware had ever known. We have already referred to it, as probably caused by the

uncommon demands of their journey abroad and the
voyage home. We did not refer, in its place, to a
severe illness which she had in Geneva, of which she
gives an account in a note some years later, and
speaks of it as very serious. Many causes thus
conspired to predispose her to this attack, which, for
the first time in her life, so far as we know, was of a
pulmonary character, and shut her up for the whole
winter, — a severe trial, where so much was waiting
to be done, and after so long a period of absence
from home and active duty. There was greater prostration, and more imminent peril, than all were aware
of, and more, we suppose, than ever before. Her
sickness must have begun almost immediately after
they went to Cambridge; for in the same month
Mr. Ware writes to Rev. Mr. Allen of Northborough,
as if he had for some time been very anxious, and was
then only beginning to hope. " I am happy to be
able to say, that Mary does seem to be doing better,
— the first day that I have thought so. Her disor
der has had transient intermissions, but never before seemed to yield. I think now she has fairly
begun to mend. But she is wretchedly weak, and a
little talking makes her hoarse. We have kept her
as quiet as possible, and forbidden all visitors; yet
she has not been as quiet as most persons, because
she does not know how to take thought for herself,
and continues her interest for all about her. She
has suffered a great deal of severe pain, and her
cough has been kept from distressing her only by
opiates. You rightly guess how great a disappointment of our hopes this has been. I have not been

without very serious apprehensions as to the result, and you may judge what must be felt, when we are apprehensive for one so perfectly invaluable as she. You know her in part, but one must know her intimately as I do, to understand half her worth." And, again, as late as November, Mr. Ware writes to Miss Forbes that Mary is not yet able to bear any visitor, not even one as intimate as she, whose society and sympathy they so much desired. And he adds, in concluding his letter to that excellent friend, " Emma," whom they had not seen since their return from Europe: " Since we met, we have all seen changes and trials, and are at least more experienced in the discipline of Providence. I esteem myself quite well; and if my cup were not dashed with the bitterness of Mary's ill health, I should have more sources of happiness than I could perhaps bear rightly."

In a few weeks, Miss F—— went to Mrs. Ware, and devoted herself entirely to the care of her for two months or more. The communion of these congenial minds was very beautiful, and will help at various points to illustrate the character of Mary. Their intimacy began early, and was never interrupted. How true they were to each other, how socially and spiritually confiding, how much they mutually imparted and received, through life and in death, can be known only to those who know all; for both their natures, even in their present exaltation, might shrink from the disclosure of some of the evidences of their tender and generous love. Their intercourse at this time, softened by the sickness from which Mary was very slowly rising, and which, we have seen, awakened many apprehensions, must have been peculiarly grateful. It was a season of precious experience to Mrs. Ware, as will be seen in the first letter she wrote, — her faithful annual to the friend in Worcester.

"*Cambridge, December* 31, 1830.

"Another year has passed away, dearest Nancy, since I last spread before me a fair white page, on which to tell you that I was still in existence; and instead of 'St. Agatha' and the disagreeables belonging to it, behold me in my own blessed home, scribbling at the same old desk. A change, indeed, and what a change, for one short year! You know it all, and I need not, if I could, recount the various causes for deep, fervent gratitude which rise to my memory in the retrospect. You can understand, without explanation, why it is that the thought of them so entirely overwhelms me that I cannot touch upon them with sufficient calmness even to write about them. I shall be less tired to-morrow morning, and will resume; but I could not let this eve, so long sacred to *you*, pass without marking it. Farewell, then, for this time.

"*January* 16. I have suffered a longer period to pass away without continuing this than I intended. I know not how it is, but I find that year after year passes off, and still the same errors are to be mourned over; and for one I begin to fear that the habit of procrastination will adhere to me through life. I was weak, and my nerves so excitable, when I began this, that I could not even recur in thought to the events of the past year, and retain decent composure. But the impression of their review has not passed away, and I trust never will; and I feel that it would do my heart good to go over the ground with you (were you only by my side), not of their external character, that you know already, but of the effect of such discipline upon the mind. Constant exposure to the weather hardens the skin, and the habit of living under circumstances of trial deadens one's sensibilities; and I could not now, if I would, be as strongly affected by them as I used to be during my novitiate. Still, I have not quite ceased to feel, and consequently to suffer and to enjoy; and I trust that the joys and sorrows of the past year have not been experienced without some beneficial result.

" I have long thought one of the greatest blessings of my life to be that singular preparation which each event has given me for that which was to succeed it; and I never realized this so fully as during my late wanderings. Habit had given me the power of sustaining easily and cheerfully circumstances which, to one less experienced, would have brought labor and sorrow; thus enabling me to pursue the one great object for which we were striving, unclogged (if I may so say) by any considerations for self, and thus lessening my trials, not only to myself, but to those around me. Now that all is over, I am conscious that the mental as well as the physical effort has been great; and I consider this ' lying by ' as advantageous to my mind as to my body. I was beginning wrong, had for some time felt that trifles were a burden to me; and although by the application of strong stimulants, such as the joy of getting home, I could keep alive my courage to act, I am persuaded that it was something of the excitement which frequently precedes entire failure, rather than any substantial good. In the delightful quiet of my own snug chamber, I have had time to look a little more into myself than I have been able to do for a long, long time. The outward exigencies of the moment had so long occupied every faculty, that it was not singular that I had become almost a stranger to that void within, which is to be known only in the 'secret silence' of tranquil thought. I have felt grateful for this repose ; and, so far from pitying me for having been arrested in the pursuit of my domestic duties, just as I was so happily re-stored to them, my friends would rejoice for me, if they knew how much I needed, and how much I have enjoyed, this rest. Don't think me quite insensible to the trouble it has caused my friends, or the loss it has been to my husband's comfort. I am not ; but neither am I sure that in the end both will not be gainers by it. I have not been *very* sick, — not so sick as to require a suspension of any of the daily operations of the household in my behalf. I could always have my children about me, and except now and then could do very well without any aid out of my family. I needed rest and quiet more than any thing ; and that did not interfere with others' pursuits. Emma has been with me six weeks ; and enacted Mrs. Gerry, Queen's jester, Cerberus, and a ' thorn in the flesh,' as she styles herself, with the perfection that belongs to such an actress. She has been a real comfort and delight to us both ; for she has the faculty of *filling in* so exactly to the circumstances of the case, that she does more good than she intends to do, good as her intentions are.

But Emma says, ' Hold ! enough ! ' I forget which of her characters she appears under now ; but I 'll punish her by making her fill this page with the bulletin of health of every man, woman, and child belonging to the establish-ment, which I was just going to give you myself.

                                        " MARY."

In February, we find Mrs. Ware still a prisoner in that chamber of sickness ; though not exactly a prisoner, for we have heard her speak of the reluc-

tance with which she left that long confinement, to
return to the glare and tumult of the world. And
from the manner in which she wrote to Emma, soon
after she had left her, it would seem that she had not
expected to return at all. Indeed, some of her language indicates a serious apprehension on her part,
of which few were aware. In refusing to let Emma
come again merely to read to her, as she had proposed, Mary says: " I allow that it would be an
especial comfort to be read to sleep sometimes,
when my opium-fed imagination is conjuring up
fancies that mar my rest for that night; and it
would be a great pleasure to have my thoughts a
little more diverted from self than I can divert them
unaided. If my disease were rapidly gaining ground,
the case would be altered. I know too well the luxury of having done ' the last' for a friend, to debar
any one from it. But although I am aware that
there are many *probabilities* in favor of the idea that
the disease never will be overcome, I see no reason
to nourish the feeling which a state of uncertainty
cannot but create. It may be that my days are to
be few. And if the ' wearin' awa of snow-wreaths
in the thaw' is to be the signal of like decay in myself, I shall surely need you more than now. At all
events, the spring must be a season of lassitude and
bodily trial to me; and if you will give me the
promised visit then, you will have no reason to be
dissatisfied with the degree of good you will do me."
Two months later than this, Mrs. Ware wrote to the
same friend, more at length.

21 *

" DEAR EMMA : —

" I have watched you from my working-chair ' out of sight,' as some of my Dublin friends would say ; and now I have taken my desk into my lap for sundry purposes, but the first that suggests itself is, to commence an *omnium gatherum* for you. I shall want to say five hundred things at least every day for a month to come ; and I don't know why I should not indulge you with one of the five hundred daily. What time so good to commence, as that in which my heart is full of twice that number of feelings of grati- tude and love towards you ? But no, this is not a good time either, for they come rushing forward with such a spirit of rivalry, each wishing to be represented first, that they blind my eyes and make my pen tremble ; so I will teach them what a good disciplinarian I am, and make them all keep silence until they have learned better man- ners.

" To-day I am as weak as possible, but free from pain. The truth is, that I am feeling, just as I told you I should, the trial of weakness much more, now that I can move about, than when I was shut up. When I knew it was my part to give up trying to do any thing, and turn my mind to the improvement which belonged to such a state of things, I had not a wish to step over my threshold, or an anxious thought about any thing beyond it. It would be time enough when I could go among people and things, I thought, and I would enjoy the luxury of idleness to the full. I did ; but now the case is changing. I am able to use my bodily powers, and feel that I ought to exert my mental energies also ; but my strength fails me, mental and bodily, and this brings to me a feeling of discourage- ment and dissatisfaction with myself, that I find it hard to struggle against as I ought. In fact, it carries me back to old Mary Pickard's spring feelings of nothingness, which I fight with in vain. I fear that I have been so long indulged in idleness, that I have lost my energy of mind, or become selfish, and a thousand other wrong things which do sometimes creep upon one without leave. You will tell me this is merely the effect, the inevitable effect, of weakness, as my husband does. I hope it is, and that I shall rise in time to my wished-for energy.

"I was glad to find you had made so good a beginning of your summer life. It is delightful to me to be able to think of you enjoying so much, and doing so much, as I am sure you will. I think it was very well to strike into the plan at once. May I ask you, too, to take one half-hour daily, with your door locked, for some little sentence and the thoughts which will grow out of it, for the cultivation of that internal treasure which you value so much, and in which you wish to feel more vital, exciting interest? I know by my own experience that we lose much of what we long to keep, by an unacknowledged but constantly operating contempt for small means, hourly attentions to the details of spiritual discipline. Having calmly, thoroughly, may I add, prayerfully, viewed one Christian virtue in the day, are we not almost secure of acting in conformity to that one, for at least twenty-four hours? And if every day we thus gain one victory, shall we not have reason to hope we may in time be wholly conquerors? But more of this in *our* pretty book, which will contain preaching enough for my share of your ear upon such matters.

"All send love, with that of your

"M. L. WARE."

In the spring, Mrs. Ware recovered, as to all apparent disease; but she continued feeble through the summer, and suffered much from her sense of inefficiency, in body and mind, — "literally unable," as she says, "to write a letter." Nor do we find any letters before October, when she wrote in full her own impressions of this important portion of her experience, with an account of its termination in the alarming illness of her husband, to whom she was summoned at a distance. His health had been constantly improving through the winter, and he had performed all the duties of his office, except preaching, which he had ventured upon but once for nearly three years, and then only on account of the death of Mrs. Emerson, the wife of his colleague and successor in Boston. In the summer vacation of the present year, 1831, Mr. Ware made a pedestrian tour, with a friend, to the White Hills; and, feeling strong enough, engaged to preach on his return at Concord, N. H. But before he could reach that place, he was prostrated with fever, and became severely, and he himself believed fatally ill. Under this full conviction, he made a great effort to write a few last words to his wife; and did write a note, which we wish we were at liberty to use, so moving as it is in itself and its circumstances, so characteristic of him who wrote it, and so touching and beautiful a tribute to her whom he loved, and whom he thought to see no more on earth.

It need not be told that Mrs. Ware went to her husband as soon as she knew of his sickness, though she had not entirely regained her own strength. He had been removed to Concord, where she joined him, and stayed till they could come home together. She seems not to have been surprised by this summons;

it being one of her principles, and a fixed habit, to anticipate all probable, even possible events, as far as she could, and make them familiar to her thoughts; not to sadden or weaken, but to strengthen and prepare her mind for the duties and emergencies to which she might be called. If the events did not occur, nothing was lost. If they came, the shock was less, and there was greater preparation and fortitude to encounter it. This is not the common course, and will not commend itself to all. Not all would be capable of it; and it may not be necessary or desirable for all. The common habit is the very opposite, and the counsel usually given, from the pulpit and in private, is to anticipate nothing, — least of all, to anticipate evil; or, as the phrase is, never to " borrow trouble." This is not the place to discuss the subject. We wish only to record our vivid impression of the delight and instruction with which we have listened to that unpretending woman, as she argued the matter with those who differed with her; not asking them to do as she did, or assuming the smallest merit for the habit, but only showing them how completely the uniform experience of a life of trial had satisfied her that this course was best for *her*. And all who have seen her in trial and sickness will testify to the reality and power of this persuasion.

The account, to which we have already adverted of their experiences during this first year at Cambridge, through her own illness and that of her husband, is contained in a letter written on the evening of the first Sabbath that Mr. Ware was able to preach in the College Chapel, when she also was able to hear him.

" MY DEAR NANCY : —

" Were you ever so weak as to omit doing a thing which you strongly desired to do, entirely because you know you could not do it thoroughly to your own satisfaction ? If you have been, you can better understand than I can describe the many foolish feelings which have, from time to time, and a hundred times, made me throw down my pen and say to myself, ' I cannot write to her now ; I have not time to say half I wish to say, or she to hear.' It is just so now ; I knew all the time it was wrong to do so, and now I am determined to turn over a new leaf with myself, at the commencement of this new year of my life ; and as your spirit has haunted my conscience more than any other, I begin by laying it with the spell of my fairy pen. But where shall I begin ? I cannot remember where I left off, or rather do not know what you have heard from others since I left you a year ago.

" Of my winter's sickness I cannot write ; it contained a long life of enjoyment, and what I hoped would prove profitable thought and reflection. I came out of my nest almost reluctantly, for I had a dread of the absorbing power of worldly cares and interests ; and for a long time my head remained so weak that I suffered from the necessity of giving my whole mind to the trifling occupations of daily life in order to perform them with tolerable decency. This has been a bane to my comfort throughout the summer ; and although I have had Harriet Hall and Mary Ware, and many of those I rejoiced to see, again around me, I have not profited much by the privilege, my mind having all its capacity more than employed by the care of our bodies. This was very humiliating for one to whom all the outward cares of life have been mere play-work; but I could contrive to keep externally quiet, and not appear fidgety; so I try to think this was conquest enough for me in my then state of weakness. The heat prostrated me very much. I began to fear I should never be able to do any two things at once again. But since my family has returned to its usual size, and the cool days of autumn have sent their invigorating influences to my bodily powers, my mind improves 'a little, not much' (as my Rob says fifty times a day). Literally, I could not write a letter through the whole summer; and now the task is so novel a one, that I cannot expect to be coherent, this being my first.

"In this state of things, my husband left me for a walk to the White Hills. I felt sure that, if pursued with due discretion, it would do him good. He was pretty well, but wanted something to give him a spring before beginning to preach. I had not the least objection to his going, but having watched him so long, so incessantly, I felt very much as a mother does the first night she weans her infant from her. In pursuance of my long-established habit, I set myself the task of preparing for any accident which might befall him, and I believe looked at all the possibilities of the case; so that when the summons actually came for me to attend him at Concord, where he was ill of a fever, it did not take me by surprise. I was, as it were, prepared for it, and could receive it calmly and act coolly. In two hours I was on my way to him, confident in my own strength, for no care of him present could be the weight on my mind which the thought of him absent had been; and the bodily exertion was not as great as I had been for some time making, having been nearly all summer without my *quantum* of help. I found him very sick, but surrounded by kindness. He soon began to mend, and we jogged homewards. Harriet had been with me, so that I could leave

my children without any anxiety; and the journey, and the
happiness which accompanied it, did me good. I have
been gaining ever since, and Mr. Ware too. I am now so
well, that I can walk an hour before breakfast, and into
Boston with ease; and to-day I have had the unspeakable
joy of hearing my husband perform all the services of the
pulpit. This is a point that I have so often thought of as
the one blessing which I dared not hope for, and have believed that, if it could be granted, I should have nothing
more to ask for, that I hardly know how I feel, now that it
is actually granted. One thing more, however, I must ask,
– that I may be truly grateful for it.

" Yours as ever.

" M. L. W."

Happy was it for Mrs. Ware if she *could* be always prepared for change and trial. For while her
life was a favored one, and so regarded by her, few
enjoying more in any condition, she was equally
alive to all suffering, and seldom knew a long exemption. So far, however, she had been spared all
trial in regard to her children. Not that they had
been free from sickness, or had caused no solicitude,
for there had been much of both; but their lives had
been continued, and at this time she was rejoicing in
their health. Three of them she had just taken to
Milton, to enjoy a week with them at Brush Hill,
where she had spent so much of her early life, but
where she had not been at all since her children were
born. Pleasantly does she contrast her present with
her former enjoyment there. Writing to her husband from this place, she says: — " I am enjoying
myself much, but find I was quite mistaken in

thinking I could turn into Mary Pickard again by the power of association. I do very well under that character through the day, but with nightfall the remembrance of *home* comes over me; the idea of the husband and child I have left there, and the three chickens who are asleep up stairs, rises before my mind's eye, as so many more blessings than poor Polly could boast, that I resign my pretensions with a very grateful heart. I am sorry, dear Henry, that you could not be a little longer with me here, (among other very disinterested reasons,) that I might read you sundry chapters in the life of that interesting personage just named, — chapters which are written about upon these trees and stone walls, and which no other place could recall. It is very delightful for me to live over those days again, and I am sure my mind will be refreshed by this visit, if my body is not. As to this latter concern, it does as well as I could expect."

This visit was made just before her summons to Mr. Ware's bedside at Concord. After their return to Cambridge, they took possession of a new house just built for them; and one of the first events that occurred in that house was the *death* of Mrs. Ware's first-born, Robert, then three and a half years of age. It was a sore trial, and well do we remember the spirit in which it was met; for it was our privilege to be staying with them at the time, and to be present at the parting. The little sufferer had endeared himself to us all by his patience and sweetness of disposition. Separated from his parents in early infancy, and remaining apart until he was two years old, they had taken him back, when they returned, as a fresh gift from God; and though another had been granted them, there was a peculiar feeling connected with *him,* which every parent will understand. Movingly now does the scene return to us, of the mother sitting silently and reverently at the side of her expiring boy; and when the gentle breathing wholly ceased, asking — still silently — the husband and father, who knelt by her, to *pray.* Faintly, tremulously, more and more distinctly, and then most fervently, did that voice of submission and supplication fall upon our ears, and fill our eyes, and lift the heart into a region which death never enters! As the voice ceased, the mother fainted; but soon she rose, stronger rather than weaker, and ready for every duty. In referring to this bereavement afterward, she says, in the thought of her husband's constant danger: "Having had so long the greatest possible trial hanging over my head, every thing else seems comparatively easy to bear; and I sometimes doubt, whether any thing but that *one* will ever wean me from the world, as I think a Christian should be." How much she felt, and how much she trusted, may be seen in her first letter after this trial.

" *Cambridge, December* 31, 1831.

"MY DEAR FRIEND: —

"Again does this anniversary find us inhabitants of this world, and again, as usual, does it present in my lot something of solemn and interesting import, upon which we may dwell with profit for a time. It is a privileged hour, and I shall use it as I have been wont to do, in the full indulgence of selfish egotism, trusting that some good may result to us both from it. What does the retrospect of the year present to me? My husband and myself have been again raised from the bed of sickness and threatened death, and I have been called upon to restore to Him who gave one of the dearest treasures which His providence had bestowed upon me. These are great events for one short year, designed to produce great effects, involving great responsibility, bestowing great privileges. My own sickness brought with it many pleasures, many pure and elevating views and feelings; and although it did not bring me to that cheerful willingness to resign my life after which I strove and hoped to attain, it thereby threw light upon the weakness of my religious character, calculated to subdue presumptuous self-dependence, and teach a lesson of humility which may perhaps be of more importance and advantage to my growth in holiness. My husband's danger renewed the so oft repeated testimony that strength is ever at hand for those who need it, gave me another exercise of trust in that mighty arm which can save to the uttermost, and in its result is a new cause for gratitude to Him who has so abundantly blessed me all the days of my life.

" And now has come this new trial of my faith, this new test of its reality, that there may be no hiding-place left for me, no light wanting by which to search into the hidden recesses of the spirit to ' see if there be any wicked way in it.' And whatever may be the result of this strict scrutiny, am I not to be thankful for it? Am I not to feel that it is indeed the kindest love that subjects me to it? We feel it a privilege that a child should have earthly parents to guide, counsel, and correct it; and shall we not be grateful to that Heavenly Parent who does the same in a far better manner? I would thank God that he has by his past dispensations taught me the duty and happiness of submission so that I can bow to the rod, and desire only to see how its chastisement is to be used and improved. I have always looked upon the death of children rather as a subject for joy than sorrow, and have been perplexed at seeing so many, who would bear what seemed to me much harder trials with firmness, so completely overwhelmed by this, as is frequently the case. But I know that upon any point in which we have had no personal experience we cannot form a correct judgment, and therefore I have never had any definite anticipations of its effect upon myself. I am thankful to find that the general views upon which my former opinions have been founded are not obscured by the flood of new emotions which actual experience brings. I can resign my child into the hands of its Maker, with as strong a belief as I ever had, that it is a blessing to itself to be removed, ' untasked, untried,' from a world in which the result of labor and trial is so doubtful. It is a blessing to be taken from the care of ignorant, powerless human teachers, to the guidance of higher and holier and perfect instructors; so that its pure spirit will not now be sullied by the pollutions of this degraded world, but go on from glory to glory until it has attained the full measure of the stature of a child of God.

" You know too well what are the hopes and enjoyments belonging to the relation of parent and child, to require to be told how hard it is to lay them all aside ; and there was something in the peculiar circumstances of the birth and life of this child, which could not but give a peculiar character to our connection with him. And so he has passed from us ; but what a comfort to know that we have not lost him ! We had a visit from Dr. Channing yesterday, in which he spoke so gloriously of the honor of having given a child to heaven, as to elevate me far above common considerations. But enough ; think of us still as happy.

" M. L. WARE "

One of the traits of Mrs. Ware's character — not named for its singularity or distinction, but simply as a fact, noticed by all who knew her — was the amount of time and strength which she devoted to her children. With all the sicknesses, which from this period came almost constantly either to her or her husband, and which are apt to make such sad inroads upon our quiet and faithful intercourse with our children, — amid all her domestic cares, of which she took as large a share, in every department, as perhaps any woman ever did in a similar position, feeling and seeing, all the time, the painful need of a rigid economy, in the midst of never-ceasing and never-limited hospitality, — her thoughtfulness and care for each child, in regard to the body, the mind, and the soul, seemed literally uninterrupted. And this care of her children reached them in their absence as well as their presence. In the summer after Robert's death, the oldest son, John, was placed at school in Framingham, where he remained several years; and seldom did he fail to receive, not only faithful letters, but a journal of daily doings, from his mother's pen, though she long remained feeble, and was now the mother of another infant, which she was compelled to put out to nurse. Another term of severe illness ensued, causing a lameness of long duration. But as soon as possible, indeed all along, she was doing something for the absent son.

"When you left home, my dear John," she writes in July, 1832, " I thought I should soon be well enough to write you, and intended to keep a journal for you of what went on amongst us, to be sent to you every fortnight; but now you have been gone two months, and I have not been able to write to you once, so little can we calculate upon the future. I have been obliged to keep my bed a great part of the time, and am not yet able to walk across the room without much pain. I have not been down stairs, excepting twice, when I was carried in arms to the front door, and rode about ten minutes, which hurt me so much that I shall not try it again very soon. I tell you all this, that you may understand how impossible it has been for me to fulfil my promise to you. I have thought much of you, and rejoiced to hear so often from you that you were happy and improving. When I have felt that I should never get well, and perhaps never see you again in this world, I have been very anxious about you, and have prayed most fervently that God would guide you in the right path, and hoped that you would live to be a comfort to your father when I was gone. . . . . .

" This is a busy week with us; yesterday being Exhibition, to-day Valedictory, to-morrow the Theological Exhibition in the morning and a public meeting of the Philanthropic Society in the afternoon. We shall have an open house, and hope to have as many friends with us as we had last year." An open house, filled with friends, all welcomed and in some way entertained by the lady of the house, who is not able to walk across the room without pain! We doubt not there are hundreds of such cases, some, it may be, more trying and more remarkable; but it does not alter the fact, nor make it less worthy of notice in a woman who did all that Mrs. Ware did.

It was a feature of Mrs. Ware's domestic character, that the throng of cares and conflict of duties seldom *worried* her. Many are they who are as diligent and faithful, but yet live in a perpetual hurry and fret. She knew the danger, and brought all her power and principle to withstand it, even in the smallest matters. Often have we heard her lamenting the necessity of spending so much of life in mere drudgery, ministering to the perishing but never-satisfied *body;* a necessity and service that devolve upon many women, and take from them the opportunity of high mental and spiritual culture, unless they carry into these daily duties and petty cares a calm spirit and a cheerful tone, with an elevated and steadfast purpose. Such was Mary's habitual endeavor. The difficulty, and the frequent failure, none were more ready to own. She never satisfied herself, but she never flagged. She never worried. Sudden interruptions, culinary disappointments, "shoals of visitors" with little of preparation, were not allowed to chill her welcome or cloud their enjoyment. There were no apologies at that table. If unexpected guests were not always filled, they were never annoyed, nor suffered to think much about it. A clergyman, who visited the house often as a student, says of Mrs. Ware: " I remember the wonder I felt at her humility and dignity in welcoming to her table on some occasion a troop of accidental guests, when she had almost nothing to offer but her hospitality. The absence of all apologies and of all mortification, the ease and cheerfulness of the conversation, which became the only feast, gave me a lesson never forgotten, although never learned."

Are these little things? They fill a large place in life, and have much to do with its solid comfort. They affect the temper, they enter into the character, and may help or hinder our best power and improvement. We introduce them here *because* they are little. There was not much in the life we are penning that was not little in some comparisons. It is the life of a plain, retiring, domestic woman. It is an example not beyond the reach of any who desire to reach it. We wish to show it just as it was; and to show, that of nothing was it more clearly the result, in nothing does its value more clearly consist, than in the power of Christian faith and simple goodness.

We have sometimes thought it would be well if all parishioners, those especially who are quick to discern the failings and slow to understand the labors of their pastor, could spend a few weeks in his house, and get some idea of the variety, complexity, arduousness, and endlessness of his duties. But from the picture which Mrs. Ware gives of the life at Cambridge, we should infer that the engagements and interruptions of most parishes were light in the comparison. "I used to think Boston life a very busy and irregular one; but our life here is far more so. There, there were some hours in the day in which, from conventional custom, one was secure of being quiet. But here, neither early hours nor late, neither rain nor tempest, are any security against interruption; and often, very often, does a whole day pass without either my husband or myself having one moment for our own occupations, or even a chance to exchange a single sentence of recognition. I do not complain of this, for it is inevitable. I must believe it is our appointed duty. But it seems sometimes a most · unprofitable mode of passing away life; at least it is very difficult to make progress in the things one most desires, when our time and our thoughts are so little at our own disposal."

Still, amid all these calls and cares, the "journal" continues, and full sheets of companion-like narration or maternal counsel go to the schoolboy at Framingham, who is having some of the trials of school-life, petty, but serious.

"Dear John, it is time you had another letter, and I am very glad to be able to write you one; it is the next best thing to sitting down by you and having a good chat. I should very much like to look in upon you, and know exactly how you get along. I hope you will continue to bear any provocation you may receive with perfect quietness and forbearance. Such conduct as you describe is not worthy of notice; and if you persevere in doing right, and show no arrogance or pride about it, you will gain their respect in time, that is, of all who are worth gaining. I am very glad you have Mr. Abbott's book (The Young Christian). I thought of you when I was reading it, and felt as if it would be very useful to you. You will find much in it which you never thought of, and much of which you will see a counterpart within yourself, if you examine yourself faithfully. It seemed to me, while reading it, that I was looking into a glass which reflected myself; for I have lived long enough to know more about myself than I used to at your age, and I often wish that I had had such looking-glasses then; I should, I think, have been saved many a feeling of self-reproach, and many a foolish and sinful action. You can hardly imagine now how great a blessing you possess in the watchful care which is extended over you by your dear father; may it never be withdrawn from you until you have learned to guide yourself by the high and holy principles of Christian virtue!"

It shows Mr. Ware's apprehensions in regard to his wife's health as well as his own, that, in a letter to the same son, he writes: "I find that your two parents are in very frail health, and probably destined to a short life. You will perhaps, therefore, be left at an early age to take care of yourself."

We learn still more of their mental and social life at this period from two letters which Mrs. Ware wrote at the end of the years 1832 and 1833; there having been little variety between, except a journey south as far as Alexandria, which they took together, for recreation and health, early in 1833, with a few later incidents referred to in the letters.

" *Cambridge, December 31, 1832.*

" DEAR N——:

" F—— prophesied, ten years ago, that friendship between married women could not be of long continuance. He did not know that there is in woman's nature something which woman only can fully understand; or his knowledge of human nature in general would have shown him that the love of sympathy will triumph over many an obstacle, which would be a perfect barrier to a less powerful motive. Who but a woman, and one too who knows the exact mould in which one's soul is fashioned, would understand what it has been to me to stand on the verge of the grave, in full possession of the whole intellectual being and prepare myself to leave such an assemblage of blessings as have fallen to my lot, — husband, children, friends, and the delightful duties which accompany these relations, — and then to be restored to them all, with an added gift! And all without one drawback, but my own want of sensibility, to make the blessing as great as it would be with a more sensitive heart. Perhaps no one can fully comprehend it who has not been placed in exactly the same situation. But you can come nearer to it than any one else, and you will not wonder that the past should seem to me one of the most valuable years of my life. I have often wished for just this experience, when I have felt how ineffectual were the monitors of Providence in awakening that deep sense of God's goodness, and that clear conviction of the reality of a future state, which are so important to the Christian life. I have almost envied those who were permitted to approach so nearly to the gates of death as to give up all expectation of a prolonged life. It has seemed as if this appeal must be irresistible; as if there could be no more deadness, or apathy, or indifference, after this. One *could* not come back to the world and be absorbed as before in its short-lived pursuits. But vain is the hope, I begin to fear, of our being raised by any thing so much above the world, as not to be subject to the power of the tempter while we live in it. The physical weakness which enables us to realize the uncertain tenure by which we are connected with this world is gradually changed into strength, and the power to act brings with it the desire; — and who shal easily set bounds to this desire? It is the all-consuming monster that cries, 'Give! give!' until we do give it every day, every hour, every thought, — until the present alone occupies us, and, alas! satisfies us too. Is this exaggeration, merely a dark picture drawn from my own sad experience? I hope it is.

"But I am going too far, filling all my paper with croaking, when I have so pleasant a picture of my 'outer man' to present to you. We are all well; that is, well enough to be free from anxiety on the subject; — neither Henry nor I good for much beyond a very narrow sphere, but free from disease. I keep very quietly at home. Indeed, I cannot do otherwise; a ride into Boston tires me so much, that I am not fit for any thing for a day after; a walk does the same. So I am fain to content myself with my home comforts; and to this end I have converted my chamber into a study, where Henry writes, I work, and Nanny plays all the livelong day. It is more like Sheafe Street comfort than any thing we have had since. My husband's social habits, and the fact of our having lived so much together for the last three years, make it particularly pleasant to him to be saved the trouble of going in search of me whenever he wants to read a sentence or say a word; and for the same reasons, it is very pleasant to me to have so much of his presence without feeling that he is taken off from his rightful pursuits by it. January 1, 1833! A happy new year to you all!

"Yours truly.

"M. L. W."

" Cambridge, December 31, 1833.

" MY DEAR N——:

" I am inclined to think that it is our inordinate estimate of the happiness of this life, and our vague, half-sceptical notions of a future state, that make us grieve so much when such spirits as Elizabeth B—— are withdrawn from us. I don't know, but I sometimes greatly fear that we do not bring home the *reality* of the future as we should do ; we are so occupied with our theories of right principles of action and correct ideas of moral conduct in this life (all very good in their place), and so afraid of falling into the extravagant exercise of the imagination, which has betrayed so many of our opponents in doctrine into enthusiasm and folly, that we lose sight of the good influences which such contemplations might have upon our hearts. This year has been to me one of less variety than any of the last six. My husband's long sickness in the spring, and the efforts consequent upon it, were the source of much anxiety, and in some points a new experience. But I have had for so long a time only to bear and submit, that my mind has settled itself into that attitude, and it is no longer an effort. It is quite another thing, when it becomes my duty to exercise my energies in positive acts, — when others are looking to me for guidance, when my habitual influence is to form the character of this child and check the waywardness of that, with all the train of active duties which devolve upon a married woman, — then I am overpowered and powerless.

" I wished you had been by my side on Sunday, while I sat in my old corner in Federal Street meeting-house, listening to that voice which is to us both associated with some of our best religious impressions. I went to hear Dr. Channing, for the second time only since I returned home, as much for the sake of recalling old associations as from any expectation of new influences; for it does me good now and then to go back to what I was, the better to understand what I am. If he had known just what I was suffering, he could not have adapted himself more entirely to my case. He was upon some of the obstacles which may prevent our use of the present moment for improvement; and he enlarged upon the tendency to rest satisfied with past attainments. Because we had at one period of our lives been deeply moved and strongly influenced by religious motives, — had performed some great acts of benevolence, or sustained ourselves under great trial with fortitude and submission, — we deluded ourselves with the idea, that we had attained a height from which we could not fall. But no mistake could be more ruinous. The past was *nothing*, except as it influenced the present. We trust too much to future improvement, to a vague notion of gradual progress, — we know not exactly how, or by what means. But as we are not conscious of becoming worse, we think we must be growing better, and shall by and by be all that we ought to be. Or we hope for more favorable circumstances to influence us, and expect to be, we know not why, in a more fit state at some other time for our religious duties.

" Had I room, I could give you a long story about this, for my mind is full of it. But I have another word to say upon the fact of our giving so much time to the mere outside of life, to the employment of our fingers, the mere mechanical employments pertaining to the body. It is a question with me, whether it is not a duty to be satisfied with a less elegant, and even a less comfortable style of life, rather than take so much from the cultivation of the intellectual and spiritual, when, as is so often the case now-a-days, we must either do the drudgery ourselves or leave it undone. I don't know, — I am puzzled. I know that if we

are doing our *duty*, however mean may be our employment, we are fulfilling our destiny, and doing God the best
service. But the question is, What is our duty? And are
we not in danger of mistaking the real nature of duty, from
too great a love of this world and the things of it? This is
one of the difficult questions, which my husband and I try
to settle. I wish you would tell me what you think. And
here comes my Willie, with an imploring look to be taken
up, — a reproving one, too, that in all this long letter neither he nor his family are so much as noticed. All are
well.

" Yours ever.

" M. L. WARE."

Unusual freedom from sickness and apprehension
was for a time enjoyed. Mrs. Ware was full of happiness and thankfulness. " It seems to me that
never had people so much reason for gratitude as
we ; and I think I never felt this more than at this
time, for I too am beginning to have the first feelings of health which I have known for a year and a
half." But a change came. And with the letter
which explains it we close this portion of the Cambridge life.

" *Cambridge, May* 4, 1834.

" My dear N——:

" .... We have had our usual variety of sickness and health
since I wrote to you in January. Soon after that, I had a visit
from my old, and I thought conquered, enemy, the cramp ;
not a very severe attack, but sufficient to make me very
good for nothing for a week, in the course of which Nanny
had a very severe fall, which for twenty-four hours made
us apprehensive that we should have to part with her. But
this trial was spared us, in much mercy ; for two days after

this, Elizabeth was very sick, though not dangerously. All this had its effect upon Mr. Ware and myself, and we have oeen the greater part of the time in the most disagreeable state of betwixity, neither sick enough to be excused from labor, nor well enough to do any thing profitable, — just good for nothing. In the vacation in April, Mr. Ware went to Portsmouth to collect materials for his Memoir of Dr. Parker, intending by the way to go to Exeter.

" The day after he went, my Willie, who had been the very perfection of health and happiness all winter, began to droop, and, notwithstanding pretty efficient measures, in a few days became the subject of decided lung fever; not very sick, but requiring constant watching and careful attention. A week from the day he was taken, he had a severe spasmodic attack, from which we thought he would never revive; and when, after various measures, he began to breathe again, we sat for four hours expecting that every moment would be his last. It was a season of severe trial, not a little increased by his father's absence, and the impossibility of his reaching home until this sweet child must be for ever removed from his sight. Yet it was not for me to learn then, for the first time, that He who sends trial always gives strength to bear it. I knew it would be so, and in that faith I rested in peace and tranquillity. But this blow, too, was averted. After a long struggle he revived, and I realized, what I had never known before, that this second birth, as it were, of a child is a far more affecting cause for gratitude and joy than the first gift ever can be. It was a great experience in many ways. It helped me to understand the feeling of those who were witnesses of miracles more than any thing I ever met with. For all human means were at an end; nothing could be done but to pray that the Almighty Power, to whom all things were possible, might yet interpose to save. And the fact of having been carried through such a trial with entire submission and calmness, — what confidence does it not give in the all-sufficient power of that religion which can alone succor one in such an hour of need! The kindness, too, which such an occasion calls forth from those around us, is not the least of its blessings. It makes us view human kind more justly than we are sometimes inclined to do, and sinks for ever some of those petty and contemptuous feelings which will sometimes rise towards those with whom we have but little sympathy.

" My husband returned after all this was over, quite sick ; but he did return without the necessity of my going to him, and returned to be the better for being *at home*, gaining every moment after he entered his house. All this was during that bright, warm interval in April, when nature seemed buoyant with joy. We had just completed our summer arrangements, and altogether it seemed to me as if I had begun existence anew. Although somewhat exhausted by the struggle, I really am better than for months past.

" Yours ever.

" M. L. WARE."

23*

XI.

LIFE IN CAMBRIDGE. (Continued.)

It is the misfortune of those who are often sick to be blamed for their sicknesses in proportion as they are active and laborious when well. Their energy is sure to be considered the *cause* of subsequent and frequent debility; and if not blamed, they find less compassion or kind considerarion than the indolent and self-indulgent. These last may be sick all the time, and it is ascribed only to nature or the providence of God. But the conscientious and energetic, who accomplish wonders for themselves or others in their brief intervals of health, and possibly in sickness likewise, are accused of imprudence and a sinful disregard of self; while in truth it may be only by extreme care and unknown self-denials that they are able to accomplish any thing.

If Mary Ware was ever severely censured, we suppose it to have been in connection with this matter of health. Few women have been blessed with a better constitution, or greater power of action. With an almost masculine frame, there was such a degree of firmness with her gentleness, as always gave the idea of more strength than was wanted. We doubt if in early life she ever thought of saving her strength, so accustomed was she to do any thing that needed to be done, without saying or thinking much about it. She who had been the sole nurse of a sick mother at the age of eleven or twelve, and, as another describes her then, "going through all the offices of the sick-room with the firmness of a woman, holding on leeches with her little hand, and performing *all* the necessary duties, not absolutely from necessity, but from so much love and so much confidence that no one else was wanted," — she who had scarcely, from that period until middle life, been free from care and toil for the sick and suffering, — might be pardoned if she became self-relying, or at least self-forgetting. And yet when at last that vigorous frame was impaired, and the overwrought energies of body and mind partially gave way, so that the remainder of her life was subject to constant fluctuations of strength and weakness, powerful exertion and acute suffering, she does not seem to us to have been presumptuous or ever reckless. It is evident now, if it was not at the time, that she made this as much a matter of sober calculation and conscientious questioning as any thing, and much more than is common. Still she tells us that she was blamed for her imprudence; and she brings instances from her own experience to show the frequent error of judging of what one does, or forbears to do, by the apparent result, rather than from knowledge or by principle. "People judge by *consequences*, or what seem to be consequences, rather than by reasoning upon premises."

It is partly to show how Mrs. Ware defended herself, and at the same time submitted to counsel and was grateful for admonition, and partly to show how singularly insulated she must have been in her early training and her self-formed character, that we introduce the following note, written to a lady who acted the part of a true friend. The date is not given, but the note itself shows that it was written the year of the journey to the South already mentioned, when she accompanied her husband at some risk to herself.

"MY DEAR, GOOD FRIEND: —

"I cannot thank you as I would for your kind note. I have not words wherewith to picture to you the joy I feel, that there is any one human being in existence who is willing to admonish me freely. If you have told me nothing new, your words are none the less welcome, for one cannot have the truth too frequently presented to the mind · and although we may have *all* knowledge, it is not often that we can grasp it all at one glance, or even that we remember the points most useful to us at the time being.

"You will not think I boast, when I say that one and all the views you present have long formed part of the rule of action by which I have *tried* to govern myself, because I know you will easily understand the deep-searching, Argus-eyed vigilance, which one wholly self-educated almost inevitably acquires. I never have had, since I can remember, a principle of action suggested to me, or a word said to show me *why* one action was wrong and another right. For many years a whisper of blame never reached my ears; and when at last it came like a flood upon me, there was no friendly looking-glass near to point out to me the deformity from which my mistakes arose. At ten years of age I waked up to a sense of the danger of the state of indulgence in which I was living. At thirteen, by the death of

my mother, I was left wholly to my own guidance, externally as well as internally; and from that time to this I
have labored night and day to know, discipline, and govern
myself, as I would a child for whose soul I was responsible.
Dr. Channing's sermons and conversation are the only
effectual human guide I ever had, until I was married.
Having no one to whom to speak, and but one friend to
whom I could write upon the subject, no wonder that my
habits of thought should have been more cultivated than of
conversation; no wonder the whole ground of self-deception, self-distrust, self-aggrandizement, should have been
gone over again and again until every root was displaced
and exposed to view; though, alas! not a hundredth part
eradicated. Now this is not to my point, but you will still
see that you have done me good by making me feel thus
loquacious and unreserved with you.

"You remind me that I omitted one item in my defence,
the mere mention of which will answer many of your que-
ries. Who can tell how often a person, blamed for the disregard of many considerations which ought to influence the
conduct, is inflamed by those very considerations, restrained
by those very motives? We see what is done; we cannot
see what is forborne. In proof of this, after I recovered
from the long illness which followed immediately upon my
arrival at home, three and a half years ago, it was five or
six months before.I felt any thing like elasticity of mind or
body; the least effort fatigued me; I looked perfectly well,
and every body was asking me why I did not go here, there,
and everywhere. I knew from my feelings that I still
needed rest, and I took it. Change of air, consequent upon
the necessity of attending Mr. Ware in his sickness at Concord, produced a great change in my whole feelings. I
seemed well again; but I knew my system had materially
suffered while abroad, and I determined religiously to abstain

from all effort of all kinds that did not seem perfectly safe
No one knew any thing about it, I was so well.   Still I
persevered.   I literally did not walk across the room, or eat
a meal, that winter, without deliberately arguing the case,
— was it best or not ?   In this healthy state, I went to Dr.
W.'s lecture, and was very prudent afterward ; yet when
my severe sickness commenced, it was all laid to tha
lecture ; I was talked to, even in its worst stages, as if tc
be sick was a crime, and I have not to this day heard the
last of it. . . . . . Again, I never in my whole life did so
imprudent a thing as undertaking the journey I did last
spring ; there was no one reason against the probability, almost certainty, of its injuring me.   I knew the risk : no one
else did.   I took the risk, because I thought the object au-
thorized it.   The result, after much suffering by the way,
was favorable, and all was well.   Had it been otherwise,
there would have been voices enough to point out that it
was wrong. . . . . .

   " There is one simple question which I wish to have answered, — How do other people attain infallible correct-
ness of judgment ?   Is it by experience or intuition ?   If
the former, have they not suffered from their experiments,
sometimes erred in their calculations, and should they not
have charity for others who are going over the same
ground ?   If by the latter, should they not pity those less
favored than themselves ?   I will not trouble you any more
with my egotism.   Remember, the best favor you can confer is, when you think I am doing wrong, to check me, ask
me why, show me wherein I deceive myself; and never
fea to speak plainly to your grateful friend,

                                   " M. L. WARE."

   There is another province into which the really
high-minded and independent will carry the same

conscientiousness, with equal firmness. It is a province often regarded as low and little. Nothing is little that involves principles and affects character. And what does this more than Dress? It is a matter to which few can be indifferent, even in a pecuniary view; and that is by no means the highest view. Love of dress is admitted to be one of the earliest passions that appear in human nature, and may be said to be a universal passion. If it be stronger in one sex than in the other, — a fact more easily assumed than demonstrated, — she is the nobler woman, wife, and mother who gives it its proper place among the elements of education, and both deigns and dares to speak of it and act upon it as a Christian.

So did Mrs. Ware speak and act. The circumstances in which she had always been placed, inducing the habit and the necessity of strict frugality, as we have seen, would alone have prevented her from overlooking so large an item in the domestic and social economy. But besides this, she had regard to the integrity of her principles, and the influence of example. She aimed evidently at two points, not easily attained together, — to make little of the whole matter of dress, and, at the same time, bring it under the control of a high Christian rule. As to her own attire, we should say no one thought of it at all, because of its simplicity, and because of her ease of manners and dignity of character. Yet this impression is qualified, though in one view confirmed, by hearing that, in a new place of residence, so plain was her appearance on all occasions, the villagers suspected her of reserving her fine clothes for some better class, — a suspicion only amusing to those who knew her, but sure to give pain to her benevolent heart. In another note to the female friend last addressed, she expresses her thoughts and describes her practice on this subject, so simply and sensibly, that we cannot hesitate to offer all of it except the specific and personal applications; while these, if they could be given, would show yet more how consistent and thorough she was.

" *Saturday Evening, January* 17, 1835.

" MY DEAR FRIEND : —

" I have such a poor faculty at expressing myself in speech, that I never feel that I have quite done myself justice in any delicate matter, when I have used only oral means. I have felt this peculiarly since I left you this afternoon, because some expressions of mine have recurred to my mind's ear, which I thought might possibly be construed by you into a very different meaning from their intended one. I do not, as you know, like to trouble my friends with the discussions of questions merely personal, and which I ought to be able to decide for myself unaided; and the whole subject of *dress* seems, at a first glance, so trifling, that most people would laugh at my having a serious thought about it. But to me, the least thing which can have an influence upon the character of my children becomes in my eyes a matter of deep importance; and for this reason I have really longed to enter upon this said subject with some one who could look at it in the same light, or who could disabuse me of my anxiety about it, if it was a foolish one. Accident has opened the door to your ear, and if you can have patience with me, and I can find words to tell you what I mean, I may some time or other try your friendship in this way.

"To go back a little. When we went to Europe you may know it was the liberality of our friends, and the good-will of the Corporation, which enabled us to undertake the expense of so long a tour. We calculated very well for such novices, but could not anticipate the great additional draft which a child's birth and the journey home would make upon our resources. Consequently we returned in debt. This debt we had hoped to liquidate by living within our salary, and thus laying by a little every year. Four years' experiment has proved this hope fallacious. Every year has brought with it some occasion of great extra expense, which has taken up what might otherwise have been laid by for this purpose. We have had, you know, a great deal of sickness, and there have been other contingencies which it is not necessary to enumerate. These may not occur again, but past experience proves that we have no right to calculate upon such exemptions; and it becomes, therefore, more than ever necessary that we economize in the strictest manner, to do all we can to free ourselves from this burden, and to do justice to others. Our children, of course, are acquainted with this state of affairs, and it is right that they should do their part, and from right motives. They know, as we do, that there are many expenses of daily occurrence in which there cannot be any retrenchment consistent with our obligations to our friends and the situation we hold in society, — such as the calls of hospitality and charity. But they ought to feel that all *personal* sacrifices are to be made that can be, according to a standard of propriety which a high moral sense would dictate. This, of course, must be in some measure an arbitrary standard, to be settled as much by experiment and example as by reasoning I have therefore had but few *rules* upon the subject, leaving to each occasion which brings up the question all argumentation, taking care to have as little discussion as may be possible, lest it become in any way the subject of too much thought. This is particularly to be avoided with regard to dress, and upon this I have been more puzzled than on any other branch, as both our elder children are just of an age to require very 'judgmatical' treatment upon it. My rule for myself is, as I told you, to do without every thing which I can *decently*, making my own ideas of decency, not others', the standard. It is a difficult matter, especially as I make no pretensions to good taste, or good faculty, about externals; but this, I maintain, does not alter the question of duty......

" I feel that I am trying your patience with much ado about a small thing. But it is my weak side to wish to be thoroughly understood by my friends, weak points and all; and it helps me to understand myself, thus to try to make others understand me. I have not a word of complaint to make. We are far better provided for than is necessary to our happiness. We could live upon our income and grow rich, were our wishes only our rule; but as we are situated, it is not easy to make 'all ends meet,' as the phrase is; and as our five children grow every day older, it becomes more and more difficult every year. Can you teach me to economize? I fear, however, that if you could, you could not insure me strength to carry your plan into execution. No one who has not experienced it can tell how great a drawback sickness is to all saving, especially when it comes upon the head of the house, and when it requires the most expensive kinds of remedy. But enough of all this. I wish you would tell me if you do not think I am right in declining your offer. I am always doubtful enough about my own judgment, to be open to conviction from those who differ.

" Yours in all love.

" M. L. WARE."

The years 1834 and 1835 are spoken of by Mr. and Mrs. Ware as peculiarly favored, having little sickness or severe trial, compared with other years. But this must have been only a comparative view; for we find several incidental allusions to a state of feebleness and inability, which most of us would consider quite enough either for discipline or release from labor. Very pleasantly, however, does Mrs. Ware speak of those interruptions and prostrations, as if they were the ordinary condition. To Emma she writes: " Could you have alighted upon us at any time within the last fortnight, you would have found yourself *at home.* Nearly all last week Mr. Ware and myself enjoyed a most social *tête-à-tête* upon the two beds which occupy my chamber, neither of us capable of reading to the other, nor, a great part of the time, of speaking; I ill from the effects of the cramp, he from the fatigue of taking care of me with it. From this state we were compelled to rouse ourselves, by having one domestic taken sick, and Nanny —— All the rest you know." This was said in 1834. In the autumn of that year a daughter was born; and for a time Mrs. Ware was so helpless, that she yielded more than was her wont to feelings of discouragement. " I did *try* to be hopeful; but the idea of so long a period of uselessness, and its consequent evils to my children and family, was dreadful to me; and I could not quite feel that I could receive it as patiently as I ought." But severely does she chide herself for this distrust, especially as the result was so much better than her fears. She regained her health, and soon enjoyed a greater sense of strength and energy tnan she had had since her marriage. And this period of exemption — though not very long as regarded the health of all the household — was one of the seasons in which she strove to make amends for lost time, and accomplished a vast deal. Not that there was any remarkable, visible product. She never labored for one object exclusively, in doors or out, and it would not be easy to point to definite results. It may be doubted if she ever thought much of results, or expected, or even desired, to see them in any sure and signal form. To do "all she could" was her only ambition; and she had the wisdom which is worth more than any other, — to be *content* with doing all she could, only taking care that that word "all" should take in something more than the thought of earth, or self. She did not forget that objects and interests have a relative, as well as positive importance; and probably all who knew her well have marked this as a characteristic trait, — that she studied the exact proportion of the different claims upon her time, and was more anxious to do justly than to do all things.

In our times, and in a position like Mr. Ware's, there were sure to be numerous calls and claims abroad as well as at home, and for a woman not less than a man. We have not inquired as to the names or number of the benevolent societies and industrial enterprises in Cambridge, in which Mrs. Ware took part. That she gained any notoriety in this way, we should be surprised to hear, both from her multiplicity of duties, and her preference of private to public activity. Yet that her influence was felt, her judgment peculiarly relied upon, and her presence always welcomed, in these connections, we know. Cases of moral want and exposure interested her most, and we have reason to think that she was never without some such case on her hands or in her heart. What she could not do herself, in the gift of time or clothes or money, she always induced others to do, *never* suffering an object of actual want or peril to go unassisted., Very far was she above the poor apology, that to do any thing for one sufferer will create more. In a multitude of small notes given us, written by her to various neighbors and friends, we chanced to see in one, so small as at first to be overlooked, a few words that fixed attention; and on reading it through, we found, in the compass of a few lines, a whole volume of illustration as to her interest, her courage, and her power of indignation for selfish excuses. We give it just as it was written to a neighbor, another right-minded woman.

" I have company, therefore cannot answer you at length, or as I wish. I should have stepped in to see you this afternoon, if I had not been prevented by callers, to say a few words upon the subject of the latter part of your note. I have to-day got at the poor man's wardrobe for the first time, and determined to *beg* for some means to supply it with a few decencies, for even they are wanting. Mr. Ware has thought it quite allowable to state the case to one or two of our rich men, to raise enough to pay the expenses of his journey; and I have just resolved to undertake the other matter. But I am full of wrath-

24 *

ful indignation at being *sneered at* for taking him in. 'You will have enough English beggars at your door, if you do so.' A good argument against relieving any distress! So let the poor suffer as much as they may, — no relief, — for others will be idle and want relief too! — M. L. W."

In another brief note, we saw a statement of Mrs. Ware, to the effect that for many years she had not been without some " case of intemperance on hand "; and a little inquiry tells us that it refers to her habit of helping the reformed and the struggling to get an honest living. A " Ladies' Aid Society " had been formed in Cambridge, with that special object; and its President, being obliged to leave home, asked Mrs. Ware to look after her " patients," when she found that Mary had long been doing privately, and by herself, what they were doing as a society.

It may seem the language of enthusiastic friendship, and our readers will deduct what they please on that account, but we must give a passage from a recent letter, written by one of the many theological students who had free access to Mr. Ware's house and family. In reference to Mrs. Ware, he writes: " I have often quoted her example since to those who make the cares of housekeeping an excuse for the neglect of all public offices. She seemed to keep house better than any body else, to exercise a larger and freer hospitality, to make her tea-table a pleasant resort, to provide more simply and at the same time more attractively, while, after all, her domestic cares were only an incident in her daily duties. She seemed to have time for every great out-door or general interest, and to be full of schemes of benevolence and kindness. And it was the easy, natural way in which she performed these double functions that gave me such a sense of her *power*."

In regard to intercourse with general society and festive gatherings, Mary Ware was often drawn to them, not less by a social, genial temper than by a sense of duty. A duty even there she recognized and regarded; a duty secondary, certainly, to many others, but involving obligation when other duties came not in the way. She believed that society had claims as well as the family, and pure enjoyment as well as religion. Her social sympathies were always calm, but never cold; subdued, but ardent, and ever ready both to taste and impart pleasure. Her interest in children was a passion, and her love of seeing and promoting their enjoyment as intense as any we have known. She could ill brook any restraint put upon the freedom and joyousness of the young, beyond the point of propriety or others' comfort. Her own convenience, her rooms, her whole house, she would give up, adding her powers of entertainment and enjoyment, rather than make life cheerless or religion repulsive. Many scenes can we recall of childish glee and hearty frolic, presided over, shared, and promoted by both the heads of that house, with which are associated some of the happiest hours of life, and the best. We will always thank God that those two hearts, which He was pleased to chasten with many sicknesses and sorrows, were as genial and joyous as they were pure and humble.

There was one form of social entertainment — if it deserve the name — with which Mrs. Ware had no sympathy, and for which she had little charity. Indeed, that "indignation" which we have seen enkindled by selfishness, though not easily roused, could not always restrain itself in the hearing of small gossip or busy *scandal*. We said in the introduction to this Memoir, that not a single line or word allied to those petty vices have we found in the whole extent of her correspondence, sober or trivial. We are sure the same might be said of her conversation. Nor was this negative only. There was a tone of decided displeasure, and, if necessary, pointed reproof, called forth at times by the spiteful or thoughtless scandal-monger. She would not allow that we have a *right* to be thoughtless; nor did she believe that we were sent into the world to scan a neighbor's conduct or impugn another's motives. In a letter written at Cambridge to a friend whom she had been to meet in Boston, but with whom her enjoyment had been greatly interrupted, she thus expresses herself.

" It is only tantalizing to meet in Boston, to fritter away the few moments of intercourse which we want for better purposes in the idle, profitless gossip of city life. Is it because I have so little interest in other people, or is it for a better reason, that I have no patience with hearing people descant upon the whys and wherefores of their neighbors' concerns; discussing their actions with as decided judgment upon their merits, as if the secret springs of thought, and all the various causes which led to them, were as fully developed to us as they can be to the Omniscient only? I know we may learn much from others' experience, both in warning and example; and to do this, we must closely observe them, and follow or vary from their course as our own conscience and judgment may dictate. But surely it is not necessary that we should be all the time speculating and gossiping with each other, upon every portion of the lives of our neighbors, or such portions as cannot from their very nature be of any importance to us in any way. Is it just to our minds so to employ them? Is it Christian charity towards others? I may see clearly my neighbor's faults, and if there be any chance of doing him good by it, I may speak of them to him freely. I may consult a friend, who I know will treat the subject with the same tender feeling that I have myself, upon all the views which could result in good to the guilty or ourselves. But to talk publicly to any and all about the matter, for no possible result but the getting rid of so much time, fostering contempt on the one hand and self-conceit on the other, seems to me the wickedest abuse of the high privilege of speech that I know of, next to absolute falsehood. And how often does this habit lead to falsehood, and all manner of injustice! . . . . . But enough. Perhaps I am too much of a recluse to judge justly of the temptations of city life, and am committing the very sin which I am condemning. Suffice it to say, that thus was my whole comfort in town destroyed, and I came home feeling that, so far as regarded our knowledge of each other's inner woman, we might as well not have met."

With all the variety of the Cambridge life, there was necessarily a sameness which makes it needless to mark every year, or follow exactly the order of events. The chief "events" of these twelve years were the death of one child, the birth of four, and the variations of health and sickness to both parents. In the experience of sickness, the year 1836 brought one of the sorest visitations. We subjoin Mrs. Ware's account of it soon after its occurrence, and her review of the year at its close.

"Cambridge, May 29, 1836.

"My dear N——:

" . . . . . You have heard, no doubt, enough of the outline of our story to have traced us in all our outward movements. But you cannot know what rich experience the last four months have brought to us, and the compass of a letter can tell you little. The first stroke was a heavy one. Henry had been very well all winter, and had gained a degree of strength and ability to labor unharmed, which, in our most sanguine moments, we never even hoped for, so that the disappointment was even greater than when he was taken ill at Ware, as the height from which he fell was greater. He was attacked, for the first time since that, upon the lungs ; and when, for the first few days, it seemed quite reasonable to expect that the consequences, if not even more alarming, would be at least as lasting as those which followed the former attack, the prospect was heart-sickening. It required the industrious use of all the few moments of thought I could borrow from my occupations, to gather strength enough to nerve me for the calm contemplation of the picture.

"His own view of the case was a very reasonable one ; and the calmness with which he looked at the improbability of recovery, was at once an aid and a source of high enjoyment to me. A few weeks, however, gave us more encouragement; the attack was not a severe one, and yielded readily to the remedies applied. And although we could not but look forward to a long confinement at that season of the year, there was much in his state to give us pleasure. His mind is always, when he begins to recover, in a very animated state, very active, and upon the most entertaining subjects. This time he injured his eyes by looking over newspapers and books, in the early part of his illness; so that, as soon as my most arduous duties as nurse ceased, I had to commence those of reader and amanuensis. I never was so literary in my life. I did nothing but read and write; nor have I done much else since, for he cannot yet do either for himself. Thus passed ten weeks, a period equal to our whole residence at Ware and Worcester; and yet, owing to the difference of the season, he could not get out of his room more than once or twice a week, when he was carried in arms to a carriage. At this time, too, I sunk for a short term, not with disease, but exhaustion from confinement and incessant effort of some kind or other. I soon got rested; but whether from the interruption which this caused to Henry's literary employments, or because the time had come for a change, I know not, — his own animation ceased, and he seemed in danger of losing all his energy and strength for the want of air and exercise I had hoped that he would be sent to a warmer re gion as soon as he had strength to get there, for air and exercise are always essential to his recovery. But he dragged on, until I was not willing to be submissive any longer; and I begged that he might go to New York at least, for a city is so much more protected than the country, that he could walk there in weather that would have kept him in here. I went to New York with him, but could not well stay ; and as he was in a second home there, it did not seem necessary. He came home just in time to sit down by a fire during this long storm ! It was most unlucky, but cannot be helped. Were it possible, I would go off with him as soon as the sun shines, to keep him from going to work. I never say any thing is *impossible*, but it seems to me next to it that I should leave home now. All my five children are at home, — to say nothing of not having attended to any of my domestic duties since last January ; — a little sewing to be done, you may fancy. Still, if it is *necessary* to go, some way of effecting it will present itself.

"Yours in all true love.

"MARY L. WARE."

"*Boston, December* 31, 1836.
Saturday Night.

"MY DEAR N——:

"What a crowd of recollections rush upon my mind as I date this letter ! It is nine years since I have affixed ' Boston ' to this annual epistle ; and the last ' Saturday night ' which found me thus occupied was eleven years ago, at *Osmotherly*, 1825 ; and the last time I wrote the whole date was to a note which accompanied a pair of pegged gloves which I sat up till midnight to finish for your brother, in 1814. What an interesting and varied picture do these dates present to my mind's eye, and how many remembrances are associated with them of joy and sorrow, of trial and happiness ! I could willingly spend hours in recalling all in detail, and I feel as if it would do us both good, should I do so ; for I find that, in the full occupation of the present, the lessons of the past are losing their power over me. Their voice cannot be heard in the busy bustle of life ; and it is only at a few favored moments like these, when all creation within and around us pauses, as it were, before taking another onward step towards eternity, that we can hear their distant, solemn murmur. It is good, then, to turn our hearts to the teaching, and to fix in them more deeply the warning and encouragement which we may thus receive. . . . . .

"I have been led lately to think more than usual of the past, by Mrs. B——'s death. I believe I do not exaggerate when I rest in the idea that she was a woman of rare powers to interest and influence those around her. My own recollections bring with them a sense of almost romantic enthusiasm with regard to her; and I am quite sure that I owe as much of my conception of the *loveliness* of a truly religious being to her exhibition of it, as to any one other source. With the thought of her in her glory, comes the remembrance of many who have been taken from time to time from our communion; and it amazes me to find how large is their number. How soon will it be, that it will become a rare thing to meet one of the companions of our childhood! . . . . . Perhaps I generalize too much from my own individual experience; but I find it so difficult to keep before my eyes the uncertainty of life, or to feel as I would do the *reality* of the spiritual world, so busy am I with the occupations of this material one, that I should like to be recalled to the subject by some irresistible voice every hour of the day.

"I have spent this evening in our old church at the North End, for the first time upon this occasion since I lived in Sheafe Street, when Henry preached; and as I look back upon the experience I have had since that time, it seems to me I have little hope of ever being what I ought to be, when all this has had so little effect.

"*January* 9. Yesterday, heard Dr. Channing preach and administer the communion, the latter of which is more

25

to me than even his best sermons, so great is the power of association. . . . . . I find I almost lose sight of some of my *best pleasures,* when I have been for any length of time free from great *trial,* In truth, all this nomenclature is wrong. Ease and prosperity make our greatest trial ; we are never more blessed than when we are said to be in affliction. It is remarkable, that not one year has passed since I began this custom of recording to you these mercies, that there has not been some striking one on the list. What is to come this year ? God knows ; and in this I can rest satisfied. Henry's eyes are useless, and mine still in requisition ; of course I do nothing else, except at odd moments, when he is away or asleep,

" MARY."

Mr. Ware's severe illness at this period seems to have been a crisis ; for the two following years, both with him and her, were probably the best of all they passed at Cambridge, in their freedom from sickness, their ability to work, and the amount of their work. We connect them in this respect, for it is not easy to separate their spheres and agencies, even in regard to his professional labors. Of course, we mean to imply nothing as to any special mental aid, for no woman ever made less pretension, or less attempt, at any thing more than could be done by every sensible and interested mind. But so completely did she enter into all his engagements, so constantly did she watch the degree of his strength and the effect of his exertions, and so often was she called to assist him directly, as reader or writer, from the failure of his eyes and his frequent debility, that her coöperation was not wholly a figure of speech,

Then, too, her heart was as much enlisted in the welfare and success of his pupils in the Theological School, as it had been in his Boston parish. All that she had a right to know, she did know; all that a woman and friend could do for those pupils, in sympathy, counsel, encouragement, or personal aid, she invariably did. A son, then a member of the School, says of her: " As a Professor's wife, I do not think father's heart was more in the School than was hers. I suspect she knew every thing about it, and was his constant assistant and counsellor. How much directly she had to do with the young men, I cannot say. They were encouraged to be at the house, came to tea constantly by invitation, and in all sicknesses she cared for them; especially M——— and B———, who were brought to the house, and C———, and also an undergraduate, sick. She did what she could for the destitute among them; and I remember her getting shirts made, &c., &c. I remember, too, the delicate way in which I was sent, on a cold New Year's evening, with a large bundle to an undergraduate who was friendless and penniless." There are others, and many, who could tell much more; and whose recollections of her delicate sympathy, generous aid, and unpretending goodness, will hardly suffer them to speak of her, but with silent tears. They felt her *moral* power; and all the more, because she seemed utterly unconscious of it. " Never have I been with her," writes one, who says he had but a common acquaintance, " no matter how short the time or slight the occasion, without the feeling of greater elevation of soul. I never knew one of whom this were truer. Virtue came out of her." And he only adds, of one connected with him, " Even now the thought of Mrs. Ware moves her more than the presence of any living friend."

While writing these passages, we have received the testimony of another of those students, more extended, but too pertinent and valuable to be abridged.

" The members of the Theological School were always sure of her sympathy. They went to her as they would to an elder sister. There was something peculiarly engaging and attractive about her, which we all felt, but could not well understand. Yet she did not encourage, as some kind-hearted women do, the morbid sensibilities of young men, which, even while apparently depreciating their own powers, almost always have their origin in an exaggerated egotism or some masked form of selfishness. Mrs. Ware's peculiar excellence was, that, without encouraging such a state of mind and without repelling those who had cherished it, she, by the healthiness of her own mind and the cheerful disinterestedness of her character, dissolved the gloomy spell, and sent away her visitors with new hope and life. It was the atmosphere in which she lived, more than any particular words or acts, that made her presence in Cambridge so attractive, and so beneficent to the young at that period of life when they are likely to be in a morbid condition. To go from our rooms to her house, when we had got discouraged or worn down, was like going into a different climate. And we went back, like invalids who have been spending a winter at the South, with new vitality in our veins.

" While connected with the School, in 1834, I had a short but violent attack of brain fever. I was in Divinity Hall, and very kindly taken care of by my associates in the School, who did for me every thing that young men know how to do in such a case. After a few days, Mrs. Ware came to see me. The bare sight of her countenance, and the sweet, gentle tones of her voice, I shall never forget. They changed the whole aspect of the room. As soon as it could be done, I was removed to her house. And the delicacy of her touch, as in my helplessness she washed my hands and face, with the air of motherly cheerfulness and tenderness, was to my diseased nerves like the ministry of one from a better world. During the months of confinement and extreme debility which succeeded, the remembrance of her kindness was a constant source of comfort, and I cannot now recall it without deep and grateful emotion."

In connection with exertions for others, it is but just to refer again to the laborious efforts, self-denial, and perpetual solicitude, to which Mrs. Ware was driven, at home, in regard to pecuniary means. The difficulty came at last to its height. They found it impossible to live as they did, and yet impossible to retrench more than they always had. We would not speak of this so freely, did we not feel — beside the light it throws upon character and results — that it is due to the professors and ministers of all denominations, whose energies are crippled, and power of

25 *

serving as well as enjoying sadly abridged, by the
conflicting facts of unreasonable demand and incompetent support.　Those of us who do not suffer, and
are only grateful, have the better right to speak for
others; and we speak in the memory, and as by the
authority, of those two unsparing and noble workers,
whose sentiments on the subject we well know, and
whose power of usefulness should never have been
hampered, as it often was, by the want of means
which hundreds were both able and willing to furnish.　Yes, willing; for it is no want of *generosity* that
we speak of; were we capable of that injustice, especially in the community and the family under review,
we should expect almost to hear the reproof of the
departed ones, whose gratitude was as intense as
their solicitude.　Not for themselves did they feel,
but for others; for the School, for the ministry; for
the students who were prevented from entering the
School, or forced to leave it, by poverty and the fear
of debt, some of whom were retained only by promises of aid, whose fulfilment cost added labor and
wearing anxiety.　There is better provision now, we
know; ample provision for those willing to accept it.
Still are there wants and straits in the actual ministry which are not duly considered.　And this it is
that is needed, — not generosity in the few, but con
sideration in the many, and the coöperation of all
If the institutions of the Gospel are worth having,
they are worth supporting.　If young men are expected to engage in a service that becomes every
year more perplexed and exacting, they must be able
to see a fair prospect of such remuneration and sym-

pathy as will at least set them free from worldly
anxiety. We believe that in no one way can the
ministry be more strengthened and elevated, than by
a consideration and provision, not extravagant, not
large, not perhaps proportioned to the labor and reward of other callings, but *sure;* and sufficient, while
it imposes the necessity of all the exertion, prudence,
simplicity, and sacrifice that should be expected and
be seen in the service of CHRIST, to save from all depression, and the necessity of other pursuits.

Is this a digression? No; for it entered into the
daily thought, and affected the life, not only of Henry
Ware, but equally of her whose life was his, and
whose spirit was always striving to allay his fears,
and nurse his powers and resources. Reluctantly
did she consent to his taking upon himself new bur-
dens and extended responsibilities, as he did in 1838,
when his father resigned to him his active duties,
by a liberal arrangement made for both of them.
" While this makes us very grateful," she writes, " it
involves more anxiety about health; but we will
trust."

Just at the time of these new offices and brighter
hopes on the one hand, and increased labor and
danger on the other, a heavy affliction fell upon them
both, in the sudden death of a sister; the first death
in thirty years of an adult member of that family,
from which six have since gone to the spirit-land.
Ought any considerations to prevent our giving to
others the Christian thoughts and high affections,
called forth from Mrs. Ware by that event? They
were many and comforting. Some she thus ex-

pressed to Mrs. Allen, a surviving sister. " The more I dwell upon what she was, of what she was capable, and how deeply she suffered from the mere load of humanity, the more I am thankful that the season of discipline is over, the more I rejoice at the thought of what she is now enjoying. Can we conceive of a higher bliss than that which must be experienced by a soul of such capacities as hers, which has struggled, as we believe, most strenuously with temptation both within and without while here, freed at last for ever from the burden of the flesh, throwing off all obstacles to its progress in a purer state, *bounding* forward to perfection? O, who would recall her here, even for the best happiness which this world could give her? But we are yet too earthly to part with our treasures without suffering. It is meant that we should suffer. It is a part, a most important object, of the dispensation; the inevitable consequence, too, of that which we esteem the best blessing of our existence, — our capacity for the exercise of the affections. It seems as if so great an event as I feel this to be must have great objects; and who can doubt that the improvement of those who suffer by it is the principal one? I have never felt this so deeply with regard to any event that ever happened to me in life. I have never had so loud, so imperious a call. O my God, give me grace to profit by this call, to be made better by the mental exercises to which it has given rise! "

At the end of 1838 we find Mary very happy, in gratitude for the past and cheerful hopes of the future, with sober but not sad thoughts of the recent sorrow.

" Cambridge, December 31, 1838.

" My dear N——:

" . . . . . O that blessed thing, Faith, — faith in the truth of friendship! Among other changes, I have not yet grown old enough to lose my youthful faith in those I love ; and between you and me, I begin to suspect that I never shall. I certainly do not find myself, at forty, one whit nearer misanthropy than I was at sixteen. Is this symptomatic of folly at the very core? Or is it only the effect of my superior good luck in life? Whatever it may be, I bless God for it, for I find in it too much happiness to be willing to regret it, even if it be a weakness.

" *January* 9. Just so far had I got, when I found my eyes so dim and my head so giddy that I was compelled to go to bed. And there have I been most of the time since, quite sick with one of my old attacks upon the lungs, which threatened to keep me there the rest of the winter, if it did not end in lung fever, so obstinate and violent was my cough. . . . . . I have been living in the past very much lately, from having many of Harriet's letters to read. Some of them, written in Exeter, have brought before my mind people of whom I had not thought for years; and circumstances having intimate connection with events in which I was immediately interested at the time, have unfolded a long and beautiful page of life before me, which I seldom have opportunity to recall. O that Past! what stores of wisdom and happiness are not laid up in it! Why should it be that the busy bustle of the Present hides it so much from our sight? Should we not, by an effort, give ourselves more to its retrospection, that we may profit more by its teaching? . . . . .

" But here we are, dear N., at the end of another year, certainly not growing younger, yet I think not at all losing our capacity for enjoying. So far from it, I am surprised to find, that, while with regard to some things my happiness becomes more and more every day a sober certainty, it does not in the least diminish my susceptibility of enjoyment from any new source that chances to present itself from day to day. In fact, it is a much more agreeable thing to grow old than I expected to find it. This is not strange, you may say, in my case, whose blessings increase with every year. Truly it is so, and I never felt it more than at this present. Never since I was married could I look back upon a year of such freedom from sickness in my own family; never was my husband so well for the same length of time in his preaching life; and if I had no more to be grateful for than my precious baby, who has been nothing but a comfort ever since she was born, that is enough for one year. One sad blight has passed over us, and it has indeed solemnized our hearts, and made us feel, as we never felt before, by how slight a tenure we hold all earthly blessings. But these afflictions serve to make us more grateful for those blessings which cannot be taken away.

"O, how I do wish you were within talking distance, that I might know whether you feel as I do about bringing up children. I have no comfort yet in my management of my little ones. I have not yet got upon the right track, and begin to think I never shall. Lucy comes and comforts me a little now and then, and if I had her power I should no doubt have her success; but that makes all the difference in the world.

"Yours ever, in true love,

"M. L. W."

Another year closed its record with similar expressions of thankfulness, though we see that it brought sickness and discipline. But these are not spoken of as trials; for Mrs. Ware appears in fact, as well as in word, to have caused sickness to change its name and its face. It had become to her a friend, whose absence she almost dreaded. "It is so long since I have had the slightest physical draw-back, that I had almost forgotten that I could be other than strong. I am glad to be reminded that I am not free from the common lot in this respect; in truth, that I am to be subject to the salutary disci-pline which the prospect of certain suffering and weakness, with all their possible consequences, brings to the soul." She had great faith in the relation of events to each other. She looked upon nothing in the providence of God as either accidental or insu-lated; every thing had a design and a connection. "If any one thing more than any other strikes me powerfully as I advance in life, gaining confirmation from every day's experience, it is the beautiful adap-tation of circumstances to accomplish the great ob-ject of existence, each succeeding event pointing to some end which the other events of life have not particularly aimed at. It seems as if we had only to keep our vision clear, to find around us all the teaching which we can possibly need to bring us to perfection." She had not much respect for the com-mon view of "circumstances," as securing all the good and accounting for all the evil in men's con-duct and character. To her mind, the responsibility was as great of turning adverse circumstances to good account, as of using well the most favoring and prosperous condition. Yet here she dealt more severely with herself than with any one else; too

severely sometimes, as may be the case with all conscientious sufferers who are at the same time conscientious workers.   They exact too much of their own
frames.   They make too little allowance for those
natural limits and occasional weaknesses, for which
many minds allow too much.   Most of us suffer the
body to be master, where it should be servant; while
they of whom we speak are apt to forget that the
body *will* sometimes rule, and affect the mind unfavorably yet helplessly.   There are various intimations, some of which we have seen already, that
Mrs. Ware was not free from all errors or dangers of
this kind, though she soon detected them.   After a
short visit to Mrs. Paine, in 1839, she says of it: " I
did enjoy my visit to you hugely; I do enjoy it now
even more; for I was fighting all the time with an
evil demon within in the shape of an uncommonly
violent attack of ' Mary Pickardism,' making me
feel that I might as well be out of the world as in it.
But that is over; and I have learnt from it that our
minds are more frequently under the control of our
physique, than we, in our pride, are very willing to
admit."

The season of exemption and favor continues;
not without qualifications and exceptions, as others
might think them, but without serious interruption
to the labors or joys of Mr. and Mrs. Ware.   And
we see the effect of it in the pleasant and playful
mood of the next letter.

" *Cambridge, January* 1, 1841, 1.20 *o'clock, A. M.*

" MY DEAR N——:

" There is some difference truly between a solitary spin

ster sitting in her quiet parlor with her desk before her, pen
in hand, without a shadow of a hope or fear of interruption
from any demand of domestic duty or pleasure, and the
mother of seven children, one of them a most agreeable
youth of six months, with a husband and nurse to boot, to
be looked after and taken care of. For instance, after a
vain attempt to get all the new year's presents finished
and arrayed in due order before the clock should strike
twelve upon the 31st of December, 1840, I was obliged at
the first date to content myself with just recording the
hour with one hand, while the other held in durance the
two hands of the above-named youth, who had been for the
previous hour exercising his utmost power of fascinating
blandishment to attract and monopolize my attention. And
now I must re-date, *One o'clock, P. M., January 3d*, being
my very first moment, since the aforesaid date, that I could
in conscience give to the luxurious employment of writing
to you. I think the said little (or, rather, large) gentleman
had a strong desire to write to you himself, or he would not
have been so remarkably wakeful upon that occasion; but
I chose to enact the part of the dog in the manger, — if I
could not do it myself, I would not let him. He is a most
bewitching creature, by the way, and there is no telling
what you may have lost by my selfishness. Nothing can
be sweeter than a healthy, bright child of his age; there is
certainly something far beyond the mere animal in the enjoyment we derive from such a creature. I am sometimes tempted, when I watch the animated expression of his
little visage, to go all lengths with the modern spiritualists,
and believe that there is a higher sense and fuller knowledge of the deep things of heaven inclosed in that little
casket now, than can be found in it after the wisdom of the
world has entered there. . . . . .

"O, how the business of life thickens as one goes on.
26

ward! I sometimes wish I knew whether there is ever to be such a thing as *rest* in this life for me, wherein to breathe a little more freely, and feel it right to forget, for a moment at least, the care of the earthly. Or I should like still better to know how far it is practicable to keep one's mind at ease, and yet do all that ought to be done. It does not seem as if it could have been intended that we should be the careworn drudges that most of us are, hardly giving ourselves time to enjoy the sight of the beautiful world around us, or know any thing of that within us. I have often great misgivings upon the subject, much doubting whether it is not, after all, more my bad management than the necessity of the case, which makes me so pressed from want of time to do what I wish. But I have looked around and within in vain for a remedy for the evil.

"I am just where I was a year ago, only a little more involved from having one child more, and that one that cannot be tended by any one who is not tolerably sizable herself. This is not as it should be, (not my baby, but my incessant occupation,) and I feel the evil effect upon my intellectual and physical too, — the one becomes utterly empty, the other too crowded. Thought is free, happily, but one uses up the material for thought if not refreshed by outward subjects occasionally ; or rather one's thoughts take too uniform a track, and become morbid. I should like to peep into some other person's mind and see how the land lies ; one is apt to think that no one is as wicked as himself, but perhaps the same causes lead to the same results. It would be a comfort to know, upon the old principle, that ' misery loves company.' Yours,

"MARY."

A change was approaching. The favored interval had been unusually long, and an amount of work had been accomplished of which we attempt not to give an idea. In had been to Mrs. Ware, as to her husband, a "golden age," in vigor, labor, and enjoyment. In the family, the school, and the community, both were busy, both happy. There was no diminution of care, rather an increase with an increasing family, unnumbered visitors, and interruptions, engagements, and claims, of every possible kind. But all this went on easily and naturally. A casual observer would not be likely to see that there was much done, or to be done. There was no hurry, no apparent exertion. Each caller or claimant was received so quietly, and listened to so patiently, that he might have thought he was the only one, or the favored. To be sure, Mrs. Ware felt, as we have seen, that there was no such thing as rest, nor time to do the half that she would. But very few saw the feeling, and it prevented neither her own serenity nor others' enjoyment. Very grateful did she feel for her husband's continued health and active usefulness. At the same time, we can see that her experienced eye and watchful heart discovered symptoms of coming change, — as in passages of her letters of different dates.

" *December* 31, 1841. I look at my husband with a sort of wonder, to find that another whole year has passed without any serious consequences to his health. I dare not look forward for him, for it seems presumption to expect that he can be long exempt. His duties are very perplexing from their variety, and I think the effect upon his system, by harassing his mind, is really worse than a greater amount of labor would be upon a more concentrated and satis-factory object. He is the greater part of the time in that dragging, half-sick state, which leaves neither freedom of mind nor comfort of body. I often think he could be happier, and do in fact more good, in a parish, than here; and were it not that men at his time of life get to be too old-fashioned and 'con-servative,' as the phrase is, to suit the rising genera-tion, I should hope he might yet end his days in the vocation which he best loves. I would not have you suspect me of a discontented spirit; but my heart leaps at the idea of parish-meetings in my own par-lor, and other *pastoreen* enjoyments. But I have no care about the future, other than that which one must have, — a desire to fulfil the duties which it may bring.

"*January* 16, 1842. I have been prevented by all sorts of things from finishing this; it is not worth while to enumerate them. I will only say, that for the last fortnight I have had little thought or time for any thing but preparing my husband for a six weeks' absence. Not that I had so very much to do for him (although it is a different thing to poor folks, to live where their clothes can be mended every day, or must go without mending for six weeks); but he has been very unwell lately, and I am so little accustomed to the idea of his going away sick with-out going with him, that I found it very hard to bring my mind to submit to it. I did not feel quite clear whether it would be right to let him go, in the hope that change of scene and occupation would do him good, or to prevent it from fear that the necessity

of the case would tempt him to exert himself, whether he was able or not.   However, he has gone;
and went too upon the anniversary of dear Dr. Fol-
len's loss.   But I have heard of his safe arrival in
pretty good case, and I hope for the best.   Yet I
am a very baby at the prospect of so long a separation.   Truly one's affections do not become blunted
by age, — do they ? "

What *her* affections were appears in the letter
which she had already written to her husband, —
written in fact the very night of the day he left her;
for her heart was full.   Its quick, keen sensibilities
told her that this was more than a common parting.
Seldom had Mr. Ware gone from home since they
were married, without being sick, or without her
going to him.   And though she had not the least
superstition, nor even indulged gloomy apprehensions, she held herself ready for the worst, and saw
reason at this time to expect some decided result
from such a journey in mid-winter, with all that had
preceded it.   Before she slept, therefore, she gave
utterance to the emotions — prayers and blessings
we might call them — which were yearning within
her.

"*Cambridge, January* 12, 1842, ½ *past* 11.

" DEAR HENRY : —

" And you are really gone ! And notwithstanding I have
looked forward to this moment for so long a time, and, as I
thought, realized over and over again all that I should feel
when it should arrive, I am ashamed to find how little all
my anticipations have prepared me for it. I do not mean
to overwhelm you with an outpouring of all my woman's

weakness, but I could not go to bed without saying, 'Good night to you, dearest.' I have a quiet faith that all is well with you, and I have much hope that this expedition will result in good to your mind and body both. I can say from my heart, 'God speed you!' And the thought that His care is over you reconciles me to having you withdrawn from mine, as nothing else could do. I feel that, in your absence, great responsibilities rest upon me, and I cannot therefore go to my solitary chamber for the first time without many solemn and affecting thoughts. But my hopes are bright, and my confidence unshaken; and I can send my mind forward with a cheerful trust, although the tear will come to my eye. So good night, again. I know your thoughts are with me, as mine with you, and that this union in the spirit can never cease, whatever may betide our outward being.

" *Friday Evening*, 14*th*. Thanks for your letter, — and many most grateful thanks to the Giver of all good for your safety! It could not be but that the recollection of the past should be present to our minds ; it was good that it should be so, and I trust it has not been without great blessing to our souls. For myself, I almost feared that I was a little superstitious, or rather inclined to forebode evil ; for I feel so much that we have been peculiarly blessed in having so many times had threatened evils averted, that, upon every new exposure, I find I am inclined to think it is presumption to expect exemption this time ; and I never felt this more strongly than now. I hope I have behaved well outwardly. I have tried to do so, but the struggle has been very great. This experience is a new lesson of trust and comfort for us. May it have its due influence !

" Farewell. Blessings be with you !

" M. L. WARE."

The result of the visit to New York is known. Mrs. Ware had not over-estimated the importance of the period. It was a crisis. The second Sunday of her husband's absence was the last time that he ever attempted to preach. He was attacked in the pulpit with bleeding, as he supposed from the lungs, and did not finish the service. It was the end of his career as a preacher, and the extinction of many bright hopes in those united minds and devoted hearts. For to Mrs. Ware, also, was this a disappointment of cherished purposes, not simply as his wife, but from her own fervid interest in the Christian ministry, and her sympathy with the aspirations and the struggles of those engaged, or about to engage, in this great work.

Her account of the change, and other changes that followed, closing the Cambridge life, may be best given in extracts from various letters, which will constitute a journal of the time.

"*March*, 1842. Mr. Ware had not been well for two months previous to his going to New York; no difficulty upon the lungs, — simply out of order from too close and wearisome attention to a vexatious variety of duty, having no rest, and not time enough to do any thing well. His system seemed disarranged, and he thought he should be most benefited by going away, changing the scene entirely, and obtaining rest to mind and body. He went. Every letter spoke of improvement, and I had made up my mind, that, in spite of all my fears, he was doing the best possible thing. So I said to his father on Sunday evening; and on Monday I received his letter, telling me of his having been taken in church with raising blood. Of course I went immediately to him, arriving at his lodgings at nine, Tuesday morning. The weather was very mild, and the uncertainty of its continuing so made me anxious to get him home. After some reluctance on the part of his physician had been overcome, we decided to return that day. So, after spending eight hours in New York, I turned my face homeward, and in forty hours after leaving my own door landed at it with my precious charge, none the worse for the journey. You may suppose it all seemed a dream to me. It was, however, a sad reality to him, a *very* sad disappointment. . . . . . Your picture of ' rest ' is a beautiful vision, — one which many of our friends have brought before our eyes at this time. But what can a man do, with seven children, and only his own hands to depend upon ?   I scruple not to say, that a ten-foot house, and bread and water diet, with the sense of rest to *him*, would be a luxury, and I trust some door will be opened to us by which we shall obtain it.   Now he is tied, bound hand and foot; and if he does not die in the bonds, it is more than any one has a right to calculate upon.   How various the trials of life! and how difficult always to feel that elasticity of spirit which is needful to make one as cheerful as we ought to be at all times!"

" *May* 1, 1842. You will hear in a few days of the change that has come to us. I have been entirely satisfied, ever since last October, that it must come to this, and I felt, the sooner Henry stopped, the better for him. But the utter uncertainty as to

the future support of such a large family, and a reluctance to leave his father's side in his declining
years, important as he is to his parent's comfort,
could not but make him deliberate. . . . . . And
now, dear Nancy, we are once more afloat on the
world's wide sea.   You will easily guess how much
there is of deep, soul-stirring emotion in all this, and.
how much more there must be before we quit for
ever our dearly loved home, rendered doubly dear by
the hours of sickness and sacred sorrow experienced
in it.   What will be our destination, I know not.
We have some plans, but the execution of any must
depend upon contingencies now hidden from us.
The first thing to be thought of is Mr. Ware's restoration to health; and had we the means, I should
like to spend a week or two in riding about home,
or in little excursions, giving him the opportunity of
doing what he could by conversation for the class
about to leave the School.   Should he ever get well,
there are some possible projects already presented
which would support us, but in the mean time all is
dark, — that is, we know nothing about it.   I am
satisfied that we have done *right,* and I am ready for
the consequences, be they what they may.   I am
not as strong as I once was to meet hard labor, but
I am willing to work to the extent of my ability ;
and I know that no amount of bodily labor can be
so wearisome as the mental struggle of the last two
years.   I feel as if I could meet any thing better
than seeing my husband declining; can he only be
spared, no matter what comes.   Do not think that
I am unmindful of the difficulties which poverty

brings, — the hindrances to the satisfactory education of children, the loss of intellectual privileges, and the wear and tear to the spirit by the uncertainties of daily supply for even the necessary wants of life. I understand it all; and I know that in all there is useful discipline for heaven, and I think for my children, that, if the means of one kind of education are denied them, they may in other ways gain the essentials for spiritual life more readily.   I cannot distrust or doubt the good providence of God under all circumstances; how can I, after the experience I have had in life? . . . . . If Mr. Ware and I should ride off anywhere, it will probably be towards Worcester.   O the money, the money! what can be done without money!   I have written to the end of my paper, and all about self; but I have much to say about other things."

" *May* 8, 1842.   I have tried in vain, dear Emma, to find time and ability to answer your kind notes, for I have longed to tell you something of the mighty movement which has been going on within our little domestic world, as well as to satisfy you of Mr. Ware's gradual progress towards health.   But for the first three weeks of his sickness, his case demanded my undivided attention; and since the day he wrote his letter of resignation, I have been, with the exception of three ' poor days,' sick myself.   Not made sick by that fact, I beg you to understand, — unless the reaction of relief from anxiety might make one sick, and the exhilaration consequent upon it act too powerfully upon the nervous system.   It is indeed an unspeakable relief to my mind, and I could see that it was also to Henry, for he began to improve at once when the deed was done. It is a great step, at our time of life, with so large a family, and so little substantial health in the acting portion of it, to be launched forth upon the wide world to obtain a support we know not how. But of what use is experience, of what value is faith, if they cannot enable one to meet the changes of life without fear? . . . . . I have been quite sick, having had a sudden and severe attack threatening fever. I felt for a little while as if I could *not* have one of my long sicknesses just at this juncture, as if I was for once too important a person to be laid upon the shelf, and I never was more truly thankful than when I found myself relieved by the first applications. I have not yet been down stairs, but expect to ride to-morrow, if it is pleasant. The breaking up will be severe, I know; but I think I am prepared for it. It is not the first time that the strong ties which bind me always to my *home* have been severed. And although I have never before felt so much that my home was indeed my own creation, the thought that it is *right* to leave it, and the oppression of spirit which the last two years have witnessed here, reconcile me to all the suffering in prospect. Don't think me a romancer, that I can feel joyous when I know not how we are to be fed and clothed. If God gives me strength, I am willing to work, and prefer that my children should be obliged to; and I have no fears but that, *if we do the best we can,* God will take care of us. He has many agents of mercy."

Mr. Ware was able to remain in office the rest of the theological term, and to carry through the graduating class, with whom his last exercises were deeply affecting. Very soon after this, in the summer of 1842, the family left Cambridge; having fixed upon Framingham, Mass., as their place of retreat, after looking at many places, and weighing all considerations of position and expense.

Of the last days in Cambridge, we have obtained the recollections of their oldest son, himself a member of the class just spoken of, as the last that enjoyed the instruction and benediction of his father. We give the account in his own unstudied words.

" That last summer was a very pleasant one, as I remember it. Things were very much as ever; if any thing, the little social gatherings of neighbors were more frequent, as all felt they must be few. The drives with father to find a place, the selection of Framingham, the pilgrimages there, occupied a good deal of the time, as also the gradual preparation, and the many adieus. The 'breaking up' was one of the gravest trials of mother's life. Thoroughly convinced of its necessity, looking forward to it as a relief in all ways, yet the whole summer was tinged by the thought of it. I remember long talks; one in particular, in which she drew nearer to me and I to her. I think that, feeling obliged to keep up before father, she yearned to confide in us. When it came to the last, it was hard. The children and all were gone. Mother, father, and I were left, and I was to be left, for I was just going into the world myself. The wagon was at the door

Father got in, merely wringing my hand, but most deeply moved. I could see it and feel it. If he had spoken, it would have been more than he could bear. I never till that moment imagined, so feverish had been his desire to get away, how much his heart was in that spot. Mother was behind, and had got down one step, when she turned round and threw her arms about my neck, and there we stood. It was one of the *moments* of life. 'God bless you, my child!' I have heard her say it many times, but it never meant more. Father could not bear it. He urged her away; the horse started at his quick word; I was alone, — and that chapter of life was ended! We never all three of us entered Cambridge together again, until the night that mother and I brought with us from Framingham 'the last of earth.'

"Since writing this, I have chanced upon father's first letter afterward. He says: 'The struggle at the last moment was a hard one; but we got composed after a while, and then found ourselves excessively overcome with weariness.'"

XII.

LIFE IN FRAMINGHAM.

It is no cause of regret that the narrative of a married woman's life cannot be separated from that of her husband. The biographer may regret the necessity of referring to familiar facts, and sometimes using materials already in possession of the public. But more sorry should we be if the history of the *wife* could be drawn out by itself; especially that history of every-day life, and idea of the inner being, which we are attempting to give. Few women, in our community, and with "troops of friends," have been more thrown upon themselves at an early age, or have led a more truly single life until life's meridian, than did Mary Pickard. But the moment she became Mary Ware she lived for another, — as unreservedly and devotedly as woman ever did. Principle and affection alone would have prompted this, as a pleasure; the circumstances in which she was placed, from first to .a*: made it a duty, and still a delight. And mo: and more, as years passed, did the duty and the delight grow, tinged only by the sad thought of *his* premature failure and sore disappointment.

It is a small trial to be summoned from one sphere of duty to another; even if it cost the disruption of many ties, still if it be a call of duty, with continued power of activity and usefulness, it is not to be called a hardship. It surely is no evil, but rather a privilege, for the faithful laborer to die at his post, with his harness on. But to die and yet to live, to have one's chosen work broken off for ever, and the strong, disinterested love of labor forbidden all exercise, with the prospect of years of helplessness at the best, perhaps protracted suffering and a dependent family, — this is trial, calling for as much of fortitude and faith as humanity often requires. It may be partiality which leads us to doubt whether there was ever *more* of fortitude and faith, in similar condition, than in the hearts of Henry and Mary Ware, as they turned their back upon the fond scenes of their labor, and, with the unavoidable consciousness of high qualification as well as affection, withdrew from all public service and peculiar trust. Nor is it too much to assume, that, while on him pressed most heavily the burden of responsibility and the grief of incapacity, it was to the wife and the mother that there came most loudly the call for exertion, for cheerful courage, a wise diligence, and unfaltering trust.

The village to which they retired was chosen partly for its seclusion combined with convenience, and partly for economy. In relation to the last, their anxieties were now relieved by a generous contribution from friends, whom it would have been wrong to refuse; though similar offers had been made and declined before, as we ought to have said in referring to their embarrassments. So long as there was the power of exertion, or a reasonable hope of it, Mr. Ware could not bring himself to accept any mere favors of this kind, — seldom so grateful as a fair requital for willing service and acknowledged ability. But now that the power of exertion was suspended, duty to those nearest, as well as gratitude to persevering benefactors, made him more than willing. " I have got rid, through the kindness of excellent friends, of all distressful anxiety for the living of my family; I can leave them in comparative peace; in that sense, my house is set in order." Thus did Mr. Ware write to his brother John, in that earnest letter in which he begs him, as a physician, to deal frankly with him, and tell him the whole truth as to the probability of his recovery or decline. And this was the state of mind in which the life at Framingham began, and continued to the end, — a state of suspense, entire uncertainty, unwillingness to be idle, but inability to enter confidently upon any plan, or engage vigorously in any employment. There is little, therefore, to be told of this period, in regard to occupation or incident. We can only show in what spirit Mrs. Ware met this new trial, — to many minds the hardest of all, — living without an object, yet striving to live cheerfully, busily, and profitably.

This may be shown best by giving brief extracts from her letters, written during the first season of their residence there.

" *July* 30, 1842. My dear Mrs. F——: You will be glad to know that we find ourselves very comfortable here. The house is exceedingly well adapted to our purpose; and though the externals of life are comparatively small matters with respect to happiness, in health, there are cases of sickness in which they must be of importance. It is a great comfort to me, in the present case, that our outward appliances are such as will aid the chief object for which we have made this change. I feel deeply that it is an experiment, and, like all human plans, has some disadvantages; but I will 'hope on, hope ever,' believing as I do that it was *right* to try it. Yet you know (none better) how much one has to feel in the detail of life, when so much is at stake. O, why can we not, with full faith and perfect peace, cast all our care upon Him, who indeed careth for us more than we can care for any being? I can for the most part feel this, but it is not easy to keep always on the mount...... Although I realize the change, and fully appreciate all I have left behind, I am perfectly amazed to find how obtuse my feelings are. I could almost fancy I did not love my friends as well as I thought I did, so entirely do I find myself absorbed by my new duties and occupations, with scarcely a thought for any thing but the best accomplishment of my immediate business, — my husband's comfort and improvement. What a blessed power of adaptation is given us, to enable us to meet the varieties of life! The fact is, in our case, never could so great a movement have been made under more favorable circumstances; and, with so many blessings about our path, it would be strange indeed if we could find place for regret."

"*August* 21, 1842. My dear N——: 1 begin to

27 *

think I shall not gain much in the way of *leisure* by this change. For although there is not the same necessity for attending to extraneous matters that there was in Cambridge, so much more of the detail of affairs necessarily passes through my hands, that I find the days all too short to accomplish half I should like to do. I cannot give up the hope, and indeed expectation, that the mode of life we have adopted will prove good for Mr. Ware; and as I view it nearer, so many of what I had anticipated as hindrances vanish into thin air, that I am more than ever satisfied with the form of the experiment. Of course, I expect to put my shoulder to the daily wheel in a new line of labor, and have fully calculated the cost. I only hope my health and strength will continue as good as they now are, and I shall do very well. I never shrink from labor of any kind. . . . . . Our children are much pleased with the place and its occu pations; and I hope to give them by the change the opportunity of acquiring the knowledge of many things, and exercising some of the virtues for which they had no chance in their former mode of life. . . . . . I have a treasure of a woman, who has been with me nearly two years, bound to me and mine by the strongest affection, kind, capable, and refined; particularly pleased with being 'monarch of all she surveys' in the kitchen, and so well informed and respectful, that it is a pleasure to me to associate with her as I am obliged to in work, and a comfort in the perfect security I feel in her intercourse with my children. It is not the least of my blessings, that just such an one should have been with me at this crisis."

This mention of the faithful domestic, "our Margaret," as she was always called, who lived with Mrs. Ware seven years, discloses another trait of character, more rare than it should be. The complaints that we constantly hear of the selfishness and "plague of servants," demand more consideration than they usually receive. The whole matter of domestic service is becoming a serious one. Even where it is wholly free, it affects materially the comfort of life, and exerts an influence on the character of both the employers and the employed. Are the employers or the employed most in fault? This is the one question which should be deliberately weighed, instead of being dismissed with a burst of passion or a smile of self-complacency. There are women who have little or no trouble with their servants, — who retain them long, secure their confidence for life, obtain from them better service than many who pay more and exact more, and repose in them the most important trusts. To this class we believe Mrs. Ware to have belonged. And the secret of her success we suppose to have been simply this: she looked upon servants as of the same species with herself; creatures of like passions and like sensibilities; as liable to be selfish, unreasonable, and easily offended, as those whom they serve, but not more; having equal claim upon kind consideration, and a perfect *right* to feel wounded and wronged, if dealt with unjustly. On this subject Mrs. Ware seems to have asked herself these two questions: Why do so many people, who are never harsh or ill-natured toward any one else, think nothing of being harsh and ill-natured toward their domestics? And why do many sound and zealous religionists forget to carry any of their religion into their intercourse and dealings with servants? It would not have been easy, we think, to discern any difference in *her* treatment of the highest and the lowest, the affluent and the dependent. Nor did she think it her duty to visit iniquity even upon the vicious, by withdrawing from them all confidence, and turning them into the streets to sin and suffer more. Not in words alone, or of one sex only, has she said, as we find her saying in an aggravated case: " I see not why a man's sins should for ever cut him off from the charities of his kind, if he is truly penitent. What are we that we should condemn, if God forgives? "

In continuing our extracts from Mrs. Ware's letters at this period, we shall draw freely from those which she wrote to the son who had been left in Cambridge, and was now entering upon the work of the ministry, feeling painfully the separation from his father, and the loss in part of his guidance and counsel.

" *Framingham, August,* 1842. At last, dear John, the great crisis has passed, the great movement is made. We have changed our home, and are no longer to live together under the same circumstances. The change is indeed great to us all, but I feel that for you it is greater than to any one else, and therefore it is that I am impelled to use my first quiet moment in expressing my deep sense of the trial of your present position, and most heartily sympathize with the soul-stirring emotion which belongs to it. To you it is indeed a very important turning-point in existence, and when one looks only upon the momentous responsibilities which it involves, it is not strange that the heart should sink, and the question should involuntarily arise to one's lips, ' How can this change be borne, how can such duties be met?' I have felt sometimes, in looking at the singular combination of events, by which you should be separated from your father, just when you were commencing the most trying and important period of life, as if it were almost too hard; and as if it would have been not only easier, but safer, to have been able to feel your way a little before you absolutely floated off under your own sole guidance. But a second thought has always satisfied me that the arrangement of Providence was the best, although for the time the most painful. Standing forth in your lot, as an ambassador for Christ to the world, you cannot be too soon led to rely solely on his teaching for direction, and it cannot but be best that you should be compelled, by the removal of earthly succor, to go only to Him who is ' the way, the truth, and the life,' for strength in the hour of need."

" My dear John: You are now passing through that ordeal which I have long looked forward to as inevitable at some period, sometimes with an almost irresistible desire to avert it by opening to you pages of my own painful experience in self-education; sometimes with an uncontrollable impatience to hasten it, that, being past, you and I and all might be enjoying the happiness it might produce. It is one of the most difficult questions to decide how far, and when, to make opportunities, or wait for them to come in the natural order of things; we should very decidedly wait, if we were sure they would come at some time, — but there is the rub. . . . . .

" It is a common and very natural idea with young people, that older ones cannot understand or sympathize in their feelings; forgetting that we have all been young, and that the struggles by which the soul is exercised in youth are never to be forgotten. The experience of different natural characters of course varies, but the fact of struggle is common to all. And upon no spot in the review of the past does one's memory dwell with so much intense emotion, as upon that thorny and tangled labyrinth through which the spirit wandered, 'bewildered, but not lost,' at the period when the necessity and duty of proving its own character first roused it to a sense of its responsibilities. You say most truly, that it is good to look at things at a distance, from new and various points of view. I have always advocated this, for my own changeful life forced the conviction upon me; and for the same reason, I would advocate free, confidential discussion of inward and spiritual experience. The mere clothing our thoughts and feelings in words sometimes places them in a different position. We take them out of the atmosphere of our own perhaps morbid fears and anxieties, and can therefore see them more clearly. Then, too, we have the advantage of another's observation, and, may-be, experience of the selfsame difficulties, to aid us in our judgment of their true character.

At any rate, we have the certainty of that warm kindling of the affections which to a loving heart is always a help in bearing the burden of life. Believe me, dear John, there is ample reward for all the effort it may cost in unclothing ourselves, in the consciousness that however the outer world may think of us, at *home*, in that sanctuary which God and nature have alike appointed as the best resting-place for the spirit upon earth, we are understood and appreciated and loved. Let us not suffer any factitious thoughts or circumstances to cheat us of this privilege, but with trusting, confiding hearts take the good which Heaven designed for us when the family-community was established in the world. . . . . . I could write more than I should care to give you the trouble to read, if I attempted to write half that I have in my heart to say."

" *December*, 1842. The going forth into the world for the first time *alone* is, it seems to me, the most trying point in the existence of any one of any sensibility. But does not the very difficulty of the case indicate the value of the experience? Are not almost all the most valuable results of effort those which require the greatest efforts for their attainment? The higher the summit to which we would arrive, the more toilsome must be the ascent. When by a prayerful, self-surrendering spirit we have sought to learn the will of God concerning us, shall we not believe that, into whatsoever path we may be led, it must contain for us the discipline we need, — treasures of experience, hidden perhaps at first, which will amply repay any toil, any suffering, in the aid we shall derive from them in our Christian progress? ..... We admire, we reverence, the spirit which actuated Oberlin and Felix Neff, and many others of the class of missionary spirits who have left all to do their Master's work in the field he has appointed for them; but we do not easily realize how much of the same spirit of self-sacrifice is called for ir what no one would think of calling missionary ground, and which yet requires as much surrender of earthly desire as their situations could, which none but the All-seeing can know."

An event which all felt, at this time, was felt by none more than by Mrs. Ware. We mean the death of Dr. Channing. The reader will remember how much he had done for her in early life, not only as a public teacher, but as a private friend, with whom her intercourse had been frequent and perfectly free. For several years she had seen little of him. And now, in her seclusion and comparative solitude, the unexpected intelligence of his death moved her deeply. To a friend in Cambridge, she writes: " You cannot imagine how trying it is to me, to know nothing of Dr. Channing's sickness and death, except what the newspapers can tell me. You know not the peculiar relation in which I have stood towards him. Do in pity tell me what you know about the event. I cannot realize it, I can scarcely believe it. There is so much to be thought of in relation to such an event, that my mind is perfectly bewildered. I cannot arrange my thoughts enough to give them utterance. But my heart goes out toward those many dear friends who will feel his loss as I do.

One is tempted to say, ' What a loss to the world is the death of such a man!' But such a man cannot die. How will his words have new power over the hearts of those who read them, from the consciousness that the spirit that uttered them already sees behind the veil, that his light can never be put out, but will penetrate still more and more the inmost recesses of men's souls! How will that last eloquent, touching appeal for the Slave gain access to the coldest hearts, when it is remembered that it was the last effort of the departing saint for the rights and sufferings of the oppressed! The impulse which such a mind gives must be felt for ever. Who can measure its power?" A fact is here suggested which there seems no reason for withholding, showing the estimate which Dr. Channing himself put upon the character and power of Mrs. Ware. A lady intimate with both of them when they were most together, says: " Dr. Channing talked with her on religious experience, to learn as well as to teach. I have known him to request her to make visits of instruction to a disconsolate person, whom *he* could not awaken to religious hope, — trusting that her gentle sympathy and clear views might shed a ray of light that would point her to the day."

The first season at Framingham was a busy one though tranquil. Mrs. Ware's bodily as well as mental labor must have been unusually great. " It is true, I do not see how we are to set all the stitches which will be necessary to prepare eight people for a winter campaign in a cold house; but I have faith that we shall find a way." They were

28

much more free from interruptions than ever before. Their new neighbors and friends were not only kind, but considerate,—one of the best forms of kindness. Gratefully does Mrs. Ware acknowledge this " How much there is in human life to interest our hearts! One cannot go anywhere without finding some cases of peculiar interest. We are here cut off from general knowledge of those around us, by having come expressly for retirement. Our neighbors, understanding this, do not call. And yet we have already happened upon some most interesting people, from whom we cannot in conscience hold back."

Thus the year closed; a year of as great outward change as any that had preceded it, and leaving them in as great uncertainty as to the future. Yet Mrs. Ware could say: " The prevailing emotion in the retrospect is one of gratitude at having been enabled to escape from the burden which before oppressed and weighed me down. The consciousness that we were spending all our strength, mental and physical, upon a vain attempt for an unattainable result, was worse to me than any degree of labor for an attainable end, or even any uncertainty about the future means of support. I rejoice that my husband is free from that incubus upon his spirits; and still more do I rejoice, that it is given to us both to feel, in the uncertainty that lies before us, such a tranquil trust that all will be well, that we have no fear, no wish. Still there is room for much mental and spiritual discipline; and I must acknowledge that there are times when the weakness of the flesh overcomes the willingness of the spirit, and I feel for the time entirely depressed by a sense of inadequacy to meet the demands of duty. I have not the power to do all that ought to be done, and I feel as if the effects of my incapacity would be grievous. I know that one has no *right* to suffer from this, because we ought to have faith to believe that the trials even of our own insufficiency are designed to accomplish some end. But the consciousness that others are suffering from our deficiencies is just the very hardest thing to bear in life. It is my cross, and always has been; and I fear I do not learn as I ought, to bear it in meekness and humility,— I need not say 'fear,' I *know* I do not."

To those familiar with the life of Henry Ware, and with its close, it is unnecessary to recount the events of the year 1843; the year that brought into stern requisition all the trust and endurance of a devoted wife. She had long seen that this trial was approaching, and had fortified herself to meet it, not by putting the thought of it aside, but by keeping it before her, and making it familiar, that it might never take her by surprise. And long had she thus disciplined her mind and her affections. For during the sixteen years that she had lived with Mr. Ware, she could never, for any long time, have failed to see the great precariousness of his hold on life. At this very period, she says: " In such alternation of hope and fear do I live, and indeed have lived for the greater part of my married life." Yet how much had she enjoyed life! and what an amount of happiness, labor, and usefulness had she *extorted* — if we may use the word in a grateful sense, as she would — from every year and every position!

In the spring of 1843 she accompanied her husband to Boston, for a short visit at his brother's; and there occurred that severe and alarming illness, which confined Mr. Ware for ten weeks, and from the effects of which he never recovered. Of this attack, and of all that intervened until his death, we will not give the particulars, but would only trace Mrs. Ware's own thoughts and feelings, as she expressed them from time to time in letters and fragments of letters to those most concerned.

" *Boston, Thursday, May* 11. Since writing to you, dear N——, I have had a season of intense anxiety. Sunday, Monday, and Tuesday, Mr. Ware suffered extremely, and it was not clear what was the nature of the difficulty that produced this suffering; one thing only was certain, — that he was very sick, and too weak to bear such distress long. It must be a long time before he is free from the effects of it, even if he have strength to hold out. So end my hopes for the present, and I must give up all thought about any thing but the care of my husband, for I know not how long. God's will be done! He must know what is best, — but it is not easy to understand how it is so in this case. And if it were easy, where would be room for Faith? . . . . . These are trying, but blessed days, for the cultivation of the spirit of faith and trust; and I know I need much to make me feel that this is *not* my home. God grant that I may effectually learn it, so as to be not only willing, but glad, to give up all that belongs to me here, confident in the prospect of a reunion in a better state! I shall write again if I can, but I have few minutes unoccupied."

Boston, May, 1843. My dear child: Father continued very much as you left him, yesterday. He does not suffer as much as he did, but his disease is a very tedious one, and it may be many weeks before he is able to get home, if it pleases God still to restore him to health. Let us pray to Him to look in mercy upon us, and spare him to us yet longer. The circumstances of our lot in life are just now very trying, and no doubt are arranged for us in order to our improvement. It is a great trial to father and me to be separated from our children so long; and to you all, this separation brings the greater responsibility to watch over yourselves, that you do in all things right, — not what is most pleasant, not what we wish, but what is *right* to do, without regard to self. Next to my anxiety about father, now, is my anxiety about you; because I feel that you are at an age when the habits are formed, and the principles of action settled for life; that your whole future, for time and for eternity, may depend upon these years. And I cannot feel happy unless I see you gaining from day to day more and more of that self-discipline and self-control, which can alone, by the grace of God, make you what you ought to be."

Mr. Ware was able to return to Framingham in June, and afterward took several short journeys among friends, one as far as Plymouth, and thence to Fall River (where his son was then settled in the ministry), and home by Providence, — his last visit to those places. In August, another and still more violent attack upon the brain prostrated him completely; and the remaining five or six weeks of his

life seemed only a vacillation between earth and
heaven, — yielding transporting glimpses of the latter, but constantly drawing him back to the former,
— and creating altogether as hard a trial for the sufferer, and those around him, as can easily be conceived.

"*August* 17. We feel, in father's case, 'how
vain is the help of man.' His system is so delicate,
that he cannot bear the administration of any potent
means. Our reliance must be upon our Heavenly
Parent, in whose hand are the issues of life and
death. Let us pray to Him, that, if it be consistent
with his wisdom, this cup may pass from us; but
let us be ready to say, and feel in our inmost hearts,
'Not my will, but thine, O Lord, be done!' . . . . .
We do not feel it to be impossible that dear father
should recover from this illness; but we know that
his repeated sicknesses must have weakened his
power of reaction, and we strive, therefore, to be prepared for any result. The very uncertainty is appointed for our good; let us use it, my dear child,
for our spiritual advancement. . . . . . God bless you!
be submissive, be patient, be *grateful*, if it so please
God that dear father should be released from the
burden of his earthly house, to be transported to his
heavenly home, where there is no more pain."

"*August* 21. It is all in the hands of Infinite Love
and Wisdom. God will order all well; let us be
willing and be thankful to place our trust in Him.
What a mercy it is to us, that He has not given us
the power of foreknowledge! But whatever may
be the event, let us not lose the benefit of this disci-

pline to our souls; let us strive to increase our faith
in God's goodness, our trust in his love. . . . . . I cannot write much, for I cannot leave father many minutes at a time, — and all the time I can get, I am
bound to devote to sleep."

" *August* 23. . . . . . Thus you see we are vibrating
between hope and fear. But it is a question whether
we have a right to allow either; for we know not
what is best for him or for ourselves."

" *August* 29. My dear Emma: I must say a few
words to you, to thank you for your most welcome
letter received yesterday. How much I have longed
for some intercourse with you, during the last two
months, you can judge better by your own experience now, than by any words of mine. I have
wished, as you do now, to know all that was passing
within the deep fountains of your spiritual life, and
nothing but the absolute necessity of the case has
kept me away from you. Now, I say, come, whenever you can; you will be most welcome to us all,
and to me your presence will be a real benediction.
I feel at times as if I should be overpowered by the
tumult of feelings to which I dare not give utterance
here, where the composure of all around me depends
so much upon my calmness. This last fortnight has
shaken to its very foundation the whole fabric of my
spiritual being, — thank God! not to displace a single fibre of the fabric. But there has been such a
heaving up of all that was hidden in the depths of
past experience, as has wellnigh conquered at times
my self-control, and I have felt that I must utter myself, or be lost; yet to no one have I dared to speak.

John's sickness here has made composure with him peculiarly important...... Happily, we cannot lift the veil of the future; we can only be ready for whatever may be in store for us, and this I trust we are...... I have been prevented from writing in the daytime, and now, at eleven o'clock, I am compelled by weariness to shut my eyes, and rest."

"*August* 30. My dear Lucy: I should indeed rejoice if you were able to be here, for I long for some communion with one who could so enter into all my views and feelings at this time as I know you would. But I bow in submission to all the discipline which God appoints for me...... In some respects the bitterness of the stroke has passed. I felt that the real separation came with the conviction, that that mind with which my spirit had so long communed in the truest sympathy was clouded for the remainder of its sojourn in the body. The sense of solitude, of isolation, I had almost said *desolation*, was for a time nearly overpowering; and there are moments when life looks so like a blank, that it is not easy to restrain the wish to go too. But the necessity of calmness for the children's sake, feeling that their state of mind would inevitably be influenced by the tone I should give it, has aided me in preserving a quiet exterior; and so we have had the great comfort of peace and entire freedom from agitation and excitement. God give us strength to preserve it! But this weary waiting from day to day, alternately hoping and feeling that there is no reason to hope, wears upon the nerves, — the days seem interminable, and the nights ages...... Long as I have looked forward to this change, it seems like a dream from which I must awake, — as if it could not be! No wonder; — for fifteen years, his health, *he* indeed, has been the first, almost the sole, object of my life. It will be long before I can turn even to my children, with the consciousness that they can now be attended to without neglecting him."

The struggle was over. Henry Ware died, at Framingham, on Friday morning, September 22. A Sunday intervened before the body was removed for burial, and that day Mrs. Ware went, with her children, morning and afternoon, to their accustomed place of worship; desiring it for their own sacred communion, and believing it most in accordance with *his* feelings. To her faith, with her habitual view of duty and death, this was probably no effort. To many it would be impossible, even with the same faith; for, unhappily, association and custom are allowed to check our highest aspirations in the holiest seasons, so that many would consider such an effort unnatural and strange. Is it not more strange, that it should ever seem unnatural for a Christian mourner to go to the house of God, in the most solemn hours of life, — especially when that house is completely identified with the life and image of the departed? Mrs. Ware was grateful also for the power of associating the idea of Death, in the minds of her children, not with restraint and gloom, but with the place of prayer and praise, and the cheerful presence of devout worshippers. It was a beautiful exemplification of her high trust, in harmony with her whole character. We honor the principle, and thank her for the act.

True, it was an altered and saddened house to which they returned, yet saddened by no gloomy aspect, disturbed by no busy preparation. There was less than usual of care and hurry, instead of more. "It was a holy season," says one of the daughters, "those days after dear father left us; no bustle, no preparation of dress, no work done but what was absolutely necessary; it was like a continued Sabbath." Then, on Sabbath evening, after a simple religious service, the "precious remains" of the husband and father were taken in their own carriage, by the wife and eldest son, to Cambridge; where, the next day, the more public ceremony of interment took place.

But of this whole experience it is right to let Mrs. Ware speak in her own letters, several of which we add. The first was written the day after the funeral, to an absent child, and the others to different friends after her return to Framingham. We take them from among many written at that time, either in answer to offers of sympathy, or as a relief to a burdened heart. Of necessity, they contain some repetitions of the same thought, in similar language; but it is best to give them as they are, that we may see in them how great was the bereavement and how deep the anguish of one whose countenance was always cheerful.

" Cambridge, September 26, 1843.

" My dear Child : —

" I use my first moment of repose to write to you, for I

know you will long to hear what we have been doing, and as far as possible to enter into all our thoughts and feelings. I want to have you know all that has taken place since you left us, and shall therefore send you a minute detail of every day, when I shall have time to write it; but now so much is pressing upon me which demands attention, so many duties which must not be neglected, and which belong to this time, and must be performed at once, that I confine myself to the last two days.

"After dear father's death, I told Uncle John that I wished all arrangements with regard to his funeral should be made in accordance with grandfather's feelings; and I gave it wholly into his hands to arrange. He came up again on Saturday, and it was decided that we should come to grandfather's on Monday morning, and have a service at his house. On Sunday we all went to meeting; we felt it was good to go to the house of God, and find peace to our troubled souls in the act of worship. About six in the evening Mr. and Mrs. Barry came to us, for I felt that I could not have father's body leave that house without

'the voice of prayer at the sable bier,
A voice to sustain, to soothe, and to cheer.'

He read to us some passages of Scripture, and offered for us and with us a prayer to Him who alone could give us strength, that he would aid us in that trying hour. We had no one with us except Mr. and Mrs. W——, whose kindness was most valuable to us during the last days of father's life.

"Then John and I brought dear father's body to Cambridge in our own carriage; we could not feel willing to let strangers do any thing in connection with him which we could do ourselves. We reached here about half past ten, having had a season of precious intercourse upon our way. We found that, in accordance with the wishes of the College Faculty, it had been decided that we should go to the College Chapel, for the service, at half past three on Monday.

"On Monday morning the rest of the family came down, and all the aunts and uncles, so that grandfather had all his children with him. At three o'clock we went to the Chapel. The students attended in their places, and the pews in the gallery were devoted to us. The service commenced by a voluntary, and the anthem, 'The Lord is my shepherd.' Dr. Francis prayed; Dr. Noyes read some passages from Scripture; then was sung the 463d hymn. Dr. Parkman then prayed for us, in his most touching, heartfelt manner, — so elevating, so soothing, so full of faith, gratitude, and hope, that it subdued all earthly emotion and took away all earthly desire. Although very minute and personal, it seemed as if one might have listened for ever without a thought of self. He loved father most sincerely, and all he said came from the depths of his heart. I had shrunk from the thought of publicity at such a time, in such a connection, but I found that the circumstances about me were wholly lost sight of; it made no difference to me where I was, or who was near me. I felt raised above all minor considerations. The services closed with 'Unveil thy bosom, faithful tomb!' We all went to Mount Auburn; that is, all the family, even grandfather and dear little Charlie. The weather was misty, but the light which it threw around was in keeping with the occasion, and I thought I never had seen the place look more beautiful. One only thing I wanted which I could not have, — the sound of the holy hymn at the consecrated spot.

"Father was laid in Mr. Farrar's tomb, — the first inhabitant; and I felt, as I looked once more upon him as he rested there, that it was indeed but his body from which we were to be separated; his spirit is still, and will ever be, with us. He seems to me nearer to-day than he has for many weeks, and the thought of his freedom from the burden of the weary flesh is sweet indeed."

" *Framingham, September 29, 1843.*

" MY DEAR EMMA : —

" I cannot write you more than a few words, I am so much pressed on all sides by matters which cannot be put off; but I must say these few, to assure you of the peace and repose which are with us, and have been, I may say, ever since you were here. O that you had been with us longer, — that you could have been with me at that still hour when the spirit was freed from its prison-house, the weary body left to its rest ! And it was rest. Could you have seen the very ' rapture of repose ' depicted upon that face, which had so long been disturbed by the pressure of disease that its very expression had been changed to a character foreign to the whole man ! All continued of the same peaceful character which pervaded our atmosphere when you were here, with the exception of a few days of a little temporary uneasiness about the time C—— R—— was here. And the last fatal attack, coming as it did at a moment of rather unusual brightness, was so sudden and so soon over, that there was no time for change. Dear little Charlie, who had just returned, was at the moment bounding, in the height of his joyous spirits, from one side of the bed to the other, exclaiming, ' Sall I buss the flies off you, father ? ' He was taken at once to bed ; and when he came down in the morning he found his dear father lying just as he had left him the night before, looking only more peaceful, more beautiful, and he took up the same thought, — ' Sall I buss the flies off father, now he has gone to heaven ? ' I felt it a peculiar blessing, that all the circumstances of the event were such as to make any movement or change in any external respect unnecessary, so that the children might have their first associations with the fact of death without any horror, and their recollection of their father uninterrupted by any repulsive details. He lay in his bed just as he had when talking with them, until he was removed from the house, and that process the little ones did not witness. I doubt not it will give a tone to their view of the subject through life. But why should I dwell upon these externals? Simply that you may dismiss from your mind any thoughts of distress connected with us at that moment; and you know all that I can tell you of the spirit *within.*

"You know how I have suffered in anticipation of this separation, but all the worst agony connected with it is yet to come. It is comparatively easy now to be calm and firm and thankful; the first thought cannot but be of him and his present happiness; and the sense of relief that the sufferings of that blessed being are over, that he has gone to his Father's home, 'to the house of his rest,' is so great, that no other thought dare intrude. I long to see you, and hope to do so soon. I go to Cambridge to-morrow, to be in Boston on Sunday. I could not deny myself the luxury of going once more to that house of his religious affections, in connection with him. That spot has most sacred, most tender associations to me, so full that it would be enough to sit there in silent meditation; and if I feared any thing, I should fear that it would be too overwhelming to be borne, to go there in public. But I have found by my experience on Monday, that the surroundings of such a moment are of no consequence. I have a quiet faith that the strength will come. O, may improvement, elevation, come also! . . . . . John leaves us soon. He and I had a holy season, as we went, in the stillness of the night, to carry those precious remains to Cambridge.

"I find it is as I anticipated,—I feel a greater nearness to my husband than I did when he lay on his couch in the next room. I am separated from that *form;* I look back to it only as the associate of the spirit in health; I do not cling to it now. Yours in all love.

"M. L. W."

"Framingham, October 6, 1843.

" My dear Mary : —

" The first moment I can call my own since my return from Cambridge, I turn to you. I know no one to whom I can so freely pour out all that is in my heart, as for the first time I pause a little from the pressure of necessary action, and realize the change that has taken place in every thing about me. . . . . . I wanted you at my side, when I stood once more at that sacred spot where we had laid our dear sister's image. You and I can never forget that moment. And, though not near, you were in close communion with the spirit in that holy hour.

" As I glance back at the period which has elapsed since you were here, one single thought takes precedence of all the rest. It is astonishment at the power of the soul to sustain the pressure of circumstances, the tension and excitement of feeling, the necessity of positive, energetic action, when the very heart-strings seem riven asunder, — and the capacity of sustaining a tranquil, and even cheerful aspect, when ' the dull, heart-sinking weight' of a vital grief is bearing us down, down, down, — one can scarcely believe there are any soundings to that *deep* gulf. Yet so it is; and does it not open our vision to the glorious truth of the alliance of the soul with its divine origin? What but that inexhaustible fountain of strength could sustain us, when the waves of trouble thus threaten to overwhelm us? Rich, blessed, indeed, is the experience which brings this conviction to our minds ; holy is that season in which we can live as it were in the light of such a faith ! And holy indeed has it been to me.

" I feel that my danger now is, that I reluctantly do any thing that shall remove me from the influence of the atmosphere which it seems as if death had created around me. Death ? transition I would rather call it. And yet let us

strive to disabuse that word of some of the horrors in which
education has wrapt it.   O, could you have seen how mercifully it was stripped of all its terrors to us, how calmly
that spirit left its earthly tabernacle, how sweet was the impress of peace and rest it left upon that face which had so
long almost lost its own expression in the veil that sickness had thrown over it!   Its last expression would have
rebuked the slightest wish to recall the spirit, had we been
so selfish as to have indulged one.   We could scarcely be
willing to be separated from that image of him we loved,
so powerfully even in death did it express his character.
Even the little children preferred being there, rather than
anywhere beside; and will, I think, all, including even
little Charlie, remember this first knowledge of a death-bed
as a beautiful experience.

"The first part of Henry's sickness he seemed quite
unconscious of what was around him; torpid, and at times
wandering in his expressions.   But the last three weeks, although still unable to exert himself to talk, — for it tired him,
he said, 'even to think,' — his mind was perfectly clear; indeed, I had reason to suppose his mind was never as much
clouded to himself, as it appeared to be to us.   The pressure upon his brain was so great, as to produce great difficulty of action of any kind; his ideas were often clear, but
the power of finding words to convey them was paralyzed.
He said little at any time, and yet I find, in surveying the
whole period, that I have many satisfactory views of the
whole state of his mind in relation to the change that he
was making.   He never had but one view of his own situation; he felt decidedly that the time for going home was
come, — 'the fitting time,' 'the best time'; and he was
grateful that the toil of sickness and inability was at an end.
And so convinced was I, that, if he should revive from that
attack, it could only be to continue to suffer still more than

be had done, from inability to do what he had hoped to, this autumn, for the good of his fellow-men, that I too felt that it was indeed the fitting time. And so intense was my suffering from the apprehension of his continuing, for years perhaps, in the half-paralyzed, half-torpid state in which he lay for so many weeks, that it was not only with resignation, it was with a sense of relief, that I saw the doubt was at an end, the prisoner was released. So strange is it, that that event to which I had ever looked forward as the one thing that could not be borne in life, came at last under circumstances which made it welcome! Do I live to say it, to feel it? But O the chasm left in my lot, in my heart! Who can estimate it! No one. No, ' the heart knoweth its own bitterness '; no human being can enter into it. . . . . . But I must stop. I hope to see you, or at least hear from you.

" Yours with much love.

" M. L. W."

" *Framingham, November* 5, 1843.

" My dear Emma: —

" 'This has been a day of peculiar trial to me. At no period, since the commencement of Henry's last sickness, have I found it so difficult to adhere to my determination not to trouble those around me by the want of self-control. This first communion service since that sacred occasion, when we together witnessed that celebration of the rite by him who can now be present only in spirit! I feel as if I needed the relief of utterance; and to whom can I go for this relief so naturally as to you, who are strongly associated with the remembrance which so deeply agitates my spirit? It frightens me, when, upon such an occasion as this, I am led to probe the nature of my feelings, to find how much the reference to him in his spiritual state is be-

29 *

coming to me a substitute for all other thoughts of heaven.
Great as was my absorption in him while he was with me
here, I find it is so far from being lessened by the removal
of his visible presence, that it has only changed its character into an idolatry of a more alarming nature. It is so
much easier for me to conceive of his presence than of that
of any other spirits, that it is the thought of his inspection
of my inmost soul that dwells perpetually on my mind,
whatever I do, or say, or think, to the exclusion, except by
an effort, of the idea of even a higher presence. What
shall I do, if this grows upon me? How shall I root out
this enemy to Christian improvement? It may be only the
first effect of the blow. Time may modify or rectify this infidelity, — I trust it will; but at present it is overwhelming.
O, how deeply do such seasons of strong emotion make
me realize my loneliness, now that I have no longer that
ever-ready sympathy, that composing, strengthening counsel to turn to, with the certainty of comfort and peace in the
turning! I do indeed feel his presence with me, but my
heart calls and he 'answers not again'; there can be no
response to my application. How deeply, how tenderly, is
he associated with all the holiest hours of existence! It
seemed to me to-day I could hear his voice in the hymn
which had so often been read by him on the same occasion;
I could anticipate the words which would fall upon my ear
as we should leave that service together, rejoicing, as he
was wont to do, that such a service had been ordained for
weak, sensual mortals, to take their souls sometimes away
from flesh and sense to the unfettered contemplation of
heavenly love. Fully do I realize, that the sense of loss
is to grow with every added day of my existence; nothing
can come near enough to supply it in the least degree;
nothing else can become so a part of one's own self. This
consciousness of desolation must press perpetually like a

weight upon my heart, as long as life lasts. And yet how
strange! I go on, and every thing goes on outwardly as
before. I eat, drink, sleep, talk, and laugh with others,
whenever it is important for their comfort to do so, as if
nothing had changed. In the midst of all, I stop and ask
myself, 'Am I dreaming?' Or is it really true that I am
alone, — that that point has been actually passed, which in
anticipation had always seemed impossible in the possession
of any power of action? I have thought that the trial could
not be borne and sense left!

"But why indulge myself in this strain? I find I cannot
write, or even think, connectedly; so I will stop.

"Your own MARY."

Language so strong as this, from a nature so calm
as Mary Ware's, means a great deal. Nor can we
marvel. For what a change is that through which
a true woman passes, — from wife to widow! Is it
not greater than even the first change? Often has
Mary referred to the difference, which few could feel
as she had, between her former isolation as to natural ties, and her adoption into a large and united
family circle. But *now* she felt the change through
which she was passing still more, — inasmuch as
she had a more profound and pervading sense of all
that is comprised in conjugal affections and parental
responsibilities. And while none can have a higher
standard of duty and obligation, very few have a
meeker estimate of their own powers; particularly
as regards the care and the training of Children.
This was to be now her great work, — the chief object and anxiety of her remaining days. And un-
feignedly did she shrink, not from the task, but from

the vastness of the trust and the burden to be sus
tained *alone.* " When I think of this large family of
little children to be left to my care, instead of *his,* it
requires a process of thought to feel so assured that
God can bring good out of seeming evil, and work
out his purposes by the weakest instruments, as
to be able to calm the throbs of anxiety, and say,
' Peace, be still!'' to the troubled spirit." True, her
ideal was high, and she could never be satisfied with
that which would more than satisfy many parents.
Years before had she said of one of her children :
" For her intellectual progress I have no anxiety, that
is, so far as the acquisition of knowledge goes ; but
how to cultivate the moral, so that it shall govern and
guide this intellectual progress into the right chan-
nels, and establish the supremacy of the *spiritual* in
the character, I know not." Again, she exclaims :
" And these are Mary Pickard's children! When I
go back in recollection to Pearl Street days, to its
long hours of lone watching, when my mind dwelt
upon the deficiencies of my condition until it had
exaggerated to a more than earthly possibility the
happiness of having something to love which would
satisfy the desires of my mind and heart, — and then
compare that longing with the present reality, — is
it strange that I can scarcely realize my identity
with that same lone one?" The time had now
come when she was again a " lone one." And this
is what we would say, — that the loneliness which
follows, is far greater than that which precedes, the
knowledge and enjoyment of such communion and
coöperation as she had known. Nor is there any

thing inexplicable in the fact, that the most conscientious, even the strongest in character and highest in aim, suffer most from a sense of their own deficiencies, and use language which seems to many exaggerated and hardly sincere. " I am so perpetually oppressed," writes Mary at this time, " with the sense of nothingness, it is so very difficult for me to realize that I am to be regarded even by my children as the leader in any matter, that it all but frightens me to have any one look to me as one who is expected to have some influence. This is no mock humility; I think as well of myself as I deserve. I am aware that it grows in some measure out of the newness of my position, and know that time and habit may bring somewhat different feelings; but it is only these which *can* do it, and I must suffer for a long time yet from this as well as from the other effects of isolation."

We are the more willing to disclose such feelings, in connection with such character, from the fact that the world is severe in its judgment of those, whose affliction is not worn as a garment or an altered visage, but whose whole aspect and demeanor, even their occupations and apparent enjoyment of life, are nearly the same as at other times. At the time of her writing the words which we last quoted, Mrs. Ware had just exerted herself to collect in her own desolate home a little circle of children and youth for their social enjoyment, in which she freely mingled, and doubtless seemed cheerful and happy. And yet she said of it soon after, that at no moment since her trial had she felt so intensely or suffered more poignantly. "Every word was an Herculean labor; and I was conscious that all were disturbed by it. For once, I must say, *I could not help it*. And shall I tell you all my wickedness? I have in vain tried to look at life with sufficient interest to care about living. It has seemed to me that my children would be as well without me, as they could be under my imperfect guidance. I could not excite in myself any of that zest in the pursuit of an object which alone could satisfy the heart. I felt *homesick* when I waked up in the morning, and would fain shut my eyes and forget that there was any thing for me to do."

How much she *did*, particularly in regard to that which we see was most upon her heart, the care and culture of her children's minds, will appear in larger extracts which we make from letters of this and the previous year, brought together as referring to the same great subject of education and domestic discipline, — the first having been written to her husband, the others to her children.

"My dear Henry:..... When I am left to the sole care of my family, there is nothing that exercises my mind more than the right performance of family worship. It seems to me that it ought to be more peculiarly adapted to the capacities of children than we are apt to make it. For the older and well-educated part of a family, other means of instruction and communion with God are open and acceptable every day; but the children and domestics must of necessity depend upon this exercise for nearly all the religious influences of the day. The simplicity of diction which would fix the attention of even little children, would not be too plain for the generality of domestics; and we all feel that the most simple is often the most sublime and affecting expression in relation to the soul's connection with its Creator. I think, therefore, that the main object should be to excite in the minds of those present some clear ideas, which will be likely to stay in their minds through the day, and work there to some definite result; and that the choice of subjects should grow as far as possible out of the peculiar circumstances of the family, — not merely the general, but particular circumstances. For instance, if they are about separating, to dwell upon the use to be made of such an event, reminding us of *final* separation and the tenderness which should grow out of that thought towards all that are left. Is one child peculiarly out of humor? It will do no harm to any to be reminded of the importance of governing our passions; and, if done in the right way, subdue the rebellious spirit more than any arguments. So, too, with regard to reading the Scriptures; it seems to me the time is all but lost if a familiarity of the words only is gained, and that the book should never be closed without having the attention fixed upon some one at least of the useful passages read, either in the way of explanation or application to duty...... I have not time now to put into shape half that is in my mind, but I really feel that we do not do justice to our children in not acting more directly upon their religious characters every day. In many instances, I believe a wayward spirit might be checked **by** having a useful current of thought opened for it, which would take off the mind from the subject of irritation."

" Dear E——: . . . . . Looking at affairs at home from a distance, I see many points in which we need improvement, and I want to talk and read more with you upon the subject of education.

" When we look back, and see and feel how much the circumstances by which we were surrounded, and the treatment of those about us, affected our views, we must bring it home to ourselves that what *we* are now doing is having the same influence upon them. God has set us apart in families to mark out for us a specific line of duty; and however we may wish that our path had been different, or our duties less arduous, as they are of His appointment, we have reason to believe they are the best for us. The longer I live, the more I realize the value of love, affectionate interest; and I think that many things, which we are apt to consider of moment at the time, ought to give way whenever they interfere with the cultivation of the affections in children. Disagreeable manners, childish though annoying ways, may be remedied in after-life, and are, after all, matters of very secondary importance in comparison with the growth of love, which is often sacrificed to them. To children the perpetual irritation of a check in trifles keeps the temper in a turmoil, and, by their standard, makes small things as important as great ones. Fault-finding is blame to them, be the subject what it may, and they will have an association of jarring and displeasure with those who keep it up, let the cause be ever so small, as lasting as if it were larger. We need change in this thing; we want a more cheerful atmosphere, a more affectionate, interested one, in which the affections may grow, and have room to expand. I do believe in Mrs. ———'s doctrine to a great extent, that *virtue* thrives best in an atmosphere of love. We should gain our object better, if, instead of finding fault with an action, we set ourselves to produce a better state of feeling, without noticing the action. Children imitate the manners of their elders, more especially of their elder brothers and sisters; for of course they feel that they are similarly situated, not always making the distinction of age which is expected of them. And I have always observed that the younger members of a household take their tone from the character and ways of the first in their rank, more than from their parents. I could name many instances of this which have come under your notice, as well as mine, and it does, as you say, make the responsibility of an older sister great. But do not feel that it is too great; be contented with doing all that you can, and not discouraged because you cannot satisfy your own conceptions. It is best for us, it is said, to aim at perfection; even if it is not to be attained, it keeps up our efforts for something higher and higher."

" My dear E———: . . . . . The old saying, that ' children will be children,' might be improved by the substitution of ' should' for ' will.' I mean in the sense, that their natural characters, which are as different as their faces, *ought* to be educated gradually; not requiring of one child any thing because another child does it, to whom the thing may be perfectly easy, or more than we can in justice require of them at their age, in consideration of their peculiar circumstances. We are to judge and discipline a child simply in reference to its own individual character and circumstances, and deal with it with the single view to the improvement of its individual character, rather than to our own comfort or even its external improvement. Now, of course, the application of this principle, in detail, involves a great deal of thought, observation, and self-denial; but if we really desire to do good, and this opportunity of doing it is in our path, can we engage in a work of more extensive good, when we consider how these children's characters are to influence a still larger circle, and how great is our responsibility to future generations as well as the present, that we do all we can to prepare the way for their best instruction? . . . . . But to come down to our own case. We all take too much notice of mere *disagreeables.* The evil of doing this is obvious; if the child is dealt with in the same way for making a noise, or for carelessness, that it is for a moral delinquency, it soon learns to confound moral distinctions; and if it is fretted by being perpetually talked to about small things, it is easily worked up to a state of irritation which leads almost insensibly, and certainly without any design, to the commission of some moral misdemeanor. I think we may often see this with all children, and it is very clear, in such a case, that their sin is as much our fault as theirs. We should watch our own state very carefully, and see how far

oui desire to check them grows out of our own peculiar state at the time, and how far that influences
our view of the offence.   We all know that what at
some times we feel to be a great annoyance, is of no
consequence to us at others; and for the same reason, in a different physical state, it is sometimes
easier for them to control themselves than at others."

"Dear E——: . . . . . I think it is good for young
people to have some variety in life.   I suffered
much from the want of it; and I trust that you have
too much good sense and right feeling to be unreasonable in your wishes, or in any measure unfitted
for the duties and enjoyments of home by the indulgence.   I know it has formerly been a great trial of
your patience to pass from the irresponsible position
of a visitor, to the occupations and responsibilities
of home.   But I trust, as you grow older and look at
life more and more with a clear appreciation of its
use and end, you will take more and more delight in
the consciousness of living for some useful object;
and, despite unpleasant accompaniments, find, in
using all your powers for the good of others, a pleasure beyond any to be derived from a mere indulgence
of taste.   We cannot, and we had certainly better
not, if we could, choose our own lot in life; we know
not in that matter what *is* best for us.   It is happily
under the guidance of a more perfect wisdom than
we can attain, and we may rest in faith that our position in life is unquestionably the best one for us, or
it would not have been appointed.   Therefore, dear
E., remember that He who appointed all 'knows
what is in man,' and in wisdom and love adapts our

trials to our wants; and the very fact that such and such things are particularly hard to bear, is a proof that we need to cultivate just those virtues which would make it easy to us to bear them."

" Most people think it as well that the young should 'fight their own battles,' as they term it, and find their own way out of their childish troubles. But I believe many a character is seriously injured by the want of *aid* in its petty difficulties, at that period when the right principles of action are most easily taught; they are as necessary to the right adjustment of small matters as of great. . . . . . I do not think as much as I once did of the loss of constant intercourse in the daily routine of life, in cultivating family affection. I believe family attachments are sometimes increased by occasional separation. But I do think a great deal of the loss, to a girl, of all domestic education, for the whole of that period when domestic occupations can best be learned. Of all objects in life there is none more distasteful to me than a *merely* literary woman; no amount of learning is a fair balance, in my mind, for the feminine graces of a true woman's character. It is not merely that she looks better, clean and tidy, or that a careful use of the needle is a preventive of waste in the use of means, — although these are considerations worth weighing. But there are internal graces connected with these external habits; and there is no higher object for a woman's life than the cultivation of those powers which make the comfort of a well-ordered household." *

---

* A strong assertion; but it is evident that Mrs. Ware's idea of a

"*December* 31, 1843. The last day of this most eventful year! Dear Annie, how many precious, solemn thoughts does the very writing its date suggest! In all the future years of our lives, be they many or few, no one, it now seems, can bring to us so great, so affecting a change in outward things, as this year which is just passing away. It is not only that the outward circumstances of our lives are to take a new course, because he has left us who was to us the leading and controlling spirit in all that pertained to our life in this world, but that we shall no longer feel the perpetual action of his character in the daily detail of the education of our souls. . . . .

" Your expressions of discouragement and anxiety about yourself touch me very much. I can enter fully into all your feelings, for at your age I was not only separated from the loved circle and influences of home, for a time, but I lost for ever my chief earthly dependence for aid and happiness in my mother's death. Thus, being left to myself, I was led to a self-inspection and care of my own character, which do not usually come for many years after. I know all the trials that beset one's path at your age, for I have had deep experience of them; and I can say with confidence to you, that they may all be overcome by a resolute will, united to a true spirit of *humility*. Not, perhaps, in one year or two; but I do know that, by the persevering use of the means which God has placed within our reach, in reliance upon and earnest seeking of the aid which he will

---

"well-ordered household" comprised all that the Scriptures mean by the direction, "Set thine house in order."

give, we shall make progress in the Christian life, the only life which can give us any satisfaction......
Seek the *truth* in your own character, and see it in others. Fix for yourself a high standard of excellence, and never 'tire nor stop to rest,' until you have put yourself in the way to attain it. Stop not then; there is no stopping in this world (or in another, I believe)...... Look your great difficulties full in the face · seek not to gloss them over, or find excuses for them. You have them as the means of excellence, by giving you something to do, a mode of applying Christian principle. Use them as such, and faint not......

" One thing I would suggest. You have been in the habit from earliest childhood, and I trust are still, of praying before you close your eyes to sleep. I am not sure that you have always done the same when you first awake in the morning. I know that much good may be derived from thus commencing the day with some private devotional exercise. The time given to it must of course depend upon circumstances; yet there cannot but be, under any arrangement, opportunity for at least the offering of a petition for light and strength, to meet the duties and temptations of the day on which you are entering, and a thought and resolution in regard to some particular fault to which you know you may be prone. I cannot but believe, that, when the day is so commenced, there is less danger of yielding to temptation than if no such act were performed."

One is perplexed to understand how Mrs. Ware, who neglected no duty, found time to write so much tor the letters here published are a small part of all she wrote, and scarcely any do we publish entire. The explanation is, that they were written after every thing else was done, at night, and very late in the night. It shows the strength of her frame, that she could follow this habit through life, till near the end. We suppose it to have been very rare that she was not up and at work beyond midnight. So was it particularly during the winter after Mr. Ware's death; when her great solace and chief occupation were found in reading and arranging the immense mass of his manuscripts and unfinished works. She says in December: " The sense of the uncertainty of life, which is always awakened by the circumstance of death, made me anxious to do a great deal with respect to Mr. Ware's papers, which no one could do as well as I; the day was too full of movement to allow an opportunity of doing this before evening, and I found myself night after night poring over manuscripts until twelve, one, and two o'clock, for weeks together." This is not mentioned as an example to be followed; nor is there reason to think that it is ever done with entire impunity. But the work to which she thus gave herself, through that lone winter, was one of pure and high gratification. "It was a touching employment, not melancholy. This living life over again, when all its sands have been 'diamond-sparks,' not dazzling, but reflecting the bright hues of heaven, cannot be melancholy; it is but a type of future blessedness."

But not for her own pleasure alone was this done. She had yielded to the earnest desire of all the

friends of her husband, that a Memoir should be
written, and many of his letters and private papers
given to the public.   Not, however, without long
deliberation and great reluctance did she give her
consent; for, as we have said in the beginning of
this work, it cost a hard struggle, and even "agony,"
to open to the public eye that "sacred inner life"
which seemed her own, and only hers.   But here, as
everywhere, she soon conquered all selfish feeling,
and, taking the largest view of usefulness and duty,
afforded every facility for a faithful exhibition of
such a character.   To her son she says: " I know
that, if the picture of what he was is to be a true
one, it must have all those beautiful lights and shadows thrown into it which come from the light of
the soul; and I hope to be able so to lay aside all
personal consideration, as to do what ought to be
done in this regard to make the work as *useful* as it
can be.   I trust you will feel so too.   In our horror
of gossip, do not let us go to the other extreme, and
be too external and cold."   In all such relations, it
was a great part of her principle and power of action,
that she had entire faith in her husband's knowledge of her motives; with the added conviction,
that, whatever had been his thoughts and wishes
under the burden of the flesh and of disease, he was
now looking only at the highest and broadest aspect,
the spiritual and eternal issues of every act.   Her
communion with his mind seems to have been as
habitual and actual as it is possible to conceive.
Again and again does she refer to it, and expresses
regret and pain when a doubt is raised, or a check

given to the full, cordial assurance of the "fellowship of the spirit." And her enjoyment of this thought was never troubled, but rather enhanced, by the thought of *another*, with whom the sharer of her affections and her existence was now reunited in heaven. Distinctly does she refer to it, in writing to one of the children of those parents who were now restored to each other. "I never experienced the sense of continued union as fully as now. It may be visionary but I know it is beneficial. Your mother and your father are as much really present with me, to my consciousness, as if Scripture had told me so, it seems to me. In his case, it is but a continuation of perfect oneness; in hers, it has always been the sense of accountableness, which has aided it."

We attempt no concealment of our wish to exhibit fully this rare and beautiful feature of a Christian's faith and love, — less rare, we would fain believe, in the reality of its existence, than in the courage that avows it. We value it, not only for its own sake, in a connection where it is needed and may be the source of peculiar happiness, but also for the evidence it affords of the power and glory of our religion. We find a letter written on the first anniversary, after Henry Ware's death, of *her* decease who had been the object of his earliest attachment, and whom every later change, in life and death, endeared the more. The letter was written to a child of that departed mother.

"Framingham, February 5, 1844.

" MY DEAR JOHN : —

" I always feel, when I get your letters, as if I wanted to

sit down and write to you at once, so much have I in my mind that I wish to communicate to you, and so much do I enjoy free communication with you. You may thank your stars that I do not give way to my inclination, for you would have more prosing than you would care to read. I am tempted now to depart from my usual custom of writing only once a fortnight, because I feel so much the want of some one with whom to commune upon the subject which cannot but occupy my mind upon this day. It is the first time for seventeen years that I have not had a delightful conversation with your dear father upon the event of which it is the anniversary. I loved to hear him tell me of your mother, for it helped to strengthen the feeling which I have loved to cherish, the sense of responsibility to her in my connection with her children. And her character was so fine a one, and her early experiences so much like my own, that I always felt that I gained wisdom as well as pleasure in contemplating it. . . . . .

" I have often wished I could convey to your mind, without the intervention of words, what I felt to be the tenderness of the relation in which I stood to you; for my views and feelings have always been so different from what I find to be general, that it was not to be expected that you should understand them without such communication. From the very commencement of my connection with your father, I have realized the truth of my long-cherished theory, that the strength of one affection does not interfere in the least with the strength of another; we love not one brother or sister or child the less *because* we have another to love; if there is any difference in the degree, it arises from other causes than number; and I know not why it should not be the same in all relations, where the soul is large enough to take so wide a range. I would thank God for this special blessing in addition, I might almost say above all others, for without it all others would have had a bitter ingredient. It has been one of the purest sources of happiness, that we could dwell together upon the memory of her who had gone, and feel an equal anxiety and interest in fulfilling her wishes towards *her* and *our* children.

" With the love of your Mother.'

One other letter we give from Framingham, addressed to the same son, in relation to the first experiences and discouragements of the ministry. Its plain good sense may be of use to some other beginners, — confirmed as it is by the fact disclosed in it, that some of the strongest minds and most successful ministers have suffered in the same way.

" *Framingham, March* 15, 1844.

" My dear John : —

" . . . . . I turn now to that for which I most wished to write, — your present anxieties in your professional duties. I cannot indeed, as you say, help you, as *he* could have done, but O how fully can I sympathize with you ! It is to my mind only the reiteration of what I have so often heard from him ; even after the ten years' experience which he had had when I first was partaker of his joys and sorrows, he suffered at times as you do now ; and the details he has given me of his trials when he was first settled would equal, if not exceed, yours. You may depend upon it, dear John, yours is a common experience of all young ministers who have feeling and sensibility enough to be really good ministers ; and you must not be discouraged by thinking your difficulties grow out of peculiar disabilities. I remember hearing a parishioner of Mr. Buckminster say, that he felt so much his incapacity to administer comfort to the sick and afflicted, that it was distressing to see him in

a sick-room. I wish you could talk freely with some ministers about it. I have no doubt you would find it more
or less so with all, according to their natural temperament.
As I have said again and again, it is well to keep one's
conscience and sensibilities tender; it is well to realize
one's deficiencies to the extent of making us humble and
energetic to improve, but not to make us despond or be
discouraged; for 'faint heart never won' the prize of
goodness, any more than of the less spiritual objects. I
know what it is to feel that more is expected of one than
can be accomplished; and it is, I grant, of all things the
most distressing. But we must shut our eyes to all such
considerations, and go on, looking only to the standard we
have in our own minds, striving with all diligence to reach
that, and be satisfied with striving, if it be but real, hearty
endeavor. . . . . . I remember there were some passages in
Taylor's 'Holy Living,' which used to be a great help to
me in your state of mind. I have not the book by me, and
cannot quote the words. Fenelon, too, has much comfort
for one thus tried. . . . . . We forget, in our familiarity with
what seem 'commonplaces,' that they really contain the
great, fundamental principles from which all strength, all
consolation, is to be derived; and of course, when the vision
is quickened by present need, they all seem to be worth
more than at any other time. And as to the other point,
it is not you that speak, — you are only the medium by
which the truths which *God* spake are conveyed to the outward ear; you are only His instrument, and, while you are
to seek to supply yourself with a full portion from the fountain of al. truth, you are to be satisfied to present it as
His, not your own; sympathizing as a fellow-Christian, not
dictating as a leader and guide. I see no other way in
which a young, inexperienced minister can have any comfort in that department of his duties. Many reasons come

to me which may account for the greater difficulty in cases of sickness, than in bereavement.

" Truly your Mother."

While looking for a place of permanent residence for herself and family, with an opportunity of doing something for their support, Mrs. Ware received an earnest invitation from a gentleman in Milton, to go there and take the instruction of three little children, in connection with her own, for two or three hours a day. On many accounts, she was inclined to accept this offer at once. But she looked well at all sides of it, and especially at its moral aspect and probable influence upon character. One is struck with her plain and practical, yet comprehensive and exalted view of the question, where so many would have looked only at the immediate and tangible advantage. " There are many things to be weighed before so great a step is taken. Expense is of course a great item, but not the greatest. The influences upon my children must be the first, usefulness the second, and the possibility of living without debt a *sine qua non* anywhere. Now I am not a very romantic person, and am not disposed to live under any less refining influences than I can help. But my children are destined to work for their living, and I wish to have them as happy in doing so as right principles and a healthy tone of mind can make them " The result of full reflection was favorable to the plan; and the wisdom of her decision, while it affected all her remaining days, became more and more manifest to the end. From that moment she had a new object, demanding and creating new energies. "I already see how I shall be a great gainer by this plan, in the strength of the stimulus it will offer to mental effort. In fact, I begin to realize that I am more exhausted mentally than I am physically, by the anxieties of the past, and absolutely need the application of salutary mental medicines, as my body would of physical, if it had suffered in proportion."

Thus another change was to be made, — and the last, in a life of change. It cost an effort. "This first going forth alone, to bear new responsibilities, to make a new experiment, unaided by *his* strength, unassisted by his wisdom, — this is indeed to realize the loss of his companionship as I have not done before. But that blessed faith! that faith in Him who is 'the strength of the lonely,' — I have a trust that it will be sufficient for me, although I cannot now see how."

A few lines to one of her children, as the last record on that sacred spot, closes the life at Framingham.

"*March* 26, 1844. I think you will like to have a few words written from this room, consecrated as it is to us, by having been the last earthly home of dear father's spirit. This is the last time I shall sit in this spot; and I feel as if all the memories of the past were concentrated in this moment of time. How much do they tell of the peaceful and holy life which was here closed; how much recall of that triumphant struggle with the weakness of humanity! Dear child, may we never lose the influence of those

last days passed in this place; may it strengthen,
encourage, quicken us to all diligence in our Christian warfare; knowing that, if we strive as he did,
we too may enter into that rest which we doubt not ·
he has attained. *This is a holy hour,* — this leaving the things that are behind, and stepping forward into a new, untried scene of life's discipline, —
alone, — and yet not alone, for the Father is with
me."

XIII.

LIFE IN MILTON.

" Life in Milton is a very different thing to me, if
you are here or elsewhere; but I warn you against
letting me cling to your sympathy, as I may if you
give me so much of it. I have such a sense of vac-
uum in life, that I am in danger of leaning upon any
one who will let me lean upon him; and my sense of
impaired powers is so constant and oppressive, that
I need to be driven to action, rather than spared it,
to rouse my energies. This is no false modesty; I
am sure that I am not myself; I have not yet come
to act freely in my new position in life; I am not
' at home,' — shall I ever be in this world?"

Thus did Mary Ware write to a friend and true
sympathizer, whose residence in Milton was one of
the great inducements that had drawn her to that
place. She had been there but a short time, and had
not yet risen from the complete exhaustion of body
and mind — the effect of years of solicitude, exertion,
and suffering — for which she made too little allowance. She had been more than mortal, if she had
not felt the effect, especially in the inevitable reaction when the great anxiety and demand ceased.
She would not allow that or any thing to plead for
her; and her danger was, as we have seen, that of

forgetting the designed and necessary sympathy between body and mind. She did not always forget it. Her balanced mind led her to suspect the true cause of the change that had come over her; and she confessed that what she had called "a stroke of mental paralysis" was only physical, though affecting for a time all the powers. Still she was inclined, through its own unconscious influence, to give it a different name. " I doubt not you will smile at my quick sensibility to every thing which is likely to injure myself; and I am deeply convinced that I am growing more and more selfish." Selfish in moral sensibility! May we not be instructed by this, as by the other aspects of her eventful life? There is good sense in the pleasantry of her words to Emma not long before, in regard to power. " I sometimes wonder whether you and I are doing ourselves or our constituents justice, — whether we do not attempt too much, to do any thing as it had best be done, — whether we secure sufficient repose of mind to keep our judgments clear, our thoughts bright, and the supply of mental food what it ought to be to enable us to have the best influence of which we are capable."

The first letter which we find dated at Milton discloses much both of the inward and the outward state.

"*Milton, June* 11, 1844.

" DEAR N——:

" You have no doubt expected long ago to hear from me. You had a right to do so, and must have wondered at my silence, as I could not but know how much you must

wish to hear of our new life. But I have purposely forborne to write; I could not have addressed myself to you,
without uttering all that was passing in my mind and heart;
and so perfectly chaotic has been the state of my feelings,
that I was sure it was best to wait until time and experience had arranged and quieted them, before I trusted myself to the slightest expression. It was as if the fountains
of the great deep of my soul were broken up, and the
waters were overwhelming every power and faculty. I
thought I had anticipated the whole amount of suffering
which my isolation was to bring to me, and vainly imagined that I was prepared to meet it with a firm mind; but
nothing but experience can picture the agonizing senso of
desolation, which entering upon a new life, unaided by the
sympathy that has been so long the light of life, brings to
me. Nothing in life can come near it, unless it be the
homesickness of a little child, when for the first time it finds
itself in new scenes without its mother's presence. At
Framingham I was but living out the plan of life which we
had formed together; the sense of association was not for a
moment lost, and it was comparatively easy to realize the
continued presence of the spirit. But on leaving that home,
I seemed for the first time to be cast upon the world alone,
and every moment's experience in Boston and elsewhere
only increased this feeling, until it reached its height in the
necessity of forming here a new plan of existence, under
circumstances of great responsibility,— alone. I used to
think I felt all of loneliness that could be felt, in that little
chamber in Pearl Street, and that humble cottage in Osmotherly; but that was nothing to this. I had then never
known what perfect sympathy was; I could not understand
as I now do its loss. I have been a puzzle to myself; but I
still am sure that I would not change one iota, the decree
of Heaven. . . . . .

" We came hither the last week in April, and find every
thing pleasant, and every body kind. As far as I can yet
see, I think I anticipated very truly the pros and cons of the
case, not excepting my own incapacity for the employment.
One would laugh at the idea of a woman of forty-five doubting her capacity to teach children their letters ; but the intellectual is the least part of the concern to my view, and I still
think I have no tact for the education of children. The little
I can do for my own is through the connection which nature
has established, not a power of my own acquisition. I have
determined to try the experiment for a year, and the result
only can decide the question of the expediency of pursuing
it another year. I must consider the good of my own
children first, of course. . . . . . My time is entirely filled,
from early rising to very late sitting. The only time I can
take for writing is at night when all are in bed, and I ought
to be ; for the constant bustle of children wearies my head
much.

" Yours, as ever, lovingly.

" M. L. W."

So far from mental infirmity or loss, the mind of
Mrs. Ware was never, we should say, more active or
energetic than at this time, as soon as she was wholly
rested. It is obvious, indeed, that the growth of the
mind had kept pace in her, as in many, with the
growth of the affections and higher aspirations. In
such a character and life, mental and spiritual are
nearly synonymous. The spiritual had been always
in exercise, sharply disciplined and expanded. And
thus chiefly, thus only, we may almost say, had she
advanced mentally. For she was not a student.
No period of her life had permitted her to be an ex-

tensive or habitual reader. Persons, and not books, events and experiences, were her study. She lost no opportunity of direct instruction, but she made it subservient, or rather concomitant, with other engagements and positive duty. And no better mental discipline, perhaps, could she have had, in connection with the communion she enjoyed with the best minds, and the lessons of her lot. We see the effect, and the progress, continually. There is a striking difference between her earlier and later letters. We have felt, in fact, that injustice may have been done, in giving so many of not only the early, but the unstudied and hurried, productions of one so pressed and unpretending. But they all serve to show her as she was.

If we mistake not, vigor rather than feebleness will be seen in her remarks upon that vast and inexhaustible subject, which now engaged her most,— education. She had always thought herself incompetent to teach; and no burden or responsibility did she feel more painfully, than that of opening, furnishing, and guiding the minds of children. This can never seem a light or easy task, unless to the superficial in self-knowledge and conscientiousness. Where the religious principle and the moral aim are like hers, we can understand any confessions of humility or distrust, in view of such a work; and we do not doubt the entire sincerity of the fear she more than once expressed, that she had almost done *wrong* in giving up the reluctance she at first felt to assume the office of a wife and mother, on account of her disqualification for so great a charge And now that it had become an undivided charge, now that her children were left to her alone, and she had engaged to be their teacher and sole guardian, she felt that the duty, the solicitude, and the happiness of her life were centred there. " O my dear child!" — she exclaims, in addressing one of them, and re ferring to all, — " when I think of what you *may be*, my heart beats almost impatiently to stretch forward; for if life is ever again to have. any zest to me, ever to seem like life, it must be through the successful struggles of my children. On them I now must rely for all I can enjoy of this world; their affection, their character, must be my sole dependence."

In a letter to Emma, a little later, she speaks of her suffering from the real or imagined loss of power, particularly in reference to the young. " I sometimes think that some strange change has taken place in my 'physical'; for I cannot otherwise account for the torpor which hangs over my mind. All the little animation I ever had seems to have departed; and, although my mind is crowded with thoughts, they are a dead letter when I attempt to use them for purposes of conversation. I feel this to be a great evil in my intercourse with children. To be sure, their own inexhaustible spirits are mostly sufficient to their happiness; yet they need sympathy, not formally expressed, but existing in the atmosphere about them. I think I have felt the want all my life of a more cheerful home in early childhood, a fuller participation in the pleasures and 'follies' of youth. I want to have my children remember their home as the happiest spot, because the most sympathetic as well as the most loving."

Of Mrs. Ware's seven children, all, excepting the oldest son, made part of the family circle, with occasional absences at school. To one of the daughters who was absent most, there are many letters containing well-defined thoughts on intellectual and moral discipline, and disclosing more fully the fact of her own trials of temper in early life, to which we have before alluded, but which many find it difficult to believe. From these letters we take the passages that follow, the first relating to a visit to Framingham.

"*Milton, October* 1, 1844. O, I did so enjoy being upon that sacred spot, living over again, as we can scarcely do but by the power of association, all the details of the holy time of which that day was the anniversary! I felt that it strengthened my faith and trust, that I could recall there something of the gratitude which I felt when that weary spirit was just emancipated. I had needed this; for as the cares and responsibilities of life have pressed more and more upon me every day I have since lived, their accumulated weight was beginning to keep down and obscure that brighter vision which faith then revealed. I had a delightful walk alone in the woods, recalling the sweet words which I had had with dear father when we strolled through those woods together. How strong is the power of association! I found that particular spots revived thoughts which he had uttered when there, which perhaps I should never again have recalled, elsewhere."

"*October* 18, 1844. . . . . . . I have determined, as a fixed principle, not to go beyond my income, for any thing short of necessity, and it is a delicate question to settle what necessity is. I choose to take it for granted that there never can be a question in any of our minds, that taste is to be held in subjection to principle, and I am not only willing, but desirous, to indulge taste, *within that limitation,* to the utmost bounds of my ability. I think a refined taste has an indirect, but certain influence upon morals; and I never can believe that one of my children will ever for an instant be pained at any restraint put upon them by a necessity which God has ordained.

" I have great sympathy with the struggles of young people in this matter. I well remember how often I had to school myself (for you know that many of my associates in early life were of the wealthy classes), when I saw my companions gratifying every wish for amusement, instruction, and dress, while I could only just keep decent enough not to shock them, and had to give up all my longings for expensive amusements and accomplishments. But I had this great advantage, by mixing familiarly with the rich, — I soon discovered that neither goodness nor happiness were dependent upon these adventitious circumstances, and I was so fortunate in the characters of those whom I thus dealt with, as to be made to feel very early in life that my own position among them was not in the least degree affected by externals. I soon began to look upon my oft-turned dress with something like pride, certainly with great complacency; and to see in that, and all other marks of my mother's prudence and consistency, only so many proofs of her dignity and self-respect, — the dignity and self-respect which grew out of her just estimate of the true and the right in herself and in the world. I can distinctly remember coming to this conclusion upon the occasion of wearing an old-fashioned, stiff, purple silk dress, with a narrow plaited tucker in it, to a party at Colonel P——'s, about the year 1808; I have never had any trouble on that score since. I did shed some tears, when I found I must give up my long-cherished hope of learning music, some years after, but they were 'natural tears,' and 'wiped soon.'

"But I have become garrulous, talking about my youth (as old people are apt to), and have wandered from the case in hand."

"*November* 8, 1844. I feel that I must have some free communication with you, for my heart is full to overflowing. That I can understand all your internal trials, I have often assured you; and, strange as it may seem to you, it is from *experience* that I am enabled to enter into them. In the solitude of my early days, the consciousness of unworthiness preyed upon my spirit, until I persuaded myself that every body despised me, that I was nothing to any one, that nobody could care for me for my own sake. Many and many a night have I lain and thought of this, and looked at life through this medium, until I wished that I had never lived, and in my agony have cried myself into perfect hysterics. Even my mother's love failed to satisfy me, for I thought it was only an involuntary feeling for an only child, not depending upon or growing out of my own deserts. O, how many precious hours of life have

I thrown away in uselessness to others, and in misery for myself, by this morbid sensibility! Would that I could recall them! Would that my example might ward off from you like regrets! I had suffered many years from this cause before I discovered the true source of my trial, or caught a glimpse of its remedy. And when at last it flashed upon me, that it was the want of true Christian humility, not the real conviction of inferiority, which led to all this, I could not at once credit my own consciousness; and many and severe were the mental exercises by which I was led at last to understand and *feel* the truth. I believe this to have been a constitutional tendency; and however much the demon may have been brought under subjection, there have been times all along life, that it has so striven for the mastery, that I have feared it might conquer. But knowing one's danger is more than half the security against it, and I have gained in happiness more than a compensation for the warfare.

". . . . . When we find ourselves disturbed in spirit, we very naturally refer to the exciting cause as an excuse for it; and however we may blame ourselves, we still feel that those whose wrong-doing irritates us are really the most to blame. But we must get away from this view of things, if we ever hope to improve ourselves. As long as we live in the world, we are to live with those who do wrong. We can never be perfect, nor can we find others who are; and our care should be, to learn so to control ourselves, that not only shall we cease to be tempted to do wrong by their wrong-doing, but also cease to tempt them by our own. And who can doubt that the best hope of improving them is by showing them the advantage of self-control?"

"*December* 12, 1844. I feel that you have begun the great work of self-education with a resolute will and I pray God to give you strength to pursue it without faltering. I do not expect, and you must not expect, that all can be done at a stroke. A whole life is too little for the attainment of all we desire; but having fairly set ourselves at work, let us go on hopefully, cheerfully, laboring diligently, ' knowing that we shall reap, if we faint not'; and remembering that, as we ascend, the prospect widens before us. And although we may be tempted to be discouraged, as we see more and more to be done, we are to look back upon the path we have trodden, and measure the steps we have taken, and find comfort and encouragement in the past, for the future. Go on, in the fear and *love* of God, in the path which he has marked out, the path of right principle, — and fear not, — all will be well."

"*January* 1, 1845. . . . . . I can scarcely realize that the year has come to an end, so little have I marked the progress of time during its passage; and yet it has witnessed a great change outwardly. But how little does mere outward circumstance affect the life within, — how do we carry *ourselves* with us everywhere! Does not this fact of experience help us to anticipate something of future retribution? The past year has been to me one of such constant, tremendous struggle, that in looking back upon it I seem to see nothing but the heaving of the waves upon which my spirit had been tost. And yet I cannot lose sight of the many bright spots, the many and great blessings with which my life has been cheered. How should we praise and thank God that our circle has not again been broken, — that we are blessed with such kind friends, and the means of improvement and usefulness! As I look forward into the uncertain future, I sometimes feel as if I longed to know how it will be with us at this hour next year; but a glance at the possible picture makes me ready to exclaim, 'O blindness to the future, kindly given!' I feel as if some great change may come, but I can leave the whole to Him who will direct it right. . . . . .

"How fully do I respond to the feeling you express of desire to see dear father once more. Sometimes, — I know not how, — for an instant an oblivion of the past comes over me, and the feeling of his temporary absence returns as of old when he had gone a journey, as if I could not wait, but *must* see him soon. Why is not our faith in the unseen sufficient to satisfy these longings? Why do we not realize more fully the presence of the spiritual? Let us remember his almost dying words: 'Body and spirit may be separated; *spirit and spirit, never.*'"

"*June* 26, 1845. . . . . . No woman can be a true woman, whatever may be her intellectual acquirements or capacity, without that womanly knowledge which will fit her for domestic life, and enable her to fill 'home,' that appointed sphere of most women's duties at some time or other, with all the comforts which alone can make it happy. I do not mean merely

the knowledge of the daily routine of outside domestic employments; but the cultivation of the domestic
affections, the habits of concession and self-sacrifice,
of delicate attention to the little things which go so
far to make up the sum of domestic happiness, and the
mechanical facility with respect to a thousand minor
matters, — all of which nothing but practice in the
atmosphere which calls them into exercise can possibly teach. I will not deny that I think a great
deal, too, of education in ' common domestic employments,' as a means of happiness and usefulness. I
hold that nothing can compensate for a wilful neglect of what may be made the means of so much
comfort to others, as order, cleanliness, and a facility
in administering to the human wants of our friends,
which is peculiarly woman's province. Now, for this
part of education, home ought to be the best place.
Of course it is impossible, while attending school
constantly, to find time for these other matters, and
all theoretical learning upon such subjects can be of
little use without practice."

Mrs. Ware had found another, new home, — a
pleasant cottage built for her use by a friend after
s :went to Milton, and entered by her and her children toward the end of the year, — her last removal.
And highly favored did she feel, both in the society
around her and the local situation. No heart could
be more alive to the beauties of that glorious " Milton Hill " than was hers. Its rich landscape, its gor-
geous sunsets, and ever-varying hues, she enjoyed intensely, for their natural beauty, and not less, if not
more, for their moral influence. The thought of her

er.thusiasm comes over us even now with subdu-
ing power, as we stand again at her side on those
beautiful heights, to which she longed to lead *all* her
friends, and see the emotion, if we hear not the utterance, of her glowing, admiring spirit. We catch again
the earnest words with which she urged a visit there,
even in the freshness of her widowed grief. " O this
glorious view! I do hope the weather will be good,
that you may see it in all its glory. I had no conception of the moral influence of the sublime and
beautiful before. I really think one must be *very*
wicked to be troubled about little things, within sight
of such a display of the Divine love; even children
feel it."

The time had come when she might be pardoned,
had she been "troubled," not indeed by "little
things," but by some of serious import. A hidden,
insidious disease, which seldom leaves its nature long
doubtful, had begun its work, and the quickened
spirit caught the first whisper of monition. Even
two years before, she had a sort of presentiment, if
not a distinct warning, of her fate, and in a pleasant way signified it to her husband, who answered
as pleasantly, and probably thought no more of it.
How much she thought of it we cannot know. But
as early as the summer of 1845 she prepared her
mind for a painful operation; and, when relieved of
the immediate necessity, wrote thus to a friend:
" You may imagine the depth of my gratitude; for
I could not doubt that an operation, even if successful, would disable me for a long time; and I could
not look upon the fact of being taken off from my

duties, without much anxiety as to how my place was to be supplied. Still I have a strong conviction that ultimately this is to end my days. But I am not troubled at the thought, otherwise than that it is a mode of decay distressing to others. But God's will be done!"

Mary Ware was not only to suffer, but to *do* God's will, to the end. And for four years longer we may follow her, and see her so busy and so cheerful, that we might think her unaware of danger, — except that we cannot fail to perceive in her letters how clear was her consciousness of all that was impending. But very few knew it. The work of life went on as usual. Her small school in the house occupied much of her time, and interested rather than satisfied her. She does not appear to have ever felt that she accomplished much in the way of teaching. She entered upon the task distrustingly. " I begin my little school to-morrow, and I doubt if any girl of sixteen, making her first essay at school-keeping, ever felt more dread of the thing. I am ashamed and almost amused at my own cowardice. The difficulty is, I have a great idea about a small thing, and cannot feel fully that it is ' little by little the bird builds his nest.' " There may have been another difficulty, — that children so young exercised only her patience, and could not call into action the higher powers, nor make her forget herself as she always wished to do. But there was another and absorbing work of mental and moral training in which she was constantly engaged, — that of her older children, for whom, by communion or correspondence, she was striving to do all that was possible in the time that remained to her.

About this time Mrs. Ware received from a friend, who knew her whole condition, the offer of a "home" for either of her children that she would be willing to spare, and for any period. She felt deeply the kindness of the offer, as will be seen in her reply to it, — where we also see her views of the wisdom of separating children, and giving them unequal advantages.

"*Milton, December* 18, 1844

"My dear Friend : —

"As I read over again your precious letter, I wonder if there is any pardon for one who could have delayed so long to answer it. There could not be, were it possible that such delay proceeded from indifference, or want of just appreciation of the feelings which dictated the letter. To neither of these charges can I plead guilty; and can only say in my excuse, that I have not had, since it was found safely rolled up in a bale of carpeting, the command of one hour of daylight, and that my eyes have been so trouble-some that I could not use them at the only time when my mind was free to write. Thus have I been compelled to put it off; until now, on the eve of leaving home, I dare not put it off any longer, and am compelled to take the hour of midnight to tell you, as I may be able, almost without eyes, how deeply grateful I am for it. You have indeed shown yourself the true friend by your benevolent proposition; what more could a friend do for another? But delightful as is the thought that any of my children could have such a home in the heart of one I so truly love, I dare not lift a finger, or say a word, which would decide such a question. I feel my own short-sightedness so much, I believe so fully in the circumstantial leading of Providence, that I could not venture to anticipate the future expediency of any arrangement, the advantages of which must depend upon a fitness of things *when the time comes,* of which we now cannot know any thing.   How little we can tell what a child may be at any future period, — what its tastes, or its adaptedness to any particular position in life, — and how great may be the embarrassment which might arise from any arrangement made in anticipation of results which are never to be reached !

"I have always had a strong objection to giving one member of a family any great external advantages over the rest.   I had rather all should stand upon the same level, as a better security for the cultivation of that family affection and sympathy which I believe to be a valuable preservative of virtue.   I should much prefer that all my children should live together, if it were possible to find any one to act as a judicious head to such a community, than risk the growth of separate interests and a feeling of superiority from any outward cause.   This, you will say, is impracticable, as, in the common course of events, one is likely to gain for himself a better position than another ; but when a strong family affection is established by early dependence, I have no fear for after influences, — I am willing to risk them.   Yet this is only an idea, and I have no hope of its accomplishment ; both the means and the person would be wanting, were I taken from them now, and I should leave them to their fate with the delightful confidence that there are many instruments in God's hands ready to do for them what may be best.   Bless you, for the satisfaction of knowing that it is in your heart to be one of them.   I have much anxiety about my children, not from any peculiar difficulty in their original characters, but from my deep sense of incapacity to guide any child in its progress

through life......I want Faith, I want Hope,—O, I
want a great deal which I ought to have gained, by this
time, to make life bearable. And yet, when I think of the
possibility of being soon taken, I can hardly say, 'I am
ready.' Pray for me that it may be otherwise when the
time comes.

" Ever yours, most truly.

" MARY L. WARE."

As the months advanced, Mrs. Ware was more
and more occupied and active, evidently feeling that
her time was short. And yet we see none of that
anxiety about the future which such a conviction is
apt to create, in reference either to the present world
or another. As regarded another world, and her approach to it, we doubt if she ever felt the slightest
dread or unwillingness to go. Not from any sense
of fitness or self-sufficiency, but with the deepest
humility there mingled the firmest trust; and a
trust that refused to separate the exercise of justice
from mercy, in God. She could trust the one as
much as the other, and she could not distrust either;
but, assured that a perfectly righteous and omniscient Being would do exactly that which was needful for her purification and perfection, she rested
there, — and left all else. We say this of the pecu-
larity of her faith, if it be peculiar, from personal
knowledge of her mind on this point, and from her
own explicit declarations at a later day. And we
refer to them at this time, to say that the same convictions sustained and tranquillized her in regard to
the future of this life for those whom she was to
leave behind. From the earliest moment of the ex-

pectation or apprehension of death, a mother's mind must turn strongly and fix intently on her children. And to most mothers this is the great struggle. Who can wonder? Who will reprove, even if the struggle be bitter, and the vision dim? He will not, who has given a parent's affections, and likened to them his own. Many a mother, who could leave the world without a pang for herself, will suffer and fear for her children. It is only the highest faith that prevents all this suffering and fear. Such, we think, was Mary Ware's. Not in commendation do we say it, — we know not that it deserves that, — but as the simple fact, that while she was always doubtful of her power to guard and train her children in the best way, she never feared to leave them with God, in reference either to things temporal or spiritual. Even when she could see no sufficient provision for their temporal comfort, she seemed unable to believe that she was essential to that comfort, or that her life would be better for them than her death. She *knew* that that would be best which God appointed. Does not this belong to the highest faith? No one could induce her to make any request, or express even a wish, as to future arrangements, the outward condition or fortune of any child. Many wishes, many prayers, did she offer for the inward condition and the spiritual preparation for both worlds, — but only the spiritual. "I could write a sheet," she says to a mother who was herself anxious, — "I could write a sheet upon the text your letter gives me, with regard to the preparation of our children for life. But I can only say, Why should we feel anxious for them when we are gone? Do we not see that the finest characters are those which are formed by the necessity of acting for themselves?" And again: "I have felt so grateful for having had health and strength to do for Henry what I was sure no one else could do, that I had nothing more to ask, and could submit to any thing. I hope I shall not find my faith fail, come what will. I do *not* feel that I am as essential to my children. I do not feel that I am competent to train them."

If we have given of late none of Mrs. Ware's "annuals," it has only been from the abundance of other material. They were continued without a single failure to the end of life. From two of them at this period, we take such parts as will help to show the state and progress of her mind.

"*Milton, December* 31, 1845.

"MY DEAR N——:

"Twenty years ago at this hour, I was writing my annual upon a pair of bellows, crouching over a small coal fire, in poor old Aunty's chamber at Osmotherly. What changes, what a variety of weal and woe, does a glance at the intervening space present to one's mind! It is all too familiar to you to make a recapitulation necessary, and you can understand, without any explanation, the wide difference between the nature of the loneliness I then felt, and that which I now experience. Have I not gained that which can never be lost, a bond of union with an immortal spirit which can never be broken? O that I could realize more the perpetuity of this spiritual union! then should I suffer less from this merely earthly isolation. But I have gained a little since last year, dear N——; either I have become more wonted by time to my condition, or the increasing care and anxiety about my children have taken my thoughts away from myself; be it what it may, I am more able to turn my mind from that one idea of change, and have acquired a more tranquil state of mind, under the consciousness of it. So far, so good; but God knows there is still enough of sin in me, to keep me from that state of quiet trust which, as a believer in Providence, I ought to have. I cannot get away from the terrible sense of insufficiency for the great work which lies before me in the education of my children, and I cannot learn to rely, as I should, upon the All-sufficient, for the supply of that deficiency. It is a living, acting Faith that I want; how shall I get it? . . . . .

"It is long since I have written to you, but I have little of variety to detail. I spent a fortnight in November, and another in December, in Boston, helping Dr. John in the completion of his work, and since my return, three weeks ago, I have been very fully employed as nurse and maid of all work; for I found C——, W——, H——, and my Margaret, all sick. E—— too has not been well. Help is not to be got here extempore, and, with the exception of two nights from a nurse, I had no aid, until within a few days I have had a little girl of thirteen. You know something about such concatenations, and need not be told, that under such circumstances one finds no time for any thing but supplying the bodily wants of those about us. Add to this, that I have been more than half sick myself all the time with one of my tedious coughs, keeping me awake at night and tiring me terribly in the day.

"Only think of Emma's trip to England, — and, good soul, that she should go and see 'Cousin Jane' for me, and George Lovell, too! Does she not always do more than any one else?

"Your faithful

"M. L. W."

" *Milton, December* 31, 1846.

" Thirty years, is it not, dear N——, since I begun to make you my mother-confessor upon this anniversary ? A long life, as some people would have used it ; a long life it seems to me, as I look back to that first hour of conscious-ness that there was one being in the world to whom I could be as egotistical as I pleased, with impunity. A long life it has truly been to me, not so much in its usefulness or improvement, as in the variety of its experiences, internal as well as external. In fact, it seems like many lives ; and as I survey different portions of it in retrospect, I can scarcely believe in my own identity with the being who appears upon the stage in each. How has it been with you ? I am anxious to know whether others are as sensible as I am of a change of character from the influence of circumstances. We are wont to say, and I think I have seen strong proof of the truth of the assertion, — that ' the child is father to the man.' In truth, he *is* the future man, in all the leading traits of his character, as well at five as at fifty years of age ; and yet I do feel as if I were not the same being that I was three years ago. Whether it is that I am growing old and losing my faculties, or whether the responsibilities of life have paralyzed my mind, or that the loss of that refreshment to the spirit which comes from the reciproca-tion of an affection for which there is no substitute, has ex-hausted my strength by depriving me of my spirit's resting-place, I know not. But certain it is, that from being a person of some decision of character, some energy, some judgment, I feel as if I were reduced to a mere child, ready to lean upon any body's judgment but my own, heart-sick and home-sick at the sense of incapacity to meet my duties. Is this want of actual power, or want of faith to use the power that is left ? I don't know. All I know certainly is this: that I find myself utterly inadequate to the duties which belong to me, and am in consequence in a perpetual state of anxiety, which incapacitates me from doing or enjoying. This is a new strain, you will say; for me, truly it is a new state of mind, and whether remediable or not, I cannot tell; can you tell me? . . . . .

" . . . . . How strangely various seem to be the means appointed to bring about the same end in life; and it is not easy to see how our various lots can all be brought to bear the same fruit of holiness and happiness. The greatest evil to me in life is the perpetual hurry, hurry, to get through the business of the day without leaving any necessary duty undone, — without a moment for quiet thought or intellectual improvement, — while here is my neighbor, it may be, at a loss how to fill up the vacant hours, thankful to resort to sleep to dispose of some of them. Does it seem as if we were both destined to the same end? The more I look upon life, the more I feel that the outside has less to do with improvement or happiness. And dissatisfied as I sometimes feel with my own position, I know not how I should improve it, on the whole. When I look calmly at my deficiencies, I see that they are not so much the effect of any outside cause, as the weakness of my own character. And if at times this brings a feeling akin to despair, it makes me less restless than I should otherwise be.

" Dear N——, I have a strong feeling that this is to be a year of change to me; not from any present indications, but that it seems presumptuous to expect that the trial which I believe hangs over me should be long averted. Pray for me, that I may be prepared for it. I fear I shall never be any better. And so I begin the year, not wishing to look to its end, but with more indifference as to what that end may be to me, than I ever felt before. I fear this is not a right feeling. . . . . .

" Yours always.

" M. L. W."

From the many letters of sympathy which Mrs. Ware wrote, we have drawn little. They were sure to be many, from her position, her large circle of intimate friends, the unreserved confidence reposed in her, and her warm affections. How warm and tender those affections were, how prompt to go out to those who suffered, and how sure to do something to soothe and cheer, many of us could tell. Or rather, it is not to be told. But the want of it is felt. There are those of that family and acquaintance, who will never weep, without the remembrance of her ready and wise sympathy. The power of sympathy is not given to all. The feeling may be in all, but not the faculty of so expressing and adapting it as to make it truly sympathy. It requires one to be " acquainted with grief." It requires a quick discernment and deep insight of character. That which is sympathy to one may not reach, or may offend, another. Mrs. Ware understood this so well, that she always accepted, for herself, most gratefully, all attempts at condolence, and at the same time adapted her own to the character and case of the sufferer. " In my intercourse with her," says one, " I felt the difference between feeling *for* and feeling *with* another." There is nothing belittling or weakening in such sympathy. It appeals to the highest, and not, as is often done, to lower motives and affections in the mourner. It does not condole merely, but rejoices with him. To a friend in sorrow she writes: " My confidence makes me rather rejoice for you, than grieve, that you should be called to such suffering. There is so much of sublimity in these *great* trials of faith, that

one feels raised by them to a nearer approach to the
Infinite, to a clearer vision of the realities of the
spiritual world, a nearness, almost oneness, with the
Father of spirits.   Who would desire to avert any
thing that will do this for us?"   There is, too, a self-
respect and decision, with which even her humility
clothes itself.   " Your case is much upon my mind,
and I cannot help wishing there .were some mental
daguerreotype, or magnetic communication, by which
I could transfer to your mind, without the intervention of words, all that is passing in mine concerning you.   ' Vain mortal!' whispers Humility, ' what
could you show her worth her seeing?'   I was not
thinking of the *worth*, but of the, sympathy and love.
I know that is worth something even from poor me.
You say, ' Why do you not talk?'   I have no habit
of talking about the internal, and I have so little
love of discussing the external, that I have no free
use of language in any way; and it always seems
to me, when I make the attempt to utter what my
mind is full of, as if my thoughts all came wrong
end foremost; and the idea of taking up a person's
time to listen to me seems so foolish, that it embar-
rasses me by making me feel in a hurry to get through
for their sakes."

But if .she could not or did not talk much, in the
way of solace, she wrote freely; and her letters,
though not original or remarkable, are drawn from
the depths of experience and faith.   We offer none
entire, but only the parts that indicate her manner
of urging upon others the great truths and principles
on which she herself relied.   The extracts that follow

are not all of one character, but such as were called forth by different experiences near the same time, — all showing the serious cast of her own thoughts, and her deepening interest in others' moral condition. The first was written to her son in the ministry.

"*February* 9, 1846. Dear John: Oh! you are but just beginning to know what life truly is in its solemn discipline. The great book of religious experience is now but opening to you; and, believe me, you will find in it treasures of happiness of which the heart of man *cannot* conceive without such experience. You say you feel something of 'fear' coming over you. I will not say, put away all apprehension; uncertainty does hang over you, but let it not produce fear. I would advocate a courageous contemplation of possibilities, for in this way, I believe, the benefits of all trial may be made greater. But let it be with a quiet trust and hopefulness, such as we as Christians have a right to feel; let it be with a steady faith, that whatever God permits has a beneficent end and object, kindly to aid us in the great work for which we were placed in this world of trial, — the preparation of our souls for that spiritual life which may be lived even while we are still in this world. Does not our Father love us with a perfect love? Does he not know better than we can what is best for us? Has he not power to fulfil all his designs of good for us, — and shall we not, if with childlike faith in that love and power we surrender our will to his, find a peace which cannot be moved? I was once most forcibly checked in some fruitless attempt to obtain peace under great difficulties,

33 *

upon false principles, by happening upon these verses
of Watts (I believe) : —

> 'Is resignation's lesson hard ?
> On trial we shall find
> It makes us give up nothing more
> Than anguish of the mind.
> Believe, and all the ills of life
> That moment we resign,' &c.

And I never find myself trying to argue myself into
acquiescence to any dispensation by reasons other
than those implied in these lines, that they do not
rise to my memory as a rebuke.   But still the struggle, — O, that struggle is great, and we must not be
discouraged that we find it so; that is part of the
discipline.   Strength comes by effort; and only think
what precious teaching this is for *your* work."

All who have read the beautiful Memoir of Robert
Swain will feel the greater interest in the following,
written from his favorite island-home, to a son in
England, about the age of Robert, when he died.

" *Naushon, September* 13, 1846.   I am glad, dear
William, to write to you from this place, not only
because I am happy in being here, but because it
must remind you of him with whose memory this
place is so strongly associated, that one cannot hear
its name without having his beautiful character
brought up before the mind.   I have thought much
of you since I have been here, in tracing Robert's
life by the memorials which are everywhere around
me, in hearing his parents talk of the formation of
his character, in reading the record of his death, and
contemplating at his grave his present life.   O, I
have felt, dear William, that to have such a child

was the highest happiness this world could give; and however great must have been the pain of parting, and dreary the void which his absence made in the earthly pilgrimage of his parents, it was all more than compensated, by the satisfaction of having begun here such a relation to so pure a spirit, which can never cease while the soul lives. And how earnestly I have prayed, that my child, too, might so understand the true object of existence, as to make his spiritual progress the first aim under all circumstances! We see in Robert's case how beautifully he was training himself for heaven, while he lived the simple life of an active boy, following all the common pursuits which belonged to his age, but doing all with a conscientious reference to the law of right. With the most devoted love towards his parents and friends, he loved his God above all, and sought first of all to obey Him. His grave is in one of the sweetest spots on the island, in a little opening surrounded by trees which he had named his 'mother's parlor'; and upon a seat which he had made there for her I have spent some holy moments, with which the thought of you was tenderly mingled. Dear son, may I have the same satisfaction in your life, which these parents have in that of their son! and should God in his providence call you also thus early to himself, may I have reason to believe, as they do, that for you the work of life was accomplished! . . . . .

"I trust you will come home ready to *begin* the work of life in earnest. When you look forward and consider that you must depend on your own efforts for subsistence, that you have a gift of mind

for the use of which you are accountable to your
Maker, and that the person with one talent is equally responsible with him who has ten, you will see
that nothing short of physical inability can excuse
you from beginning at once the work of self-education. All that can be done for you is nothing, all
the advantages with which you may be surrounded
are as nothing, if you do not set yourself to a conscientious improvement of all. I care little what path
you follow as to external life, if you only follow it
upon the basis of right principle, which shall produce
in you a manly, disinterested regard to the accomplishment of all the good you may have it in your
power to perform."

A letter from England informed Mrs. Ware of the
death of an excellent kinswoman, who may be remembered as " Cousin Bessie," the wife of George
Lovell. And she wrote of it to Emma, then in New
York, who had been her fellow-traveller in England,
and whose own health was gently but surely declining.

"*Greenhill Cottage, December* 18, 1846...... Dear
Bessie's pure spirit passed away in peace, the 22d
of November. Her mind remained perfectly clear to
the last moment, calm and cheerful. Hers was a
sweet spirit, and I love to remember the intimate in-
tercouse I had with it in times past, for there was
more in her soul than appeared to the casual observer. Her departure has added one more attraction to that spiritual state in which I hope to renew
the interchange of kind affection and holy thought.
How beautifully is it arranged for us, that, as we ap-

proach nearer and nearer to the exchange of worlds
ourselves, our interest in that to which we are going
should be so increased by the removal of so many
loved ones before us.

"It can be no new thought to *you*, that all sickness must be of uncertain result, and you understand too well the object of all the discipline of life,
to shrink from any form of it which Providence may
appoint. To you and me, strength and power seem
so much our birthright, that we hardly know how to
understand ourselves when they fail; but it certainly is not difficult to see why we peculiarly need the
gentle monitions which sickness brings to us. It
would seem as if some of the capacities for the enjoyment of the purely spiritual could not be formed
in us without them; we should be too self-dependent, too confident in our own strength, to learn how
to be the meek and lowly disciples, to whom are
promised the fruits of faith and trust. I am sure that
the sense I now have of liability to the development
of fatal disease at any time, is the source of some of
the most exalted moments of my present existence.
So far from its lessening our enjoyment of all that
we ought to enjoy belonging to life, it gives a keener
sense of it, inasmuch as it puts in their true position
all the trifles which are so apt to mar our comfort
under common circumstances. I cannot but believe
that you will derive great relief from this experiment; and if it does not reach all the difficulty, it certainly will do this good, — that, by removing some of
the causes of irritation and consequent exhaustion,
it leaves you more strength to contend with what

may remain of disease, — and, after all, that is the main thing.

".....I have had a very kind note from Miss Sedgwick, inclosing a letter from Madame Sismondi after reading Henry's Life. It was a most gratifying testimony to the influence of the truth upon a mind which had been educated to undervalue every thing proceeding from our form of faith."

The younger son, to whom Mrs. Ware had written from Naushon, had now returned from England, where he had been for his health, and was placed at school in Exeter, in the well-known Phillips Academy. From his mother's letters to him while there, we should be glad to borrow largely, but must abridge. The number and fulness of these letters, when we remember the state of her health, the care of her family, and all else that she was doing, would surprise us, if we had not seen the same, virtually, in every period and position of her life. The letters themselves are written without effort or ornament, and contain much that would be called "commonplace," because they aim only at those simplest truths and counsels which lie at the root of moral character.

During the time of writing the extracts that follow, Mrs. Ware went herself to Exeter, alone and at the shortest notice, — finding that some questions in regard to the course of study to be pursued by her son could be best determined by her actual presence. It was one of her last journeys, and, being in midwinter, must have required resolution, if it did not cost suffering.

"*January* 1, 1847. The clock has just struck one, so I may fairly date 1847. And with the recollections of the old year which has just passed away, and the anticipations of that upon which we are entering, come many thoughts of you, — affecting thoughts, for I remember my own experience at your age, and I feel that this year must be to you one of the most important of your whole existence, in its influence on your character and happiness, both for this life and for that long future which can be measured only by one word, — Eternity. It must bring to you many trials, both of feeling and principle; it must bring to you many deep spiritual exercises, and anxious thoughts with regard to your religious progress. You have come to that period of life at which one cannot escape from a deep sense of responsibility for the formation of one's own character; when with every power and faculty in a peculiarly excitable state, every nerve vibrates to the slightest touch of joy or sorrow, and one feels perpetually in danger of being led by feeling rather than by judgment. It is a period of intense enjoyment, and for the same reason may be one of intense suffering; and while it must depend much upon circumstances which shall predominate, I believe it depends still more upon our own self-discipline, in enabling us both to avoid many occasions of suffering, and to meet with a calm spirit those which are unavoidable. You are in a new position of independent action; and while, with the deep sympathy which is the result of experience, I can suffer and enjoy with you, in anticipation, I feel the satisfaction of a quiet trust that ' all will issue well.' I believe that you mean to govern yourself by the highest principle, and in that faith I can leave you to the guidance of your own conscience; hoping that you will never forget, that principle, to do its perfect work, must be applied to small things as well as great; that then only is it true principle when it regulates even the tone of the voice, as well as the most heroic action. Your mother's prayers are for you, at this solemn turning-point of life, that, when this anniversary next arrives, it may find you, whether in the body or not, able to look back with satisfaction upon the past, conscious that a true progress has been made towards that perfection of the soul for which it was created......

" You will say, you have much to struggle with in your own character, and that nothing can satisfy you while you have to contend with self so continually. But your greatest temptation is to dwell too much upon your internal trials, leading you almost insensibly to that most insidious and deceptive form of self-love, a too constant thought of self even in regard to one's faults. You will find your intellectual occupation a great help in preventing this. Do not think too much about your own deficiencies, be content to live along in the constant thought for others' good, and you will find that you have done more for yourself by your disinterested action, than you could have done by all the thought you would have given to the subject in twice the time."

" *January* 24...... Cultivate in yourself a religious spirit; read God's word to learn what he would have you do; pray to Him for power to do ft, --- and you *will* succeed. Here lies the only sure foundation. Religious principle is the rock upon which alone you can build any superstructure; all other will be like the sand on the sea-shore, — the next tide of temptation will sweep it away. And do not think that it will interfere with any of the pleasures of youth, or restrain the spirit of mirth which belongs to your age. So far from it, it will promote all enjoyment; for when we engage in that which we have decided by the standard of principle to be right, we go forth with a free spirit, to enjoy to the utmost, — without any of that under-current of misgiving which is a perpetual check upon us when we are engaged in a matter of doubtful expediency. Experience must have already taught you this in some things, and, believe me, it is equally true in all. You will have many temptations in your little world, composed, as well as the great world, of various characters. But if you once establish it with yourself to pursue only the right, and to have a strong moral courage to say 'No' to any measure of even doubtful character, you will find that you not only gain peace of mind, but win the respect even of those who may at first laugh at you. Never fear for the result, if you only do *right*."

"*January* 26, 1847. Well, it was an event for me to go to Exeter. All my associations with the place are of the most interesting kind. All the romance of my youth was connected with it; my first knowledge of your father was during his residence there, through the medium of the admiration of that brilliant circle of young ladies, in whose society he

found poetical inspiration. It was the home and the
death-place of the first specimen of the highly intellectual and spiritual form of humanity that I had
ever known intimately, in the person of your father's
dear friend, John E. Abbot; and the very name of
Exeter was sacred to me, from its connection with
the daily details of his last sickness, which I received
from Mrs. P——, then residing in her Aunt Abbot's
family. I had been there, however, only once, twenty years ago with your father, when together we
visited John Abbot's grave, and gave ourselves up
to the emotions connected with his memory. You
may believe that it was with no common feelings
that I went alone, upon such an errand, to that spot.
The sense of my sole responsibility in the care of
my children presses upon me at all times; but it
bore with peculiar power at that time and at that
place, reminded, as I could not but be, how little
qualified I was to decide the question, in comparison
with a father's knowledge and experience."

" *February* 2. . . . . . This has been an intensely
interesting day to me. What a thing is this *gift* of
life, — this strange, first union of the spiritual and
the material! How closely such an event brings
one near to the great Origin of all, and in what an
interesting, affecting relation! The tender Father,
watching over, protecting, sustaining, a feeble, mortal
child in the greatest work of creation, the introduction of a new heir of immortality to the path which
is to lead it to receive its inheritance!"

" *March* 3. . . . . . Do not for a moment lose sight
of your dear father's example. He was what he

was, not by the bestowment of great natural powers, but by the religious industry with which he used his powers, the high standard of moral and religious character at which he aimed, the disinterested devotion with which he labored for others' good. *He cultivated his conscience*, and by its light he cultivated his intellect; marking out for himself that path in life in which he felt himself most likely to be useful. And this was the secret of his great success. He was willing to do any thing he could; and he regulated that 'could' by the most unwearied industry. What cannot one do, with such a lever?"

We have not thought it necessary to speak of Mrs. Ware's peculiar interest in the public ministrations of religion. Such an interest, in a woman even of practical good-sense, is a matter of course. She could not, in any possible circumstances, think lightly of public worship, for others or for herself. Nor was she dependent upon the form and medium of worship; since, whatever her choice or taste, she thought more of the spirit than of the letter or manner. Either from hearing her quote the couplet, or from a knowledge of her feelings, we often think of her in connection with the quaint lines of old Herbert: —

"The worst speak something good; should all want sense,
GOD takes the text, and preaches — patience."

Patient she was. even interested, in all preaching that evidently came from the heart, however homely, and in all preachers who were sincerely engaged in their Master's cause. But for the lukewarm and the selfish, for those who preached not Christ, but them-

selves, and offered stones rather than bread to the
hungry soul, she found it difficult to maintain her
respect, or refrain from expressing a very different
sentiment. Her indignation at some kinds of preaching, and the abuse of sacred time, was as strong and
almost as terrible as that which we sometimes heard
from even the gentle spirit of her husband. It was
to him that she once wrote: " Mr. —— gave us a
philosophical disquisition on the nature and proper-
ties of mind and matter, containing (I suppose) a
conclusive argument against Materialism, abound-
ing in technical phrases and abstruse quotations, —
which, to a certainty, not one in fifty of his audience
could understand. What food for sinful, accountable, half-asleep souls! If an inhabitant of the insane hospital had called such a production a sermon, he might be excused the misnomer. But in a
minister of Christ to an erring world, it is nothing
short of profanation." She loved simplicity of manner, as well as matter. She loved a fervid, but quiet
utterance. Of one of the popular preachers she says:
" Such grand and momentous views as he brings together do not seem to me — it is a matter of taste, I
suppose — to need the factitious aid of such a de-
clamatory style of writing or studied mode of deliv-
ery. I want to strip them of all this, and cannot
help thinking, that in their simple, naked sublimity
they would be quite as effective, — to many minds
more so. '

As life advanced, Mrs. Ware felt more and more
the value of religious connections; and both in
Framingham and Milton she found great satisfac-

tion. Such a hearer and parishioner gives more than
she receives. Would that all knew how inestimable
is the blessing to a minister! We cannot withhold
the testimony of one pastor to her character in this
single relation: — "None could be more candid,
more kind, more sympathizing, or more appreciating.
Her seat at church scarcely ever vacant, her interest
warmly expressed by word and deed in every event
and place connected with our spiritual growth and
prosperity; reverent, and almost punctiliously faithful in her attachment to the church, its forms and its
order were cherished with a true-hearted veneration
and love, — while none could have exceeded her in
the spirituality of her religious views, or have risen
more entirely above a mere formalism. . . . . . On
those occasions, too, of trial, which will at times
arise in a minister's service, when he may be called
to speak or act with boldness, or adventure upon untried experiments, she was ever prompt and hearty
in expressions of encouragement. Instances of this
nature occur to me, where she would stop at my
house on her return from church, and leave the
benediction of a kind word of sympathy and god-
speed, uttered with all the emotion of her sympathetic nature, to assure me that one heart at least
was in unison with my own."

Of the "church in the house" we dare not speak,
— except to say, that she who was for so long a
time its only head did not believe that all religious
service must wait for a priest, nor even for a man.
Never will the sweetness of *that* voice, in devotion,

Scripture, or hymn, die away from the heart. Never will those cherished words, " To prayer, to prayer! for the morning breaks," — be so moving and uplifting, as in that dwelling, where the thought of death, just past or just approaching, served but to quicken the spirit of Devotion.

At the period now reached, 1847, the letters of Mrs. Ware continued to be nearly as many as formerly, and quite as cheerful. There is a large class of letters that have been scarcely represented in this sketch ; those which are filled with details of domestic life, personal and private incidents, and playful communications. No absent child was left in ignorance of that which occurred at home. Nothing that could interest, edify, or amuse was thought too trivial to be recorded, if it would tend to strengthen the bonds of family affection. " I believe the love of *home* to be the best safeguard to man and woman for life," — she once said; and she used every opportunity of cherishing that love, in the hearts both of the present and the absent. She had no habit of reservation or concealment with those about her, unless in regard to her own pains and trials. And as those pains and trials increased, we find no decline of general interest or free communion. More and more freely, rather than less, does she speak of herself, her expectations as to this life and another, her concern for her own strength and resources, and the character and prospects of her children. The following letter to her son was written some time in the ummer of this year.

" My dear John : —

" . . . . . I am not now as able to keep school as I was then, poorly fitted though I always felt myself. My head has been a very troublesome member for a long time, and I have had in the course of the last year and a half two distinct attacks, which, if not actually paralytic, were sufficiently like it to be considered premonitory symptoms of that affection, — amounting to loss of sensation, and giddiness, followed by a great oppression in the brain, for a long time after. Since this I have found that I soon get overpowered and bewildered in the bustle of the school, and, after a few days' trial, it is only by going at once to sleep, that I can get my head clear for the rest of the day. Besides that, the sense of hurry which I have from the daily pressure of the necessity of adhering to certain hours, in order to get through the necessary business of the day, keeps my head in a state of tension which I often feel must end in some sudden change. I work almost constantly eighteen hours out of the twenty-four; but this I could bear, were it not for the sense of hurry I have, in my anxiety to spare E—— every thing that I possibly can, while she has the labor of the school. Nor is this all. I am sensible that the trouble in my side does *not* diminish or stand still ; its progress is slow, but evidently sure ; and though there are often weeks, in which I am not reminded of it by any sensation, there are times when it produces great discomfort. I know from the nature of the case, that this may be so many years, and also, that at any moment it may suddenly come to a crisis, as in many cases I have known.

" And I feel that with the bare possibility (and it is much more) of having but a few years more to give to my children, I should be wrong to spend these few years in such a hurried life, that I cannot have time to give them an unfettered hour. This is the case now; whether from want of faculty, or an undue anxiety to spare others, or the necessity of the case, I cannot say. All I know is, that of the eighteen hours in which I am awake, I have not one commonly, free from the pressure of some necessary, imperative occupation. I may almost say, I *never* choose my employment; and as you find it, so do I with regard to my children at home, — I cannot give any of them a hundredth part of the time I would gladly devote to them. . . . . . You wonder that I cannot be more with you. You would not wonder, if you could see how little I have time to do with my children at home. This ought not to be so. But then comes the question, how am I to live, how educate my children, and pay my debts, if I give up so much of my income?

"I answer myself in this way, and I feel satisfied with the answer. If I am not to live, what now supports me will help towards this end; and if I do live, I feel justified in creating a debt for my children to pay by and by, when they are old enough to work, in order to give them the means of working to advantage. I trust they will all find a mission to fulfil, which will keep them free from dependence, and do good to their fellow-men. I will trust that I shall be taken care of; for I think the case of duty is clear, —at least it is so to me, and I feel that I cannot turn from it.

"Now do not think that this uncertainty of life troubles me, or makes me nervous, and unnecessarily anxious. I have never felt more perfect peace of mind, than I have for the last three years, with respect to death. I have felt it a great blessing to be thus reminded of the uncertainty of my life. It is a constant check upon me, and, moreover, makes all the pleasures which lie in my path greater blessings. There is an elevation in such an habitual state of mind, which takes one beautifully away from the annoying perplexities of life. I could write on for hours, but I have said enough. You will understand me, and that is all I desire now.

" Affectionately, your Mother."

Another expression of a different kind was called out at this time, by a case of bereavement in which she felt deeply concerned. We give the letter entire as to its object and argument, because in none of her letters, and in no others that we recall, is the question which is here raised so well stated and answered. It is a question which comes to every conscientious sufferer, — pertaining to the conflict between a sense of duty to ourselves and duty to others, in the season of affliction and secret communion, — the desire for repose and the call for activity. We well know what conflicts both Mrs. Ware and her husband had had, in regard to this question; and we follow her with the greater satisfaction, as she offers the result of her experience and conviction to one of another household, and of the other sex.

" *Milton*, 1847.

" MY DEAR FRIEND :—

" My visit to you this afternoon was so broken, so unsatisfactory, my thoughts are so entirely with you, and my desire to help you, at least so far as sympathy can do so, is so strong, that I must indulge myself this once in intruding my poor written words upon you, for my own relief. Very grateful do I feel to you for uttering yourself so freely to me : you do not mistake, when you believe that I can understand all your doubts and fears, misgivings and contentions. I have felt them all ; and in the knowledge which I have of all my husband suffered, I feel as if I had a double power to

sympathize with you. Well do I understand that strange
elevation of spirit which comes to one in the first hours of
bereavement, when the heart is strong to endure, and the
mind seems to act spontaneously. It would seem, when
one with whose spirit ours had become as it were identified
' passes on,' as if we too had entered ' behind the veil,' and
were also raised above the weakness and suffering of
humanity. But this cannot last long, and the necessity of
a return to the occupations of life dispels the illusion, and
then comes the struggle from which you are now suffering.
Two opposing duties seem to present themselves, — one
claiming quiet seclusion, the other impelling to great activity. We long for rest, we doubt if we have a right to
risk the loss of any portion of the benefit which may come
to us from the life of meditation and self-communion to
which our state of mind *naturally* leads us, by going back
to the busy bustle of external life. We feel that our soul
has been moved to its very depth, as it never was before,
and we long to ' hold the fleet angel fast, until he bless us '
with an increase of spiritual life, proportionate to the demands of our condition. But on the other hand, there lie
the duties of life, appointed by God for *us* to perform; in
their performance lies our mission to the world; have we
any right to neglect them for any object of self-improve-
ment? How shall we decide, when two duties, apparently
of equal importance, seem to us perfectly incompatible?

  " But here, I think, lies our great mistake. We separate
that which God has joined together; there can be no op-
position in his requisitions, and if both duties are required
of us, it must be that they may be united. What is spiritual progress? What is the benefit we believe to be intended for us by the discipline of bereavement? Is it increased love of God, reliance upon him, union of soul with
him? How shall we gain these by any process of medita-

tion, so entirely as when, contending against our desire for repose, conscious of our utter weakness, throwing ourselves with the reliance of filial affection upon a Father's love, we go forth to execute His will in the fulfilment of the duties He has assigned us, believing that His promises of strength will not fail? And did they ever fail? And do we not by this act of faith bring our souls into that union with God which we so much desire, more truly than by any abstract thought? How can it be nearer than when, in the consciousness of our human weakness, we feel that whatever strength we have is His, — that He is indeed present to us, acting in us, — and we know that, while we have this faith, He will never cease to aid us.

"But you will say you have tried this, and strength does not come; you find yourself more and more averse to effort, more and more incapable of it. But are you sure you are not aiming at impossibilities, — that you are not requiring from the nature God has given you more than you have a right to expect, and that, by striving after more than you can reasonably hope to obtain, you render ineffective the power given? Do not misunderstand me. I would not bring down in the very slightest degree the high standard of Christian excellence at which you aim; but I would have you understand truly the nature of the means which the Creator has given us by which to attain it. ' Deal gently with thine infirmity, wait God's time.' You desire at once to rise to the height to which you believe a Christian faith may elevate its possessor, and you are discouraged that the work is not accomplished when *you* think it ought to be. Put aside, my dear friend, this desire to regulate the operation of God's providence. You say you have never for a moment felt that you were hardly dealt with, in the outward circumstances of this affliction. Apply the same faith to its internal circumstances; give up your own will **as fully**

in the one case as in the other; go on, meekly relying
upon Almighty wisdom, with your appointed work, not
attempting too much at once, but selecting just that which
seems most important, increasing your labors as you may
find strength comes to aid you, and be content to use such
measure of strength as God shall give, without repining
that it is not more; and this will bring you that ' peace ' for
which you now sigh. Waste not one moment in vain regret that you cannot do all you desire. O, I could read
you such a page of suffering from this source, as would
make you weep for the sinfulness of your monitor! If I
cannot be an example, let me be a warning to you. May
I be an efficient one!

" Ever your friend.

" M. L. WARE."

How much is told in that last confession and
prayer! She who thus wrote was then in the midst
of a fatherless and dependent family, bearing a load
of duty never discharged to her own satisfaction,
wearing a face of unvarying cheerfulness, and struggling with a fatal disease, whose progress could not
be hidden from herself, though hidden from others.
That equanimity, which had always been marked
as a distinguishing trait, came out now more and
more, as the demand increased, and the difficulty
also. Every one knows the tendency of disease to
produce irritation, — sometimes imperceptibly to
the sufferer, sometimes unavoidably, and with a
painful consciousness. In no duty or sympathy
for the sick is there more need of kind allowance;
and in none, perhaps, is it more wanting. Here,
it was not needed. No irritation ever appeared.

We say this, not from that cursory and .friendly observation which so often mistakes, but from those who knew. One near her thus speaks of her equanimity: "Taking her life through, as I krew it, there were disturbing *causes* enough. Neither the lesser nor the greater seemed to throw her off her balance. I cannot recall a word or act of harshness. Disturbed, moved, sad, I have seen her, but nothing of irritation; and the first, where others were concerned, or some principle, or morality, rather than where she was herself personally interested."

Another *affliction* came, and came nearer than any other could, out of her own family circle. The decline which she had so anxiously watched in " Emma " terminated as she had long known it must; and that true friend had gone before her to a purer sphere. Deeply must Mary have felt this at any time, — how deeply then! Toward the end, all the time that could be spared, day and night, had been passed in that sick-room, where she enjoyed a communion, and exerted an influence, that few could. Perfect congeniality, perfect confidence, an intimacy of years and souls, a unity of faith and hope, with an affection unreserved and undimmed, bound them as one; and when the tie was severed, the world seemed another abode, — fast passing away.

The letters in which Mrs. Ware speaks of this change are most tender, and reveal as much of the character of the writer as of the subject. But they are too personal to admit a free use. A brief account we may take, from a letter which we ourselves received.

35

"I do not remember that I have written to you since dear cousin Emma's death. I should love to tell you of the pleasant hours passed in her chamber after her return from Europe, the precious hours of her last week with us. Her state of mind was a most elevated one, but her words were few. She could not overcome the habit of reserve upon spiritual subjects, and it was only in moments of the most private intercourse that she would utter herself freely. It was a beautiful case of great humility, united with perfect trust. She never for an instant faltered in her faith, but laid down her almost unequalled power with as perfect readiness as if she had never loved its exercise. You may suppose that her loss is daily, hourly felt, by all who belonged to her. This is not the same place without her. We constantly miss her wisdom and her disinterested kindness. Do you know that she made this cottage mine, — and more? I never received any gift which was so unexpected, or so touching. It has made this place more beautiful than ever; for the very walls have now a sacred association."

On Christmas Eve, 1847, Mrs. Ware, with some of her children, joined a family gathering at Cambridge, in the same house that they occupied during those twelve eventful years. And many were the recollections awakened there. "O, how strange it seemed to me, to be 'guest' in that house, on such an occasion! I could scarcely help a sense of responsibility, as if it were my affair. And my heart turned instinctively to the thought of all my responsibilities there, and the thought of how much *he* would have enjoyed, and added to the enjoyment of others. There was a sense of the want of his visible presence, such as I never expected to feel again, so familiar have I become with the idea of the invisible." On the last night of the year, she writes in a tone more like sadness than was common with her, though with the same tranquil trust : — " I live now so entirely among the young, who could not comprehend the results of an old woman's long experience, that I am unconsciously led to shut up the thoughts which mostly occupy me, lest any should be annoyed by what they might not understand. And there are consequently periods when it seems as if I should *stop*, from want of the sympathy and counsel of some contemporary who knew the past as well as I do myself. In the various questionings about my children, and the many doubts which will come to an insulated mind, how have I craved your ear! . . . . . It has seemed to me, since Emma's death, that every thing was giving way around me. I cannot tell you what a sense, a perpetual sense of uncertainty, appears to pervade every thing. It seems as if not merely one strong being had failed by the way, but as if strength itself, the very thing, had become weakness. And I find myself clinging more than ever to the things that remain, and more and more impatient to use opportunities of intercourse with those I love, feeling that the time is short both for them and myself. Little did I think, at this time last year, that I should be here now; and when I look back upon the interval, and remember that, instead of the sickness I anticipated, not one day of actual suspension of labor have I had, I am amazed at the small amount I have accomplished, and won- der why it is I am left. The year has been marked by less external change than usual, and yet it has brought some important changes in the progress of my children's education."

And if Mrs. Ware had not expected to see the end of that year, she could have little idea of seeing the whole of another. Yet this was granted her, — and a little more. And whatever the inward change, there was none outward, unless in greater diligence in duty, and a more earnest endeavor to make others happy. This, too, was evident, in conversation and in letters, — that while life in the present was still full and bright, there was a growing conviction of life beyond and above. It was seen particularly, as one and another of her friends departed, — when the emotions expressed were more of joy than of sad- ness, as in the case of a bereavement not long before. " O, how the holy band is gathering in that other state! And how near does it seem to us, when those with whom we have been wont to have daily inter- course enter it! I think, as I grow older, no part of my experience satisfies me so much, as the conscious- ness of an increasing *sense of union* with a purely spiritual state. Not that one loses all interest in this state, but there comes a fuller sense of the reality of another."

XIV.

THE END.

Of Mrs. Ware's last months and days we have nothing remarkable to record. They did not differ from the months and years that preceded them, except that they *were* the last, and she knew they must be. But she did not on that account seek to impart to them any new aspect, or new occupation. She had no formal preparation to make for a change, great indeed and momentous, yet perfectly familiar to her thoughts, and never dismaying. She had not left the work of life to be done after the power to do it had gone, but had used that power as one responsible for the use of all that was given her, and she continued to use all that remained, diligently and tranquilly. Had she been asked, as another once was, "What would you do, if you knew you should die to-morrow?" we suppose her reply would have been the same, — "That which I am doing to-day." And she was doing a great deal, — as much perhaps as she had ever done, in all that pertained to family and friends, the destitute and suffering. And she was enjoying a great deal, both at home and abroad, with apparently more, instead of less, freedom from that sense of "hurry" which had so troubled her. This she expresses in a note that we received from

35 *

her in the month of May, 1848, which shows likewise how fresh and full was her enjoyment of the opening year. " We are beginning to look lovely here. It seems to me the spring was never so charming; but perhaps it is that *I* am more charming than usual! Certain it is, that I have seldom been in so favorable a state to enjoy it, so free from the pressure of care and the sense of hurry, which has been the bane of my life. I am more willing to leave some things undone than I was. Is not this a great virtue in a housekeeper, whose spring-cleaning is not done, or likely to be these three months? Our school has not yet adjourned, and I shall not be quite settled until it has. . . . . . Thanks for your letter; I shall answer it, if I ever have a quiet hour that has no peremptory demand for other employment."

In those last words we see a trait which many have noticed in Mrs. Ware, and which one of her own sex, who had seen her in many situations, thus describes: " I never knew any one who had a more just idea of the due proportion which various duties and interests should bear to each other. She was never one-sided in her views, never lived for one idea alone, but took a comprehensive view of all her duties and of all her relations to her fellow-beings, and gave to each its due portion of time and attention." This habit is not uncommon, perhaps, in health and active life; but not every one attempts to maintain it in sickness and the approach of death. That Mrs. Ware was fully conscious of that approach, though yet in apparent health, appears from many circumstances. But she did not talk of it, and few knew it. She preferred not to communicate it even to her family until it was necessary, lest it should check the freedom or disturb the serenity of a happy household, preventing rather than promoting the performance of duties all the more imperative if the time were short. From a letter to an absent daughter, we take the following, so pleasantly written.

" *Milton, May* 2, 1848. Dear E——: Have not I got some pretty little paper upon which to indite my loving thoughts of thee ? It becomes me to have a fine pen, and to try and be rather refined than otherwise in my chirography! Alas for me, who have to write with quill-nibs without mending! But I have rather a fancy for these close lines, which remind me of the days of my youth, when I used to write as closely without lines. I am particularly reminded of those days, by having received to-day my own letters to Cousin Emma; and to decipher some of them would try better eyes than most people possessed in her days, so closely written, so crossed and recrossed are they. I read one of them, and have been living over again all day those singular Osmotherly experiences. I do sometimes wish that I could have had the leisure, while I had the power, to write out for the information of my children that page of my life. It was so powerful a lesson of faith and trust, that it could not fail of producing in them, in some degree, the same effect that it did upon me. In looking back upon it, I cannot but feel that it was a peculiar blessing to me, as preparatory to the trials

which were to follow ; without just such a teaching
it seems to me they would have overwhelmed me.
I often wish I could convey to the minds of those
who are coming upon the stage of life, the utter insignificance into which outward circumstances sink
in retrospect, other than as the occasion for the cul
tivation of the inner being. One almost forgets
whether outward things were agreeable or not. The
spiritual, intellectual life is the most prominent ; the
progress of our own characters, the affection which
met our affections, the satisfactions of the soul, are
all that leave any lasting impression upon the mem
ory."

By the middle of that summer, her strength had
declined very perceptibly to herself, though not to
common observers, and she felt that the time had
come for an explicit communication.   And never
can we forget the perfect composure and natural
cheerfulness with which she spoke of it to some of us
who had little idea of the whole truth, — showing a
paper that she had written to one of her children,
and asking counsel in regard to it.   The paper is of
too private a character to be given here, except a few
of the more general passages. " I have not thought it
worth while to trouble you, or any one else, with the
knowledge of this, while I was well enough to go on
as usual, and had no reason to expect change.   The
doctor has always said I might live, as many had,
for years, and die from some other cause, before this
became very troublesome ; and it may yet be so.
But within a few months the course of the thing has
changed, and I cannot but feel that it may come to

a crisis at any time, and I be suddenly prostrated. With these views, I wish not to hide from myself my danger; and I thank God for the influence which this consciousness has had upon my mind for a long time past. I have felt it good for my soul to know that I carried about with me a disease which must be fatal. It has helped me more than any thing else to put the things of this life into their true relative position. And while it has not for a moment lessened my interest or my enjoyment of any thing around me, it has saved me from many painful mo ments and anxious cares, by showing me the insignificance of much that I once cared too much for. The only evil I have found in it is a sense of hurry; feeling that I may have but little time to work in, I am tempted to work hurriedly, and thus with less comfort. I cannot tell you the many thoughts I have of the future destiny of my children...... I need not tell you how inexpressibly nearer and dearer all the children are to me every day I live, or how earnestly I pray that they may be such as their father's children ought to be."

In the early autumn, she spent much of her time at the house of her son in Cambridgeport, in whose family there occurred a case of sickness and death, which engaged her deepest sympathies and tasked her strength. Once more she became a nurse and laborious helper. After it, she sank for a time, but again rallied, and through the greater part of the winter continued strong in spirit, with great energy of will and action, interested in every thing, grateful for every thing, busily and happily occupied. Of the accounts given us by others, beside what we saw and heard of her whole bearing and conversation that winter, we can use little, lest it should seem like eulogy, — which we desire to avoid, particularly in connection with her death. But should this prevent all freedom of expression? If we may not speak from our own mind and heart, may we not from the testimony of those who were near enough to understand the whole, yet with no relation or interest to mislead them?

A lady writes: "It was my great privilege to pass a few weeks with her in the sanctuary of her own home, in the early progress of the malady which terminated her natural life. Words fail me to convey my impression of her at this period. Always serene and cheerful, there was yet a seriousness in her manner, and a depth of purpose in her words and acts, that were to me very impressive. . . . . . Every duty was to her always a religious duty; and hence we saw in her the same fidelity and perfectness in every household care, however humble or distasteful, as in employments of a more congenial character. . . . . . While her life was to me highly inspiring, it was also deeply humiliating. She seemed to me always sufficient to herself in her great resources, and I felt that I could be nothing to her. I once told her so; she smiled, and said, 'You don't know how weak I feel, and how I long to lean upon some one, and be caressed and petted like a child.'"

A near neighbor and privileged friend says: "When we learned that her days were numbered, as we did some months before her death, we of course

.ooked upon every thing connected with her with a more subdued and chastened interest. She seldom, almost never, alluded to her condition. But there were little valedictory acts to be remembered when she was gone, that showed her thoughtfulness and love. The last time I saw her at church was on Thanksgiving day, the great family festival of New England. During most of the services she was in tears, doubtless thinking of those whom she was soon to join, and of those now with her who must spend their next Thanksgiving alone. But her tears were tears of endearment and tenderness, more than of sorrow. . . . . . Gradually her walks were given up. Some unusual calls on her sympathy and strength may possibly have shortened her sufferings. ' But if I had foreseen it all,' she said, ' I should have done the same.' There was no shrinking from what lay before her, but that entire humility which neither presumes nor fears, and is content with what God appoints."

But we need not rely on others for a knowledge of Mrs. Ware's condition and temper at this time. Her own words still speak for her, and speak with the same clearness and calmness as ever. Letters and notes were written to all who had any claim, through the winter. The year was not suffered to close without one more " annual," — the last seal to that firm friendship. Portions of these letters and notes will serve as the best index to the progress of her life, — for we cannot call it the decline.

" *December* 26, 1848. Dear John : You must wonder why I have not written to you in all this age of

a week since you were here. In truth, I have not
been able to do so, for I had to give up and go to bed.
I should have been wise had I done so when I first
came home, I suppose; but I was so sure that I had
no right to expect to feel better, that I could not
think it worth while. I am better now, and am going to venture to town to-morrow. I have had but
one hour yet for accounts, and as my arm is becoming more and more useless, I dare not put off doing
what that arm alone can do. I desire so to arrange
matters that I may have only tranquillity. — no
hurry, no bustle, no irritation anywhere. I
have none but cheerful views for myself, and I desire
to be spared anxiety about the outside to mar that
cheerfulness. . . . . . I have promised to go into Mr.
B——'s, New Year's eve, and can do that with little
fatigue. Kiss Henry boy for his grandmother, and
wish him a 'happy new year' for me when the time
comes."

" *December* 31, 1848. Dear N——: Once more I
will make an attempt to write to you, for I cannot
let this season go without giving you some record of
what is passing, — as my reason tells me it is in all
probability my last annual missive. Do not, my
dear friend, shrink from this idea, as if it were some
dreadful fact which you wished not to realize. I can
write it, I trust I can bring it home as a truth, without the slightest quickening of the pulse, without a
wish to decide my own fate. I would bless God,
that in His tender love He has so gradually brought
me to the consciousness of the great uncertainty of
my own life, that all connected with that uncertainty

has been familiar to me through the softening influence of distance, and my vision can now bear the
strong light of the nearer presence without dismay.
In recalling the various circumstances in which I
have written my many annuals to you, I cannot remember one in which I have had less anxiety about
the future. I feel strangely perplexed sometimes at
this; I know that while it is *possible* my life may
be prolonged many years, yet they would be years
of suffering, of comparative uselessness, and perhaps
of great discomfort to those around me; and still
more, that the more probable prospect is a rapid, if
not sudden, annihilation of life. I have children for
whose welfare I have lived, and cared only to live
for the last five years; and of whose fate when I am
gone I cannot even guess. I have felt that my life
was important to them; and when the idea of being
obliged to leave them first came to me, I thought
I must be a great loss to them; but now I cannot
make it seem so by any process of thought. Why
is this? how is this? I cannot tell. I do not love
them less; on the contrary, my tenderness of feeling
towards them increases every day. I never cared so
much to have them with me, I never enjoyed their
various powers more. Is it that I am under a delusion,—that death is not the reality to my mind which
I conceived it to be? I confess I cannot answer sat-
isfactorily. I seem to myself, as I did at sea in a
dangerous storm, quiet, confiding, sure that no human help can aid, and not anxious to look beyond
the present. But it may be that it is only because,
while we are able to exercise both mental and physi-

cal powers in some way all the time, it is impossible to bring home the conviction that all may stop at any moment.

"One solution of the mystery comes to me sometimes. You know I have felt, ever since my husband's death, that it was the most inexplicable mystery that my children should have been left to my sole care instead of his, when I was so deficient in the power to do for them what a parent should. I could only satisfy myself by the fact, that the All-wise, All-powerful, could overrule my mistakes, and I had no right to ask why. This consciousness of inefficiency has never left me, and I cannot therefore feel that my withdrawal will be to them an essential evil. I have seen many instances of children left, as mine will be, to their own guidance, who have evidently made much stronger characters for that self-dependence. And though they may suffer, perhaps, as I did, from the loss of that affection which a parent only can give, we see so many suffering quite as much from the misdirection of that affection, where the tie is not thus broken, that we dare not say, in any given instance, which fate would be the best for a child. Of one thing we are certain; we are short-sighted, finite beings, our minds can fathom but part, 'one little part,' of the plan of Providence; and we cannot tell but what the most adverse circumstances may be made instrumental to the education of the soul, by that overruling Power which sees the end and the beginning. We understand so little of the true character of each individual mind, that we know not but that what seems most adverse is in reality best adapted to its wants. Why, then, can we not be content to give up our own desires, our own judgments, all anxieties, all plans, and trust that all will be ordered right? Not certainly to sit down passively and do nothing; but, carefully watching the indications of Providence, to exercise our best judgments in trying to further its designs, and be content with the issues."

"*January* 21, 1849. Dear Louisa: I send the above just as it has lain in my desk these three weeks, to show you that I have 'made an effort.' I devoted that last evening of the year to writing to you and N——, and began your letter first; but my arm was so painful that I soon found I could not accomplish both; and I laid aside yours, because I was reluctant to omit, for the first time in more than thirty years, my annual to her, feeling as I did that it would probably be my last. This you will pardon; but, in justice to myself, I must go back and tell you why I had not before even commenced an answer to you, because I consider the mere fact of *seeming* neglect of such a letter ought to be fully explained, for the credit of human nature in general..... I have been greatly blessed in finding, that, as the reality of what lies before me has become more and more distinct to my consciousness, I have lost nothing of the tranquil faith which made me willing to acquiesce in it. My nervous system is not touched yet in a way to affect the firmness of my views of the future. My great study now is, how to do my part towards making this experience of most value to my children. While I wish not to withhold from them

any benefit they may receive by free and full knowledge of my condition, I am sure it must be intro-
duced with a judicious reference to their different
casts of character. I am feeling my way, and earnestly pray to be guided aright. . . . . . As to my visiting you, I have not been a mile from home for
many weeks, — can only ride a little in a very easy
vehicle without suffering for days after it. But I am
content to be quiet. After such a life of activity, I
enjoy the right to be still, more than I can tell; and
I have home employment enough to fill all the
time, if it prove ten times as long as I think it
will. I hope to see you here when the weather
is warmer, if God should spare me until then.
God bless you, dear L.! I love to have your letters, but cannot promise to answer them very punc-
tually."

"*January* 28, 1849, *Sunday Evening*. My dear
Lucy: Strange indeed must it seem to you, that
your kind, sympathizing letter, written more than
two months since, should not have received an answer long before this; and if you have not, through
some of your mutual friends, heard something of the
progress of things with us since then, you must think
it perfectly unpardonable. But in truth, dear Lucy,
I have thought much of you, and longed to write,
and still more to see you; and nothing short of
physical inability has prevented me from long ago
reporting myself to you. It is not worth while now
to go back to the various causes which at first prevented my writing.

"I have lost ground greatly in the last three

months, and should I continue to do so for the next in the same proportion, I shall be a mere burden; but no one can form any calculation about it, and I desire not to attempt it. I have no wish to penetrate the future. I know all will be ordered as it had best be. What more can I need to know? I feel that I have special cause for gratitude in the length of time given me to make the subject familiar to my mind; and not less so, that the disease so far does not disturb the perfect tranquillity of my mind, or take from me any of the advantages of this long preparation. My faith is strong that He who has been the Father of the fatherless, and the widows' God, will protect and guide the orphans I must leave behind me. It is not in vain that I have had an orphan's experience. He guided me in safety through the many perils which beset the lonely one; I may surely trust Him for those to whom He has vouchsafed the aid of kindred so near and dear. My only care now is, how to do my part in giving them the full advantage of this discipline, and I earnestly pray to be guided aright...... I should love to see you, and hope to do so in the course of the winter or spring. I sit quietly at home, but have seldom a day without visitors, sometimes to weariness; but I love to see my friends, and they are many; I cannot say nay to them. I have not been to Cambridge since I first came home, and to Boston only twice for two months, and could not do it now. But perhaps, when I can take more air, I may gain a little more strength, and stay a little longer than seems probable now. Of this you may rest assured,

36 *

that, come when it may, I can say with perfect truth
' Not as I will, but as Thou wilt.' ".

"*February* 3, 1849.   Dear Friend: I know you
will be glad to have a word directly from us of our
welfare, and I therefore gladly avail myself of a kind
offer to take a note to you, though I have time only
for a short one.   I have had my ups and downs
since you were here, but on the whole do not think
there is any material change; — some days of great
suffering, and then again days and nights of perfect
ease.   So I have had much for which to be grateful
in the alternation, for the days of suffering made the
seasons of relief more delightful, and the rest enables
me the better to bear the suffering.   Much indeed
have I to be grateful for.   Never was kindness bestowed upon mortal, I believe, such as is every day
showered upon me, and nothing yet has come to disturb the serenity of my mind.   I find myself as free
to enjoy all that is passing as ever, and the 'daily
duty,' small though it be to me now, interests and
satisfies me. . . . . . I have an almost incessant in-
flux of visitors, which sometimes wearies me; but
then I love to see them, and I enjoy the occasional
quiet hour all the more.   My wakeful hours at night
are the most precious, being happily free from all
nervous restlessness; and often do I wish I had some
other wakeful spirit at my side with whom I could
commune of the passing visions.   But enough of
self.'

"Dear Maria: I did not like, in your short visit,
to occupy any time with self; but I should love to
tell you of the blessed peace which is given me in

relation to the trial which lies before me, and of the
faith and hope which shed their tranquil light upon
the future, even in respect to that most trying point,
What will become of my children? . . . . . For while
I feel that every day which is spared me makes
them all more and more dear to me, I realize more
and more that I *cannot* be separated from them."

The friend to whom those last words were written,
then a wife and mother herself, and once a cherished
parishioner of Mr. and Mrs. Ware, has since joined
their communion above. And her part of this correspondence shows how beautiful had been the influence of the life whose close she now witnessed. Indeed, the fact itself should be stated, if nothing more,
as belonging to the actual character of Mary Ware,
that the many letters and notes which came to her
in these declining days, from friends near and friends
abroad, are filled, not with empty praise, nor yet
useless and distressing grief, but with expressions of
grateful joy for the power of her faith in the present
struggle, and its power upon *them*, in the past and
always. If ever there was evidence of the reality
and influence of the Christian faith in itself, or of a
peculiar form of it, it might be shown here. The
believer and sufferer thought less of any peculiarities,
than of the essential spirit and power. But all that
she had held, she retained, and found sufficient, — un-
failingly, abundantly sufficient. And it was a blessing to her in her last days, to know that others of
the same faith felt its sustaining power, and shared
with her in its peace and joy. The friend to whom
we have just referred writes: " Scarcely an hour

passes in the day, that I do not think of you with so much tenderness and sympathy as I have no words to convey to you. The thought of you does me good. I know what is passing in the depth of your soul, and it gives me strength to go on. Will you pray for me, that while I live I may do what is right, cheerfully and submissively, if not joyfully?" She begs Mrs. Ware to write down, or let another write, some passages of her life. "Your experience has so blessed me, that I long to spread its influence. I can never thank you for what you and our sainted friend, with whom you seem now more than ever 'one,' have done for my soul." Another, who was herself the widowed wife of one of the best of men, writes to Mrs. Ware of their former intercourse and communion: "There has been no alloy mingled in this cup of blessing; we can carry it all with us to our Father's house. With my whole heart I rejoice that you are able to act out your highest convictions, that your disease so gently looses the bonds to earth, as to leave your spirit free to bear its testimony to the last to the power of your faith in the goodness of God, and the reality of everlasting life. 'He that liveth and believeth shall never see death.' With you and me death has lost its sting. Are we not willing to go where those we have loved so truly are gone? Shall we not gladly make their home our home? It is not the fear of death that ever presses upon me, but the fear of not being worthy of the unutterable happiness of a reunion with those that have gone before me; so I welcome pain, hoping it may purge me of my sins, and make me more fit for heaven. Sometimes, when the idea is very clear and strong in my mind of eternal life with the good and great souls that I have known here, I gasp for breath, and, like the disciples, 'cannot believe for joy.' And surely, dear Mary, the love that has been perfect love cannot be quenched or turned from us in the land of spirits to which we are tending, — in which you seem to me now to be living."

These sentiments are the reflection of her mind, who had done so much to form or invigorate them. They were some of the blessed fruits of the faith that she and her husband had cherished, — the faith that still bound her to him, and to all whom she loved. As such, she welcomed them. But the moment the partiality of friends carried them beyond this, and implied the least merit or power of her own, she was pained. " I thank you for this note ; yet — shall I say it ? — it pained me. I do not like to feel that my friends are attributing to *my* efforts that which I feel is the direct action of a higher power. Knowing as I do how great are my deficiencies, how far I fall short of the 'perfect stature,' I cannot but feel humbled by such expressions. . . . . . Please thank Mrs. —— most gratefully for her kind offers of aid. I seem to be so overwhelmed with comforts, that I have nothing to ask for myself. O, how great is the goodness of God towards me !"

It is a touching incident, that one letter came from England just too late. It was from 'little Jamie,' the motherless boy, now a man, whose life Mary Pickard had been instrumental in saving, during the dreadful sickness at Osmotherly. She had never heard from him. But he now wrote a long and grateful letter, thanking her for her kindness to his dying parents and to himself, of which he had heard so much, as well as for her continued remembrance of his aged grandmother as long as she lived. Had the letter come a few days sooner, it would have rendered still more fervent the thankfulness which filled and animated that deathless heart.

We offer nothing more from Mrs. Ware's pen. She used it as long as she had strength, forgetting no friend, keeping her personal and domestic accounts, and leaving nothing to others that she could do herself. Attention to things temporal was with her not even secondary, but part of religion, all of which was primary and essential. Essential also, in her view, was the duty of cheerfulness, and of making others happy. Thoughtfulness for others, and a participation in all their joys, were among the latest manifestations, as prevailing in sickness as in full health. She wished no household duty to stop for her, no happy face of youth or manhood to lose its brightness. The song of the birds, and the song of the children, were glad notes even to her decaying sense. " Never did a sick-room have less of the odor of sickness than that," says one of her children. " It was the brightest spot on earth. Nothing was shut out from it, but the door stood wide for all the joys and hopes of all, even to the last."

In this connection it deserves to be mentioned, that Mrs. Ware found a true and most devoted friend in her physician. She knew the worth of such a friend; and it was one of her last acts of thoughtfulness and gratitude, to beg her children to remember the kindness of the Doctor.*

The last letter that Mrs. Ware wrote, or rather dictated, was in behalf of an aged and destitute clergyman, whose family she had often taken to her home, and for whose benefit the provision made by some generous friends, partly as a solace to her own departing spirit, shed upon that spirit a serener and brighter radiance. To him who told her of it, she said, joyfully, "I hope to have some spiritual ministry given to me; I have been able to do little here, but I hope to do more."

With great clearness, and in words that were retained, she had defined to a friend and clergyman, a short time before, her views of the world to which she was drawing near. "I find myself thinking very little of the future world as to its 'circumstances.' I mean, I am surprised to find how little *curiosity* I feel about it. I trust myself with my Father, both now and hereafter. Whatever is best for me then, as now, I feel sure will be ordained. . . . . . If we suffer here, it is by a Father's hand, it is in wisdom and mercy. If we suffer there, it must be no less so. No, I desire to suffer in the coming world, as in this, if He pleases, if He will that I should. I have a perfect trust and confidence in God. . . . . . Ah, Mr. H——, it is the *self-surrender*, a renunciation of our will for God's, which is the thing. If we can only do this truly, it is all. But how much it

---

* Dr. C. C. Holmes, of Milton.

means! · It has relation to the whole of life. It in
cludes action as well as endurance. It is a perpetual
act. At times we feel strong to do it, — to do it in
one great act. But in the details of life we come
sadly short. . . . . . There are some who seem to
think of self-surrender as implying and inducing a
certain weakness of the spirit, a giving up of power,
a lessening of the soul's activity. · But it is not so.
Far from it. It implies no lessening of activity, of
energy or power of character. It is that these are
out of *self*, and in and for GOD."

"The afternoon of the day before she died," writes
her pastor, "I was told that she had expressed a
desire to see me. As I entered the room, her face
was perfectly radiant. She knew that her hour had
come, and she would say a few last words of kindness to us all. 'I wish to thank you,' she said, 'for
all that you have done, — every thing. And it is all
here,' placing her hand on her breast, 'it is all here.
This peace, this peace! it is all here.' 'Yes,' I re-
plied, 'if we seek we shall find it.' 'I have not
sought it,' she said quickly. 'It came. It was
sent.' . . . . . 'Come with a *smile*,' she said to one
whom she had called to bid her farewell. And her
chamber then seemed to us more as a forecourt of
heaven, than a painful approach to the tomb."

On a lovely April day, the windows of her room
all open that she might breathe freely, she looked up
at one who entered, and said with a smile, "What
a beautiful day to go *home!*" Near the end, one
at her side said to another, in tears, "How much
stronger she is than we are!" "I am so much nearer

the Source of strength," she whispered. Her suffering was acute, but her thought and care were more for others than herself, to the last. Much of the time she held in her hand that sacred note which her husband had written to her when he thought himself dying, at a distance. And precious, very precious, must have been to her those last, parting words from one to whom she was now going. "Dear, dear Mary, if I could, I would express all I owe to you. You have been an unspeakable, an indescribable blessing. God reward you a thousand fold! Farewell, *till we meet again.*"

In the evening twilight of another balmy day, — GOOD FRIDAY, — that spent frame was laid by the side of *his*, in the hallowed rest of Mount Auburn. And as we turned away, we felt that another tie to earth was broken, and heard another voice calling us to heaven.

With regret, rather than gladness, we lay down the pen which has attempted to record the life of a humble Christian. Delightful has it been to renew our communion, and extend our intimacy, with one whose presence was always felt as a blessing. If we have transgressed the bounds we set for ourselves in the beginning, and given expression to feelings as well as facts, we can only say that we have repressed more than we have disclosed of the recollections and emotions awakened by this intercourse.

37

A true portrait may seem to be praise, but less than that would be injustice.

We draw no character, in the end, but only refer to the two facts which seem most worthy of note. First, the amount of happiness enjoyed by one whose life was passed in the midst of sickness and trial, and who for six years felt that a fatal and distressing disease was consuming her life, — yet could say of the whole, " It has been a beautiful experience." " I have been so happy, — no one can tell how happy." And, next, the illustration here seen of the large sphere, the vast power, and imperishable work, of a woman who never left the domestic relations, nor aspired to any thing that is not possible to every daughter, wife, and mother. If this appear, it is enough, — that religion, with or without rank, wealth, beauty, rare endowment, varied accomplishment, or any singularity, can lift WOMAN to the highest distinction and confer the most enduring glory, — that of filling well, not the narrow, but the wide and divine realm of HOME.